LEGENDS OF ALLYOSHMAR

THE DREAMS AND THE DARKNESS

LEGENDS OF ALLYOSHMAR

THE DREAMS AND THE DARKNESS

CALEY BISSON

2014

Dedication

For Kaity, who provided the inspiration to begin this story, believed I had something to say, and continued to encourage me, even when our paths had diverged.

For my Family, who provided the support and basement to finish, regardless of how much I complained about the weather.

For my Peers, who provided the feedback and ideas to refine, humoring even my most tedious lines of questioning regarding their experiences reading my book.

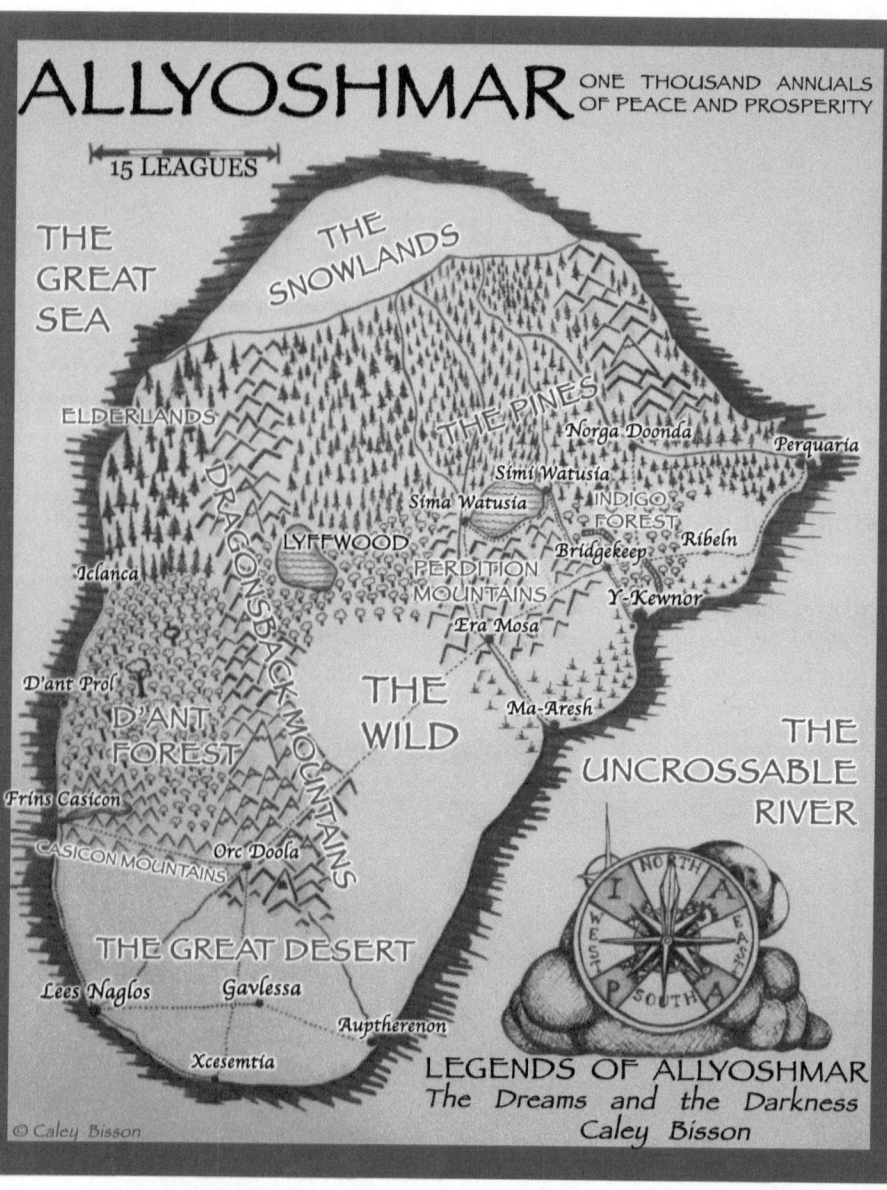

Contents

PART ONE

THE PRINCESS AND THE MILK BOY

LEES NAGLOS

Princess Teryessa's only memory of her mother was a lie and she knew it. She remembered a beautiful woman lifting her from her crib in the middle of the night, tears glistening in the light of the two moons, to kiss her on her forehead. It was a false memory constructed by her mind when she was still naive enough to believe the stories. Teryessa was complicit in the lie because the truth was too painful. Her mother wasn't a brave and powerful warrior who left Lees Naglos, in the name of The Divine Empress, to heroically defend the kingdom and all of Allyoshmar from The Dark One; she was a mad woman who, unable to bear the dull confines of motherhood, abandoned Teryessa and her father, a heartbroken king who did his best to raise her. As Teryessa grew, she learned to ignore the paradox of this false memory, but, as her own departure from her kingdom approached, she found herself unable to suppress the thoughts of her life without a mother.

Teryessa, eyes vacant, approached the large iron tub silently, as though she was made of nothing but ether. Her white silk robe glistened like silver over her warm golden skin. She knelt on a red velvet pillow beside the tub and dipped her slender hands into the water of her morning bath.

"Temp-tur suit you, Your Highness?" Lionara, her beloved nurse, asked.

Teryessa nodded and flashed a contained smile as she stood. Lionara straightened her own ancient knees, standing to remove the princess's robe. A bit of damp castle chill whipped through the arid Lees Naglos air, spreading goosebumps across Teryessa's nude body.

Even in the warm water, the princess trembled. Sand rushing to the bottom of the sunglass on the mantle echoed loudly, while the water dripping from Lionara's porofungi as she washed Teryessa's back sounded as distant as the crashing waves and seagulls of the Great Sea where the bath water would eventually be deposited. As Lionara bathed her, Teryessa imagined a life where everything wasn't already decided. She thought of swords and horses and dragons. She thought of doing something for her kingdom other than being its whore.

The distant gaze of Teryessa's hazel eyes reflected like gold in the solitary beam of sunlight cast upon her through the room's one narrow window as she nodded to whatever small-talk Lionara attempted to make. She didn't intend to be cold to her loving nurse. She wondered if her mother felt so adrift, but the princess knew she'd never benefit from the absent woman's counsel. She knew what her prince would do to her, but Teryessa loved her kingdom and would endure this sadism; she had no choice. With her jaw clenched to control her emotions, Teryessa's gaze glistened with just enough briny moisture to well in the bottom lids of her eyes. Lionara dabbed the tears away with the corner of a silk cloth.

"There, there, love."

With a sudden explosion of fury, Teryessa brushed Lionara caring hand from her face and threw a bar of soap across the room, smashing a porcelain vase.

"I'm being sacrificed," Teryessa screamed. "I want someone to be responsible!"

"I know, love," the kind nurse said, arms wrapping around the princess to subdue her struggling. "I know."

As Teryessa wept in Lionara's arms, she stared at the large silk tapestry of a phoenix hung from the stone wall beside her: the Palidnia family crest and the seal of Lees Naglos. Nine stars surrounding the Palidnian Phoenix represented nine-hundred annuals of peace and prosperity. The scroll in its left talon represented the civility and knowledge of the Palidnian people. In its right talon, the Flaming Sword of Justice symbolized power and mocked Teryessa every time she gazed upon it. She was a member of the Palidnia line, but she never felt any power.

After Lionara dried her, dressed her, and brushed her hair, Teryessa descended through the cold corridors and stairs of the castle to her father's throne room. Spying on the conclusion of her father's morning council through a crack in the heavy wooden doors, she prayed for clemency. Her father, King Noldar Palidnia of Lees Naglos, paced around the massive round table where the Knight Generals, his most valued military leaders were seated. Niveous Snew, Noldar's advisor, a perfectly groomed man seated with the Knight Generals, stroked the thin mustache that only accented his disdainful grin, as he waited to speak.

"I humbly disagree," he sneered with shrill detachment. "The casualties of a northern campaign would be sustainable and, if we control the water, perhaps we could choke them out of the desert."

Noldar turned to Snew. His huge muscular body towered over the sniveling little man.

"This is not an empire, Snew!" Noldar barked. "Peace and prosperity cost the blood of generations and, unless my back is to the wall, I'll not sacrifice a drop more!"

"Is that the rationale you use to pacify yourself into slumber each night, as your daughter's wedding day approaches, Your Grace?" Snew asked.

"You imagine my sleep as restful, Snew?!" Noldar roared. "Do you not believe I would go to war with those monsters in the beat of a heart, should such actions not imperil the lives of every man, woman, and child in this kingdom, including my daughter?! I'll have no more of this discussion."

Teryessa's stomach twisted into knots, but she opened the doors and entered, averting her eyes as she curtseyed to the bows of Snew and the knights shuffling out of the throne room. Red faced, she curtsied to her father and took a seat at the round table.

"I've often wished for an heir to join me at this table," Noldar said, sitting next to her in the utilitarian chair of a Knight General.

"I've often wished that, myself, father," she said, knowing where her father's thoughts went when he looked upon her in that grim, disconsolate manner. "Will you tell me about her again?"

Her father hesitated, wincing as he looked into Teryessa's nearly golden eyes, eyes she had always been told resembled her mother's.

"I was a young king at the time," he said. "My father had recently died. She was barely alive when I found her in the sandy cactusia fields to the east of our kingdom. She was the most beautiful woman I had ever seen. She told me she had been injured fighting a dragon. I was young. I believed her."

Teryessa smiled. It was only a story, but she always loved the part about her mother fighting a dragon.

"You were a baby. It was Vari-Matera-a. I told her she must stay inside, but your mother was headstrong. She said she heard a voice calling to her. We fought. Your HighnessYour HighnessYour HighnessYour HighnessI locked her away in the tower. As soon as the sun rose the next morning, I hurried to the tower. She was gone."

"Do you hate her for leaving us?" Teryessa asked.

"Your mother was as true to us as she could be," Noldar said, kissing Teryessa on the forehead.

The light of the palace library felt dimmer than usual to Teryessa, who's hands shook as she scratched her quill across the parchment with ink-smeared fingers. Her eyes struggled to scan the text of the tome before her, but her concentration barely endured the length of each sentence and the words were forgotten as soon as they were read. She closed the book with her remaining strength and rested her head on the cover.

"Tell me about dragons," she murmured to Lionara, who was knitting on the other side of the table.

"We shouldn't be towkin' 'bout such fowl beasts, Your Highness," Lionara said, looking up from her tangle of yarn.

"Please," she said, lifting her head from the book. "They say my mother fought a dragon. I'm sure I can handle hearing about one."

"But you already know the stories, Your Highness."

"And I enjoy them told with your words most of all, sweet Lionara," Teryessa pleaded, desperate for a distraction.

"Well, you must be feeling better," Lionara replied, setting down her needles. "You're back to flatt'ren' poor old Lionara to get er to tell you a story."

Teryessa smiled. Knowing Lionara couldn't resist an invitation to tell a tale, Teryessa gave her nurse her undivided attention.

"Well, some say dragons is worstest beasties there is, that a dragon's wings can stretch fifty paces, an that dragons is covered by mixamatched rusty metal scales. They say dragons hide their hideous flesh with clothing made from the skins of their victims."

"Well, I should be certain to stay clear of any dragon if I saw one. I'd lock myself in a room, but a dragon could probably break down the door."

"If it ad to. Their claws can shred through rock an their breath can melt iron, but it usually don't come to that. You see, dragons is crafty creatures, known to lure young missus to em. To most young missus, a dragon might seem like a mountain o gold or an endless smorgasbord o delicious food, but usually young missus see the dragon 'bout to kill em as a beautiful young man. The dragon seduces em an the young missus don't realize it's a dragon until it't too late."

"That's horrible!" Teryessa gasped. "You've never told me that version of the story before, Lionara."

"Well, you're older now," Lionara replied. "I figured you could andle the growed-up version."

"I'm not sure I like the grown-up version, Lionara."

"I'm not sure I like the growed-up version, meself, love. I think that's enough story time."

"Lionara, do you actually believe in dragons?" Teryessa asked, crawling beneath the billowy silk blankets of her canopy bed later that night.

"I do, but I believe in heroes, too. An true love."

"Well, heroes are never what their cracked up to be and true love is nothing but a fantasy for little girls."

"Perhaps, Your Highness. O course maybe you simply aven't met the right hero yet."

"Well I haven't met a dragon yet, either, and I'm certain neither of those things is rather likely."

"Time will tell, love," Lionara sighed, blowing out the final candle in Teryessa's chamber. "Time will tell."

Teryessa thought about her father and her mother meeting. She imagined her mother as a brave warrior battling a dragon. She imagined her own dragons and heroes and love. For a moment, her heart sang.

"Stop it, Tery," she said to herself, opening her eyes. "Stop your wandering mind. You are Princess Teryessa Palidnia of Lees Naglos. You have a royal duty. You will turn off your heart and do what you have to do. Your mother wasn't special. She was a selfish woman who abandoned you and your father. There is no such thing as dragons or heroes or true love. Now, stop acting like a little girl and go to sleep."

And she wept until she did.

VARI-MATERA-A-SHOL

A mellow red glow highlighted the web of white frost on the cold glass. The first bit of lazy light hit the window and warmed the hue of the small space. As amber flush permeated darkness, the chamber's simple furnishings became apparent. Wrinkled rags of clothing tumbled out of a simple wardrobe made of cedar in the corner, littered the crude planked oak floor, and hung on hooks fastened to the flimsy pine door. A cheap, rusty saber with no sheath leaned against a white clay wall. Closest to the window was a bed. The wood was old and the mattress stuffed with straw, but it was sturdy and off the ground. In the bed slept a curious young man with a pure but restless heart.

Aiwren Wayde always woke first every morning and the morning of Vari-Matera-a-Shol was no different. Aiwren's days began early and the beams of light beckoned him to open his eyes and move.

Aiwren dressed quickly and without bathing first. His family owned a bathtub, but his chores would leave him covered with filth, so he preferred to bathe afterwards. He grabbed his rugged canvas work trousers from under his bed, put his feet in, pulled them up as he stood, and fastened their grommets. He pulled a baggy thread-bare shirt over his head and slid his feet into his beat-up old boots. Leaving his little room, he grabbed a bulky wool overcoat.

The quiet kitchen, prepped the night before for efficiency, patiently waited for the activity of the morning rituals. Oats and honey absorbed water in an iron pot hanging over a pile of unlit wood in the fireplace. Madeline Wayde would start the fire as soon as she awoke. On a heavy wooden table, sat another iron pot filled with water, vegetables, and herbs for the stew, the family's dinner. Beside the stew pot was a parchment ledger, a quill, and an ink well. Cillian Wayde's first task of the day would be compiling a list of items for Aiwren to pick up in town after breakfast. A stack of metal pails waited on the worn-smooth wooden floor beside the table.

Entering the small kitchen, Aiwren grabbed his wool cap from the back of a chair. Most villagers considered it vulgar to wear a hat indoors, but the Waydes eschewed that custom and Aiwren didn't think twice before pulling his over his shaggy brown hair to keep the cold away on that chilly autumn morning. The Wayde family defied the traditions of Ribeln at just about every opportunity. His family's eccentricity fostered a desire to fit in and, doing his best to act like everyone else in his small corner of the world, Aiwren's differences went unnoticed for nearly eighteen annuals. Inquisitive, intelligent, and ambitious, Aiwren wasn't like the others. He was a dreamer, but regardless of his dreams, the cows needed milking, so Aiwren grabbed the stack of pails and headed to the barn.

In their modest barn, the Wayde family cared for their cows, loved them, and treated them well. In return, the Wayde cows produced the best milk in Ribeln. The extra care increased the cost required to operate the small ranch, so, although they were the top milk providers in Ribeln, keeping the budget balanced was difficult.

"Good morning girls!" Aiwren bellowed.

The cows responded with a chorus of gleeful mooing when Aiwren entered. The boy set the stack of pails on the ground, grabbed the top one, and headed over to the closest stall.

"How about I start with you, Persephone?"

The beautiful brown bovine batted her big eyelashes at him and mooed as Aiwren entered the stall, pulled up a tiny stool, and milked. Aiwren usually tried to keep his attention on the cow at hand, but, having recently received a letter from his best friend, he found it especially difficult to concentrate that particularly morning.

Leicester and Aiwren had been best friends nearly their entire lives. Four annuals earlier, when the boys finished schooling, Leicester left Ribeln to apprentice with a tailor in Y-Kewnor. Unable to afford an apprenticeship, Aiwren remained in Ribeln, but enjoyed Leicester's letters about his adventures in the big city.

Aiwren took a break from milking to re-read Leicester's letter, as though another glance would change the situation. He pulled the folded parchment from his trouser pockets.

Dear Aiwren,

I hope this letter finds you well. Things are splendid in Y-Kewnor. I have completed the penultimate stage of my apprenticeship with Ulysses James Cutter and he's offered me the Master Apprentice position in his shop. It's just a beginning, but Master Cutter is probably the best tailor in Y-Kewnor. In addition, I have recently begun courting a lady. Her name is Wanda. She is the most beautiful creature I have ever laid eyes on. Unfortunately, this means I will not be returning to Ribeln; however, I hope to continue our correspondence.

Your Friend,

Leicester Wiggleby, Tailor

Aiwren folded the letter and returned it to his trouser pocket. He was happy for Leicester, but lonely. He wished he, too, could enjoy such an exciting adventure. He reminded himself to stop thinking about such preposterous dreams and return to the task at hand, milking cows. Aiwren did dream of going to Y-Kewnor. He dreamed of leaving his family's ranch, but he didn't dream of being a tailor. Aiwren Wayde dreamed of being one of The Divine Empress's Knights. He dreamed of the applause he would hear as he rode into town after a heroic success, armor shining spectacularly in the sun. The crushing blow of reality reminded him he wasn't a knight. He wasn't even a great swordsman. He was scrawny and uncoordinated. His dream was ridiculous.

After he finished milking all the cows, Aiwren took the last bucket of milk with him and returned to his parent's little house for breakfast.

"Good morning, son." Madeline sing-songed to Aiwren.

"Morning, mum," Aiwren responded, wondering how she could be so content with this life.

Madeline's beauty defied the rags circumstance required her to wear. Her dark hair cascaded from her wool cap down to the middle of her back. She had bright blue eyes, like oceans, filled with life, knowledge, and power. Her sincere smile contained a tongue predisposed for irreverence. Unusually strong for her stature, she easily heaved the porridge pot to the table.

Cillian Wayde, a bull of a man sitting at the table, peered up from his ledger with bright black eyes, twinkling with wisdom, as the wooden peg he wore instead of a right leg rapped against the floorboards as if to punctuate the line he had just written.

"Perfect timing," Cillian said, putting away his work as his wife set the porridge on the table. "Smells delicious."

"Same as I've made every morning, love," Madeline responded as Cillian kissed her on the forehead.

"Still smells delicious," he replied.

After breakfast, Madeline started the stew and routine guided the Wayde men out to the barn. At the far end of the barn, after the cows, the resident old mares, Agatha and Sabrina, resided in the final two stalls. Aiwren fetched the horses while Cillian finished loading the wagon. The two lazy horses preferred to stay in their stalls all day, but always acquiesced agreeably when Aiwren hitched them to the wagon for the daily trip into town. Cillian secured the ropes around the crates of milk. The flasks would keep the milk cool for a little while, but Aiwren and his father had to hurry to deliver it before it spoiled. Aiwren hopped on the wagon and Cillian snapped the reins to begin their daily journey.

Less than a league away from the town of Ribeln, the proximity of the Wayde Ranch and Cillian's discipline made fresh milk delivery possible in this small town. Every morning Cillian would head into town with his son in the back of the rickety old wagon to make sure no milk spilled. Bouncing their way along the path repetition of travel had worn for them, Cillian called for his son to join him up front.

Aiwren obliged, climbing over the unstable backrest he felt like he just repaired.

"Your mother and I didn't always live in Ribeln."

"I remember, Pop. You were a guardsman in Y-Kewnor."

"Right. Well, not everything is what it appears to be in the city. Many things in life may seem shiny on the outside, but they're rusted in their core."

"It's all right," Aiwren reassured his father. "I know this farm is the place for me."

"Do you believe that's why I told you that?" Cillian asked. "I understand having dreams, son. So much about you makes me so proud, but so much about you makes me so frightened for you. Not everyone has the heart you do, which is why you must be especially vigilant."

"Don't worry, Pop. I know I'm safe here."

Cillian never said another word. After a few moments of silence, Aiwren returned to the back of the wagon, wondering why his father told him that, wondering what his father wasn't telling him. Then his thoughts turned to his dreams again. He loathed the safety of the ranch. He didn't want safety; he wanted adventure.

As the wagon progressed across the rolling hills, Aiwren and his father observed the leaves on the trees changing color. The beautiful autumn foliage, bright red, orange, and yellow, was breathtaking, even for Aiwren who had seen it his entire life. For that moment, he was content with his unimpressive, but comfortable destiny.

One hand of the sun later, Cillian and his son arrived in Ribeln Square. The little village was humming with regular activity. Farmers from just out side of town struggled to navigate their carts and wagons through the congested town square. The market buzzed with the cacophony of good-natured bartering, bickering, and squabbling over prices. Most of these people had known each other their entire lives.

Cillian and his milk wagon wobbled away, leaving Aiwren behind in the town square. Rather than staying in the market, he delivered the milk to each home, himself, and had been doing it this way for annuals. Customers had offered to meet him at his wagon, but

Cillian, a stubborn man, insisted on walking the milk up to each front door. As his father disappeared into the bedlam of the market, Aiwren took in his surroundings, how the town differed from the country. The houses were taller and made of fine materials: polished solid wood walls, tile or tin shingles, and leaded windows. Cobble stones paved the Ribeln street, rather than the dirt and gravel of the country paths. The townsfolk were well groomed, well dressed, well fed, well manicured, and well bathed. The countryfolk stood out.

Aiwren glanced at the list. He had two sunhands and ten copper coins to shop for the essentials on the list, but he would need only a half sunhand and eight copper coins. His father had given him extra copper and time. The additional extra coins were certainly intentional and likely an early Vari-Matera-a gift, Aiwren decided, as he rushed through his mandatory shopping.

Within a half sunhand, Aiwren had filled a large burlap sack with the provisions from the list and he still had two copper coins left. Although he hurried though his shopping, he made sure to take note of any personal items catching his attention. He planned on returning to the tanner to spend his two copper pieces on a leather sack with a shoulder strap. This would be a wise purchase, he thought, until something new caught his eye, a group of town boys wearing blue silk scarves around their necks. The scarves were thin at the top, wrapped around the neck under the collars of their shirts, and were tied in some strange triangular knot in front. The beautiful blue scarves draped down, covering their shirt buttons, and came to a neat little triangular point at the bottom. He wondered if Leicester had made those scarves.

"Fancy one a them scarves, do ya?"

Aiwren whipped around, startled by Bonishara, an old Nomasha woman who lived in a brightly painted wagon and came to town to sell her wares.

The villagers speculated wildly about the Nomasha, believing that they were half lyff, or that they were once spirits, or that they had struck a deal with The Dark One in exchange for magics. These things were considered to be tales for children, yet most adults were still wary of them. Some towns had banned the Nomasha from entering, but Ribeln welcomed them. The Nomasha were mysterious and they could all benefit from a little mystery in their dull lives.

"The finest neck scarf, straight from Y-Kewnor," she said.

"I planned on purchasing a satchel," Aiwren replied.

In a flash, Bonishara pulled a scarf from her pocket. It was blue and fabric, but that was the extent of its similarity to the scarves town boys wore. While the town boys' were smooth silk, Bonishara's was some sort of rough canvas. While the town boys' were expertly died and hemmed along the edges, Bonishara's appeared as though she had painted it with the blue paint she had used on her wagon and trimmed it with garden sheers.

"Finest neck scarf," she repeated, waving the impostor scarf.

Aiwren knew that, if he wore this poor replica of the current fashion, he, too, would be an impostor. A rough edged country boy mimicking town fashion. But he didn't care. He wanted to feel as though he fit in, even if just for a moment.

"Two copper," she said.

"That's all I have!" he exclaimed

"Two copper," she demanded

Aiwren dropped the coins into Bonishara's outstretched hand. She flashed him a toothless smile and extended her hand to offer him the rough neck scarf. He reached for it, but as he grabbed the scarf, the old woman grabbed his wrist. Bonishara's toothless grin vanished. Panic flashed in her eyes.

"Only the Crystal Blade can save you!" Bonishara exclaimed. "She haunts you! You've been marked!"

"I don't know what you're talking about," Aiwren said.

"Don't lie to me, fool boy!" she commanded. "The Dark One is upon us! Only the Crystal Blade can save you! Only the Crystal Blade can save us all."

"I don't know what a Crystal Blade is," Aiwren said, "but The Dark One is just a myth."

Bonishara released Aiwren's wrist and bolted, disappearing into the crowd. Aiwren laughed at himself for paying the Nomasha woman a second thought. He laughed at the blue neck scarf and shook his head, realizing he didn't have a collar on his shirt and he didn't even know how to tie the thing. Aiwren did his best to tie the rough blue rag around his neck and headed towards where he usually met his father.

"Nice scarf, milkboy."

Aiwren recognized that voice. Quinntonn Sutherfield, the only son of the wealthiest family in Ribeln, took delight in his family's success and even more delight in the suffering of others, especially Aiwren.

Aiwren kept walking, but he heard chuckling. Quinntonn always travelled with two or three of his friends. Aiwren told himself that, if he ignored them, they'd lose interest and go away.

"I said, that's a nice scarf, milkboy."

"I think he's ignoring you, Quinnt."

"Well, that's not nice."

"Perhaps we ought to teach milkboy some manners... civilize him."

Aiwren kept walking, pretending not to hear the words, ignoring his anger. Then he felt the push. It came from behind. Aiwren stopped dead in his tracks and turned around, facing Quinntonn Sutherfield and his four friends, well-dressed young men with contemptuous grins, malicious eyes, and blue scarves around their necks.

"He doesn't even know how to tie a neck scarf, Quinnt," a bully said.

"Leave me alone." Aiwren warned.

"I don't think he knows his place either."

"That true?" Quinntonn asked, pushing Aiwren in the chest. "That true, milkboy?"

Quinntonn pushed one more time. This time, he pushed Aiwren to the ground.

"That's your place, milkboy. In the dirt."

This humiliation and abuse was a common event in Aiwren's life and typical of his trips into town. Normally, he would ignore it, let the town boys bully him, then go about his day, but, something inside of him snapped that morning. Aiwren charged. The force and the surprise of Aiwren's tackle knocked Quinntonn to the ground. The young town-boy didn't stand a chance.

Aiwren's first punch landed hard. Right on Quinntonn's jaw. His second punch landed even harder. Then, a boot crashed into Aiwren's ribs. He lost his breath. He tried to grab the leg of the assailant, but another kick crunched in on his other side. Two of the town boys pulled Aiwren off Quinntonn and pinned him to the ground.

Quinntonn retaliated without hesitation. Aiwren, out numbered, didn't stand a chance. One punch. Then another.

"You wanna sass, milkboy? We put up with you and your cripple old man coming into town, but we don't like it and we expect you to be thankful for the gift of being around civilized people. Maybe we need to teach your whole family a lesson."

Quinntonn spat in Aiwren's bloodied face and stood up, giving Aiwren one final kick as he walked away. Aiwren laid motionless for a moment. He wished he had a sword. He would have cut down all five of them.

Cillian finished his milk rounds just before noon. Aiwren, sulking on a stoop, held his head low, ashamed of the dried blood caked below his possibly broken nose and the gash over his swollen left eye.

"Get in," Cillian said.

Cillian and Aiwren, avoided conversation almost the entire way back to the ranch. The silence provided Aiwren time to think and he couldn't stop wondering about his conversation with Bonishara. As the wagon approached the gate, Cillian pulled on the reins, stopping the two tired old horses.

"I don't care how much coin those town boys have or who their fathers are," Cillian said, looking Aiwren in the eyes. "You're twice the man any of them will ever be."

"Hey, Pop?" Aiwren asked. "What is a Crystal Blade?"

"Why do you ask?" Cillian asked.

"Someone mentioned it in town today," Aiwren replied.

"Bonishara, no doubt," Cillian laughed. "That old bat will tell her foolish Nomasha tales to anyone willing to listen."

"Have you heard of it?" Aiwren laughed.

"Aye," Cillian confirmed. "The Order of the Crystal Blade. From what I remember of the myth, back in the days of lyffs and orcs, the Order of the Crystal Blade were a group of heroes who protected Allyoshmar from The Dark One. But those are just stories."

"Why have I never heard of them before?" Aiwren asked, fascinated by this tale.

"Well, folks like Bonishara would tell you the truth has been concealed," Cillian said. "But I recon it's because the people have moved on. They don't care anymore."

For a moment, Aiwren father stared off distantly, but then he regained his focus flashed Aiwren a loving grin. With his usual earnest expression, he snapped the reins and the wagon wobbled away.

"What's that rag around your neck? Some cruel joke those bullies pulled on you?" Cillian chuckled.

Aiwren laughed and said, "It's a neck scarf. I bought it from Bonishara for two copper."

"It's hardly worth one, I recon," Cillian replied, as the wagon rolled into the barn. "Unload the empties. I'll prepare your mother for the sight of you. Do me a favor though, son. Don't bring up the Crystal Blade with her."

***

Vari-Matera-a, the night of two moons, the biggest celebration of the annual, was once believed to be the most dangerous night of the annual, the night all The Dark One's creatures were free to prowl Allyoshmar as they pleased. On Vari-Matera-a, everyone remained indoors from sunset to sunrise of the following day, feasting and exchanging gifts. Fear of The Dark One's creatures had faded generations earlier, but the tradition of the night of two moons remained. Vari-Matera-a-Shol, the night before the night of two moons, held great importance as part of this traditional holiday. On Vari-Matera-a-Shol, communities gathered to enjoy what could be a final feast together and celebrated around a large bonfire of cedar logs and the green hay that people once believed provided protection from evil. For many, this once terrifying night, was their favorite night of the annual.

Many young women loved Vari-Matera-a-Shol because, on this night, a young lady bestowed a kiss upon the young man whom she most wished to survive Vari-Matera-a. This tradition also evolved over the ages and became an excuse for shy young ladies to be forward and for forward young ladies to be even more forward. The excessive consumption of sweet delicious honeymead, believed to be the spirit of young lovers, silenced inhibitions and exaggerated emotions.

Finally a young woman of age allowed to attend the festivities without parental chaperone and kiss the young man of her choice, Vannoria Nillhalla had been thinking of this Vari-Matera-a-Shol for the last four annuals. She knew who she was going to kiss: the boy with whom she had been in love for as long as she could remember; she was going to kiss Aiwren Wayde.

The Nillhalla family, immigrant farmers from beyond the Uncrossable River, specialized in roots and tubers. When Lyal Nillhalla's first child turned out to be a girl, he and his wife, Lhyr, tried again. Five daughters later, the couple gave it one more attempt, birthing Vannoria, the closest thing to a son Lyal ever had, an attribute her poor family desperately needed, but also looked down upon. The only of Lyal's daughters to help in the field, Vannoria loved the outdoors and, though never appreciated for it, liked being helpful. Maturing into a young woman earlier and more awkwardly than the other girls her age, the boys began looking at her differently. She hated feeling so different, but it was for Aiwren, most of all, that she wished she wasn't so foreign, and thin, and awkward, and boyish.

The countryfolk had no desire to celebrate Vari-Matera-a-Shol in Ribeln with the townsfolk, so each annual, they held their own celebration, digging out a fire pit and erecting a banquet tent in an unused field.

Except for the old men who ignited the logs at sunset, Vannoria arrived at the Vari-Matera-a-Shol bonfire before anybody else in her little community that night, fiddling at her clothes, peering up the road, and pacing nervously outside the banquet tent as other guests arrived. For the first time in her life, she wore a dress. It wasn't a beautiful gown, but it fit her nicely. Her thick dark hair fell over her shoulders and her smooth olive skin was bathed and clean. Her brown eyes twinkled in the green light of the fire. As a familiar silhouette approach, Vannoria smiled.

"Happy Vari-Matera-a-Shol, Aiwren!" she exclaimed, immediately wishing she'd done so in a more lady-like manner.

"Happy Vari-Matera-a-Shol, Vannoria," the boy replied with a cool, relaxed smile.

Vannoria took in Aiwren's outfit as he approached. His blue dress trousers and blue jacket fit loosely over his lean frame. His shaggy hair was parted and combed. He looked perfect to her. Then she noticed his face and reached for it tenderly.

"Some of the town boys," Aiwren said, moving neither towards or away from Vannoria's caring hand. "It's not so bad."

"I'm glad you're fairly good, at least," Vannoria said. "I'd have been miserable, were you too injured to attend my first unchaperoned Vari-Matera-a-Shol."

"Of course," Aiwren congratulated. "You're an adult now."

"I am," Vannoria continued, inching closer to Aiwren. "Do you know what that means?"

"Honeymead!" Aiwren exclaimed, breaking the moment.

As Aiwren led the way to the honeymead, Vannoria hated herself for losing her nerve. What if another girl kissed Aiwren that night? What if no girl kissed Aiwren, but The Dark One's creature took him the following night? If she intended to kiss Aiwren, she decided she had to stop thinking like a child, summon her courage, and actually kiss him.

***

It wasn't that Aiwren didn't like Vannoria. They had known each other since childhood, played in the fields together, caught fish together, and built forts together. Besides Leicester, Aiwren considered Vannoria to be his best friend. It wasn't that Aiwren didn't notice when Vannoria blossomed from a girl to a young woman, either. He found Vannoria to be quite beautiful. He also found her to be the kindest, smartest, and most individual girl in Ribeln. What prevented Aiwren's friendship with Vannoria from growing into a romance was that she had always been his friend and he didn't want to tarnish his image of her with impure thoughts.

Aiwren did have impure thoughts, though. Once, several annuals earlier, just as Vannoria began to blossom, Aiwren had walked over to her house to invite her to take a rock collecting walk with him. As he approached her family's little farmhouse he heard her singing and assumed she was playing in the back yard; however, as he walked around the corner, he saw her in the pond. He was about to yell her name, until he realized she was naked. He had forgotten her family didn't own a bathtub and took turns bathing in the pond. He wanted to close his eyes, but he couldn't. He wanted to run away, but he couldn't. He wanted to yell for her to put her clothes back on, but he couldn't. Frozen, all he could do was stare at her nude figure, at her skin, wet and glistening in the sun, at her budding breasts with nipples pert from the cool water. After a moment, he snapped out of it and ran home, swearing to never think of Vannoria that way again.

Several long banquet tables filled the banquet tent from end to end. The ranchers and farmers contributed enough food to cover a large buffet with a variety of dishes. The parents and grandparents usually remained in the tent, while the under-aged children played nearby. Outside, a huge bonfire burned the green fire of cedar and green hay. Anybody who played an instrument always brought it along and played music until the fire went out. Once a young man or young woman was of age, the bonfire became the real draw of the evening. They would wolf down their meals and hurry out of the tent to join the party at the bonfire with their friends. This was usually a joyous night.

"The music is growing rather loud," Vannoria said, leaning towards Aiwren over the plates of food they had devoured and a stack of empty honeymead goblets.

"Yes, it is," Aiwren replied, distracted.

"An awful lot of laughing, too," she continued.

Aiwren glanced around the large tent. At one end the children played and laughed. At the other end, the parents and grandparents sat, sipping honeymead as they relaxed and discussed farm life. Outside, the others his age, young adults, laughed and sang. Aiwren wondered where his place was, but Vannoria longed to celebrate and he had no intention of ruining her evening with his introspection.

"Let's suss out the bonfire," Aiwren said. "Shall we?"

"Yes!" Vannoria exclaimed. "If you like."

As he stood and walked outside, the effects of the honeymead became immediately apparent to Aiwren, warmed from the inside as he and Vannoria stepped into the cool autumn night. The bonfire burned especially bright, the joyous music filled the air, and life, he thought, wasn't so bad. He opened a bottle of honeymead, took a sip, and smiled.

"Would you care to dance, Vannoria?"

Aiwren and Vannoria danced for hours. Aiwren wasn't thinking about romance or desire. He was drunk on honeymead and enjoying himself with a friend. Celebrating. As the night progressed, the crowd dwindled. Drunk and exhausted, Aiwren and Vannoria took a break from dancing and sat on a short stone wall in the field.

"This is the most fun I've ever had at Vari-Matera-a-Shol!" Vannoria exclaimed.

"Me, too," he smiled back.

"I have something for you," Vannoria said, trembling.

As she leaned close, Aiwren knew what was about to happen. He could have stopped it, but he didn't. Their lips met and his thoughts melted away for a moment. He thought of the day he saw her naked. He wanted to touch her. He thought of her breasts. He felt himself losing control. He thought impure thoughts. He thought dark things. He thought of a voice in the back of his mind telling him to take her. But he didn't. Aiwren snapped out of his mind and regained control of his thoughts. He pulled away and said the first thing that came to his mind.

"Thank you."

"The pleasure's mine, Aiwren Wayde. I've wanted to do that for a long time now."

"I'm glad you did."

"I should probably go home now. My sisters will tell on me if I'm late."

"Yeah. Me, too."

"Happy Vari-Matera-a-Shol," Vannoria said, hesitating to leave. "I hope The Dark One's creatures don't take you."

After Vannoria disappeared over the hill, Aiwren's thoughts changed. He wondered if he really liked Vannoria. He wondered, if he didn't, why he was trying so hard to convince himself he did. So much of life was so confusing to Aiwren. He wanted so badly to have answers, to have some sort of sign. He sat on the wall and watched as young adults coupled up, kissed goodnight, and parted ways. He wished he was capable of enjoying the simple pleasures of life. As the last of the group left, Aiwren walked into the field, laid on his back in the tall grass, and soaked in the stars, hoping for answers. Varishanta-a, the blue moon, cast a pale blanket of its wraithlike light upon Aiwren, illuminating his grey eyes. Was nobody else destined to sense the sweet seductive mystery?

***

For her entire life, Vari-Matera-a-Shol had been Princess Teryessa's favorite night of the annual. She loved being the most popular at the grand Vari-Matera-a-Shol Ball. From the old noblemen who danced jigs with her when she was a child to the young knights who waited to waltz with her as an adolescent, she enjoyed the smiles on the faces that always seemed so serious. Afterwards, at the festival, her father would beam with pride from his throne as she blessed the honeymead to the applause of the guests. At the end of the night, after dancing around the green fire until her feet throbbed, Princess Teryessa would retire to her chambers, already anticipating the next annual's celebration. This annual everything was different. Vari-Matera-a-Shol meant the ominous expectation of impending doom, a deathbird circling above her head. This annual, Vari-Matera-a-Shol would be the eve of her wedding.

As the sun set, the grand ballroom was already filling with royal guests. Enormous banquet tables inundated with overflowing plates of food and decanters of honeymead lined the walls. Brightly colored tapestries smothered the stone surfaces. There was a small dance floor at the far end, but nobody was in a dancing mood this annual. Two trumpeters stood by the massive entrance, bugling a dour cadence every time a guest entered. The room was buzzing with activity, but none of it was gleeful. The trumpeters began their most regal tune, silencing the room for Princess Teryessa's entrance. Her long blond hair flowed from beneath her small tiara, splashing onto the shoulders of her green gown. All eyes followed her as she walked up the red carpet to her father.

No sooner had Teryessa arrived at the royal table, when the doors flew open again, the trumpeters sounded a daunting cadence and the envoys from Gavlessa entered the room. While the people of Lees Naglos had clean skin, golden complexion, and fashionable attire, the Gavlessans entering the ball room had filthy skin, pale complexions, and wore the loin clothes and garish accoutrements of barbarians. The two kingdoms couldn't have been more different and those differences only started with appearance. Finally, Prince Monnon Grell entered the ballroom with a legion of guards. Every overdeveloped muscle in his lean sinewy body rippled as he walked into the room with his head held high. The long stringy hair dangling down to his shoulders had already turned white, a sign of power and esteem to the people of Gavlessa.

Teryessa was disgusted by the sight of Grell and the thought of him touching her made her want to vomit. She hated him and everything he stood for. She hated him for imposing his will upon her people, upon her father, and upon herself. She wished for someone with the courage to stand up against him and the barbarians of Gavlessa. She saw him notice her from across the room and begin advancing towards her. Her fate was sealed, but she had no intention of hurrying things along and had every intention of delaying the inevitable for as long as possible. She ducked into the small hallway leading to the courtyard and crept down the corridor.

"Have you received any further instructions from the Master?" she overheard.

"My portion is quite under control," another voice replied. "King Grell is aggressive, but he's old and his son will be easily persuaded with the promise of power."

The voices sounded old and one sounded familiar to Teryessa. She crept closer, straining her ears to learn who was conversing so surreptitiously in the corridor. Peering around the corner, she could see one man, but not the other. The man she saw was Niveous Snew.

"I'm more concerned with things in your kingdom," the other man said, squeezing Snew's hand tightly. "You have not responded to my communications."

"I have been meaning to," Snew said, wincing in pain. "Everything is going as planned. Noldar has been preoccupied with the betrothal of his daughter. He won't realize the noose is around his neck until he's swinging by it."

"If anything goes wrong, it will be you that's hanged, worm," the other man said, letting go of Snew's hand.

Teryessa crept closer, until she could see the other man, dressed in black from head to toe, was Vregg Plale, the chancellor of Gavlessa. Teryessa didn't understand the conversation, but it clearly wasn't good. She had to tell her father. She ran back the way she came, but, as she emerged from the corridor and into the ballroom, she ran right into Grell. He grabbed her by the shoulders.

"Going somewhere, beautiful?"

"Grell!"

"Prince Grell," the man hissed, grabbing her arm.

"I was just on my way to speak with my father."

"I think you were about to join me for a dance."

Teryessa struggled to get away, but Grell pressed his terrible lips pressed against hers. The more she struggled the more viciously he pressed, his filthy wandering hands groping her bosom.

"Let go of my daughter, Grell."

Noldar had lumbered up behind Grell, towering over the twisted young man.

"Step away, old man. She's mine now."

"She's her own. She's made a decision to sacrifice herself for the good of her people but she's her own."

"Sacrifice?! Wedding the prince of the most powerful kingdom in Allyoshmar is now considered a sacrifice?! Quaint sentiment, Noldar, but the sacrifice will do no good. My people will take your land no matter how many of your royal whores you offer us."

Noldar grabbed the young man by the neck and threw him against the field-stone wall of the ballroom. Teryessa coughed and rubbed her sore throat, relieved to be free. Grell scrambled to his feet, dusted off his jacket, gathered his pride and approached the huge king.

"You've just made a huge mistake, old man. That girl is mine. It's only a matter of time. Just as it's only a matter of time before the streets of Lees Naglos flow with a river of its citizen's blood."

Noldar said nothing, locking eyes with the barbarian. The horrible young prince turned to Teryessa.

"Insolence, my dear, is not an act I'll suffer without retribution."

Grell reached his left arm across his body and, with the back of his hand, smacked Teryessa across the face. Her jaw throbbed. She had never been struck before. Her father raced to her aid, but Grell's gnarled blade was already drawn and pointed at Noldar.

"You may be king of these weak wretches, but you're nothing to me. If you take another step, it won't be just your blood and your daughter's, but your entire kingdom's."

Quivering with rage, her father reached for his sword. Around the ballroom, she saw the faces of the innocent people who would die if she allowed him to followed his instincts. She reached out and lowered her father's hand from his sword.

"When we return to Gavlessa, Your Highness, our marriage will be consummated in the most uncivilized way," Grell growled at her. "Then, after you've wiped the blood from your loins, I'll put you to use fulfilling the desires of my most savage soldiers. The whores in the streets will look down on you in pity and throw copper at your feet with disgust."

Grell sheathed his sword, spun on his heels, and walked out the doors to the ballroom, his barbarous entourage in heel.

Teryessa shook with anger, not for herself, but for her father. She met her father's eyes with her own in an attempt to shift his gaze from the welt on her cheek. Her pain melted into a numb hopelessness. She tried to maintain her brave mask of dignity, but the future seemed bleak and her serene facade cracked as she gazed upon her forlorn guests. Without saying another word, she exited the ballroom, silent as a ghost.

***

Wurm Ahkk-Rhall wasn't filled with hate. He wasn't sad and he wasn't angry. He wasn't motivated by emotions such as revenge, by human emotions. Nor was he insane. He knew exactly what he was doing and he enjoyed it. He did it because he wanted to. He did it because he could. Wurm Ahkk-Rhall did it because he was a dragon.

The young girl before him, whose name Ahkk-Rhall hadn't bothered to learn, stopped screaming days earlier. Filth and grime covered her nude body. Purple bruises stretched along her arms and legs and around her neck. The scratches on her back, puffy and pink from infection, spread across to her ribs, around to her breasts. One of her nipples was badly mangled and the other was sheered off. Blood dripped from her wounds and mingled with the blood and slime matted in her long raven hair. Blood flowed from her vagina, drying on the inside of her thighs and trickling into a small pool on the stone table she was shackled to. Her eyes, two empty voids where fear, panic, or hatred ought to have been, stared vacantly. She was nearly gone, but Ahkk-Rhall knew she had some enjoyment left in her.

The heartless dragon approached. His four enormous prehensile claws ground into the stone floor, crunching rocks into gravel with every step, as he swaggered across the dark cave on his long, lean, muscular legs. His slick grey skin was covered with spidery blue veins, white scars, and festering blisters with yellow puss oozing from them. Haphazardly scattered over his legs were clusters of rusty metal scales with mold and rot growing in the cracks between them. His torso was covered with thin pieces of hide stitched together with bundles of twine. The twine was made from the hair of young girls and the leather was their skin. From beneath the back of the grotesque suit, grew a slender gray tail, swaying back and forth and curling before whipping to the other side. His skin was taut across his long bony skull. Nostrils flayed as sulfuric rotting steam erupted forth. Stubble sprouted from his long pointy ears. His mouth contorted, smirking, to reveal his dagger-like teeth. His eyes were red.

Ahkk-Rhall laughed with a roar. His for-claw reached towards his human-skin clothing and untied a bow. As he pulled at the human-hair twine it slid through the grommets and the human-skin clothing fell to the ground like a corpse. He stretched out his colossal bat-like wings. Nearly translucent skin spread over his boney ribs and bloated gut. Ahkk-Rhall stood on his hind two legs and climbed on the stone table, bearing his horrific, barb-covered erection.

Ahkk-Rhall knew this would be the last time with this girl. After this she'd be dead and he'd have new materials to create his art with. They didn't all die. Some of them lived. Some of them went on, soulless for the rest of their days. It didn't matter to Ahkk-Rhall what happened to them; they meant nothing more to him. They didn't all die, but most of them did.

"Are you ready?" Ahkk-Rhall asked, in a voice gurgling like brimstone.

The pitiful girl, panting with desire and writhing with the expectation of what she perceived to be orgasmic pleasure, beckoned her ill fate and responded with a barely audible, "Yes."

Wurm Ahkk-Rhall mounted the girl one last time and howled with satisfaction as he ended the girl's life with his brutal sex.

VARI-MATERA-A

On the morning of Vari-Matera-a, Aiwren awoke to a bad dream. A nightmare. The worst kind of nightmare. The nightmare that haunted him his entire life. He was behind Vannoria's house, at the edge of the pond, but the pond was filled with blood and the woman with no skin was grabbing at him. Pulling him below. Whispering horrible things to him. He fought her, but she persisted. He was drowning. Then, he woke up, drenched with sweat and shivering as he opened his eyes. Every time Aiwren had this dream, terror invaded the very core of his soul.

Aiwren's terror vanished when he remembered what day it was. He rushed out of bed to sprint through his chores and gather the gifts he had for his parents. Rushing into the kitchen, Aiwren was shocked by the silhouette of a person sitting at the table. Aiwren stopped, dead in his tracks. Heart pounding, his breath abandoned him and his stomach twisted inside his body.

"Up early."

Aiwren was relieved to see his father at the table. A flint struck and the wick of the oil lamp ignited. Cillian Wayde, pulled out a chair, indicating to his son to sit.

"I wanted to get my chores out of the way," Aiwren replied. As a rule, Aiwren never lied to his parents. Sparing them the knowledge of his nightmares was the only exception to this rule.

Cillian said nothing. Aiwren sat in silence. Did his father know about his nightmares? What would he think if he knew the horrible things Aiwren dreamt about? Why was his father so somber?

"There are things in the night, things so horrible that we never speak of them," Cillian said. "I always hoped this life would be enough for you, son. Sometimes hope isn't enough, I recon."

Cillian dropped something on the table with a thud. It was wrapped in dirty old rags.

"If your mother found out I gave you this, she'd skin me."

Cillian slid the bundled object across the table. Aiwren pulled it close and began unwrapping, revealing only glimpses at a time. Dull. Dark. Worn. Iron. Then, the last rag fell to the floor. The sword was nearly three steps in length and bulkier than anything Aiwren had ever wielded. The handle had old leather wrappings and a chipped pomme. The blade was dull and ordinary.

"It doesn't look like much, but that sword has a lot of power, goodness, and history."

"I don't understand," Aiwren stammered.

"For now, hang on to it, son. Hide in the barn."

Aiwren, speechless, grabbed the rags from the ground and wrapped the sword. He didn't understand the abrupt gravity of his father's instructions, but he obediently hurried the sword out of the house.

In the barn, Aiwren hid his new sword in a pile of hay between the stalls, right by the presents he had bought for his parents. While he worked, Aiwren thought of his father, wondering about the sword he'd given him. Why did he do so in secret? Why couldn't his mother find out? Why was his father so somber about such an ordinary weapon? These questions burned in his mind. After Aiwren finished his chores, he returned to the hay-pile hiding spot to retrieve the presents for his parents and to steal another look at the sword. He hoped answers would be revealed with a second glance. He grabbed the bundle of presents for his parents and covered the sword.

Later, after a delicious, but uncharacteristically quiet Vari-Matera-a dinner of roasted turkey, mashed potatoes, carrots, and cranberry chutney, Cillian, Madeline, and Aiwren finished scraping the last sweet gooey crumbs of apple pie into their mouths. A moment lingered. Then, without saying a word, the three of them slid their plates away, and hurried into the parlor, leaving kitchen clean up for later. His mother immediately handed him his first present, a soft bundle. Aiwren ripped though the parchment wrapping like a mad-man. He expected a new shirt, but nothing as fine as the white silk shirt he received.

"Thank you," Aiwren said as he stood up to hug his parents, "Now you open one of mine."

The first present Aiwren had for Madeline was a large tube. Aiwren's wrapping job wasn't as neat as his mother's, but she smiled at his attempt. She lifted the heavy object.

"My word," Madeline uttered. "What on earth?"

Madeline unwrapped a roll of thick parchment.

"That's the Farmer's Almanac for this entire annual. If you read that, you'll know everything that happened across the lands since last Vari-Matera-a, but the best part is that a courier will deliver you a supplement every fortnight to keep you updated on the world. You'll have to keep me and pop notified of any important news."

"I recon we have our own town crier, now!" Cillian joked.

"I realized you're always reading the same stories," Aiwren said. "I didn't know what other stories you'd like, so I figured the news would be good."

"Only good news!" Cillian joked.

"I love it, Aiwren," Madeline said, choking back tears as she hugged her son. "I love it."

"Okay, now you, pop."

"Oh. My turn?" Cillian said, feigning disinterest. "I'd lost track."

"Here," Aiwren said, handing his father a gift.

Cillian looked as stumped as Madeline when Aiwren handed him his gift, a peculiarly shaped package. Skinny at one end and wide at the other. Peeling away the wrapping, he almost dropped the gift. Beneath the parchment, the golden hue of beautifully stained wood stared at him like an old friend. He slowly tore more wrapping away, revealing four strings traveling down a darkly stained neck interrupted incrementally by bronze frets. The strings arrived at four pegs on the head of the delicate instrument. Cillian ripped the other way. The parchment fell from the smooth curved body of the mandolin.

"Mum used to tell me how you used to play. I thought perhaps you'd like to again, but if you don't mind, please sing the romantic serenades to mum when I'm not around."

Cillian tried to speak as a lifetime flashed across his face and his fingers gently touched the wood.

"This is a wonderful gift, my son."

"Play us something, father. Please."

"Been some time," Cillian said, looking at Madeline. "Perhaps later."

A little disappointed, Aiwren nodded, but also noticed that his father didn't put the instrument aside, keeping the mandolin on his lap as though that was its home.

Madeline diplomatically reached for another present and handed Aiwren two bundles tied together. Aiwren's jaw dropped at the fine trousers and beautiful blazer.

"They're incredible!"

"Look in the pocket," Madeline said.

Aiwren reached inside the pocket and pulled out a beautiful blue neck scarf.

"My idea," Cillian confessed with a wink.

Aiwren knew his parents couldn't afford the expensive clothing they'd given him. As his parents opened their gifts for each other, mostly mundane items for around the ranch, Aiwren's thoughts drifted to the joy he would have strolling into town in his fine new clothes.

"You've a few more gifts, son," Cillian said, tossing a large backpack to Aiwren.

Confused Aiwren carefully opened the pack. It was filled with traveling supplies, a rugged shirt, work trousers, new riding boots, and, at the bottom, a sack of coins. Aiwren opened the sack to count the copper, but it also contained silver and even a few gold.

"Should be enough to get you to Y-Kewnor," Cillian said. "We know you want to go."

Aiwren was speechless. He had no idea how his parents had afforded this.

Madeline continued, "You have to leave tomorrow. We've already paid your fees. You'll begin your apprenticeship in four suns."

"I'm going to Y-Kewnor," Was all Aiwren could say. It was a dream-come-true for Aiwren. No more farm. No more town-boys picking on him. He was going to Y-Kewnor to learn a trade. He would return to Ribeln as a respectable man. He would return a tailor.

"Perhaps I'll read about all the wonderful clothing you'll design in the almanac you gave me," Madeline said.

Cillian picked up the mandolin. His wife and son stared attentively while he tuned it. Without introduction, Cillian's fingers plucked the strings. He'd seen the other farmers play their fiddles or pipes, but never anything like this. He watched his father's large fingers dance magically across the strings, creating the most beautiful sound Aiwren had ever heard. As Aiwren was about to applaud, thinking his father was finished, Cillian opened his mouth and sang as he played.

Aiwren sat with his parents in their parlor for the remainder of the afternoon and into the evening, playing games, singing songs, eating, drinking and having fun. Although he was lost in the moment, a moment of bliss with his family, in the back of his mind, he was imagining the future and his life about to change.

***

Princess Teryessa was weeping in her wedding gown when Lionara entered her chambers. The young princess looked up to her nurse for answers, for encouragement, for reassurance.

"The way I see it, you've got two choices o what to do when that barbarian tries to ave is way with you. Now, e may be gentla with ya if ya let im do what e wants ta do, but suppose ya don't cooperate with im. What do you think e's gonna do?"

Teryessa wanted so badly to run, but Grell's guards were certainly right outside her door, waiting, hoping for her to attempt an escape. She was trapped.

"I think he'll probably be rough with me."

"You're probably right, but maybe, if you put up enough of a fight, he'll think twice about avin' is way with ya the next time. And maybe, after a little while, e'll decide it ain't worth the bother and e'll leave ya be."

"Do you think so, Lionara? Truly?"

"I don't know ow those barbarian's minds work, love. That may make im like it more."

Lionara put her hands on Teryessa's chest.

"Never ever let go o what's in ere. You lock this away if you ave to. You bury this deep deep inside if you ave to. But don't you dare let im touch what's in ere. Don't you let im get to your eart."

A huge reed organ played her favorite wedding march when Princess Teryessa walked down the aisle later that morning, stepping in time with a morose dirge, as though marching to her own execution. Prince Grell waited for her at the altar, flashing her a sickening smile that told her she belonged to him; he won. She reached her fiancé. The music stopped.

The service was crude and over in moments. Teryessa nodded meekly in acceptance of her vows. Then, Grell grabbed her, pressed his face against hers, and drove his slimy tongue deep into her mouth.

At the reception, Teryessa sat next to Grell. She needed a moment to tell her father what she heard the night before, but he was at the other end of the table and Grell was watching over her like a hawk.

Guests from Gavlessa lined up to congratulate Grell and Teryessa smiled as she was supposed to. Eventually, Chancellor Plale approached their table. Teryessa recognized him immediately as one of the conspirators from the previous night.

"Congratulations, Prince Grell. Your new wife appears to be a virgin. I wish you enjoyment in breaking her in."

Teryessa fumed.

"Thank you, Chancellor. It will be my pleasure."

The chancellor continued, "There are matters I'd like to discuss. I'm sure you'll be pleased with what I have to share."

Like a snake erupting from its coil, Teryessa reached across the mugs and dinner plates, grabbed the chancellor by his collar, and slammed his face into the table.

"What ever you have planned, forget about it, or so-help-me, I will skin you alive."

So focused on Plale, Teryessa didn't have time to react to Grell. The back of his hand struck her hard.

The chancellor chuckled as he rubbed his sore neck and said, "She certainly has some fight in her, Prince Grell. I'm sure you will enjoy your new wife, indeed."

"Yes," Grell conceded. "This one should definitely prove to be enjoyable."

"Well, I hope you don't beat all the fight out of her before you open her services to the public."

Grell smiled as Chancellor Plale bowed to him. As soon as the Chancellor's back was turned, Grell grabbed the meat knife from his plate and, with a flick, had the blade pressed hard to Teryessa's neck.

"You think you're cheeky, little girl? You think you can embarrass me before my servants without any punishment? Mouth off again, and I'll slit your throat from ear to ear. Do you understand?"

Teryessa nodded and Grell pulled the knife away.

"Good," he said, handing her a bottle. "Drink this."

"What is it?" Teryessa asked.

"When I tell you to drink something, you drink it. Have I made myself clear?"

Teryessa nodded.

Grell gestured towards the bottle with his head. Teryessa gingerly reached for it. Hands shaking, she uncorked it and looked at Grell. He nodded. She brought the bottle to her lips and drank.

"That's numbendria," Grell smiled. "It should make the remainder of the evening more pleasant for both of us."

Grell's words and the world faded away, receding behind a curtain of fog in Teryessa's mind. Her arms tingled and melted down to her side. Her eyes opened inquisitively wide at passing objects blurring by her. Nothing mattered. Her cares evaporated. The rest of the reception dissolved into a haze. Faces faded into one another. She wanted to sleep, but her eyes refused to close. She wanted to cry, but she didn't know why and she didn't feel particularly sad. Drugged by the numbendria, she was simultaneously present and absent. At one point she found herself dancing with Grell on the ballroom floor. At another point she found herself eating an enormous leg of turkey with her bare hands. At another point she found herself lying on the floor behind the table. These isolated moments resonated briefly, then evanesced seamlessly into her emotionless drugged blur.

Finally, Grell stood to address the crowd and said, "Ladies and Gentlemen of Gavlessa and Lees Naglos, thank you for joining me and my new bride this evening, to congratulate us on this arrangement and wish us a happy future. I am confident that my strength and her obedience will blend to form a perfect union. Right, princess?"

Before Teryessa could willfully react, she found herself responding a monotone, "Yes, my prince."

"Already she's learned how to respond to my whims. Are you my royal concubine, my princess?"

Again, as though she had no control of her actions, Teryessa said, "Yes, my prince."

The Gavlessans in the crowd cheered and applauded, while those from Lees Naglos shifted uncomfortably.

"Would you like a demonstration of my wife's submission?"

The Gavlessans in the crowd laughed and cheered as the guests from Lees Naglos worked their way towards the door, extricating themselves from the tasteless situation.

"Are you my hound, my princess?"

"Yes, my prince."

"Show me, my princess. Bark like a dog."

Without hesitation, Teryessa barked like a dog. Almost aware of the situation, but not quite, she realized she should feel horrible, but she didn't. She felt numb. Careless.

"Not only is my bride obedient. She is also beautiful and will make a wonderful addition to my collection. I was going to wait until after the consummation of our wedding, but would anyone here care to see what I'm getting out of this marriage before, I try out her gifts for myself?"

With the Lees Naglos citizens shuffling toward the exits, the remaining Gavlessan crowd cheered, this time the loudest of them all. Men pounded their goblets on their tables, stamped their feet on the floor, clapped their hands, and howled at the top of their lungs.

"Well, my princess. What are you waiting for? Remove your gown. Show our guests your bare bosom and your treasures down below!"

Teryessa almost stopped herself, but something inside of her forced her to continue. She reached behind her back for her dress's laces.

"Enough!" Noldar's voice boomed from the back of the ballroom. "I will not have you make a mockery of my daughter in my own hall!"

Teryessa froze, her hands still on the laces of her dress. She didn't want to take off her clothes in front of these strangers, but she couldn't think of a reason why not to. She wanted to be thoughtless, wanted to be absent, she wanted to ride the high of the numbendria. Seeing her father approach, Teryessa's spirit crumbled, but still frozen, unable to cry or even frown, she only stared forward with dead eyes.

"Your army may be more brutal than mine, Grell, but I could cut you down in a heartbeat right now, which is what I aim to do, unless you end this humiliation at once," Noldar whispered to Grell loud enough for Teryessa to hear. "I suspect a military success will provide you with little joy if you are cleaved in half. I am going to take a moment to say good-bye to my daughter in privacy and then you will leave my castle. I suggest you make good use of the time I'm allowing you and saddle up before I change my mind."

For a moment, fear appeared to penetrate Grell's cool façade. His eyes narrowed. Sweat beaded on his brow. Then, he gathered his wits and let out a laugh.

"You think you frighten me, old man?"

"I care not if I frighten you, barbarian, but sure as the sun, I will cut you down. The decision to live or die is yours."

"The reception is over! Everyone go home!" Grell announced, staring at Noldar. "I'm ready to return to Gavlessa to consummate my wedding."

Grell and his guests quickly exited the ballroom. Only the king and his daughter remained.

"I don't know what to say to you, Teryessa. This is my fault."

Something in the back of Teryessa's mind decided to fight the mindless apathy of her numbendria high and, for a moment, she won.

"There is a plot. A horrible plot."

"That beast drugged you."

"No! Please, father. Listen."

"Okay. I'll listen. What is it?"

"It's a plot... a plan... a... what is the word? Last night. I overheard... The Chancellor and... and a man. I know him... His name... He says he is serving you, but he isn't; he's serving himself. They... they're going to..."

The fog in Teryessa's brain took over again.

"I love you more than anything in this world and I fear I've made a mistake I cannot amend," Noldar said. "If I see that monster with you again, I will kill him, and, though I care nothing of my own life, in seeking revenge, his father would kill every man, woman, and child living in Lees Naglos. Though I can not improve your situation, I can do my best to curb my fury so your sacrifice isn't meaningless. I am so sorry, sweet daughter. I love you."

Noldar hugged his daughter one last time, then hurried out of the room.

"I love you, too, father."

The ballroom doors slammed open. Teryessa didn't flinch.

"We're going!"

Teryessa was about to go to her husband, but she didn't react quickly enough for him. He grabbed her by her hair and dragged her.

Out the front doors and into the square, hundreds of guests watched, as the Gavlessan prince dragged their beloved princess, high on numbendria, out of the castle. Teryessa found one familiar face in the crowd. Lionara. She had tears in her eyes. As she was being dragged, Teryessa wondered, out of casual curiosity, what her beloved nurse was so upset about.

The doors to the carriage flew open. Grell pushed her in and climbed in after her. Plale, already in the carriage, sat opposite of him.

"I'm delighted you rearranged your transportation back to Gavlessa on such short notice, Chancellor."

"It is an honor to share a carriage with the prince on the night of his wedding. What can I do for you, Your Highness?"

"I want Noldar dead."

Plale chuckled. Teryessa couldn't believe what she was hearing. She wanted to respond, but her mouth wouldn't work.

"Do you think this is appropriate conversation, considering the present company?"

Plale nodded to Teryessa. Her eyes opened wide.

"Don't worry about her," Grell snapped. "That man made a fool of me in front of everyone. He needs to be an example for others who would cross me. Is this a problem, Chancellor?"

"No," Plale responded. "I think you and I can definitely arrange a mutually beneficial agreement. This might require a little something of you, however."

"What is it? Name the price."

"I merely wish to suggest that, if we are going into the business of making examples and killing kings, perhaps another assassination is over due."

"To even suggest such a thing is treason," Grell snapped. "You're his chancellor!"

"I could be your chancellor."

Grell turned to Teryessa. "Do you like that? King Monnon Grell?"

The young princess nodded in apathetic agreement, sitting silently with her new husband in the carriage as it travelled east, unable to stop thinking about her father. There was no way to warn him. He was going to die.

Outside, the sun was setting. Varishiva-a and Varishanta-a, the two moons of Vari-Matera-a, were rising. The demon moon and the ghost moon created a hazy purple glow that crept across Allyoshmar as night descended upon the land.

VARI-MATERA-ESHU

When the sun rose on Vari-Matera-Eshu, the day after the night of two moons, Aiwren Wayde woke up with the exuberance of a young man with the thrill of adventure coursing through his veins. He raced through milking and feeding with a song in his heart and a bounce in his step, crooning to the dairy cows who enjoyed the music, especially Persephone, who coquettishly mooed along with him and received a kiss on the nose for her part in the duet. As the Wayde family cows were sent off to pasture that morning, Aiwren laughed at them gleefully galloping out into the expansive green field, marveling at how surprisingly spry the simple lumbering beasts could be when treated to freedom.

On his way back in from releasing the cows out into the field, Aiwren visited his little hiding spot in the barn again to steal another moment with the sword his father had given to him. After a glance over his shoulder, he unsheathed the sword and swung wildly with it. He wasn't particularly athletic and he hadn't a lick of formal training, only what his father had taught him, but the weight balanced perfectly in his hands.

Aiwren was already in the kitchen when Madeline entered. He had started the porridge for her. Pleased with himself, he glanced over his shoulder, beaming a proud smile at her. She threw her arms around him and hugged tightly.

"I will miss you with all of my heart, my son," she said, refusing to let go. "Please stay safe."

"Of course, mum," he said, hugging her back, "I'll miss you, too."

Soon Cillian had joined them for breakfast. After finishing their food and discussing traveling routes, the three left the table. It was time for Aiwren to leave.

After hugs and kisses and several false goodbyes, Aiwren finally headed out the gate and down the path on foot. When he crested that first hill on the little dirt road, he turned to look at the only home he had ever known. Cillian and Madeline, still at the gate, holding each other, watched their only son, with an enormous pack on his back, wave at them one last time before he disappeared over the horizon.

The first leg of Aiwren's journey to Y-Kewnor would be a familiar one. He would head into town the same way he and his father often did, but instead of turning around and heading back he would continue on. As he walked towards Ribeln, his thoughts drifted to fantasies of fighting Quinntonn with his new sword. He had packed away his city clothes since he didn't have time to hem them and he didn't want them to get dirty from the road, but part of him wished to strut around town in his new outfit.

As Aiwren passed the Nillhalla farm, he thought of Vannoria and wondered if he should stop by to visit. He stopped at her gate, at the road and still far from her home, and contemplated. Reaching for the gate, he thought of Vari-Matera-a-Shol. Of their kiss. Of the dark and disturbing thoughts he had. He didn't want those thoughts again. He decided it would be best to avoid her. She would be fine here, happy, but he had to go to the city. He had to move on and saying goodbye would make that difficult. He continued walking and told himself he would send her a letter from Y-Kewnor.

Ribeln was quiet that morning. It was usually quiet on Vari-Matera-Eshu. The children showed off their toys to one another near their homes, while the adults remained in doors, suffering the results of their Vari-Matera-a indulgences. Aiwren was content with an empty town as he headed towards Ribeln's west gate, so lost in his thoughts that he didn't notice Quinntonn and his lackeys following him until it was too late.

Aiwren's face hit the cobblestones hard. The crunch and the searing pain told him his nose had been broken. Blood poured from his nostrils and, before Aiwren could react, Quinntonn was on his back, forcing his face into the ground. Aiwren struggled, unable to free himself.

"How do you like that, country boy?"

A loud crack rang out. Quinntonn had been knocked off of him by something. Aiwren scrambled to his feet.

Bonishara stood above him holding her staff ready to strike again as Quinntonn climbed to his feet, nursing the new welt on his jaw.

"You'll pay for this old woman," Quinntonn threatened as he and his lackeys ran off, "I'm telling my father."

"Then I'll turn your whole family into the jackasses you are. You'll be lucky to escape with your lives."

Surprisingly strong, she helped Aiwren to his feet.

"Thank you," he muttered, humiliated by the bullies.

"You must find Crystal Blade," Bonishara replied.

"That's absurd," Aiwren said dismissively. "I appreciate your help, but it was unnecessary."

Bonishara shrugged and shuffled off, leaving Aiwren alone by the western gates of Ribeln. He wanted to casually exit his village, to pretend it wasn't important in making him who he was and to pretend that at least part of him didn't believe Bonishara, but as soon as he was certain nobody was looking, he ran.

Aiwren ran until, certain the town boys hadn't followed him, Ribeln shrank into the distance behind him. Content with his safety, he sat to catch his breath and convince himself everything would soon be better. He was going to Y-Kewnor to be a tailor and it would be nothing but fun and excitement. After resting for only a few minutes, he stood and continued down the little dirt road that stretched across the farmlands west of Ribeln and into the Indigo Forest.

Aiwren walked strait through until lunch, passing by farmers he knew and farmers he had never met but recognized from town. He passed a camp of Nomasha, with their brightly painted wagons clustered in a circle around a camp fire. Eventually he stopped and sat on the fence of a farm. The last farm in the Ribeln County. Beyond this was the Indigo Forest and all the other places he had never been.

Aiwren ate his lunch and stared into the Indigo Forest. He thought about Y-Kewnor and what city life would be like. Then, thumbing the edge of his sword for a moment before getting up, he thought about Bonishara. He told himself that she was just a crazy old woman, but he wondered for a moment if there really was a Crystal Order. Chuckling at his own childish fantasies, he stood and headed into the forest.

The Indigo Forest was named after the rich blue color of the leaves of the indigo willows that populated the forest. Along their blue dangling tendrils, grew bright white flowers. The flowers made a delicious and refreshing tea, the soft skin under the bark was good for relieving pain, and the leaves were good for treating wounds to prevent infection. As Aiwren entered the woods, he hurried past several Nomasha women gathering the various tree parts and putting them in baskets. The branches of the indigo willows stretched overhead to create a beautiful blue and white tunnel over the damp dirt road, with beams of sunlight slipping between the leaves. To the side of the road, large moss-covered boulders peppered the grassy ground between the trees. Continuing west, these mossy rocks grew into the Perdition Mountains, but Aiwren planned to head south at a fork before then, where he also planned to camp for the night.

The day passed quickly for Aiwren, who imagined how exciting Y-Kewnor would be as he strolled down the road, occasionally stopping to view the scenery or smell a flower, until it was time to set up camp, a simple bed roll, the dinner his mother made for him, and a fire to treat himself to some tea from a handful of indigo willow flowers he had picked.

***

By dawn, with the grass still dewy and the sky still dark, the hooves of the Nameless Rider's steed were already pounding into the damp country gravel. What did he care of the traditional Vari-Matera-a quarantine? He didn't know fear. He only knew purpose. By the light of the moons, he, on his mount, a massive black horse with fiery eyes, galloped across a vast savanna towards the small town on the horizon. He knew it wouldn't be long. The Nameless Rider's eyes narrowed with singular determination.

In the dark, he and his horse appeared to be only a dark flash whipping across the plain, but as the light spread, his figure became more pronounced. A deep, dark hood cast an impenetrable shadow over his face and his black cloak rippled in the wind behind him. His gloved hands tightened into fists around the reins. He was man. At least he may have been at some point. He wasn't sure what he was anymore or what base moral turpitude shaped what he had become. He had no memory of such things, but it didn't matter. What mattered was serving his Master and, on this morning, that meant finding the Boy at all costs.

Small farms with lamps not yet lit passed by him as he rode hard across the plain, but life in the outskirts of the county of Ribeln was awakening. An old woman walked along the side of the road with a bucket of eggs in each hand. She turned to see who was galloping so fast so early. She turned as white as a sheet, dropping her buckets of eggs in a frozen panic, when she saw him, but he whooshed by and she hurried back to her home, slamming the door shut behind her and leaving her eggs by the side of the dirt road.

Well into the morning, the Nameless Rider approached the Boy's farm. His horse slowed, then stopped and waited for him. The Nameless Rider examined the farm. A puff of mist bellowed from his steed's nostrils like dragon smoke. Emotionless, the Nameless Rider watched the small dairy farm and listened. The Boy was gone. He didn't understand the mechanics of how he knew that, but it didn't matter to him. The only thing that mattered was the Boy. The Nameless Rider rode on.

The ground moved quickly beneath the hooves of his horse, a beast nearly as terrifying as the Nameless Rider, himself. As the sun rose and baked the earth, evaporating the dew on the narrow dirt road, clouds of dust enveloped the ferociously galloping rider; failure was never an option for the errands he was tasked with.

The small town of Ribeln was protected by old magic, magic the people of the town didn't even know was protecting them, magic that kept out creatures like the Nameless Rider. So, as he drew close and felt the power of the unrecognizable glyphs written on the wall, faded but still potent, he knew he would have to circumvent the town.

The horse charged more fiercely than ever around the town and on the road to the west of town. He didn't know what was special about the Boy; he only knew the orders of his Master and, as he approached the Indigo Forest without a sign of the Boy, he knew these orders would take him into the woods.

Riding through the Indigo Forest was slower, but, as a creature of the shadows, the canopy of blue leaves blocking out the light brought the Nameless Rider comfort. Trotting slowly, he focussed on the road to his right, looking for the Boy. The beams of light piercing between leaves, limbs, and flowers eventually dimmed. As the sun set and the visible sky relinquished itself once again to star-speckled inky black, the Nameless Rider caught his first glimpse of the Boy arranging a bedroll for the night and sipping tea by a small fire. He had found his target; now, he would wait.

***

Teryessa stared out her little window, her mouth open and drooling, as the sun rose before the carriage, silhouetting the barbed rusty metal towers on the horizon. Out her tiny circular window, a blurry view of sand whisked by her. She wondered if it was the window or her vision that was blurry. After focusing on the details of one particular smear of grime, she decided it was the window, but she didn't see the point in knowing. Time ebbed by pointlessly as it grew brighter and brighter outside of Teryessa's blurry little window.

Eventually the carriage slowed down. Chains and gears clunked and clanged, but Teryessa saw only desert. Then, there was darkness, as the carriage disappeared into the subterranean city. The sudden darkness broke Teryessa's fixed gaze, but before her eyes could adjust, a large iron door slammed into place behind the royal carriage. She looked around the carriage. For a moment, there was nothing, then Teryessa noticed a dim oil lantern. It was inches from her face. Beyond it was Grell's face. He looked at her hungrily.

"Welcome home, Princess."

Three large guards, wearing nothing but filthy loin clothes and stinking of putrid rot grabbed Teryessa and pulled her from the carriage. Hands grabbed all over her body, but she didn't fight, even when the shackle ratcheted around her neck. With a ferocious rip, her wedding gown, torn in two, slid to the ground. She stood in her undergarments, numb and blank.

Below Teryessa's feet was a street, not of cobblestone, but of sand compacted to nearly the hardness of stone. Buildings lined both sides of the street, not the little thatched roof buildings she was accustomed to, but tall buildings that seemed to have several stories, like a castle. These buildings were made of the same packed sand as the street and they didn't have thatched roofs. Instead, they climbed right up to the top of the cave. The whole city was inside one giant cave. Nearly a mile away, at the end of this underground street, was a castle. It was also made of the sand, but it was also ornamented with buttresses, arches, spikes, barbs, and trimmings made of twisted rusty metal. Just like the other buildings, the castle had no roof; no beautiful minarets, onion domes, or spires. Instead, its decaying metallic towers and walls thrust right up into the ceiling of the cave.

Standing beside the castle was another massive structure, the Pitt Stadium, an enormous colosseum where Gavlessans went to bet on and participate in vicious blood sports.

Word of the arrival of the carriage must have spread. Gavlessans poked their heads from their buildings and poured into the street. Teryessa had witnessed the peasants of Lees Naglos rush to welcome her or her father, but it was nothing like this, nothing so savage. A primitive craving illuminated their maddened eyes and ran a chill up her spine.

Gavlessan guards lined up on either side of the street. These weren't anything like the Royal Army in Lees Naglos, with discipline, self-control, hygiene, and polished homogenous armor or the glamorous Divine Empress's Knights, armored in elaborate silver or gold. Each of the Gavlessan guards had a different piece or armor. A bracer here. A shield there. A chest plate here. A helmet there. Most of their bodies were unprotected. The armor wasn't polished either. It was painted. An illustration of a decapitated head. A nude woman. A dragon. A skeleton. The most frightening thing about these guards to Teryessa, however, was their ice cold faces of pasty white skin looking upon her menacingly.

As Grell exited the carriage the place erupted with noise. Screams and howls. Clanging of metal. Sounds that shouldn't come from people. Sounds that should come from animals.

The princess heard the low grumble of dunebeasts, scores of them. Horses weren't well suited for the desert terrain or climate, so the Gavlessans, back when they were nothing more than nomadic raiders, domesticated the dunebeasts. They were enormous lizards, closer to the ground for a lower center of gravity than horses on the shifting and unstable sand, with long horns on their head that the Gavlessans held onto as they rode the creatures. The creatures were protected similarly to the Gavlessan Guards with a smattering of mismatched armor here and there. The end of each beast's tail was fashioned with a weapon: Giant Ax, Huge War Hammer, or Gigantic Spiked-Ball and Chain. These creatures appeared slow and cumbersome, but, although they weren't very nimble, once they started charging they were fast and powerful juggernauts.

"Let's go, Princess!" Grell growled.

With a leash in his hands connected to the shackle around her neck, he began walking towards the castle. When the leash ran out of slack, Grell gave a firm tug and, almost falling to the ground, the dazed Teryessa stumbled after him. The prince's royal guard fell in line after her. Looking over her shoulder, she marched on and the dress, trampled by the royal guard, grew distant.

For most of her shameful walk, Teryessa remained disconnected from the world around her. She was thankful for the numbendria. She concentrated on its effect on her, allowing the fear and sorrow to melt away and dissipate. Had she been more alert she would have heard the foul tongues of the Gavlessans as they insulted her and ridiculed her, but locked away inside her mind, unable to feel humiliation or fear, she heard only wordless voices and felt nothing.

The princess wasn't sure how long she'd been walking. Time blurred together, compressing and expanding until meaningless, but all the elastic time seemed to catch up with Teryessa in an instant when she arrived at the Pitt Stadium.

Rather than becoming overcome with dread, Teryessa thought back to her history lessons, remembering with emotionless fascination how essential the pitt was to Gavlessan society. Originally a loosely associated group of pirating nomads, the Gavlessans, even when organized into an empire, centuries prior, had retained their freedom to loot and pillage individually. A Gavlessan would raid a party traveling across the desert and return to Gavlessa with his plunder. Driven by greed and jealousy, the Gavlessan raider would be unsatisfied with his loot and take it to the pitt. The pitt was an on-going gladiator tournament. It never stopped; there were always bloody fights for Gavlessans to bet their loot on. Each fighter and his record would be examined by the probabilitists, a group of men working directly for the chancellor, who would determine the odds of each fight. If the betting Gavlessan betted correctly, the amount of loot he would win would be determined by the odds of the fight he had bet on. If he won, he could significantly increase his wealth. If he lost, he could lose everything. If he could not pay his debts, he would be forced into service as a Pitt Fighter. These Pitt Fighters forced into service by debt were called Fradats. One could also volunteer to be a Pitt Fighter. These volunteers were called the Ravusas and were among Gavlessa's deadliest warriors; many were Gavlessan Beast Raiders, themselves. Ravusas would be rewarded for each successful battle and could also bet on themselves to increase their reward further if they won. The other way a man could become a Pitt Fighter was by capture. In a raid, Gavlessans rarely killed all of their victims. The strongest and best would be brought back to Gavlessa, sold to the probabilitists, and forced into pitt fighting. These Pitt Fighters were called Vlases. Between the Vlases, the Fradats, and the Ravusas, there was a seemingly limitless supply of fighters. The pitt fights had drawn the Gavlessans together long ago and were still the foundation of Gavlessan society. Since the chancellor controlled the probabilitists, he controlled the odds and, therefore, the wealth and power. No matter who was king of Gavlessa, the chancellor would always be the one pulling the strings.

Prince Grell led Teryessa into a room with hundreds of cages, cages no bigger than her own bedroom. Cubes forged from rusty iron, surrounded by torches for the viewing pleasure of the audience, betting from rickety rotten benches as they watched their own fate unfold in the cage before them.

As the princess walked by a cage, a savage man with one eye crushed his opponent's head to pulp with an enormous spiked club. Blood showered the spectators. A drop landed on Teryessa's cheek. It may have been the grizzly sight or it may have been because the numbendria had run its course, but Teryessa's heart raced, twisting her stomach into a sour, convulsive panic.

"Enjoying my work, princess?" Plale hissed, slithering up to her. "Would you like to make it go away?"

Teryessa nodded to Plale who tossed her a bottle. The princess uncorked it and took a large sip.

The wave of numbendria swept over Teryessa again and the sights of the pitts blurred by her. The guards opened a heavy stone door and Grell led her onto a small platform on the rim of a massive pit, an arena populated by hundreds of blood-thirsty Gavlessans. At the edge of the platform, a thin bridge made of rope and wood stretched over the arena to a similar platform on the opposite side.

Grell stepped to the edge. Below, a large horn bellowed a resonant note. The Gavlessans erupted with cheer for Prince Grell. Teryessa hesitated for a moment when Grell stepped onto the small bridge, but he yanked on her leash and she followed. High above the arena, the world spun for the princess. She gripped the ropes on either side of her, struggling to put one foot in front of the other. On the other side, Teryessa found herself on another small platform over the arena.

At the back of the platform, an open door led to a small stairwell. The stairs looked ancient, carved of stone from another time. An overwhelming darkness radiated from the chasm.

"Teryessa. Come to me," the princess thought she heard someone say, but when she peered into the darkness she saw nothing.

Grell tugged on her leash and she followed him as he climbed up the flight of stairs, glad she wasn't forced to descend into the darkness.

There were two sets of enormous doors on the upper level, each guarded by a pair of Gavlessans. One set of doors seemed to lead back into the arena. The other set, presumably, led into the castle. The guards standing by the arena doors opened them.

Grell dragged Princess Teryessa onto another brightly painted platform with five thrones and a railing standing between her and the arena below. Each throne was a disgusting collage of intricately twisted iron. In the center was the largest throne, obviously for a king who was absent. To its left was a smaller empty throne for a queen. Plale sat in an even smaller throne to the left of the queen's throne. To the right of the king's throne, and nearly as grand, was Grell's throne. Finally, next to Grell's throne, was the smallest and plainest throne of them all. Teryessa knew her place. She sat.

Behind them, the guards closed the doors again. Grell stood and, in a bellowing voice, addressed the crowd.

"People of Gavlessa. I have returned from Lees Naglos, where their feeble king has offered me a gift, the hand of his daughter. He thinks this bribe can persuade us to overlook his kingdom in our conquest of Allyoshmar, but no kingdom shall ever be spared in our campaign for domination. Gavlessans don't wait for gifts or bribes! We take! And nobody will ever stand in our way."

The Gavlessans leapt to their feet, cheering loudly.

"In celebration of our fearlessness, I present you with... the Royal Pitt Battle!"

Again, the Gavlessans cheered. This time, their cheering cued the music, a course fanfare of horns, drums and some sort of bagpipe. Over the music, Grell continued.

"Merciless warriors of Gavlessa, this warrior has killed hundreds in the arena and on the battlefield. He's known and feared for dismembering his opponents! Savage, brutal, and ruthless, he is a true Gavlessan hero. Gavlessa: Ovyrr-Keel!"

Below, in the arena, an iron door burst open. From inside, a positively terrifying man emerged. It was Ovyrr-Keel, a terrifying example of a Ravusa. Huge plates of armor haphazardly clung to his impossibly enormous body. Gripping a huge battle ax in his giant hands, he lumbered to the center of the arena. Gavlessans cheered. He thrust his ax into the air and they cheered even louder.

"Merciless warriors of Gavlessa, this warrior travelled all the way here from Auptherenon as a threat to our people. He has killed scores of our best warriors and wants to prove that the Auptherenese are the best warriors. He spits in the face of our people. His name is Ryz Scor!"

While Ovyrr-Keel was just massive, Ryz Scor was lean and muscular. His plated armor was more streamline. His weapon was a long staff with a large blade at the end, the halberd. The Gavlessans booed as the proud man strutted from his cage.

The two warriors met in the middle of the arena, ready to battle.

"Fight!"

Ryz was the first to strike. He swung his halberd. Sparks flew as the blow glanced off of Ovyrr's shoulder plate. Ovyrr laughed like boards breaking. Ryz swung again. Ovyrr effortlessly knocked the halberd aside with his battle ax. Sensing an opening, Ryz thrust forward, but Ovyrr grabbed the staff of his halberd. Panic rushed into Ryz's eyes. Ovyrr was already swinging his ax. The blade came down hard, crushing more than slicing. The shoulder plate crumpled as the ax ripped diagonally through Ryz's body and a shower of blood sprayed into the air. Ryz fell to his knees as blood spurted from his mouth. As his knees hit the ground his torso fell from his body and into the sand, exposing the spine and entrails of his lower torso before that, too, fell. Ovyrr thrust his ax into the air. The audience leapt to their feet and cheered.

"That's power," Grell sneered.

Princess Teryessa found herself being dragged, by leash, out the back door and into the great room of Grell's palace, a museum to Grell's father's conquests. For all the dinginess of Gavlessa, Grell's palace was lit with an abundance of bright colors: red, pink, blue, purple, orange, and yellow. There was no order or pattern, no attention paid to matching or aesthetics in any way. A bright mural wrapping around the room documented King Grell's rise to power, complete with a section detailing him slaying the previous king in battle and another section graphically depicting Prince Grell being conceived. A series of brightly colored tapestries illustrated women being sodomized in various ways. Another series of tapestries celebrated the violence of the pitt. The centerpiece of the great room was an enormous statue of King Grell. The room was lit with a variety of mismatched torches, lamps, and lanterns. The whole nauseatingly gaudy place blurred by Teryessa as Grell dragged her through.

Passing through a confusing maze of narrow, twisting passages and corridors, Teryessa found herself in the throne room. In the throne at the far end of the room slumped King Grell. Unlike, Teryessa's father, Grell was an old king; however, rather than rightfully inheriting his kingdom in his due time, King Grell was an ambitious Ravusa who seized power for himself. From her lessons, Teryessa remembered how he confronted the previous king to a Pitt Challenge and how everyone speculated that the chancellor, who had several confrontations with the previous king, had fixed the fight in the senior Grell's favor. Shortly after his coronation, Grell enslaved the most beautiful woman in Gavlessa and impregnated her. Nine moon cycles later, his son, Monnon Grell, was born. The king ruled for over thirty annuals, during which time the world feared Gavlessa more than ever before. He rewarded cruelty on the battlefield and punished weakness or mercy. King Grell believed the only way to wage war was with brute and relentless force. Other than the strength of Lees Naglos, which was dwindling, the only thing preventing Gavlessa from spreading its empire of terror was King Grell's lack of strategy.

The large king dozed off in his throne. A scar ran across his face, from his left eye to his right ear. His long grey beard, littered with chunks of meat, gravy, and gristle, twisted and curled like a briar patch, down to his bare, rotund, gut. He wore silk loin cloth that flowed from a ruby-encrusted gold belt. On his massive arms, he wore heavy gold bracers. Even asleep, he was a terrifying beast of a man.

Prince Grell stepped towards the throne, letting go of Teryessa's leash on the way. As Prince Grell reached for his father's shoulder, his cruelty momentarily vanished; he was a son looking for his father's approval. The king opened his eyes. In one swift motion his blade was drawn and pressing into the prince's throat.

"You're lucky I didn't slit your throat, boy."

The boy in Grell's eyes vanished and was, once again, replaced by the monster.

"I apologize, Father," he said, with an edge as sharp as a razor. "I've returned with my bride."

"Perhaps, with this wench, you won't fail to provide me with a grandson. Step forward!" the king barked. "Step forward so I can examine you."

Princess Teryessa did as she was told. As the disgusting old king leaned forward, Teryessa feared whatever he was about to do. The old man pulled her close and sniffed between her legs.

"She's a virgin."

"Yes, Father. Noldar's word was true."

"Very well. Your sheets will be red tomorrow morning. If not from her blood, then from your own."

Prince Grell nodded. He grabbed the leash and walked away, tugging hard on Teryessa's neck as he left, leading her into his own throne room. It was smaller than the king's and decorated with many luxurious tapestries. Grell threw himself in his throne. Teryessa didn't know what to do.

"Sit!" the prince screamed at her. "On the floor, dog!"

Teryessa sat on the floor.

"Ruthillo!"

Grell buried his face in his hands. A moment later, a muscular man entered. His skin was dark. He had no facial hair and his head was completely bald. He was dressed in loin cloth and had a large curved blade attached to his waste, a scimitar.

Ruthillo stood before the prince, at attention.

"Your Highness?"

"Update me on what's happened in my absence."

"The king has been making increasingly erratic decisions, Your Highness. In celebration of Vari-Matera-a, he had seven of our best soldiers executed for no reason what-so-ever."

Grell stood up and started pacing.

"Damn it! What else?"

"Quirilla, your fifth wife, attempted an escape on Vari-Matera-a-Shol, but we captured her before she reached the surface."

"Have you punished her yet?"

"No, Your Highness. We were waiting for your instructions."

Grell approached Ruthillo. He stroked the man's head and closed in on him, faces almost touching.

"You are such a good servant, Ruthillo. You always cater to each and every one of my needs, anticipating my desires. Why can't anyone else serve me as well as you?"

The two men stood face to face for a long moment.

"Bring me the wretch!"

Without at word, Ruthillo exited. Prince Grell turned to Teryessa.

"You're in store for a real treat, Princess, a front row seat to witness Gavlessan justice."

Ruthillo returned accompanied by two guards dragging a young girl. The young girl struggled and squirmed. Her dress was ripped, torn, and dirty.

"Hold her!" Prince Grell shouted, approaching the girl.

"Quirilla, you disappoint me. I make you a part of my family, and this is how you repay me?"

"Please, Your Highness," Quirilla pleaded.

"Let her go," Grell told the guards. "She doesn't want to be with me. I shall give her what she wants."

The guards released the girl.

"It's too bad," Grell said. "I'll miss you."

Grell turned to walk away, but, as he took his first step, he drew his blade and swung with one swift, arcing motion. A thin red line appeared on the girl's throat. Her eyes widened. The line thickened. A crimson bead crashed to the floor with a nearly audible drop. She grabbed for her throat. She opened her mouth to scream, but no sound came forth, only air. Blood trickled from between her fingers. Her silent scream gurgled with liquid. She coughed. Blood spurted from her mouth. A veil of haze fell over her eyes as life slipped from her body. As she dropped to the floor Grell turned to Teryessa and smiled.

Ruthillo handed Grell a silk cloth. The prince wiped the blood from his blade and sheathed it at his side.

"Clean up the mess," Prince Grell said as he walked towards the door, gabbing Teryessa's leash on the way.

Grell dragged Teryessa into the next room, his private chambers.

"This isn't where you'll sleep, but it is where you'll do my bidding to provide me with a son."

Reality crashed down on Princess Teryessa. She knew this moment would come, but nothing could have prepared her for it.

"Undress."

Teryessa's hands trembled as she reached for her undergarment laces. She untied them and let the fabric slip off of her. She pulled on the ties to her bodice and it, too, fell to the ground. Standing in her chemise she trembled. She wanted to vomit. She loosened the tie around her neck and the chemise slipped away. She made no attempt to cover her nude body; modesty, at this point, was pointless. Tears slid silently down her cheek. Grell looked her up and down. Not the way a man would look at a woman he desires, but the way a buyer inspects a horse he has just purchased.

"Turn around," Grell said.

The princess did as she was told. Behind her, the prince's sword clanged against the ground as his trousers and belt fell from his waist. Teryessa turned to look and Prince Grell, noticing her gaze at his nude body, punched her in the face, dizzying her and crashing a jolt of pain through her numbness.

"Don't look at me!" he screamed. "Don't you fucking look at me! Turn around!"

Rattled, Teryessa turned back around, frightened for what he would do next. She braced herself as Grell's arm wrap around her waist, her pounding heart erupting from her body with dread. The world slipped from her grasp as darkness fell upon her.

Inside, Princess Teryessa's mind raced. She flew over desert, over plains, over forests, and over mountains, until an enormous white canvas of snow stretched out beneath her, twinkling in response to the stars overhead. She flew towards a brightness that forced the night to recede behind her as its form materialized on the horizon: a palace made of light. Princess Teryessa flew into the Palace of Light, not through a door, but right through its very essence. She was standing, it seemed, in a throne room, so beautiful, right, and pure. At the far end of the room, a woman waited for Teryessa. Nearly translucent, she wore a long flowing gown made of gleaming brilliance. A silvery waterfall of hair cascaded from her head, glistening over her porcelain skin and rose-petal lips. Her eyes were like molten gold swirling through the abyss of space. Without moving her mouth, she spoke and her voice was a song.

"Hello, Teryessa."

"Where am I?"

"Your body is still in Gavlessa, but part of you is here, in the Palace of Light."

"How did I get here?"

"I brought you here."

The woman reached for Teryessa's face with a touch as gentle as clouds. Teryessa's skin tingled warmly. A wave of peace washed over her body.

"You're The Divine Empress!" Teryessa said, falling to her knees, dropping her head in reverence.

"Please, stand, my child."

Teryessa stood on her feet again.

"Why have you summoned me, my Divine Empress?"

"You will have important decisions to make, my child."

With a graceful wave of her arm, The Divine Empress and Princess Teryessa glided through the walls of the Palace of Light. The two of them stood upon the edge of a giant glacier. Every color imaginable swam and swirled in sky above above, wavering and pulsing, overwhelming Teryessa with their splendor. Beyond the luminous swirls, the stars twinkled brightly in a night sky.

"The Source." Teryessa muttered.

"It is time for you to leave."

"But I've only just arrived. Can't I just stay here with you forever?"

"I wish you could. Things would be much easier that way. Unfortunately, what is easy is not always what is right."

Teryessa realized she was once again flying.

"Will I ever see you again?"

"I hope so, my child. I hope so."

Teryessa was now high in the air, floating towards The Source. The waves of color engulfed her, embraced her, and entered her very being. Everything flickered. Light flickered brighter and brighter, until she couldn't stand it anymore. She clenched her eyes tight as the light consumed here, then slipped away as though it had never been there.

Princess Teryessa opened her eyes to find herself looking into Prince Grell's cruel eyes. She was in his chamber, on his bed, on her back. Grell was pumping his waist into hers with no satisfaction or release. Her loins burned from friction, but weren't bleeding.

"I told you not to look!"

Grell pushed himself away from her and Teryessa realized that he was still limp. A fist crushed down fast on her, followed by momentary darkness, followed by pain in her nose. She reached for her face as blood gushed from her nostrils and onto her hands. The prince grabbed Teryessa's face and squeezed her mouth violently.

"If you tell anyone about this, I'll slit your throat like the dog you are. Ruthillo!"

The door opened. Ruthillo entered.

"Wake Plale. Bring him to my meeting room."

Ruthillo nodded obediently and exited as Grell pulled up his trousers. Before he put his shirt on, however, he grabbed a chair and threw it in a fit of rage. It hit hard against the wall above Teryessa's head, showering her with splinters. He grabbed his jacket.

"Dress!" the Prince screamed. "Stop looking at me."

Frightened, Teryessa scrambled for her clothes and, cowering in the corner, she dressed. When she was finished, Grell grabbed her leash and dragged her out of his room.

Chancellor Plale was already waiting for them in the Prince's meeting room when he and the Princess arrived.

"What is it, Your Highness?" Plale asked.

"Tonight is the night." Grell barked.

"Your Highness-"

"I don't care if I have to do it myself," Grell sneered to Plale. "He won't wake another morning!"

Prince Grell stormed away. Plale's thin lips curled into a dastardly smirk as he followed the prince out of the room. Ruthillo picked up Princess Teryessa's bottle of numbendria and handed it to her.

"Just let me know, Your Highness, when you need more."

Princess Teryessa narrowed her eyes at Ruthillo with burning contempt.

"I won't use the leash if you promise to follow me."

Princess Teryessa found herself waiting outside a door, while Ruthillo unlocked it with key he wore on a length of twine tied around his neck. He opened the door and she entered.

"I'm going to have to lock this door, Princess."

The princess said nothing as she entered the room.

Ruthillo nodded and closed the door behind her. With the click of the lock, Princess Teryessa knew she was alone in the small, bare room. Rats scurried from beneath a mildewy cot in the middle of the room, across the damp stone floor, and into a hole in the wall. It wasn't a room. It was a cell.

Princess Teryessa realized how exhausted she was. She fell into her bedbug-ridden cot and closed her eyes. As she drifted off to sleep one thought resonated through her mind. It wasn't her father. It wasn't being captured. It wasn't the several murders she'd witnessed that day. It wasn't being raped. It wasn't The Source. It wasn't The Divine Empress. As reality faded away, Princess Teryessa thought about the voice in the stairs and, before she fell asleep, she though she heard the voice again.

BALYSH-PAH

The night mellowed into dawn and Aiwren Wayde found himself far from the road or any path, wandering through a dense fog that clung to the earth and wrapped its wispy tendrils around him as he walked, inexplicably, deeper into the Indigo Forest. An eerie silence surrounded him. No crunching of leaves. No morning birds singing. Only silence. Silence, save for the sound of his beating heart and a voice calling to him, suffocated him like a blanket. The female voice, alluring and mesmerizing, called his name and he, unable to resist, mindlessly followed.

The grove of trees vanished in the distance, giving way to a clearing even more enveloped in the soupy mist. It was from this clearing that the voice was calling him. Silhouetted, the figure of a nude woman stood in front of a pond much like the pond behind Vannoria Nillhalla's home. As he approached, unable to observe any details of her identity, she stepped into the water. The closer he walked to the water's edge the further she waded, until she submerged and his toes dipped into the still murky water.

He found himself kneeling beside the water, intent on taking a closer look, unexplainably fearful of it. He called out, but his voice made no sound. He drew closer to the water, peering into its depths as though he would find some answer beneath its surface, but the mysterious pond remained opaque. It frightened him to his core and he shuddered as the hair on his arm stood on end, yet he found himself reaching to touch the inky surface. His finger made the tiniest ripple.

A hand exploded from the water, latching on to Aiwren's wrist like a talon snatching a rabbit with enough force to break its neck. The hand gripping Aiwren's wrist was slick with blood. Cold and slimy it grabbed tightly. The hand was covered in blood because the skin had been completely removed. The hand's owner, entirely skinless, herself, erupted from the water, grabbing Aiwren's neck with her other skinless claw.

The Skinless Woman ripped Aiwren down into the water, immediately leagues over his head. He flailed wildly, his mouth filling with bloody water, fighting to escape the clutches of the Skinless Woman dragging him down to the bottom.

His eyes popped open. Covered in sweat, he trembled in his bedroll, too terrified to move. A bird whistled in the distance. His heartbeat quieted as his anxious breath corrected itself. He was in the woods, at his little camp, and relieved to be alone... until the face leaned over him. He screamed.

***

Vannoria was exhausted from running all through the night. She had no backpack, no coins, no food, and no water. Though common sense and exhaustion constantly told her to stop, rest, and return home, she was driven by the fear of losing her one shot at the young man she was certain was her soul-mate. She knew, given her late start, running though the night would be her only chance to catch him and confess her love. Her heart yearned for the chance that he would love her, too, and invite her to journey with him to Y-Kewnor, where they would marry and have children and live the rest of their lives together. She knew she didn't have princess-dreams or desire fancy dresses like the other girls, but that didn't mean she didn't love. She loved Aiwren Wayde with all of her heart and, although she was furious he left with out saying goodbye, especially after the kiss they shared, she was not going to let him go. So she ran.

Vannoria didn't learn Aiwren had left until after lunch the previous day. Surprised at having not yet been visited by Aiwren on Vari-Matera-Eshu, she walked to his house. She remembered rationalizing that he must have been gifted something extravagant from his parents, since, although they were country folk, with their books and plumbing and city-speak, the Wayde family was fancier than the other countryfolk around Ribeln. She couldn't wait to find out what Aiwren's gift was, but when she arrived at his house, his parents told her he left for Y-Kewnor. Her mind swirled as she stumbled away, not sure what she mumbled as a response. She collapsed onto a large stone by the road and wept until her tears aggregated into resolve and, clear-eyed, she stood and ran.

She ran without stopping. Though Ribeln and across the fields west of Ribeln. As the sun set, she entered the Indigo Forest. Once in the forest, she was forced to move slowly, groping her way on the edge of the road. She had tripped several times. One trip sent her tumbling down a rocky embankment, scraping her hands, shins, and face as she fell. After climbing back to the road on bloody hands and knees, she continued with her heart as her compass.

As the night was ending, she saw a campfire. She hoped it was Aiwren and, though sore and tired, this hope motivated her to keep pushing forward. Then, something happened and she knew it was Aiwren. She heard his screams.

***

For most of the night, the Nameless Rider watched the Boy and waited for the signal. His missions were always the same, death, but for reasons beyond his understanding, the details mattered to his Master. It had to be him taking the life and the timing had to be precise. He had located his target. He would abide the signal to deal his death and return to his sleep. Until then, he would wait and keep his target safe from anything but him.

The Nameless Rider thought little about the mechanics of his job. He was a pawn, a dark pawn on a giant chess board. His existence was a simple one. He was a shadow and shadows obey the darkness. He wondered about this boy, though, wondered why he had to die. The Boy seemed insignificant. He also wondered about wondering. Had he ever wondered before? He couldn't remember. He couldn't remember anything before galloping across the plains less than a day earlier. He was certain he had existed before the previous morning, but he had no recollection of it. The tunnel of purpose once again ratcheted into place, focusing his attention on the task at hand.

Close to dawn, the Boy murmured, twisted, and turned. The Nameless Rider wondered if this was the signal. He had no recollection of the signal from previous missions and wondered what his punishment would be if he was too late. The Boy screamed and the Nameless Rider rose, certain it was the signal.

He left his dark steed and slowly approached, drawing his dark sword forged out of a black metal shining with darkness. He walked towards the Boy, prepared to reap his life, but a surprising thing happened.

***

The shock of the dream disoriented and paralyzed Aiwren. He didn't know where he was, what had happened, or why this face was so close to his.

"Aiwren! Are you all right?" Vannoria asked, sitting at Aiwren's side, holding his face.

"Vannoria?" Aiwren muttered, sitting up, as bits of reality locked into place out of the jumbled mess in his mind and dream fragments slid off into the ether of the early morning, nebulous and unreachable. "What are you doing here?"

Without hesitation, she slapped him hard across the face, shocking him into full alertness.

Looking just as shocked as he was, Vannoria sat back on her haunches and said, "I wasn't sure if I would do that or not, but it just sort of happened."

"I deserved that," Aiwren said.

"You left," she said. "You left without a good-bye."

Aiwren sat silent for a moment. He felt horrible for hurting her and wondered why she didn't understand how hard this was for him. He wondered why things couldn't remain forever unsaid.

"I didn't know what to say," he said. "I'm going to Y-Kewnor."

"Your parents told me."

"I went to your house. Stood out front for a while, but I lacked the courage to knock at your door and tell you. I tried to. I did."

Vannoria smiled, touched his cheek gently, and said, "It's okay."

"It is?" Aiwren asked, quite shocked.

"Yes," Vannoria answered, "because I'm going with you."

"What?" Aiwren asked, standing up, shocked.

"Think about it!" Vannoria said, climbing to her feet. "What is there for me in Ribeln? I'll always be in last place to my sisters, I don't want to farm, and you're the best friend I've ever had. It all... makes sense!"

Vannoria threw her arms around him for a hug and Aiwren knew she was hoping for another kiss, but he didn't kiss her. He was still upset by the dream he couldn't even remember. The day had only begun and he was already overwhelmed.

"I'll make the most fantastic travel companion ever!" Vannoria exclaimed as she released Aiwren from the hug.

Aiwren told himself to accept what was happening. He cared about Vannoria. Besides Leicester, she was his best friend. He should have been happy she was joining him on his journey. On the other hand, he was aware of her romantic expectations, but dealing with this, he told himself, was something he could delay.

Aiwren shared his breakfast with Vannoria. He had more than enough food to get to Y-Kewnor and she was famished from her run. He offered to let her rest for a bit before starting off, assuring her they could get to the fork in the road by nightfall, but Vannoria refused the rest, insisting she would be fine and had no intention of slowing him down. So, after Aiwren gathered his belongings, the two of them set off down the road.

The first part of their journey that day was uneventful. It wasn't until lunch that things took a turn. They were sitting by the side of the road, eating some of the food Madeline had packed for Aiwren, when Vannoria spotted a doe no more than fifteen paces from them. Sandwich in hand, she tapped Aiwren on the knee and pointed.

"Here ya go," Vannoria said, slowly standing, offering her sandwich.

The doe cautiously approached and gingerly nibbled Vannoria's sandwich. Vannoria slowly reached her other hand out to gently pat the doe's head. The doe quickly moved its head away, but it didn't run and, after a moment of hesitation, it, once again, nibbled at the sandwich. Vannoria looked over her shoulder, smiled at Aiwren to encourage him to approach. Curious about the doe, he slowly stood and joined his friend by the peaceful creature. The doe didn't seem to be afraid of them, but suddenly her head shot up into the air and her tail stuck straight up to reveal its white underside. Ears perked, it stared up the road, stone still. Then, it bolted off into the woods south of the road.

For an instant, Aiwren was in tune with nature, and understood that they might want to fear what ever it was the doe was afraid of, but then he laughed at himself.

"That doe gave me an idea," Vannoria said. "Rather than heading south at the fork, we should simply cut across the forest diagonally. We'd cover a greater distance, allowing me a few extra winks of sleep tomorrow morning, while still remaining ahead of your schedule."

"I don't know," Aiwren said, "These are unfamiliar woods."

"It's the Indigo Forest," Vannoria pleaded. "If there were something dangerous here we would have heard about it. What are you afraid of? Another doe?"

Not wanting to have his courage scrutinized anymore, Aiwren reluctantly nodded in acquiescence to the plan. Vannoria clapped her hands with glee, grabbed Aiwren's hand, and led him from the road, southwest, into the woods.

The trees blurred by Aiwren, who stumble over logs and under branches, unaware of anything other than his hand, the hand entwined with Vannoria's. Lost in thought, his blank stare betrayed the fierce dilemma he was wrestling with. He told himself he hated this; he hated holding hands with this girl. He wondered, if he hated it so much, why he wouldn't just let go. His hand would drop to his side. Her hand would drop to her side. They would continue walking, as friends, as they had always been. He told himself he would let go, but his grip remained in tact. He leveled with himself and admitted Vannoria's affections felt good, but he wondered, if these affections felt good, why he didn't want them. He wondered if enjoying Vannoria's affections was the very definition of having affection for Vannoria, himself. He wondered, if he did have affection for Vannoria, why he was working so hard to convince himself otherwise. Was it the dreams? Was he afraid of the thoughts he had the night they kissed? Was he simply more interested in Y-Kewnor? Ultimately, he rationalized that they were just holding hands, that they were just friends in the woods holding hands, and, if it should feel pleasant, that was fine, but it didn't bind him to any relationship.

"I don't think we should hold hands," Aiwren said.

"Okay, neither do I," Vannoria quickly replied, letting go of his hand.

"It's just... if we trip," Aiwren quickly interjected, "we ought have our hands free to catch ourselves."

"Of course," Vannoria said with feigned nonchalance, "naturally."

Aiwren was so preoccupied with hand holding that he lost track of time and direction. After a little while longer, Vannoria asked if they ought to have intersected with the south road by then or if Aiwren thought they had cut too far south and not enough west. Aiwren said he wasn't sure and they kept going in the direction they were going.

Roads are meant to be travelled upon, not circumvented; when traveling on a road, travelers can be certain someone has been that way before, but when travelers leave the road they are likely to find the things roads were built to avoid. This was the lesson Aiwren learned when his heart sank at the sight of the moss-covered stone wall in the distance. He hoped it wasn't as tall as it seemed, but as they approached, his hopes were dashed; it was taller.

The Wall of the Ancients bisected the Indigo Forest diagonally and, if Aiwren hadn't been so preoccupied with hand holding, he might have remembered this earlier. Nobody was sure who had built it, but the popular story was that it was from long before their histories were recorded, that an ancient people built it, and that it used to be a league high. Now it was only forty or fifty paces tall, but still taller than any building Aiwren or Vannoria had ever seen and, most certainly, unclimbable. Of course, when they approached, Aiwren immediately knew what it was and hated himself for not thinking of it.

"Perhaps there are openings," Vannoria suggested. "There must be an opening where the roads intersect."

"It's possible," Aiwren said, not wanting to make Vannoria feel too accountable for a mistake that was clearly her fault. "Perhaps if we head north."

"You mean south," Vannoria replied with a laugh. "Y-Kewnor is to the south. Remember?"

"Yes," Aiwren snapped, "but the roads are to the north. And who knows how far south the wall goes? What if it goes all the way to the Uncrossable River? Then what will we do?"

"So you're suggesting we backtrack the way we came?!" Vannoria argued.

"No," Aiwren replied, trying to remain calm. "What I'm suggesting is that we follow the wall north, which would actually be northwest. If we come across an opening, we'll take it. If not, at least we'll be back on the road and you won't have gotten us too far behind schedule."

"Me?!" Vannoria said, her temper rising. "You and I both agreed to go this way. We made the decision together."

"Just so you recall, we wouldn't have had to if you didn't want extra sleep."

"Well, don't let me hold you back, Aiwren Wayde!" she snapped. "Just so you recall, I wouldn't have needed the sleep if I hadn't run all night to catch up with you."

Not having the sense to say nothing, Aiwren retorted, "Well... why did you do that?!"

"Because... I love you, you... ass!" she shouted, before bursting into tears.

Aiwren didn't know what to say. If he didn't say he loved her, he would hurt her. If he said he loved her she would not believe his words were sincere. He didn't even know if he did love her. He crouched down next to her and said, "I'm sorry."

Vannoria sniffed back her tears, doing her best to regain composure as she stared at the ground. "I didn't mean that."

"It's okay," Aiwren said, kissing her forehead.

This forehead kiss caused Vannoria to look up, nose running and eyes still wet with tears. Aiwren found himself close to her face. Winded from their argument, their breathing synchronized, sharing breath. He reached for a smudge of dirt on her face with the honest intention of wiping it away to break the tension, show he cared, and get them out of this moment. His thumb did drag across the smudge of dirt, but his hand remained on her face and the moment remained unbroken. He found himself leaning towards her, overwhelmed with guilt as soon as his lips met Vannoria's, but allowing the kiss to linger, nevertheless. Afterwards they both exchanged awkward apologies and headed northwest, along the Ancient Wall, their hands intertwining once again. This should have been okay, Aiwren told himself, thinking his affections for Vannoria were possibly real, but he couldn't shake the nagging question eating away at his gut. He wondered if the voices he heard made him kiss her and he feared they did.

The shadows had grown long, reminding Aiwren the end of the day was quickly approaching. Soon, it would be too dark to start a fire easily. They kept pushing bit by bit until Aiwren stopped walking and plopped down his backpack.

"The sun's setting. I don't think we're going to find anything tonight. Let's camp here and start again tomorrow morning."

Vannoria didn't want to sleep unsheltered in the middle of the woods. She offered to gather kindling and she began wandering up the path collecting the right sized sticks, leaving Aiwren behind to drag some larger logs together for a fire. The sun was very low, the woods were getting darker, and the shadows were long and deep when Aiwren heard Vannoria's scream. He grabbed the sword his father gave him and bolted, branches snapping in his face as he sprinted through the woods with complete disregard for his own safety. Running with blind speed, Vannoria and Aiwren collided with enough force to knock them both the ground.

"There's a break in the wall," she exclaimed, "an opening!"

A few minutes later, Aiwren and Vannoria had gathered the rest of their things and were at the opening in the wall, but this was no crack in the wall, top to bottom, through which you could see the other side. This looked more like the mouth of a cave. It was a semi-circular opening a little taller than Aiwren at its tallest point and just as wide, if not slightly wider. It didn't seem to be caused by erosion or man-made destruction. Stones locked together around the opening with a keystone at the top. This was built into the wall.

"What do you think?" Aiwren asked, peering in. "Camp on this side tonight and try crossing in the morning?"

Vannoria thought for a moment, then said, "Might be safer to camp with some walls and a roof over our heads."

This sounded like a good idea to Aiwren, thinking they would sleep better inside with walls and a roof to trap the heat of the fire.

"Not too deep though," Aiwren said, "we don't want to trap the smoke in there with us and choke to death."

Aiwren dragged the logs into the entrance, close enough to the edge to let the smoke out, but far enough in to benefit from the shelter. A compromising distance, he thought. Vannoria helped with the logs and grabbed the kindling from outside as he arranged them. With the kindling Vannoria gathered and the sparks Aiwren's fire rock made when he struck it against his sword, it took only a few minutes for them to get the fire going.

The fire cast enough light to reveal that the chamber was wider and taller than the entrance and deeper than they originally imagined, which led them to wonder how wide the Ancient Wall really was. Outside, the sun had set, but Aiwren still had enough light to run out and return with a long stick, which he thrust into the fire. After a moment, the end ignited and Aiwren removed it from the fire. It wasn't a proper torch, but if he moved slowly he could keep it lit and take a look around. The room was a good twenty feet wide and twenty feet tall. The stones were warn, but clearly assembled with advanced masonry. The strangest thing he noticed was the cleanliness of the room. No pieces of bird nest. No bat droppings. Not even a spider web.

The two of them walked twenty feet deep and saw no end to the room or signs of an opening on the other side. Finally, nearly forty feet away there was an opening the size of the opening they entered from. Aiwren gave Vannoria a look, telling her to wait as he investigated, which she responded to with a nod of understanding and agreement.

Aiwren poked the flaming stick and his head into the portal at the far end of the room. He hoped it would lead to the other side of the wall. Instead, it lead to a small chamber with a portal to his left, another portal to his right, and a stairwell curving up to the floors above and down to the floors below. It was safe, so Vannoria joined him in the little room, but they both agreed they should decide what to do in the morning.

After eating quietly by the fire, Aiwren offered his bedroll to Vannoria.

"Where will you sleep?" She asked.

"I'll be okay by the fire," he responded. "Nights aren't too cold yet, but I want to make sure you're warm."

Vannoria laid on the thin mat and pulled the blanket up over her as Aiwren laid perpendicular to her by her feet. Comfortable in the warmth of the fire, Aiwren quickly fell asleep.

Later, as the fire cooled, Aiwren was woken by his own shivering. He thought about getting up to add another log to the fire, but he didn't want to wake Vannoria. He subdued his shivering as much as he could, but eventually she woke up.

"Come here," she said and, after a moment of hesitation, he did.

Aiwren crawled under the blanket with Vannoria. They were facing each other. She rubbed her hands on his shoulders, then took his hands and blew her warm breath into them. Aiwren looked up. They were face to face. So close. Chests rose and fell harmoniously. Urges pulled him towards her, urges he had to stymie.

"Good night," Aiwren whispered.

He had the intention of rolling onto his back and drifting off to sleep, but his intentions counter balanced with his urges kept him frozen in equilibrium. It wasn't clear who made the first move, but a small amount of motion was all it took for his intentions to lose and his urges pulled Aiwren toward her, urges Vannoria would satisfy on that cool night inside the Wall of the Ancients in the middle of the Indigo Forest.

***

The Nameless Rider followed the boy and his female companion to the mouth of a cave. He kept his distance, but, through dark things unknown to him, he was able to track the Boy effortlessly and the youthful travelers were so loud, as they crunched through the forest, they would have been easy to track even without the aid of unseen powers.

Riding on his steed granted, or perhaps forced, the Nameless Rider time to reflect, an uncomfortable activity for someone with only one day of memories. He thought of the mayfly, a small insect that lives only one day, performs a function, and dies. He thought, with the exception of the function, he and the mayfly were quite similar. He wondered what he was doing two days ago. Was he kept in hibernation until his duties were required? Or did he have a duty to perform two days ago, which he returned from only to have any memories of it erased before being sent off on this new task? He wondered how he even knew about things such as the mayfly. Was he allowed to keep knowledge, but not memories? Mostly, he wondered, aware of his thoughts, if he had ever thought before.

The Nameless Rider, while silently traveling through the woods, remembered a curious thing the Boy and his companion did when they left the road. As they walked, they had held on to each other by the hand. This clearly made it more difficult for them to walk and he wondered why they traveled like that. He wondered if it was a game? They wouldn't be playing games if they knew he was following them. They didn't seem to be aware of very much though. Perhaps, he posed, that was what creatures without purpose did, play games all day and night, unaware of their peril until it is too late.

The Nameless Rider, once again, wondered how long it would be until he would receive the signal, ride in, reap the Boy's life, and return to where ever it was he came from. Were his duties normally so prolonged? He wondered if this duty was a punishment for failing at his last task.

Eventually the sun set and the Boy and his companion found refuge inside the large wall. From a hilltop near the entrance, he watched them build a fire and explore the dwelling. The Boy and his companion shed their clothing and moved together. Touching. Moaning.

When the Boy and his companion were quite still and their breathing steady for some time, the Nameless Rider, confident they were asleep, approached the wall. The wall, he instinctually knew, perhaps as the result of some archaic knowledge his Master permitted him to retain, was called the Wall of the Ancients, but this spot on the wall, this portal, was an entrance to something else. There would be stairs inside, descending deep into the earth, to a room best left undisturbed.

"Balysh-Pah," he said quietly, surprised by the sound of his own voice, surprised he even had a voice, not sure why he said it or what it meant, but he did know that whatever Balysh-Pah was, it was down there, beneath the wall, older than ancient, and dangerous.

The Nameless Rider backed away from the Boy and his companion, from the wall, from the entrance leading to Balysh-Pah. He returned to the little hill where his dark steed remained waiting for him.

***

If there were windows in her little cell in the palace in Gavlessa, perhaps the sunrise might have pierced through the pane, cast its light on Teryessa's face, broken her from her slumber, and freed her from the horrible dreams that kept her tossing and turning all night, twisting her sweaty body in the coarse sheets of her moldy mattress, but there were no windows in her little cell and, even if there were, no light could have reached her that far below the surface, in the underground city, so it was Teryessa's own screams that woke her that morning, her first morning in Gavlessa. She opened her groggy eyes and rubbed her throbbing head. Poison tingled heavily in her veins as she slowly sat up, poison far more poignant than any numbendria withdrawal, poison far more poignant than anything natural. This place was evil. Evil, somehow, beyond anything Prince Grell was capable of. It was an older, deeper evil.

A key turned in the door. Teryessa wrapped herself in the blanket and braced herself. Ruthillo slipped into her room, closing the door behind him. He carried a rusty metal dish in one hand and a dim oil lantern in the other.

"I thought you should eat."

"I'll never touch it," Teryessa snapped venomously, "no matter how hungry I am."

Approaching slowly, Ruthillo set the plate on the edge of Teryessa's bed and backed away. It was some sort of gruel, slop unfit for a princess of Lees Naglos, but this was Gavlessa and there were slightly different standards here.

"It's not poisoned," he said. "It's gloatmeal. What it lacks in taste, it makes up for in nurture."

"I don't trust you," she shouted, throwing the metal dish of goo across the room, where it clanged against the wall, stuck for a moment, and slid to the floor. "I'd rather starve than eat such disgusting rubbish!"

Ruthillo, crouched to the floor, picked up the dish, and scraped his fingers through the remains of the gloatmeal.

"At least one of us won't starve," he said, licking the food from his hand. "Forgive me. I'll know better than to share with you next time, Your Highness."

"Share?"

"This was my breakfast. The cooks were told not to feed you until you've learned obedience."

"I haven't much of an appetite, anyway," Teryessa mumbled apologetically. "Thank you."

Ruthillo nodded his reply as he ate more of the Gloatmeal. Teryessa looked around the room, noticing, in the dim illumination from Ruthillo's lantern, that it was, indeed, a cell. Clarity ebbed into her numbendria-fogged mind. She remembered everything. She remembered her dreams. She couldn't decide which was worse. At least the dreams weren't real, she thought. Ruthillo finished his breakfast in silence, uncorked his hip-flask, took a sip, and offered it to Teryessa.

"No," she replied. "Thank you."

Ruthillo took another sip from his flask, closing his eyes in a manner Teryessa recognized as a small prayer for emptiness made by a heart incapable of indifference. He was not there to do her harm.

"I am sorry if the noise this morning woke you. It seems there was a commotion."

"I wasn't woken," Teryessa said. "What commotion?"

"Last night my master made a Pitt Challenge to his father. Everyone in the palace has been scrambling to make the proper arrangements."

"A Pitt Challenge!?"

"He and his father will fight to death in the arena today. If the prince wins, he'll become king. And you will become one of his queens."

"As long I produce an heir," Teryessa said, knowing Prince Grell's impotence would make an heir impossible.

"If you can't produce an heir, there would be no use for you," Ruthillo admitted.

Teryessa swallowed hard.

"And if the king should win?" she asked.

"If the king wins, all of the prince's wives will be killed to be sure they don't produce heirs to a deceased and dishonored prince."

Teryessa's stomach turned. She couldn't even scream. The blood rushed from her face. The room spun.

"Well," she said, "it appears as though, the ending of my story is fixed regardless of the outcome. On second thought, I think I should like a sip of whatever's in that flask."

"Of course, Your Highness" responded Ruthillo as he handed Teryessa the flask of numbendria.

The princess uncorked the flask. She smelled its contents. She remembered the smell of numbendria from the previous night. It smelled like cloves and cinnamon, but tickled her nose in a funny way. She hesitated for a moment, brought the flask to her lips, and took a sip. She tasted the spicy tingle in her mouth as soon as the liquid touched her tongue. The mellow heat spread down her throat and through her veins and in her belly. It was wonderful and shameful and delicious and sad. Her second sip went down with little hesitation and a haze cascaded across her mind like a muslin curtain filtering her reactions, dulling her emotions, calming her, making her affable. She smiled.

"The elixir you call numbendria is from my land, but my people call it vision water and they don't use it to control each other... or to avoid emotions. It is a spiritual drink used in ceremony."

"Where are you from?" Teryessa asked, sipping.

"I am from a far away land, Princess. On the other side of Allyoshmar. I am from beyond the Dragonsback Mountains, beyond the Wild Plains, beyond the Freelands, and beyond the Uncrossable River, in a land you call the Wasteland, a land we call called C'ar-Ifa."

"C'ar-Ifa?"

"It means hidden treasure. All you see is desert, but my people recognize the life there, in the plants, the secret plants. Every plant has a secret, a story, a treasure. The Sacred Animals know. They tell us the stories of Allyoshmar and of The Divine Empresses."

"Divine Empress. You mean," Teryessa corrected. "The Divine Empress is the Creator. The Giver of Life."

"Allyoshmar is ancient beyond comprehension. It has been countlessly peopled and unpeopled and peopled again. There have been more Divine Empresses than there are stars in the sky."

"You certainly have an interesting set of beliefs. I'd be careful not to speak of them within earshot of a high priest. He'd probably have you sent to a sanitarium."

"Yes, Princess."

Teryessa watched Ruthillo. There was such pain in his eyes. Such longing. Such a sadness. A sadness, not of one man, but of a people. Wisdom. Kindness. He was looking away and didn't seem aware of her scrutiny. She looked at the scars on his back too numerous to count and the strange markings on his arm. The weathered creases around his eyes. His dark skin.

"How old are you, Ruthillo," she asked.

"Too old to count anymore. Perhaps eight score or nine score of your annuals. We count differently in C'ar-Ifa."

"Nine-Score?!" she exclaimed. "You don't look much older than me. Do you have any children?"

"I had a mate and a ward, but they were lost."

Teryessa looked in Ruthillo's soulful eyes, certain there was more to his tragic story. His eyes were beautiful. Dark brown irises surrounded huge black pupils, pupils accustomed to bright light, pupils more accustomed to life in the sun than life underground.

"Would you like to go for a walk, princess?" he asked.

Teryessa nodded. Ruthillo stood and tossed her a folded fabric. It was a robe. She remembered she was still nearly nude. Teryessa pulled the robe over her head. It was simple, course, and too big for her. She guessed it was Ruthillo's. It felt good to be wearing something other than her undergarments, a little less exposed, a little less vulnerable.

A moment later they were in the hallway and Ruthillo was locking the door behind them. The palace was buzzing with terrible excitement. Countless chefs, harem girls, maids, probabilitists, and accountants were rushing around. Everyone was hurrying to set something up, rushing to find a way to benefit from the Pitt Challenge.

"Does it matter to any of them who wins," Teryessa asked Ruthillo as they walked away from her room.

"Only if they have a bet placed," answered Ruthillo.

"How horrible."

"Would it matter to you if you didn't have something at stake?"

Teryessa didn't answer, but asked, "Do you think I should be grateful to be here?"

"I understand your situation, princess. As I understand theirs. As I understand the prince's. As I understand my own. We are all doing what we can."

"How did you get here?" she asked.

"I was taken as a slave by the horsemen of Woscom and sold to a wealthy and cruel land owner who would often beat me. I was willful and that only made things worse. I was his slave from when he was a young man to when he was an old man. One day, the poor rose up against the wealthy and beheaded them in the market square. All the slaves were set free. I headed west across the Uncrossable River."

"Why did you head west? Why didn't you go back to your home?" Teryessa asked, passing through the great room, so engrossed in Ruthillo's story, that she paid no attention to the gnashing jaws of the large saberbeast being led by an obese man with a loin cloth and a mask on his head.

"There was nothing left for me at home and I don't remember why I headed west, I'm afraid," he replied.

Teryessa thought she detected a hint of shame in his voice. She also thought he wasn't being entirely truthful.

"It doesn't matter anyway," he continued, "for, as I was heading from Orc Doola to Frins Casicon, I was captured by the Gavlessans."

"How tragic, you were freed only to again be enslaved," Teryessa replied.

"I had a healthy taste of freedom."

"Is that how you became the prince's servant?"

"I was put into the pitt. If I won enough, I could buy back my freedom. I was about to win my freedom, when I was challenged by the prince, himself. He defeated me but spared my life and made me his servant. He owns my life now and I must always serve him."

Teryessa was about to ask another question as they descended the stairs towards the Pitt Stadium, when Ruthillo stopped her. He put his finger to his mouth telling her to be silent. Once she was still and quiet, Teryessa, too, heard the voices. Grell and Plale were in the royal box overlooking the arena.

"How dare you set the odds against me?!" Grell hissed. "Do you think I'll to lose against that old man?"

"I told you to wait longer before challenging your father. Your pride gets the best of you."

"How dare you insult the prince?!" Grell snapped. "Soon, I'll be king and you will be beheaded!"

Teryessa held her breath. The door opened a bit. It was the chancellor. He was leaving. Teryessa gasped. Ruthillo pointed down a second set of stairs.

"Stay quiet," Ruthillo whispered. "Don't move."

Teryessa moved down the stairs quickly and quietly. When she got to a second landing she stopped and listened.

"Ruthillo," Grell said.

"Yes, my master," Ruthillo replied.

Then, she heard a voice whisper, "Teryessa, I've been waiting for you. Come to me. Come to me now."

She spun around. There was nobody there. She was alone.

"Teryessa, I've been waiting for you. Come to me now."

It was the voice she had heard the night before. This was the stairway she had heard it from. She dared not ask who was speaking, for fear of Grell hearing her. Instead, she peered further down the stairs. It was dark. She had never experienced such darkness. Even absence of light has some radiant quality, but this darkness was complete absence. It wasn't a natural darkness. It was something deeper, something older. Something scary. If she waited, Grell might catch her, she reasoned. On the other hand, there was something alluring about the voice. Though terrifying, something about it intoxicated her. She decided she wanted nothing more in life than to hear that strong, soothing voice. She had to find the voice in the darkness.

She took a step. Then another. Then another. Once she was far enough that Grell's nasal tone faded from her ears and mind, she quickened her pace. She groped along, keeping one hand against the wall and one hand in front of her. The dark was blinding, but it didn't matter; she wasn't being led by sight. She was being led by desire, a desire she could smell; it was musky. Desire crept into her body. Her heart beat rapidly. Heat spread through her veins. By the time she reached the bottom of the stairs, she had forgotten about her fears. She was curious and helpless and the power of the voice made her insane with passion.

In a trance, she wandered further, one foot in front of the other, until she saw the faint speck of the glow of a dim light. She hurried towards the light, a lantern sitting on the ground as though someone had left it there for her, knowing she'd be coming. She picked up the lantern. Turned up the wick to provide more light. After a moment her eyes adjusted. She was in a cave. It wasn't an engineered cave like the caves throughout Gavlessa. This one looked like a natural cave. It didn't feel natural, though, not at all.

"Come to me, Teryessa," the voice said.

She followed it. She would do whatever the voice told her to do. Her breath echoed through the cave, which seemed to continue forever, sloping deep into the earth. Then, as suddenly as it had begun, the cave ended. Teryessa stood before a wooden door with writing carved into its surface. It had one word.

"Gallery," Teryessa said, aloud. "Who would put a gallery down here."

She assumed it would be locked, but her curiosity, or something else, forced her to turn the knob. She entered.

Inside was a long hall. It was an art gallery with paintings hung along the walls, but her lamp wasn't bright enough to illuminate the art. As she approached, she could make out the beautiful gold frame, but she couldn't identify its subject wasn't until she was right in front of it.

It was a painting of a dragon so lifelike, she shuddered, fearing the beast would leap from the wall and devour her. The dragon was sitting on his haunches and holding a lance in each of his fore-claws. Each lance was stabbed through several knights. Looks of anguish were frozen on their dead faces. Beneath the dragon was a pile of bodies, women, with blood flowing from their genitals into a river of blood raging by in a deep red torrent. Teryessa shuddered and moved to the next painting. It was another dragon, as were many of the paintings.

Some of the paintings were of dark shadows. These shadows were devouring humans, and leaving nothing behind. Although they were less gruesome, they frightened Teryessa even more than the dragons.

One painting was of a nude woman in a town square. A red gown laid by her feet. Her long red hair cascaded down, covering her genitals. Some of the townsfolk held her still, while others skinned her alive, revealing bloody muscle, tissue, and sinew. The woman looked young and beautiful, but something was wrong. The woman was smiling. Teryessa gasped at the terrifying smirk and swore the woman in the painting laughed at her. She quickly backed away from the painting.

She peered further down the gallery, but it was too dark. She continued apprehensively. Her gut told her to turn around, but she proceeded as though she was compelled to. She wanted to go into the darkness. She wanted it to consume her.

"Come to me, Teryessa. Come to me."

She stopped. Another sensation spread through her body. Not fear. Not the darkness taking over her body. She felt light. It was inside of her. It was anchoring her to the spot. She was stuck. If that light hadn't begun to glow inside of her, she would have gone into the darkness. She wanted to leave, but she didn't have the strength. She couldn't move.

A hand grabbed her shoulder.

Ready for anything, Teryessa whipped around.

"What are you doing down here?!" Ruthillo demanded. "This is very dangerous. We have to go."

"I-" Teryessa began, but Ruthillo grabbed her by her hand and whisked her away.

They rushed back through the gallery and through the door, which shut behind them. They hurried through the cave and up the steps. They hurried through the chambers and halls and never looked back until they made it to Teryessa's little cell.

Ruthillo slammed the door shut and locked is as Teryessa dropped to the floor. She was drenched in sweat. Ruthillo sat down next to her. He, too, was sweaty, his eyes filled with panic.

"Never ever go in there again, Princess. Ever!"

"I'm sorry, I don't know what came over me," she pleaded. "What is that place, Ruthillo?"

"The Gallery of Nestellishma. It is an evil place and you must never go there ever again!"

Teryessa shrank like a scolded child. Ruthillo uncorked the bottle of numbendria, took a sip and handed it to her. As she sipped, he began the tale.

"Many annuals ago, ages upon ages into the past, at the beginning of this peopling of Allyoshmar, before this desert was a desert, there was a kingdom called Allustria and it was ruled by King Hesia. King Hesia was a powerful man. No kingdom dared challenge Allustria's power. At the same time, there was a great artist. This artist was a mystery, but everyone could recognize his paintings."

"Nestellishma?" Teryessa asked.

"Yes," replied Ruthillo. "One day, King Hesia asked his seer who the most powerful man in Allyoshmar was, certain his seer would tell him he was, but the seer told the king it was Nestellishma. Outraged, the king had his guards bring him the painter. He told Nestellishma he must only paint for the king, or else he would be hanged in the town square. Nestellishma agreed."

Ruthillo stopped, took another sip of numbendria, and continued.

94

"So Nestellishma moved into the castle and started painting for the king. At first Hesia was only concerned with keeping Nestellishma away from the public, but he, too, grew obsessed with Nestellishma's paintings. He would ignore his tasks and spend entire days starting at his painter's art."

"Why? What was so great about it?"

"Nestellishma wasn't always such a powerful artist, but he had made a deal with The Dark One to serve him through his art. The Dark One put his magics in him, allowing him to paint better than anyone ever had before. So, in painting, he was serving The Dark One and in loving his paintings above anything else, he was loving The Dark One above anything else."

"So when Hesia was growing more and more obsessed with Nestellishma's paintings, was he growing more and more obsessed with The Dark One, too?" Teryessa asked.

"One day, the king asked the painter how he became so incredible. The painter told the king about his deal with The Dark One. That night the two men, made a pact. They would do whatever it took to serve the paintings; they would do whatever The Dark One wanted so they could enjoy that art. King Hesia decided to build a gallery. In this Dark Gallery he would display the best of Nestellishma's work. Through his paintings, Nestellishma told forgotten stories and awakened demons, which was exactly what The Dark One wanted."

"He was tricked."

"They were both tricked. They were tricked into doing The Dark One's work. One day, Nestellishma went into the Gallery and never returned. King Hesia went to the Gallery to inspect the work and he never returned either."

"What happened to them?"

"Nestellishma was tricked into painting a portrait of The Dark One, himself. They say he was incinerated completely as he made his final brush stroke. King Hesia, they say, went mad when he gazed upon the painting. They say he picked up Nestellishma's brushes, and gouged out his own eyes with them, before stabbing the brushes into his own heart."

"That's horrific, Ruthillo."

"It is, but that's not the end. The painting freed The Dark One and, once free, he sucked all the life out of the kingdom, devouring it, himself. Every man, woman, and child died. Every beast was killed. Every tree. Every bush. Every blade of grass. Every building. They all turned to sand, creating this desert. The only thing left was the Gallery. They say it was discovered again during Gavlessa's construction and that anyone who has ever looked at that painting has gone mad. Originally they tried to seal the room, but it was impossible. Nothing can destroy the Gallery. It is a Balysh-Pah, a Forgotten Place."

"Are there any other Balysh-Pah?"

"Yes. Too many."

Ruthillo tilted his head to listen. He leapt to his feet, swung the door open, and grabbed. It was a page, a scrawny little boy.

"I were jus a knocking on accounta da news."

"What news?" Ruthillo demanded.

"The king's been stabbed. Chans'lor Plale said Prince Grell did it an e ad im locked op on accounta misconduction ov da Pitt Challenge."

Ruthillo let go and the boy scrambled out of the room. Ruthillo slammed the door shut and locked it.

"What does this mean?" Teryessa asked.

"I don't know," replied Ruthillo. "I don't know."

SERVANTS AND MASTERS

Vannoria was startled when she awoke that morning. Struggling to catch her breath, she was terrified and she didn't know why. She had a dream, a nightmare already forgotten. She was angry that night terrors would ruin the morning after the wonderful night she and Aiwren had shared. Still unable to shake the fear that latched on to her belly and squeezed the breath from her throat, she turned to Aiwren for reassurance, to vanquish her bad dream, but that's when the horror shook her too her core. Aiwren was gone. Vannoria leapt to her feet. Aiwren's backpack was still by the fire, but Aiwren's sword was gone.

Pacing around the small stone room, now filled with light, Vannoria did her best to gather her wits. She reassured herself that he must have woken up early, gone ahead to check out if the ruins led to the other side of the Wall of the Ancients. She hurried over to the portal at the far end of the room and whispered for Aiwren, but he didn't respond. She called his name louder, still met with only silence. Listening towards the stairs, she waited. Then she heard a faint voice calling her name.

"Aiwren," she said, "don't worry. I'm coming for you."

Vannoria rushed back to the fire, hoping to find a lantern in the backpack. Dumping the contents to the ground, she shuffled through a pile of paper, rope, some old clothes, and various other supplies, but didn't find a lantern. She did, however, find a jar of lamp oil. She dunked one of the shirts in the jar, wrapped it around a stick and ignited it with some of the embers from the fire. She hurried towards the portal at the back of the room.

Some of the light from outside the Wall of the Ancients reached back to the corridor with the stairs. Vannoria looked to the right, certain it was north, and that Aiwren would have gone in that direction, but she was certain he had called her from down the stairs. She told herself he might have already tried going to the right, only to meet a dead end, and decided to try his luck heading north on a lower level. She began her descent.

Vannoria wasn't a fearless type of person, but she was stubborn. She held the torch in her right hand as she took her first step, but her left hand shook with fear, so she grit her teeth and grasped the torch with both hands to hold the light steady. If she couldn't be fearless, she was damned sure going to act fearless.

The narrow stairwell spiraled down into the dark. No paintings or tapestries decorated the walls. No wooden beams arced overhead. Just stone, each piece locking perfectly with the next, like scales. The stones were worn, but not nearly worn enough, Vannoria thought, for a building as old as the Wall of the Ancients was. Vannoria moved slowly and carefully, but soon arrived on the landing of the floor below the one she entered on.

The landing had no corridor to the left or to the right, but it did have a room with similar dimensions to the room she and Aiwren had slept in. There was no furniture or decor; however, at the far end of the room, directly below where the entrance was on the level above, there was a pile of earth and stone; this room was not always under ground. Under different circumstances, this may have been interesting to Vannoria, but singularly focussed on finding Aiwren, she left.

There were several floors like the first subterranean floor Vannoria explored. They each had entrances at the far end that were covered and increasingly deep beneath the surface, but none of them contained Aiwren, so Vannoria kept descending.

Eventually Vannoria ran out of stairs, and found herself facing a wooden door with no sign of wear or rot or age. The door had one word carved into the surface: "Gallery." Something inside of her wanted to run back up the stairs and all the way home, but, when she heard her own name whispered, she told herself Aiwren was inside and she had to help him.

When Vannoria opened the door. The walls of the room were lined with torture devices and lit by torches she assumed Aiwren had lit. There was another door at the end of the long room and, from beyond that door, Vannoria thought Aiwren was calling her. She walked by the various torture devices without pause. She passed a bed of nails, a head crusher, an iron maiden, and other horrific contraptions, before arriving at the door. Filled with dread, Vannoria reached for the door.

"Vannoria. Please help."

Vannoria took a deep breath and opened the door, revealing the greatest horror yet. Aiwren wasn't there. The room was small and almost empty. The only furniture was a stone altar at the far end, with a mirror on the wall above. The stone was a deeper black than she had ever seen. She peered into the mirror.

At first, as Vannoria gazed into the reflection, all she saw was her own face, but then the mirror gave her answers, not the answers she wanted, horrible answers. Aiwren wasn't down here. He never was. He had left her. Gone to Y-Kewnor. She had given him her body. She had given him her love. He, in return, discarded her like rubbish. She was hideous: huge nose, drab eyes, thin lips. She saw something else in the mirror. In a flash, her gaze was returned by a skinless woman, sneering at her liplessly. She realized, to her horror, the Skinless Woman was her.

Vannoria screamed and smashed the mirror with her fist. Cracks spread across the pane and several shards fell to the altar. Blood trickled from her left hand and onto the infinitely black stone. She would punish Aiwren for how he had treated her. She would have her retribution. She knew what she needed to do. She slowly removed all of her clothing and stared at the cracked mirror, calm and determined, but burning inside with hatred and rage. She raised a shard of black glass from the altar and began removing her own skin.

***

Early in the morning, a scream snapped the Nameless Rider to attention. Unshaken by his strange awareness that it was a dangerous place, he unsheathed his black sword and headed into the wall after the Boy, entering the world of stone made by men and things far worse.

The Nameless Rider walked though the empty debris of the Boy's camp, to the back of the room, and into the corridor. There were four choices: left, right, up, and down, but the typically clear and decisive pull abandoned him, leaving him irresolute. On one hand, everything he knew, told him the Boy traveled to the right and it made sense. The Boy was traveling to Y-Kewnor, was searching for a passage through the wall, and a passage to the right would minimize the distance between the wall and the road. On the other hand, something inside of him told him he was supposed to go down the stairs. Perhaps, his mission had changed. Perhaps the Boy had gone to the right, but had been killed at the wrong time by the wrong means and now his purpose was to reap death upon the Boy's companion, the Girl. Perhaps it was necessary for them both to die. For the first time he could remember, he didn't automatically know what to do and had to make a decision, but for creatures like the Nameless Rider, decisions were very rarely left to free-will alone and a voice nudged him in the direction of the stairs.

Not stopping to investigate any of the other floors, the Nameless Rider found himself at the bottom of the spiral staircase, entering the Gallery. The torture devices lining the walls didn't frighten or disturb him at all; even if he couldn't recall specifics, he was no stranger to death. What bothered him was the door at the far side of the room, the door calling to him.

The Girl was nude and her back was to him. Blood trickled down her leg. A rough incision cut the top of her left arm from her elbow to her wrist. Holding a broken chard of glass, she fixated so intently on prying her fingers beneath her own skin to tear it off, she had no idea the Nameless Rider had entered the room or how much blood she had lost. She was going to bleed to death. The means and the timing of this death were wrong. His Master would not be pleased. He sheathed his sword and approached. He grabbed her shoulder and turned her to face him. Her greatest laceration went from her chest bone, between her still youthful breasts, down to her naval. The cut was deep and just one of many she had made. Enraged by the interruption, the Girl swiped at him with the broken piece of glass, but he caught her hand, and knocked the piece of glass free. As soon as the glass fell, she collapsed into in the pool of her own blood on the floor.

Without thinking, the Nameless Rider threw the Girl over his shoulder and left.

He left the Wall of the Ancients before dressing the Girl's wounds. He had grabbed the boy's backpack on the way up to the hill where his horse waited for him and laid her onto the moss. The Boy's supplies contained suitable materials for cleaning and binding her wounds, but she would still have a fight for her life. After he had treated her injuries, she opened her eyes a sliver.

"What happened?" She asked.

"You have injured yourself," the Nameless Rider said, unable to recall if he had ever spoken to a person before.

"Who are you?" the Girl asked.

The Nameless Rider didn't know how to answer this. Not exactly sure what she meant, he tilted his head.

"Aiwren!" she screamed.

"The Boy's gone," he said.

The Girl's eyes darted around and she tried to sit up, but the Nameless Rider held her still and she slipped, again, out of consciousness.

The Nameless Rider knew he had to bring the Girl with him because, when he received the signal, he would have to kill her. As he loaded the supplies back into the backpack, he came across a folded sheet of paper that said, "Vannoria." He stuffed the letter in his cloak and returned to the Girl. He heaved the her over his shoulder and lifted himself into the saddle. Moments later, the Nameless Rider and the Girl galloped away. For the moment, she was safe, but the Nameless Rider had noticed the tiny sliver of black glass in her left index finger and knew it was working its way to her heart.

***

Aiwren's dream was the worst he had ever had. He was in the woods again. Again, fog reduced his visibility to almost nothing. This time, he was following Vannoria. She was only a few feet in front of him and she kept glancing back to smile at him, laugh playfully, and make sure he was still behind her. A creeping feeling of dread seeped into his gut.

Vannoria entered a clearing and approached a pond, the pond from behind her house, the pond Aiwren had watched her bath in. He remained at the edge of the clearing, but she walked up to the water and peeled off her clothing. He yelled for her, but made no sound. He tried to run to her, but his feet were stuck.

Vannoria, completely nude, stepped into the water. Aiwren watched her walk deeper and deeper, unable to warn her, unable to move to stop her. When the water reached her waist, she turned around to face him. He waved his arms to warn her, but she only laughed, unaware of her peril.

Suddenly, panic flashed on Vannoria's face. In an instant she disappeared beneath the surface of the water. She struggled and floundered. She came up for air and, for a moment, appeared as though she might have been safe. The Skinless Woman, emerging from the water behind Vannoria, grabbed her, wrapped one arm around her neck and, with the other arm, ripped the skin off of her face.

By the time Aiwren reached the water, wading out to his waist, the Skinless Woman and Vannoria had submerged again and all that was left was the same bloody water Aiwren's dreams always ended with. Desperate to find Vannoria, Aiwren splashed his arms through the water. A hand reached up from beneath the surface. He grabbed it and pulled, but the hand went limp when he lifted it from the water. It was the skin of Vannoria's arm, but Vannoria was gone.

Aiwren sat up, relieved to find Vannoria nestled next to him, safely asleep. He slipped away, walked to the far side of the fire, and watched her. She was so good. So pure. He knew he cared for her and that frightened him. What if he didn't love her? What if he did love her, but fell in love with another woman in Y-Kewnor? What if his dreams meant something? What if the Order of the Crystal Blade was real and they were the only way he'd be able to rid himself of the Skinless Woman? If he truly cared about her, he had only one option. He had to leave her.

Aiwren, rushing to leave before she awoke, quickly packed what he needed. He left her all the food, the backpack, all of the supplies, a few coins, and some clothes. He only took his sword and a small sack tied to his back which contained his new city clothes and the rest of his coins. Finally, he wrote her a brief letter:

> *Vannoria, I cannot take you where I'm going. You are a good person. Go home.*

He signed the letter, folded it, wrote her name on the outside, and left it in the top of his backpack for her to find when she woke up. He grabbed the lantern, filled with oil, and headed to the back of the cave. Before leaving the room, he cast his eyes upon Vannoria, silhouetted by the entrance, one last time and whispered, "I'm sorry."

In the corridor, Aiwren already knew he would be going to the right, so when the voices called out for him to go down the stairs, he reminded himself that they were only in his mind and that the best course of action from then on would be to ignore them. So we went to the right, away from the voices, and to the exit to the other side of the wall.

Aiwren's small lamp was running out as he walked down the seemingly endless hallway. The walls, floor, and ceiling were all stone and mostly nondescript. The only outstanding detail to him was how finely they were crafted and how little wear there had been. He wasn't about to waste too much time exploring though. He had always been curious about things, a born adventurer, but Y-Kewnor was the adventure he was supposed to be on and he didn't want any distractions getting in the way of that, so he hurried.

Just as his lamp began flickering to warn him of the dwindling fuel, a light glimmered ahead, faint and small, but clearly a light. His lantern extinguished a few moments later and he spent the rest of his journey down the corridor, groping his way towards the light at the end.

Certain it was daylight, Aiwren ran. He had never been so relieved by the sight of daylight. The light was coming from the left, the west side of the wall. As Aiwren Wayde stepped out into the Indigo Forest he thought he heard a scream. He tipped his head back inside and listened. He waited for a moment before deciding it was only his imagination and leaving the Wall of the Ancients behind him. He was free.

The Indigo Forest looked pretty much the same on the west side of the Wall of the Ancients as it did on the east side and because he had travelled so far north inside the wall and since the wall was on a diagonal, relative to the roads, the south road was only a brief walk west from where he exited. As soon as he found the south road, he picked up his pace and headed south, towards Y-Kewnor, planning to arrive later that night and didn't want to stop to rest until he arrived. With this goal in mind, Aiwren pushed hard down the south road.

***

Teryessa awoke alone and frightened. She had spent the long terrifying night comforted and protected by Ruthillo's strong embrace. His absence that morning was jarring. A hand grabbed her shoulder. She screamed.

It was only Ruthillo. Then she saw his eyes and her relief was replaced with fear. She knew it was time to go. Teryessa brushed the sleep from her eyes.

"It is unsafe," Ruthillo said, snapping his scimitar into its scabbard. "We must hurry."

"What is it?" Teryessa asked. "What's going on?"

"Revolution," he said, tossing her a robe. "The king has died. Plale and his followers are waging war against Prince Grell and his followers for command of the city."

"And Grell?"

"Escaped."

Teryessa stood, drawing the strings of the robe tight. As Ruthillo unlocked the door, Teryessa drew the large heavy hood over her face. The door opened and a body slumped into the room. It was the messenger from the night before. He was dead. The hallway was a bloodbath. She covered her own mouth with both hands. Her eyes widened at the sight before her as she followed Ruthillo down the hall.

***

Like pried open jaws of an enormous beast, the entrance to Gavlessa was agape before the figure. He was adorned in ornate gold armor, glistening in the hot desert sun. His long blond hair flowed through the bottom of a beautiful gold helmet. He knew gold wasn't the strongest metal, but he wore it for what it represented.

The Gavlessans had a reputation for their barbarism. Most knights would be terrified. He was not. He was calm. He stepped into almost complete darkness, cast in shadow, a silhouette with a golden corona, he drew his mighty sword, a sword most would need two hands to lift.

His destiny called him inside. That was what brought him to Gavlessa. Destiny. Of course orders had been given, but there were always orders. He didn't do what he did for the orders. He did it for the thrill. He did it because he could.

As the Gold Knight set forth, a mysterious gleam flashed in his eyes, a glow, perhaps. He knew what he needed to do. Find the princess.

***

Teryessa and Ruthillo had come to a corner in the corridor. Ruthillo put his hand up for the princess to wait. She did. She held her breath helplessly as Ruthillo left her alone in the darkness. His steps faded into the distance. Then, silence and darkness engulfed her. Her head spun erratically. Was this the numbendria? She thought she heard something, a whisper.

"Ruthillo?" She whispered in response. Nothing.

"Teryessa." the whisper called.

Teryessa gasped. Held her breath. Was it the Gallery? Was it calling to her? How? Why? Just as Teryessa's head started spinning, Ruthillo rounded the corner.

They followed the twisting and the winding of the dark dirty hallways, until they reached the huge heavy doors of the great room. So far they had not seen a single person. Ruthillo mimed for her to be silent. She nodded. He slowly opened the massive door, careful not to create any creaks. He poked his head in. Turned back. Nodded.

Ruthillo and Teryessa slowly crept into the great room, her bare feet padding their way across the cold stone ground. In the distance something snapped, a small lantern flickering on. Teryessa hoped it was the end of this room. A hallway. Hope. Ruthillo paused. He gave her a comforting glance.

It only took an instant for everything to change. The flicker grew enormous. A torch had been lit. Then, all around the room torches ignited, one after another. Ruthillo grabbed Teryessa's hand tight and bolted for the far door. From out of nowhere there was a smack. It was a glancing blow, but enough to knock Ruthillo to the ground.

A huge Pitt Fighter lunged in to bring his massive club down hard on Ruthillo's head, a strike that would have surely crushed his skull. He rolled quickly and, with a crack, the club smashed into the stone ground, sending dust and splinters into the air. The Pitt Fighter swung the club down again. Again, Ruthillo barely dodged it, but this time, as he dodged, he quickly scrambled to his feet, drawing his blade with one fluid motion. The Pitt Fighter took one final swing at Ruthillo, a wild and desperate swing, the swing of someone not accustomed to having to swing more than once. As he did, Ruthillo spun towards him, effortlessly averting the club and swinging his sword down gracefully as he completed a full rotation. The club fell to the ground. It took the Pitt Fighter a moment to realize his hands had been severed from his body. He staggered back in horror as Ruthillo's blade sliced from his belly to his chest. The Pitt Fighter dropped so quickly, Teryessa was not quite able to put it all together. Ruthillo fought with blazing speed, grace, and agility. It was unlike anything she had ever seen.

A dozen more Pitt Fighters advanced on them and two more barricading the door they had entered from.

"Stop."

Plale, cast in shadow, sat on the throne, wearing black robes with the hood drawn over his head.

"We wouldn't want anyone to harm even a solitary hair on the princess's pretty little head. Why don't we drop our weapons and discuss this civilly."

"You think I don't know what would happen to me?!" she said. "I don't care if you have a coup. I wouldn't bat an eye if you barbarians all killed each other, but if you think I'll die civilly then you are sorely mistaken."

The Pitt Fighters made an advance.

"No!" Plale shouted. "The Master wants her alive."

"Master!" She laughed. "You have no master. You had your master killed, then turned on the man who did it."

"Oh, I have a Master, Princess, the only true Master," Plale said, slowly approaching. "You think this is about rebellion? The petty disputes of one small, barbaric, and utterly unimportant kingdom?"

Plale was so close she could feel him breathing on her.

"Oh, no," he continued, removing his hood to reveal that his face had been grotesquely disfigured.

Plale smiled at her reaction to his appearance and continued, "This is about you, Teryessa. And you, like everyone else in this land, will do my Master's bidding whether you like it or not."

An enormous shadow approached. Even more terrifying up close, Ovyrr-Keel obediently waited for Plale's orders.

"Bring her to my chambers," Plale said over his shoulder, adding, "Kill the slave."

As Plale walked towards the exit Ruthillo whispered in Teryessa's ear, "Wait for my signal, then run for the door at the far end of the room and don't look back."

"What?" She asked, but it was too late.

Ovyrr's ax was screaming towards them. The massive slab of iron was dull and heavy. Ruthillo shoved the princess away and dodged the blade. The iron bit into the stone floor, ringing like a horrible bell, showering sparks up in the air, and, for a moment, sticking. A Pitt Fighter with a sword and a Pitt Fighter with a trident seized the opportunity and closed in. Ruthillo easily dodged a sword, drawing his own across the throat of his attacker. As the Pitt Fighter lunged with his trident, the backswing of Ovyrr's giant ax crunched into his body, sheering the man through the gut, showering the floor with his pulpy viscera. Ruthillo ducked just in time for the blade to skim over him, cleaving a Pitt Fighter with a net right in the face, splitting the man's helmet and head.

Teryessa's eyes met Ruthillo's.

"Now," he whispered.

The fighters charged toward her. It was her only chance. She ran. As she reached the far doorway, she glanced over her shoulder at the mob of Pitt Fighters closing in on Ruthillo. She stood there, helpless and frozen with panic, as a sword plunged into him.

"No!" she cried.

With his final breath, Ruthillo screamed for her to run, and she did. Her heart beat hard and fast as her bare feet pounded down the steps. She was completely defenseless, cast in darkness, and utterly alone. She reached a landing, the landing with the door to the balcony that overlooked the pitt arena. She reached out for the door. She had one more flight of stairs and she'd be out of the palace. She fumbled her way to the next descending flight.

"Down the stairs! Get her before she escapes," someone called from above, followed by the clanking of metal boots.

She scrambled. Tripped. Overcompensating, her weight crushed over her right ankle as it slipped out from under her, sending her tumbling down the stairs. Time stretched and warped to accentuate each and every moment of contact on the slick, filthy rock. Reaching to protect herself, her hands hit first. Pain surged up her arm. Her face cracked down onto a stair, crushing the bone above her right eye. Her shoulder took the rest of her body weight into the ground as her feet, flailing over her head slammed onto the steps. She slid the rest of the way down, the sharp edges ripping through the back of her robes tearing into her back, the back of her head hitting every hard step until she reached the bottom landing.

"Teryessa," whispered a voice.

Blood trickled into her right eye and fire seemed to course up her left arm. She was so close. She had to escape.

Her right ankle throbbed with pain as soon as she stood, refusing to carry her weight and buckling beneath her. It was already swelling. Tears streamed from her eyes. She had never known such excruciating agony. She crumbled back down to her knees.

The footsteps grew closer. She had to get up. She forced herself to her feet. Keeping as much weight as possible on her good ankle, she limped to the final door. The door to her escape from this palace. She hoped the coup had created enough chaos in Gavlessa for her to escape undetected.

She paused for a moment. She wasn't sure what it was, but something inside of her bound her to that spot. She heard her name and whipped around to find herself staring at the door to the Gallery. The voice from within was calling to her.

Resisting the voice, she turned to the exit, the door leading her away from the palace, and grabbed the handle. It was cold. She slowly pulled it open.

"Leaving so soon, Princess?"

It was Grell. She was face to face with him. He was bruised, beaten, and broken, and even more maniacal than ever. She froze. He took a menacing step towards her.

"This is all mine," he raved. "This city. This palace. You."

She had nowhere to go. He grabbed her wrist. Her left wrist. The pain throbbed. She squirmed.

"How dare you deny me, you disgusting little pig?" he screamed, shaking her. "How dare you?!"

Teryessa thought, for certain, Grell was about to kill her, but his rage overtook his malice and, instead, he shoved her. Hard. The next thing she knew she was hurdling across the landing. Then contact. Her body slammed into the door to the Gallery. Reaching up, she grabbed the handle and twisted, slumping over as it opened, collapsing onto the timeless, dust covered ground of the Gallery. Up the stairs, Grell's silhouette approached. She picked herself up and, as quickly as she could, shuffled down the dark forgotten hallway.

Teryessa wasn't thinking about the terrifying paintings she had seen the last time she unwittingly visited the Gallery. Nor was she thinking about the story of King Hesia and Nestellishma and the lost city of Allustria or the whispers or the darkness. She was panicked and desperate and thinking only of escape. She hurried past the paintings. The light in her heart silenced by fear, she pushed on, into the darkness, allowing it to consume her. She knew she was at the door. She reached out, turned the knob, and opened it. As she entered, the torches on the walls burst into flame.

Though she had only walked through a doorway, Teryessa felt as though she was somewhere far away. The room was small. Smooth black marble walls. Smooth black marble floor. Seamless. Other than the torches, there were only two other items in this room. A painting

112

and the black marble altar before it. The painting wanted her to come closer, so she did. She stared at the painting, mesmerized, in a trance. She didn't know how much time had passed and she didn't care. She was lost in the painting. The painting was black. Solid black, contained within a gold frame. The paint appeared to be wet. It was slick and shiny like oil. She reached out to touch it and it seemed to reach back to her. Slowly. Then. Contact. She quickly drew back her hand. It was cold. Wet. Black.

"Grell is coming, Teryessa. When he finds you he is going to kill you. Do you want that?"

"No," she said. "No."

"Then kill him."

"I'm defenseless."

"The altar."

Teryessa's eyes darted to the alter, spotting a dagger, black and smooth like everything else. Mesmerized, she grabbed it and reached her finger out to touch the razor tip.

Just then, the door burst open. Teryessa snapped out of her trance. Startled, she plunged the tip of the dagger into her finger tip, her black painted finger tip.

"Looks like you've reached a dead end, Princess."

Teryessa, held the dagger out with two hands and braced herself for an attack.

"So the little bird is going to defend herself with a knife."

"Stay away." Teryessa pleaded, "Please."

"You're mine, Princess," he said as he slashed out with his slender sword, cutting her leg through the robe. "I'll do with you as I please."

Teryessa gasped and looked at her leg. Grell laughed. She grit her teeth and lunged at Grell with the dagger. He easily grabbed her, laughing even louder. With his arm around her neck, he held her close. She struggled to escape, but he was too strong. She sank her teeth into his arm. Blood rushed to the surface of his skin and trickled out around her teeth, but he wasn't even fazed. He forced her to the ground. She fought to bring the dagger up to his throat, but he turned it back onto her own.

Teryessa something squished and Grell looked at her with shock, eyes bulging from his head. Thick blood gurgled out of his gaping mouth. She glanced at the black dagger, wondering if she had done this. It was dry. There was no blood on it. Through Grell's chest was the blade of a sword, only missing her by inches. He collapsed on top of her spraying his last breath all over her face, speckling her with bloody flakes. A knight in elaborate gold armor stood above Teryessa.

"You're safe now, Princess," he said, as he pulled off his helmet to reveal gold hair shimmering in the torch light and a face more beautiful to Teryessa than the finest sculpture. "But we must go now."

The Gold Knight offered Teryessa a hand to help her stand. She was taken by the swirling mystery in his eyes and was so relieved to be rescued, she barely noticed her own blood on the altar or the torches sputtering out as they left or the dark ink coursing through her veins. The door slammed shut behind them as they left and darkness, once again, engulfed the room at the back of the Gallery.

Teryessa fell asleep soon after she and the Gold Knight began galloping across the desert on his horse. She felt safe with him and she was exhausted. They travelled faster than she had ever travelled before and, in her delirium, for a moment, she thought she was flying.

***

The sun had already set, when Aiwren Wayde arrived at Y-Kewnor. When the staggeringly huge citadel first crept over the horizon, he had discarded any sense of exhaustion and began running. He couldn't wait to find Leicester and surprise him with his arrival.

Through the city, he ran. He found the small building Leicester's letters had been addressed from. It was a bachelor house and Aiwren had the number memorized. He ran up to the front door and knocked. Some other young man answered. He thought it must have been one of Leicester's new city friends. The young man hollered for Leicester as Aiwren waited out side.

A few moments later, Leicester, overcome with excitement, practically tore the door off its hinges to greet Aiwren, but, as the young man stepped outside, before he could lift Airwen off the ground in a bear hug, something else caught his eye and his face went from glee to horror as he looked up at the sky behind Aiwren.

***

The Nameless Rider knew he was closing on the Boy. The Girl, laying across the horse, slept as he rode. Then the gates to Y-Kewnor closed. He had missed his opportunity. The Boy had entered. There was no longer any point in speeding towards the city. It was protected from him. He had failed.

The Nameless Rider dismounted. He would wait until he was given the signal, then he would kill the Girl and return to his slumber, where he would surely be punished for his failure. Until then he would treat the Girl's wounds and make sure she didn't die by any incorrect means or at an incorrect time. He lifted her from the horse and laid her on the ground.

The Girl creaked open her eyes and, gazing past the Nameless Rider, said, "Pretty."

The Nameless Rider turned to see a great fire burning in the sky. Bright flames engulfed the citadel. Around its blazing summit swarmed four enormous dragons.

PART TWO

THE MANY TWISTING PATHS

Y-KEWNOR

Rheozarccio Rheodo thought nothing odd of his day when he woke up the morning of the attack on the Citadel. No signs, gut feelings, or foreboding omens ominously warned him doom was descending upon Y-Kewnor, the city to which he pledged his allegiance, and the Citadel, the heart of the The Divine Empress's Knights to which he swore his life. As Rheozarccio's bare feet touched the cold stone floor of his sparse but private quarters in Knights Keep, he stretched and focused his attention on drawing in the first breath of what he believed to be a day as wonderful as any other. He had no reason to believe otherwise.

Life had been hard, but kind to Rheozarccio Rheodo, who went by Rheo to his friends, which seemed to be everybody he knew. Rheo's parents were hard workers, a carpenter and seamstress, from Xcesemtia, a kingdom operating under a feudal system neither kind nor generous to its serfs. So, while Rheo's mother was pregnant with him, she and Rheozarccio's father traveled north through the

Dragonsback Mountains, across the Wild Plains, and into the Freelands. They settled in Y-Kewnor, where they learned new skills and worked their fingers to the bone, thankful for the confidence that their son would have a life free from the tyranny of a cruel and vindictive king. Rheo quickly learned Kewnorian, the common language of Allyoshmar, and, because of his gift for people, the children at school overlooked his olive skin, short black hair, Xcesemtian accent, and green eyes, earning the gregarious young Rheo a popularity that only increased as he grew into a strong, tan, handsome young man with emerald eyes.

Rheo was thankful for the city and thankful for The Divine Empress who, he was certain, had a hand in making his life so blessed. This was why, as soon as he had finished his schooling, he decided he would test for The Divine Empress's Knights. This way, he figured, he could serve The Divine Empress, the city of Y-Kewnor, all of the Freelands, and all the people of Allyoshmar, many of whom were less blessed than he was. His natural athleticism secured his acceptance in the Academy of Knights and developed into a skill with swordsmanship unparalleled by his peers.

Graduating early from the Academy, Rheo assumed his petitions to the High Knights of the Council would almost immediately prove triumphant and he would soon be a High Knight, himself, but, after petitioning to almost every High Knight of the Council, Rheo was only met with disappointment. Eventually, only one High Knight of the Council remained unpetitioned, Sir Vincent Ackaback, who had never accepted another knight-son since losing his first knight-son many annuals earlier. It was Vincent who became Rheo's knight-father.

As he had done every day for the past five annuals, after dressing in the decorative silver armor all High Knights wore in public and eating the simple breakfast of grains and cream prepared for him in the Hall of High Knights, Rheozarccio journeyed to meet his knight-father in the Citadel. On this day, however, as he did once every seven days, he would wake early and make a stop along the way. As he lumbered, encumbered with five annuals of too much food and not enough exercise, through the halls of the Knights Keep, knights acknowledged him with jocular greetings, embraces, and salutes; they loved him and he loved being loved. Although his home life had been stressful and painful, he often missed his parents, who had eventually succumbed to poverty's burden, and wished they might experience this with him, but he was confident that, since he was so loved by The Divine Empress, his parents, too, were loved by Her and they were, no doubt, by her side, proudly watching him from The Source. Thinking of them watching over him beside The Divine Empress always brought him peace. The Divine Empress's Knights were supposed to be content; Rheo was comfortable.

The motto of Y-Kewnor, the crown of the Freelands, was, "no birthright." Nearly a thousand annuals earlier, The Divine Empress's Knights led the people of the kingdom of Argratos in an uprising against the tyrannical, King Slyvos Argratosius. This revolution sparked a change across Allyoshmar and the flags of rebellion flew in almost every kingdom. Battles raged until the people defeated Argratosius and Argratos was renamed Y-Kewnor, the city with no king. Weakened, other kingdoms fell to their own revolutions. By the end of the war, the last great war, most kingdoms east of the Realmsend River experienced complete shifts in power and became known as the Freelands. West of the river, the kingdoms maintained their hold over their people, but many of them compromised to change the ways their kingdoms functioned. In Y-Kewnor, the lords, all powerful land owners, created the Parliament of Lords, electing a

119

new High Lord of Parliament once every ten annuals. People believed, with hard work, any Kewnorian could become a Lord, a Lord of Parliament, or even the High Lord of Parliament. The Kewnorians were a motivated, productive, and industrious people. Y-Kewnor thrived as the heart of business for all of Allyoshmar. It was a city built on business, a city built on dreams.

The palace, an expansive white building with ancient scorch marks all across its top, stood in the center of Y-Kewnor's sprawling businesses, apartments, and homes. In the absence of a king, the palace became the Parliamentary Palace and housed the business chambers for the Parliament of Lords. Rheozarccio arrived at the Parliamentary Palace early for his scheduled meeting with Lord Archibald Plune, the Lord of Finance.

Lord Archibald Plune, the wealthiest man in Y-Kewnor, had been elected as the Lord of Finance. Rheo's knight-father was the liaison to the City of Y-Kewnor, a seemingly reputable position, but as impotent as the knights had become to the Kewnorians. One of his duties was collecting regular tithes from Parliament, an act for which Ackaback was made to feel like a beggar and it seemed as though Lord Plune made extra effort to aggrandize the benevolence of his donations to The Divine Empress's Knights. Rheo knew Sir Vincent hated dealing with Lord Plune, so Rheo usually volunteered for this task.

Across from the Parliamentary Palace, Harry Haggard's Haggis boasted the best Sour Sausages in Y-Kewnor. Sour Sausages, one of Rheo's favorite foods, reminded him of a Xcesemtian dish his mother used to make. Rheo's routine visits to Harry Haggard's may have accounted for a significant measure of the heft he had acquired. The old men, mostly from neighboring shops, would laugh and welcome Rheo before returning to what ever politics they had been arguing about. Rheo would exchange grunts with Harry, the choleric old man at the counter with a bloody apron, grey hair sprouting wildly from beneath his leather cap, and a scowl on his face as sour as his sausages. Harry would always slide Rheo one more sausage than he had paid for, surreptitiously winking at him, as if to acknowledge that they were getting away with something deviously clever. Rheo would always respond with the same appreciative grin and eat his sausages while the old men in the shop grilled him for information, only to have whatever he told them dismissed as being the opinion of one too young to know any better. He would tell them they were old fools, before wiping his mouth and crossing the street to conduct his unpleasant business at the Parliamentary Palace. Rheo loved real connections; they were authentic, unlike his meetings with politicians, which always felt so fraudulent and duplicitous.

Though sparse in comparison to the opulence it once had as the king's palace, the Parliamentary Palace still illustrated a level of ostentatious extravagance most Kewnorians didn't have the privilege of enjoying even a fraction of, themselves. Lord Archibald Plune's chambers overlooked Y-Kewnor, high in the northwest tower of the building.

"Apparently The Divine Empress's Knights have little appreciation for punctuality," Lord Archibald Plune sneered without looking up from his ledger, as one of his servants opened the door for Rheo, "or attending to business matters in person."

"I extend to you my most humble apologies, Lord Archibald," Rheozarccio said with a bow, knowing Lord Archibald Plune's sole intention of making this insinuated false accusation was to illicit a response. "I'm afraid Sir Vincent had matters requiring his attention."

"As usual," Plune said, as he closed the ledger and looked up, grinning condescendingly through strands of stringy black hair. Lord Plune made it clear that the taxes Y-Kewnor spent on The Divine Empress's Knights were an especially bitter annoyance to him. He slid a bag of gold across the table and returned to his ledger.

Rheo picked up the bag of gold. These donations had been thinning for a while, but this one seemed as though it had half the gold of the previous week's.

"I beg your pardon," Rheo said, "but I believe there may have been an accounting error."

"Are you a banker now, Mister Rheodo?" Archibald replied dismissively, his gaze remaining fixed on his calculations.

"No, Lord Archibald, I am no banker." Rheo replied, still standing in front of Lord Archibald Plune's desk, fists clenched.

"Well, Sir Rheozarccio Rheodo, with children to feed and roofs to keep over their heads, the people of Y-Kewnor, are becoming less interested in paying real gold to pretend soldiers who accomplish nothing productive other than parading around town dandy'd up like a troop of actors. Perhaps you and your thespian warriors ought to consider a vocation other than begging for gold coins from those who can't afford suits of silver armor. Remind me your father's trade. Carpentry? Perhaps it's time to abandon the toy sword and wield a real hammer."

Rheo mustered his restraint to chill the heat of anger coursing through his veins.

"With all due respect, Lord Plune," Rheo said, as evenly as possible, "although the houses carpenters construct are important, I believe Kewnorians understand that the protection of those houses is also important."

"From what?!" Plune snapped, looking up from his ledger, thoroughly irritated, "Monsters?! We have real problems and they can't be solved with stories about magic. They require rational thought, resources, and the men who actually protect our homes, the Kewnorian Guard. You and your knights are tolerated, Sir Rheodo, not welcome, and that tolerance is waning. If you or your perpetually absent knight-father have any further grievances to air, perhaps you ought to go pen a play about it. I'm too busy keeping this city running to cater to the complaints of fools from another time who are no longer necessary."

Rheozarccio, who wished only moments earlier for politicians to be more sincere in their discourse, didn't find Plune's honest expression of hatred to be the breath of fresh air he expected. In order to prevent himself from drawing his sword, he took a breath, thanked Lord Plune for his donation, and left.

After his brief, but infuriating meeting with Lord Plune, Rheo decided to purchase more Sour Sausages before going to the Citadel. He told himself, as he stuffed his mouth, that he ought to eat less and exercise more. Rheo sucked the last bit of grease from his fingers before wiping his hands on his satchel, the satchel containing the bag of gold from Lord Plune, and opened the door to the Citadel.

The Citadel, was an enormous tower built next door to the Parliamentary Palace for The Divine Empress's Knights, who had been invited to make Y-Kewnor their primary headquarters. For a long time this arrangement benefitted Y-Kewnor and The Divine Empress's Knights. The knights had a home to house and train recruits. Y-Kewnor had the protection of the knights. Over time, the army of rebels became the Kewnorian Guard, responsible for protecting the city and for keeping the peace within its walls. Meanwhile, the knights continued receiving taxes from the Kewnorian people. They had become sacred merely for the ideals they represented. Eventually, even that importance dissolved and many Kewnorians believed the once esteemed protectors of the realm to be a waste of tax money.

As Rheozarccio climbed to the ninth floor of the Citadel, his concerns about the future of the knights puzzled him. Being disliked by anyone shocked to Rheo. He had always attributed Plune's hatred of the knights to the Lord's nasty disposition, but to hear Plune say the entire city had turned against him and his brothers was a dizzying contradiction that sent his world spinning. They were wrong and someday they would be thankful the knights were there to protect them. Or perhaps, he worried, they would be sorry the knights weren't there. If the latter were the case, he mused, it would serve them right for turning their backs on The Divine Empress.

Winded from his climb, Rheo took a deep breath and reminded himself that a Divine Empress's Knight oughtn't have such bitter thoughts. Unmotivated by money or fame, their code demanded they do the right thing, regardless of appreciation. He never considered the notion that the knights might have all grown as comfortable as he had grown. Complacent, even. They were well clothed, well fed, and hadn't been called to duty in a generation. Rheo never considered this possibility as he stopped on a landing to catch his breath.

Like all of the High Knights of the Council, Sir Vincent Ackaback had served as a Knight and then a High Knight for many annuals before retiring to the bureaucracy of the Citadel when his own knight-father, Sir Deleronis Stegos died in his sleep at the age of one hundred. Although elderly, himself, he would have preferred to have been in the field, but he understood the importance of his role, especially in a world increasingly more dependent on politicians than heroes. Unlike the other High Knights of the Council, he had only one knight-son, Rheo. The other High Knights of the Council had scores of knight-sons in their houses, most of them took a knight-son as soon as they were promoted to the Council and adopted at least one knight-son every annual, since. Each house had been named for a virtue: Chastity, Temperance, Charity, Diligence, Patience, Kindness, and Vincent's house, Humility. Vincent was stern, but he made his adoration for Rheo's company no secret. They shared a bond not entirely based on their love of food, but that was certainly a contributing factor.

Rheo entered Vincent's chambers on the ninth floor of the Citadel, greeted by the sight of a banquet table spread out and waiting for him.

"Rheo, my boy! Just in time for breakfast!" Vincent bellowed with glee, but the crumbs of scones falling from his flowing white beard onto his round belly made it clear breakfast had already begun. "Don't tell me you've already eaten!"

"I have," Rheo chuckled. "Twice. Actually, thrice."

Vincent's twinkling blue eyes frowned. "Well," he said, taking a breath, "throw that damned miser's gold in the corner, pull up a chair, and start from the beginning."

Just being in Vincent's presence, all of Rheo's concerns and anxiety and confusion slipped away. Sir Vincent Ackaback always had everything under control. Not like Rheo's birth father, who targeted Rheo when he frequently succumbed to frustration and anger. Perhaps it was the consistent absence of cruelty that put Rheo at ease, but Rheo wasn't the type of man to ponder his own motivations; he preferred to view the complex world in the simplest way possible: Vincent was the closest thing to family he had.

At the end of Rheo's story and the end of their meal, Sir Vincent took one final bite of quail egg before pushing his plate away, looking up at Rheo and saying, "Well, if he's right, what do you suggest we do?"

"He's not right," Rheo exclaimed, flabbergasted by the thought of this and confused as to why Vincent would even suggest such a thing. "The people love us. They must!"

"Well, let's examine this," Vincent replied. "We expect the Kewnorians to make these sacrifices for the greater good, but how clear is our understanding of the needs of the Kewnorians?"

"We ask for nothing more than a little bit of gold," Rheo shouted, standing from his chair out of frustration.

"A little bit of gold might mean the difference between the life and death of a carpenter's young son," Vincent reminded him, motioning for a servant to remove the dishes.

"We understand the needs of the people because we are guided by The Divine Empress who created all of Allyoshmar," Rheo exclaimed, pacing tempestuously. "Who better would understand these needs than Her?!"

"Rheo, my boy," Vincent said, remaining calm while Rheo seemed determined to work himself into a fit, "it's important to understand the people and where they come from. The Divine Empress's Knights serve all of Allyoshmar, but the Lords of Parliament serve only Y-Kewnor. To whom, do you suppose, would the Kewnorians pledge their support? Think of the Parliament. Do you suppose they think it's wise to take money away from their own army in order to fund a foreign military presence in their city? The Lords of Parliament require popularity in order to maintain their positions and the people are suffering now, more than they have in a long time, which doesn't make the Lords popular."

Now shaking with frustration, Rheo threw up his arms and replied, "Which is why they need their leaders to lead, not follow. The people may not want to part from their gold now, but what if something terrible were to happen? Then The Divine Empress's Knights would be sorely missed. Then the Kewnorians would wish to The Divine Empress, Herself, that they had parted with a few coins to remain under our protection!"

"Be careful with your tongue, my boy."

"I apologize, knight-father." Rheozarccio said, rushing to Vincent's side and kneeling, "I meant no anger."

"Your apology is unnecessary, my knight-son," Vincent replied. "The Divine Empress created an astoundingly complex world, with landscapes that shift in appearance as perspectives change. Examining these issues, thinking through them, and learning to explore them from many points of view is a hallmark of wisdom."

"Wisdom, it seems, is a quality I'm deficient in," Rheo said, head hung low.

"Patience is a quality you're deficient in and only time will answer how you fare with wisdom," Vincent said, putting a hand on Rheo's shoulder. "I'm on my way to visit with General Boomswift, but, while I'm gone, I'd like you to go to the library and pick a history, any one you haven't read yet, and spend the day reading. The council meets at sundown. Please be punctual."

Rheozarccio took his time walking to the library. In losing his temper, he worried he failed his knight-father. To assuage his concerns, he stopped for a leg of mutton and munched on it joylessly as he shuffled down the street. Spiraling into even more self-deprecation, he thought of what Lord Plune had said and he couldn't help but notice the Kewnorians who's paths he crossed, the thankless way they looked at him. Lost in thought, Rheo didn't notice the glob of mint mustard dripping from his mutton until it dropped onto his chest, greenish yellow sauce sticking to his silver armor. He stopped and pulled a rag from his satchel. He had to remove this stain; if he didn't everyone would be certain he was nothing more than a bumbling buffoon. Scrubbing at the sauce in the middle of the promenade, passing strangers scolded him for being in the way. Rheo stood frozen in the street as the world swam around him and he wondered how he, all of a sudden, had become so unloved.

The library provided Rheo with relief. By the time he was in the Academy and first forced to attend the library, Rheo, certain he didn't enjoy reading, struggled with words. He thought everyone else already had a head start on, an advantage over him, but when he realized how many books the library contained, rows and columns stacked to the ceiling, his perspective changed. He told himself it was impossible, even for the most well-read person, to have read all those books. The difference between the little he knew and the little even the most learned men knew didn't seem so big; the library had become an equalizer. He soon found, without the pressure of competing against people he thought were more intelligent than he was, he actually enjoyed reading. After his stressful morning, Rheo looked forward to escaping his life and entering the life of some person from long ago.

Despite Sir Vincent's instructions to read something he hadn't read, Rheozarccio went straight to the section he always went to first, the section of recent history containing the story of his knight-father. It was always difficult to get any information from Sir Vincent about his past. Most of what he had heard was from other young knights only repeating stories they had heard, stories Sir Vincent referred to as "gossip and hullabaloo." The story of Sir Vincent's previous knight-son always perturbed Rheo. Perhaps, because his knight-son's name had been redacted from all of the volumes or because Sir Vincent refused to talk about him, Rheo often wondered about what ever tragedy happened to Sir Vincent's first knight-son. Rheo took the leather tome to a table and, once again, read the story.

The book described chapter upon chapter of details on Sir Vincent's many exciting adventures with his own knight-father, Sir Deleronis Stegos, but the writing became vague and concise near the end. Rheo always made note of the final volume's author, swearing, if he had ever met M.W., he would certainly have some words with him about omitting such important information. Once again finding the text unsatisfactory and unfulfilling, Rheo closed the book.

Still long before sunset, Rheo arrived at his usual impasse of missing information. Rheozarccio perceived life in a linear fashion and horizontal thinking was a strategy that annoyed him, so he returned the book to its shelf and searched for a more ancient text, something from when Allyoshmar was an exciting place, when battles waged between a clear good and a clear evil.

Rheo walked all the way down to the first shelves, the most ancient of texts available to peruse without the supervision of a librarian. At the end, next to a cart, stood Greta, the librarian, shelving books. Greta, though young, had already read more books than any of the other librarians. As saucy as she was brilliant, she always made extra time to converse with Rheo.

"Have any suggestions today, Greta? I'm looking for something old."

"Hmm. Ow does the romance of King Julian an Queen Marigold sound to ya?" She asked him with a wink.

Rheo flashed a disgusted scowl.

"Wut?!" She replied, "Bout time ya start thinking a doin' some romancing, yerself!"

"Now you're offering unsolicited advice on my love life, too?"

"Ya got other ladies talkin' bout your love life? I'm jealous! Who are they? I'll scratch out their eyes!"

The two of them laughed for moment, before one of the older librarians tilted her head around a corner, scowling disapprovingly.

"Oh, mind yer own business, ya old crow!" Greta barked at the librarian, then giggled at Rheo.

"Here," she said, handing him a tiny book in such disrepair, the binding crumbled when he touched it. "This is one of my favorites. It's so old, nobody even know when it was written."

Rheo thanked Greta for the book and brought it back to his table hoping it might describe exciting battles or introduce him to a knight he had never read about before. The book was called "The Last Magics," and it was, indeed, ancient. He flipped it open, turning the pages gently to prevent them from completely disintegrating.

The book told of a group of The Divine Empress's Knights who journeyed to Allustria, a kingdom Rheo had never heard of, to battle the evil King Hesia. Hesia, no ordinary King, was a cruel and powerful dragon, who took delight in butchering anyone who stood in his way. He was known for spearing as many as ten knights on each of his two enormous lances and for raping and torturing countless women. He was aided by the necromancer, Nestellishma, a man with the ability to consume life and use it to power his spells. Together, King Hesia and Nestellishma had created a giant machine, fueled by the blood of their foes. They used this machine to raise and command an army of death savages, living corpses more powerful than mortal men. The heroes dared to attempt what all others had failed, to defeat the dragon king, Hesia, and his necromancer, Nestellishma. To accomplish this task,

The Divine Empress, herself, granted them each a magical sword. When they reached Allustria all that remained of the city was sand and dust, but, with their blessed weapons, they defeated Hesia and Nestellishma, freeing all of Allyoshmar from the reign of terror.

Distant, Rheo closed the book's flimsy little back cover and imagined a battle like that for himself, but, when he looked up, panic struck him like an anvil. Through the stained glass window high above the marble floor, the sun was setting.

Rheozarccio left the little book on the table and bolted from the library. He bolted to the Citadel. His knight-father specifically requested he be punctual and that the meeting began at sundown.

Though he pushed his muscular legs hard, he already had an unshakable feeling of dread that he was going to disappoint his knight-father. Heaving his way across Y-Kewnor, barreling though crowds on the promenade, Rheo sprinted. When the last shaft of sunlight extinguished on the horizon, Rheo still had several more blocks to travel. He had failed.

Rheo stopped running and, bending at the waist with his hands on his hips, worked to catch his breath. The thought of fabricating an excuse occurred to him, but he immediately dismissed it. He would accept full responsibility. Once again in control of his breathing, Rheo jogged the rest of the way to the Citadel.

As he lumbered up the spiral stairs of the Citadel, the twisting pattern of the stone threw Rheo into a dizzyingly vertiginous trance. His sweat chilled him as his field of vision circumscribed to a narrow beam and he felt the weight of the white marble Citadel rocks crushing down on him. He couldn't breathe. Paying too little attention on where he was going, Rheo ran right into someone coming down the stairs.

Rheo stopped to help the man back to his feet, but the man shook off Rheo's hand and said, "Someone out to tie a bell around the necks of you lumbering fools so the jingling alerts people not to enter an otherwise safe stairwell when some giant oaf is charging up it."

Rheo took a step back and realized the man was Lordson Jocund Plune, the son of Lord Archibald Plune, a thin young man with black wavy hair, pale skin and the same vicious blue eyes as his father. Jocund's neck tie was loose and his shirt disheveled beneath his sport coat. He clutched a bottle of wine, which he had almost certainly spent the day drinking. Before the Academy, Rheo had gone to school with Jocund. He didn't like the entitled lordson then and he didn't like him any more now.

"What are you doing here?" Rheo asked, unable to think of an obvious reason for Jocund to be in the Citadel.

"That's my business," Jocund responded. "I'd prefer if you minded your own, Rheodo."

"Sir Rheodo." Rheo corrected. "Sir Rheozarccio Rheodo, of The Divine Empress's Knights, knight-son to Sir Vincent Ackaback of the House of Kindness."

"House of Kindness?!" Jocund laughed venomously. "That's precious. Unfortunately, I haven't the time to explain irony to you this evening."

Jocund stumbled down the stairs. It was clear to Rheo that Jocund was quite intoxicated, though, according to rumors, Jocund was always intoxicated. Rheo watched Jocund's clumsy descent and wanted to stop him and yell at him for blaming their collision entirely on him when the fault was clearly shared, but his thoughts were interrupted when the building shook.

Three more tremors, in rapid succession, followed the first one. Rheo almost immediately heard the screams. His eyes narrowed and he sprinted up the stairs. As he grew closer, the screams grew louder and Rheo smelled the burning of wood, the melting of stone, and the distinct and horrifying charring of flesh.

Rheo arrived at the top floor, the Council Hall. He heard the cracking of timber and the crackling of fire as smoke billowed from beneath the thick wooden door. He grabbed for the handle, but the door wouldn't budge. Rheo heaved his giant shoulder into the door and the wood creaked as the metal of his armor clanged against it and the door opened enough for him to see the collapsed burning wooden beam blocking it. As his body crashed into the door again, he saw, through the small opening, a man on the other side, engulfed in flames. Rheo threw himself against the door again. Several more people, set ablaze, scrambled for their lives as fire swallowed the room. Rheo slammed against the door again and he could see the deceptively peaceful looking starry night though the openings in the wall where the stone had been melted down to pools of magma with flames licking at the remaining ruins and, to his horror, he saw people leaping from these openings. Finally the beam tumbled over and the door opened.

"Over here" Rheo shouted! "This way!"

Several High Knights of the Council, old men in gold armor, exited the room with the aid of their knight-sons, but Sir Vincent remained missing.

Rheo charged into the enormous burning room. A high knight in silver armor struggled to free his foot from beneath a collapsed wooden table. His wide, panicking eyes darted around the room desperately for something to grab onto while he mindlessly pulled at his leg in an attempt to free himself. Rheo grabbed the table and flipped it over, his muscles invigorated by the crisis-fortified blood coursing through his veins.

"Can you walk?" Rheo asked.

The knight nodded, unable to speak.

Rheo spotted a young squire crawling across the floor, groping his way with his hands, his boiled eyes oozing from his skull. Rheo told the knight he freed from the table to help the blind squire out of the room and, limping, the knight rushed to the squire's aid.

Rheo scanned around again for his knight-father. The large room was now mostly cleared of people struggling to escape. Everyone capable of escaping had. Everyone else he came upon was clearly dead, either burned to a crisp from direct contact with the flames or blue from suffocation. Then, off in the distance, something moved.

Chunks of rock and burning wood fell down on Rheo as he ran towards the movement. The ceiling trembled, threatening to collapse. The distance seemed to stretch before Rheo's eyes and the path became increasingly obstructed with burning rubble. Finally, through the smoke and fire, it was clear. A man in gold armor laid still, trapped beneath an enormous wooden beam. It was Sir Vincent.

As Rheo arrived at his knight-father's side and immediately started clearing the smaller debris to free the beam and lift it from his knight-father's body.

"No!" Vincent said, but Rheo kept working.

Rheo grabbed on to burning rock, flinging it wildly across the room, oblivious to the pain of it searing through the skin on his hands. He finally gripped the beam. Nearly five paces long and two steps thick each way, in ordinary circumstances this enormous plank would have been impossible for him to lift, but charged with emotion and determination to free Sir Vincent, Rheo slipped his burnt, bleeding fingers beneath the ashy timber and heaved with all of his might and lifted the beam from Sir Vincent. Without hesitation, Rheo threw his knight-father over his shoulder and headed towards the door.

Rheo hustled across the room with Sir Vincent over his shoulder, bombarded by a shower of rocks the size of his fist, denting and marring the armor he had worked so hard hours earlier to clean mint mustard from. Beams cracked and split, dropping avalanches of burning wood and deadly payloads of molten stone from above. Something crashed behind him. He glanced back. The ceiling in the center of the room had completely caved-in and the already weakened floor collapsed beneath its weight to create a hole in the ground that was quickly spreading. Rheo cleared the door to the stairwell just as the final piece of ceiling collapsed, snapping down like a guillotine that Rheo and Sir Vincent only narrowly avoided.

Rheo, didn't stop when he reached the stair well. Nor did he stop on the next floor. He hurried down the steps with Sir Vincent over his shoulder until he got to the ground floor and outdoors, where all of Y-Kewnor panicked. Knights and guardsmen franticly rushed to the scene to take arms against a long-gone enemy. Rheo placed Sir Vincent gently on the ground.

"Rheo, my boy," Sir Vincent muttered, his voice raspy and weak.

"Knight-Father," Rheo cried, "this is my fault. I shouldn't have been late."

"You're always so punctual," Vincent whispered. "Had you been on time, you'd have only been in the same pickle I'm in. You saved many lives tonight, Rheo. I've never been more proud of-"

Vincent's speech was interrupted by a coughing fit that resulted in gobs of blood flowing from his mouth.

"Where are you injured? What can I do?" Rheo asked, hollering, "Help! Somebody help me!"

"Shh," Vincent said. "Something terrible has begun. Something, I feared was eminent, but hoped I had taken measures to avoid."

"You can tell me when you recover." Rheo insisted.

"Tell me, Rheo, what did you read at the library today?" Sir Vincent asked.

"I read your history again," Rheo admitted, tears streaming from his eyes.

"Bah," Vincent scoffed, "gossip and hullabaloo."

"I know you told me to read something new," Rheo said, "but I wanted to know what happened on your last great adventure and all the information is either missing or redacted. I have never read such an uninformative history."

"This land is filled with secrets and lost history," Sir Vincent replied. "Crystal Order."

"Crystal Order?" Rheo asked, half believing his knight-father's speech to be delusional, half hanging off of his every word. "What are you talking about?"

"You have made me proud more than any father or knight-father could wish. You'll be a knight-father soon. A great evil is coming and I have left you with a terrible burden, but I have faith you will-"

Sir Vincent Ackaback, High Knight of the Council of The Divine Empress's Knights, knight-father to the House of Kindness stopped speaking. His chest sank, but didn't rise again. His blank eyes stared off into the inky black, star-tinseled sky. He wasn't in pain, but he wasn't at peace, either; he simple wasn't. Sir Vincent was dead.

Rheo's sobs echoed throughout the square in front of the Citadel, its fire burning out after consuming the thirteenth floor and destroying the twelfth and eleventh. He threw his body over his knight-father's and wailed. The gathered crowd watched him as he put his burnt and bleeding hand over Sir Vincent's eyes and closed them. He squeezed Sir Vincent's lifeless hand, wiped the tears from his eyes, and stood. Turning away from his knight-father, Rheo stripped off his armor as he walked away, leaving a trail of burnt, dented, and bloody silver. By the time he reached the street, Rheozarccio Rheodo was completely naked, the cacophony of the chaos behind him silenced by daze.

INFECTION

The Nameless Rider sat in the ruins of Old Argratos and stared at Y-Kewnor as the sun rose across the river before him. He had spent the night, leaning against what was once a castle wall, watching the flames in the Citadel until they died. With daylight spreading across Allyoshmar, the building still smoldered. He had been in that building, in the now incinerated room on the top floor, but had no recollection of his experience there. He didn't mind what he had forgotten as much as the bits of memory reminding him he had forgotten something. Like the ruins of Old Argratos; the little structure remaining rendered it impossible to discern detail, but served as somber evidence that something once stood there.

The Girl slept fitfully though the night next to the Nameless Rider. A lethal fever burned in her little body. The corruption on her finger spread quickly to her hand. The skin was peeling away, disintegrating like the stones of the lost city she rested in. The cuts on her arms, face, and body were also infected. He knew his medicine wouldn't be enough; in order to save her life, he'd have to stop waiting for instructions and make a decision.

The Nameless Rider thought more about his nebulous mission. He wondered why he hadn't yet been given permission to kill the Girl and return to his sleep. Unable to recall any of his previous tasks, he could not imagine what his signal would even look like. He had spent all night hoping the stars would re-arrange or spell out some message or an ethereal disembodied head in the flames of the Citadel would speak and tell him it was time to complete his assignment and come home, but he received no message.

"My Master, I have still not received your signal," he said to the rising sun. "Perhaps you are punishing me for allowing the Boy to escape, but this Girl is dying. I will do what I can to keep her alive until you tell me the time is right, but I don't know if I'll succeed or if you even want me to. I wonder, perhaps, if it is your wish to allow this creeping death to consume her. I will do your bidding, but I must know your will. Please, Master, speak to me."

The Nameless Rider waited, but there was not a sound. No wind. Not even the subtlest change in the river.

"There are things I know that I do not know how I know. Perhaps these are fragments of memories you wish me to have so I may perform my duty. I can only hope I am pleasing you."

The world remained still.

"I have thought of a way I might save this girl's life. I have thought of a man who may help her. I do not know how I know this man, but my mind tells me he may be able to help. My mind tells me he might be able to revive her if I get her to him in time, but my mind denies me proof that this is what I am supposed to do."

The Nameless Rider still heard nothing.

"Please, give me a sign. Otherwise, I"ll have no recourse other than to preserve this life to the best of my ability until I receive notice. If you fail to speak to me I will leave. I will leave this instant and go to this man."

The Nameless Rider made up his mind. He threw the Girl over his shoulder, climbed onto his black steed and rode off, electing to ride west directly across the marshlands rather than taking the indirect route of the roads.

***

Aiwren awoke on Leicester's floor. Leicester had lent some blankets to him and to all of the apprentice tailors who were sleeping on the floor of the tiny parlor in the tiny apartment in the bachelor house, finding comfort in being close together.

So much of the night was a blur for Aiwren. He remembered Leicester's expression changing and how the light from the fire flickered in his peripheral vision before he turned to see the Citadel burning. He remembered people running from their homes. He remembered racing across Y-Kewnor with Leicester to find his fiancée, Wanda, who lived near the Citadel. He remembered how, when they passed the Citadel, he saw a man stripping off his armor and walking, nude, into the night. He he remembered how, when Leicester went up to Wanda's apartment, he overheard a man telling a Kewnorian Guardsmen it was dragons. He remembered meeting Wanda, who sobbed and shook as Leicester helped her walk down the street. He remembered how, when they returned to Leicester's apartment, Leicester's friends were waiting. He remembered how one of the boys had a bottle of a liquid he referred to as numbendria. The last thing Aiwren Wayde remembered was taking a swig from a bottle.

The other boys were waking for the day. The light renewed their courage and they returned to their own apartments in other parts of the bachelor house, leaving Aiwren alone in Leicester's parlor. Aiwren thought of how amazing it would be to be one's own man, living in a city, having one's fiancée sleep over, regardless of social customs. Aiwren thought about Vannoria, reassuring himself that leaving her behind was for the best. Telling himself she had already returned to Ribeln and would forget about him, he found himself thinking about the Crystal Order.

Aiwren's thoughts were interrupted by the door to Leicester's bedroom opening. Wanda, wearing nothing but a short slip, crept from the room. Worried she would realize he saw her and that it would be inappropriate, he closed his eyes, pretending to sleep, sighing with relief when she entered the water closet without noticing him. When the door opened again, Aiwren held his breath, telling himself to hold still until Wanda returned to Leicester's bedroom, but she didn't return to Leicester's bedroom.

In her slip, Wanda walked over to the little pantry area and began opening cabinets, making little effort to be quiet.

"Breakfast?" she bellowed in her charmingly raspy voice.

Aiwren wondered who she was talking to, but he didn't want to peek his eyes open, fearing he would get nabbed for pretending to sleep. He heard grains and cream being poured into a ceramic bowl. Then he heard Wanda return to the door to Leicester's room. She opened the door, mumbled something, then closed the door. Aiwren sighed.

Then he heard walking again. Wanda remained in the parlor. Her bare feet padded by him. A window opened and the sounds of the city filled his ears. Then, she plopped herself down on Leicester's little sofa... right above him.

"Deep sleeper," Wanda trumpeted and Aiwren realized she had been talking to him the entire time.

If he replied, she would certainly catch him pretending to sleep. If he didn't reply, he wondered how much longer he'd be forced to maintain the charade.

She kicked him playfully and said, "Help yourself to breakfast."

The kick was Aiwren's opportunity. He sprung up, as though he had been startled.

Nonplussed by Aiwren's dramatic reaction, Wanda continued casually chomping as though she could care less who saw her in her nightgown. She was a short young woman with reddish hair, freckled skin, and big green eyes. Her finger nails and toe nails had been painted the same color green as her eyes. She seemed as though fire was constantly coursing through her veins, swaying her freely expressed emotions beneath a veneer of nonchalance. Wanda was a city girl and a modern young woman.

"There are grains and cream in the pantry," she smacked, between bites. "I wish we had more to offer, but neither Leicester, nor myself, can cook worth a shit."

"Thank you," Aiwren said, thankful she hadn't noticed his fake sleep and for the reason to leave the room and not worry about averting his eyes from Wanda.

"You overplayed your charade of sleep, by the way." Wanda chuckled.

Thankfully, Leicester interrupted the uncomfortable moment. Unfortunately, Leicester was dressed as minimally as Wanda, making Aiwren's task of averting his eyes twice as difficult. Leicester and Aiwren always had much in common. Both of them grew up on farms, so they weren't accepted by the townsfolk, but they were both small and drawn to the more intellectual pursuits, so they weren't accepted by the countryfolk. They had forged a friendship over not being accepted, but Leicester's time in Y-Kewnor had given him the confidence of a young man who's gawky appearance was, in his current social circle, considered artsy and modern.

"I'm so glad you and Wanda are bonding, Aiwren," Leicester said as he fixed his own breakfast. "Did I mention Wanda is an actress? We met when I was stitching costumes for one of the plays she was in."

"You had mentioned that. Yes." Aiwren said, still recovering from embarrassment.

Leicester put his bowl on the counter, gave Aiwren a huge nearly-naked hug, said, "I'm so glad you're here," and walked into the parlor, where he snuggled up next to Wanda.

Having no recourse but to join the scantily-clad pair, Aiwren returned to the parlor, himself.

"So where are you from, Wanda, before journeying to Y-Kewnor to pursue acting?" Aiwren asked.

"The north, Sima Watusia," she replied, "but I hated it. The place is full of petty, small-minded people, and my parents were the worst of them all. Y-Kewnor, I've found, is also flawed, but there are wonderful people here, too."

Then she sobbed and Aiwren looked to Leicester, not knowing what to do, and Leicester replied with an awkwardly helpless shrug.

"I apologize," Wanda said, continuing, between sobs, "I keep trying to be brave, or forget, or pretend as though nothing happened, but then I think about last night."

Aiwren and Leicester were both trying not to think of the previous night's attack also, but since Wanda brought it up, they were left with no recourse but to discuss it.

"It hits me in waves," Leicester said, suddenly somber. "Little moment here, small thought there, eroding away my resolve to remain optimistic and, each time I think about it, the waves of those thoughts crash down upon me. It's as though my world changed the instant I saw the fire, but my mind is still catching up. And I slept last night. I slept. And now I'm burdened with the guilt of that slumber."

Aiwren was relieved his friend spoke so candidly. He had never discussed such serious subjects with anyone before. He didn't know how to explain that he, too, felt guilty. Although he stopped himself every time he thought about the dragons, part of him was already consumed with torment. He had been haunted by nightmares of a Skinless Woman, ignored Bonishara's warning, abandoned Vannoria, witnessed a vicious attack by four insidious creatures, and he focussed his strength on insisting to himself these things weren't his fault, but his strength was waning and he needed to be reassured. So he asked, "Why?"

"They were dragons, Aiwren." Leicester said. "That's just what they do."

Aiwren didn't realize this would be a trigger for Wanda, who, in an instant, flipped from devastating melancholy to furious rage.

"I'll tell you why," she said. "The Divine Empress's Knights. Those knights reap the tax money from the people simply so they can perpetuate the comfortable life styles they have built for themselves with the labors of the masses, contributing absolutely nothing to Y-Kewnor or Allyoshmar, in return. And the Kewnorian Guardsmen are no better, save for the fact that at least they really are servants. Unfortunately, they aren't servants to the Kewnorians, but are, instead, servants to the lords of Y-Kewnor, who are the absolute worst of them all. Kingless city! What a cruel and disingenuous joke! Tell that to the people toiling until they bleed so the lords can live as extravagantly as they do. Active feudal systems flourish from the blood of the serfs all over Allyoshmar! Sima Watusia is supposed to be a city of the Freelands, but it still has a king. The king of Lees Naglos just sent his own daughter off to marry some Gavlessan barbarian! He sent her off, against her will, to marry this Gavlessan prince. What do you suppose will happen to her, enslaved by those barbarians? Can you imagine how horrible that must be for her? I'll shed no tears for the loss of even a single lord, or guardsman, or knight, but so many innocent people died last night. Servants! Squires who had already suffered enough beneath the thumb of the powers that be. I've no idea where those dragons came from, but I'm certain the knights or lords brought this on and the regular people are the ones who paid the price."

Aiwren and Leicester sat stone silent at the end of Wanda's impassioned tirade, which ended when she, once again, broke down into tears. Leicester consoled Wanda, leaving Aiwren to his own thoughts. He was glad to have Leicester and Wanda near him. Everything felt so much bigger and more grown up than he had ever thought of himself as being.

Breakfast time flew by for Aiwren, Leicester, and Wanda. The few hours spent in Leicester's parlor were burdened with the tragedy they witnessing the night before. The reality of the situation would, as Leicester had said, hit them in waves. They spent the space between those waves trying to live as normally as possible, thankful they had only witnessed the event. Before too long, Wanda was dressed and leaving for rehearsal, while Aiwren, dressed in his new city clothes, headed out the door with leicester, to begin his apprenticeship.

Cutter's Fine Fabrics, a humble shop with a tiny storefront on the Avenue of Craftsmen, was considered one of the finest clothing stores in Y-Kewnor. It was on the east side of town, like Leicester's bachelor house, so it wasn't much of a walk. Ulysses James Cutter, the shop master had built a reputation of using the finest fabrics and stitching with the greatest skill. Not as flashy as some of the newer designers, popular with the lordsons and lorddaughters, his clothes were high quality, conservatively styled, and a favorite of the lords, themselves. Leicester and Aiwren dilly dallied the short distance, stopping to take in some of the sights along the way. Aiwren was worried about being late, but Leicester assured him this wouldn't be a problem.

Ulysses James Cutter, a thin but muscular old man, stood at the far end of the little shop with all of the employes crowded around him silently as he addressed them. Leicester motioned for Aiwren to remain quiet and for the two of them to surreptitiously join the mass of tailor apprentices.

"Wiggleby! You're late!" Cutter barked.

"I'm sorry, Mister Cutter," Leicester stammered.

"Thinking of an excuse? I'll return to you in a moment. Who's your friend? You think this is some kind of theatre? You some fancypants lordson come here to watch where clothes come from?"

Leicester appeared to be thrown even more off kilter by this, desperately attempting to calculate how best to react.

"My name is Aiwren Wayde, Sir-"

"Sir?!" Cutter scoffed. "Do I appear to be one of those wishy washy knights to you?"

Some of the apprentices chuckled, which distracted him from the question and left Aiwren wondering if they were laughing at his mistake or Cutter's description of a knight. Always assuming the worst when it came to other's opinions of him, Aiwren decided the tailors were laughing at him.

"No, Sir. I didn't think you were- I mean no, Mister, I didn't think you were a knight," Aiwren stammered. "I'm the new apprentice.

I just arrived in town last night, so it's probably my fault Leicester and I are late."

"Late on your first day?!" Cutter snapped, "What manner of imbecile are you? Don't answer. Wiggleby, have you fabricated some sort of sensible excuse yet?"

Leicester and Aiwren both looked up, dumbfounded.

"The behavior Mister Wiggleby and his friend were kind enough to demonstrate for us this morning is a perfect example of the kind of behavior that will no longer be tolerated in this shop," Mister Cutter said, turning his attention back to the group. "In case you were too busy with your modern living to notice, Y-Kewnor was attacked last night. Now, anything other than the free and easy life might be impossible for any of you to imagine, but you woke up today in a different city state than the one you went to sleep in last night. It's a shitty new world, boys and girls. Our shop is going to have to produce twice as much for half as much money and much of my time will be occupied by other responsibilities. Rollins, you'll be responsible for the shop when I'm away."

"But I'm the Master Apprentice," Leicester said, without thinking first. "Shouldn't I be-"

"You can't even show up on time, Wiggleby," Cutter interrupted. "Mister Thompson has requested a smart and responsible apprentice to learn the crafts of leather and chain-mail armor, but I'm sending him you instead."

Leicester slumped breathlessly against the wall.

"Everyone else," Mister Cutter continued, "get to work. Other than the fact that I'll be driving you like slaves for the foreseeable future, it's business as usual. Go."

As the crowd dissipated, Aiwren, shocked by what was happening, confused about why his best friend appeared as though someone had just died, and terrified of Cutter, slowly raised his hand.

"Yes, Mister Fancypants?"

"Mister Cutter," Aiwren said cautiously, "to whom should I report for my first lesson?"

"Do you know how to stitch?" Mister Cutter asked.

"No, Mister. My mum has always stitched my clothing." Aiwren responded.

"Well, perhaps we may offer a position to Mister Fancypants's mother. Would anyone care to volunteer to teach Mister New Boy how to stitch, keeping in mind that, should you not finish your own assignments today, I will most certainly beat you within an inch of your life?"

The crowd of apprentices scampered off to do their work, leaving Cutter alone with Leicester and Aiwren. Mister Cutter grabbed a broomstick and approached. Aiwren was almost certain the surly old tailor was going to beat him with it. Instead, he handed Aiwren the broom and said, "Sweep."

"Yes, Mister Cutter," Aiwren said, taking the broom. "For how long?"

"How long!?" the man bellowed. "Until I tell you to stop."

Aiwren slowly walked away as Mister Cutter approached Leicester, but he couldn't hear the conversation. He didn't like to see his friend so distraught and he didn't like Mister Cutter at all, so he was concerned, but not as concerned as he was about what would happen to him if he didn't start sweeping.

Aiwren swept all day. His stomach began grumbling after four hours, but nobody seemed to be stopping to eat and he didn't want to get in even more hot water with his new boss, so he swept all day without eating. It was already dark when Rollins told Aiwren he was done for the day. When Aiwren stepped outside the shop Leicester was waiting for him.

"How was it?" Leicester asked.

"It was sweeping," Aiwren replied. "How was your day?"

"Well, I'm trying to make the best of it," Leicester said, as the two young men began their walk to the bachelor house. "Mister Cutter said, because of the increased demand right now, Mister Thompson was going to focus on training me to make armor, so it would be an annual of an armory apprenticeship condensed into just a few moons and I'd be a Master Armorer by the time all this military nonsense is done and over with. He also said I'll be able to return to his shop to finish my tailor apprenticeship. So, perhaps I'll be able to create the most fashionable armor in the history of Allyoshmar."

Aiwren smiled. One thing he loved so dearly about his best friend was Leicester's ability to imagine the bright side of almost anything. He had the ability to turn situations around simply by changing his perspective.

"Oh, Leicester," Aiwren said, "I am so thrilled to be in Y-Kewnor and to be spending time with you and meeting Wanda, but I must confess, I'm already less than excited about sweeping all day."

"I'm sorry, Aiwren," Leicester said. "I wish things were different, but I promise you, it isn't ordinarily like that. Of course we swept, but we learned, too, and enjoyed our days. I'm certain, once the Guardsmen eliminate the threat of these dragons, everything will return to normal and you'll have a positively wonderful time. You just have to be patient. Please don't return to Ribeln."

"Don't worry, old friend," Aiwren said. "I have no intention of returning to Ribeln just yet."

After making Leicester promise not to laugh, Aiwren told him of Bonishara and Order of the Crystal Blade. He even told Leicester about what had happened with Vannoria. Aiwren didn't tell Leicester the part about the Skinless Woman, worrying even his best friend wouldn't understand.

Aiwren finished his story as the bachelor house was in sight and Leicester said, "So you bed Vannoria Nillhalla and left her in a cave in the middle of the Indigo Forest?!"

Aiwren had never thought of it in those exact terms, but, "Yes," he admitted, "It seemed like a good idea at the time. Am I a terrible person?"

"Your decision makes sense," Leicester began, "but I'm not certain she'll follow the same reason."

"I wrote her a note," Aiwren said.

"I don't know if that makes things better or worse," Leicester laughed. "She's always been in love with you."

"I suppose part of me has always known and I love her, but I don't know if I love her like that. Also, I feel as though I'm supposed to do something here, in Y-Kewnor, and I didn't want things to be any more confusing than they already were."

"Hey, you," a voice said, gruffly.

Aiwren and Leicester turned around to notice a group of three young Kewnorian Guardsmen approaching, a short, pig-nosed guardsman, flanked by a muscular young man and a rough-looking young woman.

"Yeah, you," the rough, female guardsman said.

Aiwren could tell, by the aggressive tone, this guardsman intended to cause trouble and he wondered why he seemed to always attract such ruffians.

"You know what happened last night?" asked the piggy one.

"Yes," Leicester said, "the Citadel was attacked."

"Do you know what that means?" the piggy guardsman asked.

Aiwren and Leicester were both at a loss for the correct answer to this question.

"It means," the guardsman continued, "until these dragons are slain, Y-Kewnor is in a state of war."

"Yes," Leicester said. "We'll be sewing from sun up to sun down to keep up with the war effort."

"Sewing?!" the guardsman laughed. "What kind of cowards are you?!"

"Actually," Leicester said, "I'll be making armor so guardsmen don't have to go after dragons in their skivvies and get their balls burned off."

"What's your name, tailor?" The guardsman asked, clearly not appreciative of Leicester's humor.

"Leicester Wiggleby, and technically I'm an armorer."

The muscular guardsman punched Leicester in the gut. Leicester doubled over in pain as the guardsman moved on to Aiwren.

"What about you?" The guardsman asked.

"I'm Aiwren Wayde," Aiwren said. Emblazoned to mischief by the stress of his day, he said, "And I'm just a tailor, so I can't protect your balls, but, hopefully, you'll look fashionable as the dragons melt them off."

Aiwren's humor only resulted in a punch to the gut from the female guardsman.

"I'm Roderick Blakely," the pig-nosed guardsman said. "Remember my name. Someday everyone will know it. And while you two are cowering here in Y-Kewnor, I'll be slaying dragons and becoming a hero."

Roderick spun on his heels, and marched off with his lackeys.

"Don't pay him a second thought," Leicester said, leaning on the steps of the bachelor house for support, "If such a fool were ever to encounter a dragon, he'd either piss himself or get roasted alive or both."

Aiwren picked himself up. Perhaps it had been his stressful and demeaning day. Perhaps it had been how similar Roderick was to Quinntonn, the bully who had always singled him out in Ribeln. Perhaps it had been the nagging sensation that he was supposed to do something, but Aiwren was paying Roderick a second though. In fact, although he didn't know it yet, Aiwren's mind was already made up.

When Leicester and Aiwren hobbled up the stairs and into Leicester's apartment, they were shocked to find Wanda looking as down trodden as they were.

"What's wrong?" they all asked, simultaneously.

"No performance tonight?" Leicester asked.

"No!" she screamed, thrusting a piece of paper at them. "They closed the theatre. The Kewnorian Guard is using it as a recruitment center.

"I'm sorry," Leicester said, "but I'm sure we can find you another job."

"I'm not worried about the coins!" Wanda said, "This is just infuriating. Why should the people have to suffer for battles and skirmishes caused not by them, but by Lords and guardsmen and knights and kings?! The whole system is corrupt! It's an infection!"

Leicester and Aiwren were silent, not entirely sure how to react to Wanda's indignation. She stood there, fuming, not necessarily at them, but in their direction.

"So what happened to you?" She asked.

"We were accosted by some roughnecks." Leicester began.

"I'm joining the Kewnorian Guard," Aiwren announced, interrupting Leicester's story and surprising even himself.

***

Jocund Plune's eyes slowly creaked open. The light bursting though the window caused immediate pain in his head.

"What hand of the sun is it?" He groaned, deciding this was absolutely the worst hangover he'd ever had.

There was no response. He lifted the arm draped over his naked chest and let it go. It dropped like a dead fish. The arm was dainty and naked and female. He traced it back to the body it belonged to, a woman sleeping on her stomach, draped over him on his left. He lifted the covers to inspect her body and frowned with satisfaction.

"Past high hand," a woman sitting up in bed to his right said. She was, he presumed, nude as well. She was certainly topless and not bashful.

"It's past high hand," she said, continuing, "Recon you know what that means, m'lord?"

Jocund looked around the completely unfamiliar room. The blinds were pulled down. Empty bottles littered the floor. What appeared to be some kind of strawberry or raspberry preserves blotted the drab wall paper and Jocund vaguely recalled believing the room required decoration. He had no explanation for the white rabbit sitting on a worn out old dresser, twitching its nose, but he wasn't surprised by it, either.

"Correct me if I'm wrong," Jocund said, "But I believe it means we had one positively fantastic evening."

"It means you owe double, m'lord," the woman said, flatly, "and I ain't takin no blame on accounta damages to this room neither."

"Of course," Jocund said, "judging by my exhaustion, you performed your job well and judging by her exhaustion, I performed my job exceptionally well."

He flashed the woman a charming smile that didn't charm her at all and said, "Be a doll and fetch me my satchel, will you, good woman?"

As the woman got out of bed to get Jocund his bag, he smiled at her nude body and said, "Oh how I wish I recalled more of last night."

"You always say that," she said, tossing him his satchel.

"Well," he said, handing her a stack of coins, "that must explain why I keep returning to you."

The woman snatched the coins and started counting.

"Perhaps you could remind me?" Jocund suggested.

The woman responded by sticking out her hand for more coins, which Jocund didn't hesitate to reach for in his satchel, but the door bursting open interrupted the transaction.

The woman screamed, waking the sleeping woman, who hesitated for a groggy moment, then also screamed.

"Terrific," Jocund said, more annoyed than frightened.

***

Rheozarccio awoke early from his restless sleep. As his eyes opened, he felt confused and tired and sad, but he couldn't quite remember why until he saw the gold armor next to his bed and the reality of the night before came crashing down upon him once again. Someone must have entered his quarters in the middle of the night and stacked it neatly on the floor. He laid on his side and stared at the armor. He asked himself how he could possibly be living in a world without his knight-father. He squeezed his eyes shut, as though, if he tried hard enough, the world would be set right again when he opened his eyes; his armor would be silver again and none of yesterday's tragedy would have happened, but when he opened his eyes the armor was still gold.

The armor went on easily. After he buckled his leg plates on, he grabbed the chest and back pieces. He held up the large metal plates and realized that, although it was beautifully finished and coated in gold, the metal beneath the gold was thin and flimsy; it was just for show. This was all just for show. Lord Plune was right; The Divine Empress's Knights were a joke and, the previous night, a great life was lost as the humorless punchline.

When Rheo entered the High Knight Dining Hall, he realized many of the other knights must have also slept poorly because the room was busier than it usually was at that early hand of the morning. The din of chatter silenced. All eyes turned to him. In a sea of silver armor, he was the one man in gold. He expected the knights to return to their breakfasts, but they continued staring at him, waiting for something. These men in their flimsy silver armor, members of an order who were once the most elite warriors in Allyoshmar, had never seen battle, never bled, never lost a brother. These knights were frightened.

"We lost a great knight-father last night," Rheo announced in a loud baritone, more bitter than empathetic, "and many other great men. Eat your breakfast and stay focussed so the same thing doesn't happen to you!"

His speech certainly didn't instill any confidence in the High Knights, but Rheo had addressed their attention so they returned to whatever it was they were doing before he entered. Sitting alone, Rheo wondered if it was always like this, if every knight-father had to spend his first day pleasing others and not dealing with his own grief. Unable to eat, he left his bowl on the table and walked out of the hall.

Rheo knew returning to the Citadel would be difficult. As he approached, the painful memories came rushing back to him with gruesome and vivid detail. The enormous white column of a building, the once pristine pillar, was sullied, its top charred and broken. Part of him wanted to leave, to run away and never come back, not because he was afraid of another dragon attack, but because he was afraid of entering Sir Vincent's chambers, chambers that were now his. As he climbed the stairs, nearly every passing person either greeted him with condolences or applauded his heroism, but he didn't know how to respond. Distracted by memories, his mind pulled him elsewhere. Images of the previous night flashed before him.

The room was, for the most part left how it had been the day before. The dishes had been cleared from the table, but he could clearly imagine Sir Vincent sitting there, offering him a meal. Or perhaps, Sir Vincent would enter from the bedroom or water closet and tell him what the plan was for the day or assign him reading or ask him to run an errand. This, he knew, would never happen. Rheo had cried the previous night and that was all he would allow himself.

A moment later a squire entered and told him the Council of High Knights would soon be convening in the Grand High Knight's chambers and he was expected to attend. On top of losing his knight-father and becoming a knight-father, himself, Rheo had also become a Hight Knight of the Council and would be, for the rest of his days, spending most of his time with his least favorite knights, a pack of grouchy old bureaucrats who did nothing more than sit around a table arguing over money and politics. Was this the life he had imagined for himself? All alone, hated by the Kewnorians, in a job he hated?

Rheo sighed, did his best to gather his spirits, and stood. As he was headed towards the door, Rheo was struck still by the memory of Sir Vincent's mysterious final words. He touched the table where he and Sir Vincent had shared so many meals, and meetings, and stories and Rheo made a decision. The Divine Empress's Knights may have resigned themselves to being bureaucrats, Rheo told himself, but Sir Vincent didn't live that way and neither would he.

There were always seven High Knights of the Council, the knight-father of each of the seven Houses of Virtue. The senior-most member was given the honorary title of Grand High Knight of the Council. He ran the meetings and he delivered the decisions of the Council, but these decisions were all determined by the votes of the seven members.

Sir Leopold Leonard, the Grand High Knight of the Council for the past twenty annuals, was the knight-father of the House of Patience, and his even temper matched the virtue of his house. Revered for his wisdom, wisdom matched only by Sir Vincent, his confidant and close friend, Sir Leopold possessed the prudence of objectivity, a trait Sir Vincent lacked, which may have been why he held Vincent's passionate council in such high esteem.

Rheo entered Sir Leopold's chambers and was lead by a servant from a vestibule just like Sir Vincent's into a dining hall, also much like Sir Vincent's, but with less colorful decoration. Six men were already seated at the large table. The six men stood when Rheo arrived and watched him join them at the table.

"Before we begin," Sir Leopold Leonard said, "we must recognize Sir Rheozarccio Rheodo. Ordinarily this would wait until after the funeral services, but, in an effort to instill confidence in The Divine Empress's Knights for the people of Y-Kewnor, it would be wise to create a sense of order in a timely manner, given our circumstances. Sir Rheozarccio, please kneel."

What Rheo heard confirmed his concern that this was all for show, but he knelt before the Council, with his head down and his palms out, to show he accepted what ever fate, present or punishment, gift or execution, The Divine Empress saw fit for him.

"Do you, Sir Rheozarccio Rheodo, High Knight of the House of Kindness swear to serve Divine Empress and accept any fate She has created for you, from this moment forth, until the end of your days, no matter how brief or lengthy they may be?" Leopold asked him.

"I do," Rheo replied.

Leonard stepped away and Ordo Ollycanterer stepped forward. He was a short and heavy-set man from Frins Casicon. He knelt in front of Rheo and laid his sword across Rheo's hands.

Sir Ordo stepped away and each of the other five members took a turn leaving Rheo with their sword. Sir T'Ethal La-al, the knight-father to the house of Charity, a muscular man from Ma-Aresh with dark skin and no hair on his body went next. Sir Arowyr Malegon, of Era-Mosa, the knight-father to the House of Humility, a man who's armor was always perfectly polished and who always wore white gloves, followed. After him, Sir Sigfried Illanto, from Lees Naglos, knight-father to the House of Diligence, approached. Sir Allesander Montgomery, a Kewnorian and knight-father to the House of Temperance, was the last before Sir Leopold returned to perform the ritual, himself, leaving Rheo with six swords laying across his hands.

Arms out, holding the swords, Rheo stood and said, "I, Sir Rheozarccio Rheodo, recognized by the Council as knight-father to the House of Kindness, have sworn my service to The Divine Empress and the virtues She represents: Patience, Temperance, Diligence, Humility, Chastity, Charity, and Kindness."

As Rheo spoke each virtue, the knight-father to the House of that virtue retrieved their sword. When all of the swords had been retrieved, Rheo drew his own blade and held it out, tip to the ground.

"As you would trust me with your swords," Rheo said, "so would I trust you with my own."

"Then, in the name of The Divine Empress," Leopold said, "Sir Rheozarccio Rheodo is now recognized by the Houses of Virtue and The Divine Empress, Herself, as a High Knight of the Council and the knight-father to the House of Kindness."

The Council of High Knights sheathed their swords and, without any congratulations or further discussion, took their seats at the table to begin their meeting.

"We all know what we saw," Sir Leopold started, "but there are details that don't make any sense. Would anyone like to begin?"

"Immediately, several things strike me as odd," said Sir Sigfried, glancing at the notes in his journal, "there hasn't been record of a dragon in twenty annuals."

"If you believe the late mad queen of Lees Naglos' account," interrupted Sir Allesander. "Going by reliable sources," he continued, "it's been over a hundred."

"Either way," added T'Ethal, always coming right to the point, "It has been a long time. So what do they want now?"

"Excellent question," Sir Sigfried said. "Which leads me to my second point. These dragons didn't take anything. Dragons, even when they were abundant, attacked for specific, immediate, and selfish reasons. Gold. A woman."

"What about revenge?" Asked Sir Ordo. "That's a specific, immediate, and selfish reason."

"What, pray tell, would they be avenging?" Asked Allesander, condescendingly.

"Well, for my third point," added Sir Sigfried, "May I remind you there were three, possibly four, of them. Dragons aren't known for their cooperative dispositions."

"We were all up in that room," offered Ordo, "If it hadn't been for Sir Rheozarccio, we'd all be dead. Who would benefit from the destruction of the Council."

"I had the same thought," said Sir Sigfried, "so I made a list. So we have the Sima Watusian princess going missing an annual ago."

"It's most likely the Simi Watusians killed the princess." Allesander said, "Everyone knows this, including the Sima Watusians. If they were going to hire dragons to attack anyone it would have been the Simi Watusians. We weren't even involved."

The five men debated back and forth while Leopold absorbed their conversation and Rheo's head spun. There was so much to think about and so little action. He wondered why it even mattered who sent the dragons; they had to be killed regardless of who sent them. Wasn't that most important?! Then he realized that he did have something to contribute. He knew who would benefit from the downfall of the knights.

"The Kewnorians," he said, silencing the room.

"Don't be preposterous, boy," said Allesander.

"As I was walking up the stairs, I saw Plune's son." Rheo explained, "Perhaps he didn't orchestrate the attack, but he and his father must have had something to do with it."

"Our relations with the Kewnorians are strained, in deed," said Allesander, "which is precisely why accusing the son of the most popular lord is an unwise decision."

Sir Leopold brought the issue to a vote. Ordo and Arowyr were more hesitant, but, eventually, sided with the rest of the council, voting to wait. Rheo was the only vote opposed to waiting. Furious, when the meeting was adjourned he immediately left, knowing they'd change their minds if he could prove Jocund's involvement.

Rheozarccio, accompanied by a dozen knights, kicked down the door to the bedroom in the brothel just after noon. Jocund was naked and in the company of two prostitutes.

"Oh, terrific," Jocund said.

Jocund's smugness infuriated Rheo. Anybody else would have been in a panic, should The Divine Empress's Knights burst into their room, but this man found it only to be an annoying inconvenience. This man, and the those like him, thought themselves to be above the law, Rheo thought, as he did his best to control his temper.

"In the name of The Divine Empress, I, Sir Rheozarccio Rheodo, High Knight of the Council of The Divine Empress's Knights, and knight-father to the House of Kindness, do hereby place you under arrest for conspiracy to attack the Citadel and the resulting loss of life."

"What?!" Jocund said. "What are you talking about?!"

The knights pulled Jocund, nude, from the bed, wrenched his arms behind his back, and brought him to Rheo. The prostitutes screamed.

"I don't know what your involvement was," Rheo said, "but I saw you in the Citadel last night and intend to get to the bottom of this."

A knight asked if they ought to arrest the prostitutes, but Rheo said to let them go.

"We ain't been paid yet," one of the prostitutes said.

"That's a lie!" Jocund said. "I just paid you."

Rheo grabbed the bag of coins from Jocund's satchel and tossed it to the prostitute. There was no reason why, he thought, an innocent woman should be made to suffer for Jocund's wrong doing. As the two prostitutes ran from the room with their giant pay day, Jocund screamed for them to alert his father.

Beneath the Citadel was a dungeon. The Divine Empress's Knights had made an agreement when Y-Kewnor was established, that they were allowed to conduct their own investigations and make arrests in the name of The Divine Empress, but they wouldn't interfere with the law and order of the city. The dungeon consisted of a dozen or so cells that were, with the exception of one, empty. Rheozarccio stared through the bars at Jocund.

"I already told you," Jocund said, now clothed, "I had nothing to do with the attack. I was in the Citadel on personal business for my father."

"What was the personal business?" Rheo asked.

"Personal," Jocund answered, approaching the bars. "Look, were I to plan an attack by dragons, don't you think I would have had the sense not to be present at the time?"

"You were a weasel when we were children and you're a weasel now!" Rheo said, grabbing Jocund and slamming him into the bars. "I know you were involved in this, Plune. I just don't know how."

"Rheozarccio!" Rheo heard, turning as Leopold approached.

"Sir Allesander just barged into my quarters to tell me he had just spoken to a livid Lord Plune. I insisted you would never disobeyed a council decision. What, in the name of The Divine Empress, are you thinking?"

"This man is guilty!" Rheo insisted.

"This man is not your concern," countered Leopold. "Free him at once."

Rheo unlocked the door, allowing Jocund to step out and say, "Rheo, as always, it was a pleasure to discuss old times."

Jocund gave Leopold a nod and sang a bawdy song as he walked out of the dungeon.

"Our Citadel was attacked by dragons, not Plunes!" Leopold scolded, once the Plune lordson had left. "The Divine Empress's Knights aren't as popular as we used to be. We need to focus on being in the good graces of the Lords and we need to wait until our services are requested before we muscle our way into the investigation."

"Vincent was my closest friend," Leopold said, putting an arm on Rheo's shoulder. "I wept in my wife's arms last night and tonight I shall do the same, but during the day I must wear the gold and maintain order, and, despite your grief, so must you."

Rheo had nothing to say. Leopold walked away and left him alone in the dungeon with his thoughts. The word, "order" stuck with him and he remembered Sir Vincent mention the Crystal Order, so headed to the one place he hoped could give him answers.

It was already late when Rheo arrived at the library and walked directly to the help desk. Greta, organizing books on a shelf with her back to Rheo, said, "Closing up soon, so don't get too comfortable."

"Sir Rheo," she said, when she turned to the counter with a stack of books, dropping the books and reaching for his hand. "I'm so sorry."

Rheo was touched by this expression of support and emotion. Not one other person had really reached out to him. He realized Greta was his one true friend and he smiled because that was one more friend than he thought he had.

"I'm thankful I'm for your compassion," he said. "I'll persevere; I have responsibilities so I must. It is a seemingly random question, but I knew, if anyone knew the answer, it would be you. Are there, in the library, any books on the Crystal Order?"

"Sounds familiar," Greta said. "You ave any idea whens it from? I'd need to know the era in history so I can add it to the Need List."

"Need List?" Rheo asked?

"Sure," Greta continued, "it's a list o all the subjects people ask 'bout that we ain't got. This way we can ask other libraries if they got it. An if some scribe appens to come in ere trying to sell us some story o this or some istory o that, we can look on the list. If it ain't on the list, we ain't interested in buying it."

"So, look," Greta said, pointing to an entry in the Need List, an enormous leather bound book on the counter. "You asked for more details on Sah Vincent, so I added it to the list. Every library as the same list an we update each other once a moon or so. If one o them other libraries ave something useful they send it to us. Them scribes musta been lazy then coz lotsa information is missing from all over Allyoshmar that annual."

Rheo remembered Sir Vincent telling him, as he died, that the land was filled with secrets and lost history.

"What else is missing?" Rheo asked.

"Look," Greta said, flipping the book around, "The great flood o Sima Watusia. All them trolls vanishing in Bridgekeep. Good riddance, I say. Some giants attacked Norga Doonda. Of course, the disappearance o that crazy queen in Lees Naglos. We even got some from beyond the Uncrossable River. We been liaising wif some o the libraries over there lately. I don't care too much for liaising wif them Woscom folk. Even their librarians is scary."

As Greta read the list, Rheo's mind raced. It was as though some secrecy had eaten its way though history, like an infection, an infection that spread throughout all of Allyoshmar. He didn't know what it was, but he knew it was big, he knew Sir Vincent was trying to tell him about it, and he knew it was his duty to Sir Vincent, The Divine Empress, and all of Allyoshmar, to put the pieces together. Unfortunately, none of it made any sense to him. He needed to figure out how all the pieces fit together. He didn't have any answers, but he was emblazoned with purpose and determined to solve this puzzle.

***

The night his daughter left, King Noldar Palidnia sat in her empty room all night, drinking every drop of numbendria he could find. He sat through meetings despondently silent and spent the rest of his days staring vacantly from his throne. He was a perfect target for assassination and, were Sir Truson Everly not there, he would have died.

Sir Truson was a High Knight in the House of Diligence stationed in Lees Naglos. Since the kingdoms of the west maintained their feudal systems when the cities of the Freelands abolished them, there were few cities west of the Realmsend River that housed chapters of The Divine Empress's Knights; Lees Naglos, the western ally with the largest army, was one of them. Nearly one thousand annuals earlier, Lees Naglos was called Palidnia, for the family to whom it belonged and it was a ruthless empire. After annuals of fighting during the Great War, Lees Naglos brokered a peace deal with Frins Casicon, the enlightened city, which had always been structured more like the city states of the Freelands and had amazing engineering, but a weak army. They would build a canal from the water-abundant Casicon Mountains down to Palidnia. Palidnia could maintain their crown and throne, but had to relinquish their empire and adhere to a more peaceful system of government. The Kingdom of Palidnia accepted this deal and became Lees Naglos, "The Light of Peace." The Divine Empress's Knights stationed in Lees Naglos served as diplomats from the Freelands to Lees Naglos. Truson, being the highest ranking knight was responsible for this diplomacy and, for most of his career, the relationship had been a relatively stress-free one.

Gavlessa's recent attacks on nearby city states and unincorporated villages posed a threat against Lees Naglos. Lees Naglos had asked for the aid in defending itself against Gavlessa, but The Divine Empress's Knights and the City States of the Freelands all declined, not wanting to become mired in a western conflict. Lees Naglos was forced to make a peace deal, offering Princess Teryessa to Gavlessa. A deal for which, King Noldar was resentful of The Divine Empress's Knights and the city states of the Freelands. This strain in the relationship between The Divine Empress's Knights and Lees Naglos, made Sir Truson's job more complicated.

Sir Truson was born in Y-Kewnor, but was sent to Lees Naglos as soon as he became a High Knight and, being in Lees Naglos for fifteen annuals, he had become close with the royal family, who accepted him lovingly. King Noldar had treated him as his own son, a relationship which was, since the East rebuffed Lees Naglos, on the rocks. Truson disagreed with the council's decision to remain uninvolved, but there was nothing he could do. Regardless of his shame, however, when he learned of the king's despondency, Truson felt obligated to pay him a visit.

The morning Truson entered the palace, not a guard was in sight. According to the guards at the door, King Noldar had dismissed everyone, demanding to be alone. Expecting silence, Truson was shocked when he heard a voice. At first, he thought, it was the voice of the king. He was still distant and its was difficult to tell, but as soon as he got closer, he could tell it was not the king.

Knowing the king was in peril and any noise would only increase the risk, Truson needed the element of surprise, so he removed his silver armor and, blade drawn, crept down the stone corridor towards the throne room.

As Truson peered around a corner into the throne room to assess the threat, he saw the Gavlessan assassin, sword drawn, standing before the king Truson wondered how such an eyesore could have snuck into the palace without being noticed. The barbarian was getting increasingly aggressive and threatening, so Truson had to act. If he had run in, the barbarian would have been able to kill the king before Truson could have reached him.

Truson pulled his bow off of his shoulder, nocked an arrow, drew the string, and fired. The arrow buried itself into the assassin's leg and, by the time the barbarian turned to look, Truson had already let fly another. This one struck him in his chest. As Truson had feared, threatened, the barbarian approached the king, who did nothing as the barbarian limped towards him with his sword drawn. Truson couldn't risk another non-lethal shot or potentially hitting the king instead of his target, so, without armor, he grabbed his sword and sprinted across the throne room.

The Gavlessan's giant sword came down fast towards King Noldar's head, but Truson's blade diverted the attack just in time. Judging by his reaction to the deflection, Truson assessed that this warrior was gifted in strength and willing to die for his cause, but had little skill. Truson, on the other hand had been nicknamed "The Mathematician" back when he was in the Academy, not because he was an actual mathematician, but because he had understood fighting and strategy like a mathematician understands numbers. His mind worked rapidly and he could imagine options in battle no other fighter could. He wasn't the strongest or most physically gifted swordsman, but being able to predict any move a fighter was going to make and having such accurate and completely unpredictable attacks, himself, made him almost impossible to defeat. He had the demeanor of a scholar rather than a warrior and his opponents never presumed how formidable a fighter he was until it was too late. Truson's blade severed ligaments on the assassin's legs, causing him to cry out, but continue fighting; however, despite the difference in size, Truson also sliced through the tendons on the assassin's arms, leaving the assassin unable to lift his heavy sword. As the assassin crumbled to his knees, Truson kicked the sword out of his hands. Unarmed and unable to move, the attacker laid on the ground.

"Guards!" Truson yelled as he approached Noldar.

"I suppose you expect my thanks," Noldar muttered.

"No, Your Grace," replied Truson, tongue tied with how to proceed with the conversation. "Damn it, Your Grace. May I have your permission to speak freely from my heart?"

The king shrugged apathetically and Truson chose to accept this as consent.

"I can't imagine the weight of the burden on your shoulders to make the sacrifice you made. I want you to know I detest the Council's decision and I tried as hard as I could to get them to listen because it was the right thing to do and because, Your Grace, you have never been anything but kind to me. I wish I could have done something to change the outcome, just as I wish I could do something now to lighten your spirits."

Noldar looked up to Truson, but said nothing.

Noldar walked closer to Truson and the young knight could feel the king's breath as he waited for a reaction that likely could have been an execution order, but the king touched Truson's cheek with his enormous hand and nodded.

A moment later, the guards ran in and Truson told them to bring the would-be assassin to the dungeon, lock him up, and guard him to make sure he didn't kill himself.

For a moment, Truson's protection of the king and his gesture of friendship, appeared as though it might help, that eventually, the king might mend, but this hope was lost when the messenger arrived.

The messenger told the king about the revolution in Gavlessa, that Chancellor Plale was now ruler, and that the royal family had all been killed, including, they presumed, Princess Teryessa.

King Noldar Palidnia clutched the arm of his throne for support, but was too weak to stand and his legs buckled. He fell to his knees and released a beastly scream that shook the very walls of his kingdom. Sir Truson Everly's heart broke for the king, but despite his compassion and his own sadness for the young princess he was always fond of like a little sister, Truson was mostly afraid of how the king would react.

***

There was a pulse to the drops of water. A steady metronome of reality stretching into her dreams wrapping its tendrils around her throat. As reality started pulling her closer and closer, her eyes still shut, Teryessa heard a voice.

"Do you know where you are?"

Teryessa opened her eyes. Leaning over her was the Gold Knight, his beautiful hair cascading down around his high cheek bones, masculine chin, and piercing eyes. Realizing she was laying down, she tried to sit.

"You're still too weak," he said, helping her relax. "Save your strength. You'll need it."

"Where am I?" Teryessa asked.

"You're in my home," the Gold Knight said.

"Thank you for your chivalry and bravery. My name is Teryessa." Teryessa said.

"Yes, I know," said the Gold Knight, putting the palm of his hand gently on her cheek. "Princess Teryessa. You've been through so much and I'm afraid it's only going to get worse before it all ends. Far worse."

Teryessa was confused.

"You know... Princesses..." the Gold Knight said, adjusting the shackles on Teryessa's wrists, "are actually more delicious."

As she heard the clanging, Teryessa became aware of the shackles on her wrists and ankles and she realized how hard the surface was that she was laying on.

"What have you done?" she asked. "Why am I shackled?"

"I don't know what it is," the Gold Knight said, "perhaps it's the way you've been preserved like veal in your gilded cages, but you can actually taste the difference. And your skin," he said, slowly dragging the back of his fingers across her cheek, "is the smoothest I have ever felt."

"Let me go!" Teryessa demanded, now becoming fully aware of her predicament, panic setting in.

She struggled and lashed about in the shackles and tried to sit up, but her neck was shackled, too. "Why have you done this?"

The Gold Knight stepped away from the stone table where Princess Teryessa was restrained. Calmly removing his gold armor, he chuckle smugly.

"They always ask for a reason," he said. "As though, if I provided one, they'd welcome the torture. That's what's going to happen, by the way. I never understood why they never ask what I'm going to do before asking why."

Teryessa screamed at the top of her lungs.

"Oh, right," the Gold Knight said, removing his clothing, "Scream all you like. Nobody will hear you."

Teryessa struggled to free herself, but the iron shackles were too strong; she was not escaping.

"As I was saying," the Gold Knight said, putting his hand firmly over her mouth, "I'm going to brutalize you. You'll wish you were dead for quite some time before your body finally consents."

Teryessa let out a muffled scream through the Gold Knight's fingers, her eyes wide and filled with terror. Her mind raced, hoping desperately for a way out.

"Why?" The Gold Knight asked, stroking Teryessa's hair, "Because it feels good. Sorry if that's not a grand enough rational. I know you royal types love your complex plots and it seems as though, with necromancers and depositions, conspiring is everyone's favorite hobby these days, and you're quite popular with all these grand-minded idiots, but my motives are simple. I feel like it."

Teryessa shook her head free from his hands, which he allowed, chuckling as he walked away from her.

"What kind of monster are you?!" Teryessa demanded.

The Gold Knight smiled; that was the question he had been waiting for. Standing, nude, beside the stone table, the Gold Knight's smile widened as his face elongated, bones popping and stretching, neck elongating, horns bursting through his skull. He screamed in pain as his spine lengthened and he fell to his knees, laughing as his ribs broke and repositioned, taking a new form. His hands and feet seized and contorted as they metamorphosed into razor sharp talons. The flesh of his back ripped apart, spilling blood everywhere as giant wings, slick and slimy, tore through his skin. His spine continued growing, carving its way out of his body into a long, whipping tail. Festering lesions grew out of his flesh, many popping to reveal chunks of rusty metal boring their way up to through surface of his miry grey skin. He closed his eyes and when he opened them again they were red. He was a dragon.

"This is the kind of monster I am." the dragon laughed. "I am Wurm Ahkk-Rhall!"

Throughout Ahkk-Rhall's transformation, Teryessa stared, transfixed with horror, horror for the sight, horror that such unspeakable beasts exist. As Ahkk-Rhall approached her, though, her panic and desperation became more personal. She was helpless. Rather than screaming, she closed her eyes, begging for The Divine Empress to take her away, inside her mind, to the Palace of Light, to shield her from experiencing this violation of her body as She had shielded her when Prince Grell raped her, but as far as she reached out into the darkness of her mind, The Divine Empress never responded, and Princess Teryessa endured every moment of seemingly endless abuse, completely conscious and aware, until, after hours of brutality, pain, and horror, her constitution finally relented, allowing her to drift into darkness, darkness that had been waiting for her.

DRASTIC MEASURES

The Nameless Rider rode through the day and the night with the Girl, unconscious, in front of him on his horse. He rode across the marshlands in sunlight and in moon light, to prevent the Girl from dying before her time and to deny himself an opportunity to sit and think. It wasn't his place to think or question or wonder or yearn; he was a servant; it was his place to unquestioningly do the bidding of his master. He knew the Girl wouldn't benefit from stopping. She couldn't hold down food, she slept while they were riding, and the only thing that would save her was help as quickly as possible, if it wasn't already too late.

As the sun rose behind the Nameless Rider, a glint of something appeared on the horizon. Being a marsh, these were flat lands with mucky ground. He knew whatever cast the reflection was distant, but he rode with caution. He was heading into the land of people with magics that could do more than just keep him out of their city, magics that could prevent him from doing his job.

The Nameless Rider came upon a bog and had a decision to make: go around or cross through. The bog was shallow, but wide. If he went around he would loose time, but should he cross, he and the

Girl would be vulnerable for the duration of the crossing. He decided to cross.

The muck on the bottom of the bog was thick and stuck to the hooves of his horse, who never whinnied or nickered about the discomfort, but snorted and grunted as it pushed on. The Nameless Rider knew, if he was going to be attacked from behind, the attackers would wait until he was almost to the halfway point before making their move. He passed the halfway point without incident, but he certain he was being watched and had a feeling something was about to happen.

The Nameless Rider saw the glimmer again. It was the glint of steel reflecting the sunlight, the tip of a spear. It was being held by a man on the back of some creature. By the time he got closer, dozens of men with very little clothing covering their dark skin came into view. Most of them were armed with spears, though a few of them were wielding tridents, nets, or any other weapons that could double as a means to catch food in the marsh. The creatures they rode were giant alligators. These were the Ma-Areshi Bayou Men. Long ago, the Ma-Areshi, wishing to trade with the other cities of Allyoshmar, founded the city of Ma-Aresh in marshes on the east bank of the Realmsend River; however, some of the Ma-Areshi rejected city life and remained in small communities out in the Bayou. They were known to others as the Bayou Men, the Marsh Men, and the Gater Men, but they just considered themselves to be Ma-Areshi. They were powerful warriors and had powerful magics, but they were few in number and, like when the city was built, they had no intention of involving themselves in the affairs of war or cities or politics. They were a peaceful group unless defending their territory.

These were the men the Nameless Rider needed. He raised his hands in the air and waited. The alligators the Ma-Areshi rode on high-walked until they approached the shore, when their legs spread out and their bodies descended and they slipped into the water, floating across the top easily, gracefully. In only a few moments, the Nameless Rider was surrounded by the Ma-Areshi and their alligators, who's bodies alone were easily twice the length of his horse. They were silent, disciplined. Even the alligators were still, as one old man on a white alligator even bigger than the others floated up to the Nameless Rider.

The old man gazed upon the situation for a moment. He was a small man with dark skin, long white hair, and a long white beard. His skin was covered with black markings, tattoos of symbols scattered all over his body. The other Ma-Areshi had these symbols on their skin, too, but none had as many as him. The old man looked at the horse, then the Girl, then the sword still sheathed at the Nameless Rider's side, then the Nameless Rider, himself.

"You wish for me to save this girl?" the man asked.

"Yes," replied the Nameless Rider.

"Tell me, Shadowman. Do you remember me?"

"No," he said, "I do not."

"Then why have you come here?" the old man asked.

"To save this girl."

"How do you know she is not meant to save you?"

The old man was speaking in riddles and the Nameless Rider had no idea what he was talking about.

"Very well," the old man said with a smile, "I will help you, old friend. I already put a crab stew on the fire for you this morning."

The Nameless Rider somehow knew that the old man's name was Uq-artt D'Russeaux, but everyone called him Mister Uncle. He was the elder of his Family and, it was believed, he had abilities and knowledge hidden from others. Some said he was as old as the swamp.

Mister Uncle's home was a small cabin, up on stilts, to protect it from the frequent flooding of the marshy area it was in. The Nameless Rider had been there before. There was a porch around the house with a pair of rocking chairs. Hanging from the rafters of the porch were all kinds of herbs and medicines picked from the marsh and hanging upside down to dry.

The inside of Mister Uncle's house was simple but neat and clean. There was a small table and a cabinet at the end near the fire place, which did have a crab stew cooking. On the other side of the room were two beds, one for him and one for any patients he had to monitor over night. Mister Uncle directed the Nameless Rider to put the Girl on the patient bed.

The Girl laid, unconscious, on the bed, her forehead dripping with sweat. The wounds the Nameless Rider had dressed were inflamed again and blistering. Her hand looked even worse. The skin had peeled off entirely from the big knuckle down and black veins stretched all the way up her finger and across the back of her hand.

"Where was she?" Mister Uncle demanded. "Where was this girl?"

"In a room beneath a wall," the Nameless Rider said.

"This poor little teeffah has been infected by darkness. It has spread all over her body. Drastic measures never attempted to this extent must be taken and, even then, I make you no promises."

Mister Uncle picked up the Girl's hand and inspected it closely. He grabbed a pair of tweezers and reached into the decaying flesh. Inside, a long shard of black glass had splintered into her flesh. He dragged over the table and put the Girl's hand on it, asking the Nameless Rider to hold her hand there. Mister Uncle raised a large cleaver over his head and recited a chant. Then, without hesitation, the little old man brought the blade down hard, severing the Girl's finger. He used the knife to scoop the finger into a jar. Once the finger was removed, Mister Uncle worked fast to first stop the bleeding with a hot poker from the fireplace. That was the easy part. The little old man prepared his inks and his razors and began the process.

Mister Uncle finished as the sun was setting. The Girl had been wrapped in bandages and was still unconscious.

"Now it is up to The Divine Empress and her spirits," Mister Uncle said. "How many sunbirths can you remember?"

"Today was my fifth." The Nameless Rider answered.

"I have never known you to have so many sunbirths before returning to your sleep," Mister Uncle said, handing the Nameless Rider a bowl of crab stew.

"I don't think I eat," the Nameless Rider said.

"You say that every time, old friend," Mister Uncle said with a laugh, insisting he take it.

The Nameless Rider took the bowl of crab stew.

***

Aiwren's day began with determination and zeal. Remembering Wanda's theatre had temporarily become a recruitment office, Aiwren knew where to go. When he arrived at the theatre, he was surprised to find there was already a line. Aiwren chose to view this as a good sign. He thought about how all these young men were noble for committing themselves to defending Y-Kewnor, just like him. He was going to be a Kewnorian Guardsman, a hero with the respect of all who he met. As the sun rose, the line led Aiwren into the theatre and face to face with the recruitment officer.

"Do you own a sword?"

"Yes."

"Training?"

"No official training, but-"

"What is your name?"

"Aiwren Wayde."

"Aiwren Wayde, you are now a Kewnorian Guardsman. Take this document and report to this address."

The whole interview lasted only a moment and Aiwren was on his way to report for duty. He wondered what he would learn about dragon slaying. He was looking forward to using the sword his father gave him. He walked east across town to the barracks, excited about his new life.

The north and east sides of Y-Kewnor were fortified by a stone wall. The Kewnorian Guard had built their barracks along the length of the wall, adjacent to the flanking towers and battlements, to keep the Guardsmen close to the wall and ready for attack. This crescent-shaped part of town was where all of the Kewnorian Guard's towers and garrisons were located. Because of its shape and purpose this part of town was referred to as the "Guardsman's Smile." Many annuals earlier, in a desire to expand the size of the guard, but not increase the cost, the barracks were converted to extensions of the battlements and the Guardsmen were required to find apartments within the city. The Guardsmen were pleased with this freedom, but it allowed for a decrease in discipline among soldiers and an increase in the frequency of them having to arrest each other at pubs and brothels late at night.

With Y-Kewnor gearing up for a war, the Guardsman's Smile was bustling with activity. The Kewnorians had, almost over night, constructed a small internal wall delineating this military complex, keeping the Kewnorian citizens away from military business, increasing security, and more clearly defining the shape of the Guardsman's Smile. It was like entering a city within a city.

A guardsman stationed at a gate in the wall between the Guardsman's Smile and the rest of Y-kewnor, asked to see Aiwren's papers before allowing him passage through the security checkpoint. Practically shaking with excitement, Aiwren proudly showed him his papers. The guardsman, still not accustomed to these suddenly harsher times, casually glanced at document and directed Aiwren to the proper barracks.

Aiwren noticed, as he approached the destination scribed on the note, that it was nothing more than a tent erected between two buildings. He also noticed the stack of cloth bags piled up next to the entrance. Before entering, he peered in one of the bags. It was filled with uniforms. He was certain this was where he was to receive his uniform. He couldn't wait. He was certain he would look positively heroic in it. Looking over his shoulder to make sure nobody was watching, he opened one of the bags slightly to get a peek at the uniforms. Stained with blood, torn, and covered in soot and mildew, Aiwren frowned with disappointment at the uniforms' state of disrepair, but told himself he didn't know much about the military and hoped this was normal.

Inside the tent, a meeting was already underway. Three dozen young men stood, with their backs to him, intently listening to the speaker at the other end of the tent. Aiwren strained to see who it was.

"Mister Fancypants," Mister Cutter said, interrupting his own speech, "do you always arrive late?"

"No, sir," Aiwren said, completely confused, "not always."

"Sir?!" Mister Cutter shouted, but Aiwren tuned out for the rest of his berating.

"As you may know," Mister Cutter started, changing the subject, "there are a great many things to accomplish to prepare for war. Wars require specialists with specific skills to accomplish specific tasks. Most of you were sent to me because you possess the skill of tailoring. While some of you were sent to me because you possess no skills at all; I'm looking at you, Mister Fancypants. We have an important responsibility in preparing our fellow guardsmen for war. The bags outside the door contain the uniforms used the last time we had any sort of battle, so they are, you will find, quite distressed. It's our job to wash, mend, and repair these uniforms. We don't have much time, so get to work."

The sewing soldiers went to work and Aiwren finally made sense of the situation. These were apprentice tailors from various clothing shops all over the Avenue of Craftsmen. When Cutter said he had other responsibilities for the war, this was what he was referring to. His shop was selling new uniforms to the Kewnorian Guard and he was in charge of the soldiers tasked with repairing the old ones. With the influx of recruits, this would be the only way the Kewnorian Guard would be able to provide all of them with uniforms.

"Mister Wayde," Mister Cutter shouted, as the group dispersed to begin their work, "We've already established you know nothing about stitching, so pick up that broom and start sweeping."

Aiwren, too shocked, confused, and defeated to respond, picked up the broom and, for the second day in a row, spent the duration of the sun sweeping up thread and muttering to himself.

When Aiwren noticed the other stitching soldiers quitting for the evening, he leaned his broom against the wall and walked towards the tent's exit, but was interrupted by Cutter's harsh voice.

"Mister Fancypants," he shouted, "did I give you permission to put down that broom?"

Aiwren said nothing, picked up the broom with his blistered hands, and kept sweeping. He had to explain that sweeping wasn't what he had signed up for and that he wished to be transferred. Finally, when everyone else left, Mister Cutter told Aiwren to go home, and Aiwren approached the gruff man.

"Mister Cutter, I've been thinking," Aiwren said, "and I'm not sure sweeping up thread is really the means by which I would like to contribute to the war effort. Perhaps I might transfer to another unit."

"Really?" Cutter said, "How would you like to participate?"

"Well," Aiwren replied, "perhaps something requiring a sword rather than a broom."

"A sword which you, according to your papers, do not know how to use?"

"Well, I thought I would learn."

"And you think the front line of a battle is the best place to learn swordsmanship? If you're so determined to die without having contributed anything, perhaps you ought to throw yourself from a naval tower into the Uncrossable River. At least this way, we won't be wasting a uniform."

"With all due respect, Mister Cutter, I don't think I would simply serve as fodder."

"Okay." Cutter said. "Let's see you use your sword."

"But you're an old tailor and you don't have a sword."

"Then it should be an easy task," Cutter said, grabbing the broom. "Disarm me and I'll transfer you to the front lines."

Aiwren was confused and unsure of how rough he should go on Mister Cutter. He didn't want to hurt him, but seemed like a fantastically easy way for him to be transferred to a unit with more glory. He drew his sword and took his fighting stance. He should have known, by the slow and controlled way that Cutter took his fighting stance with the broom, that he was in trouble.

Aiwren charged in. His plan was to engage his blade with Cutter's broomstick with a circular motion so that it fell from the old man's hands. Everything happened so quickly and was all so wrong. In a blink of his eyes, Aiwren found himself disarmed with his sword more than five feet away, sticking into the ground.

"My apologies, Mister Fancypants," Cutter said, "it appears as though you weren't prepared. Best out of three?"

Aiwren picked up his sword and charged in again, this time his plan wasn't to out-finesse the tailor, but to overwhelm him with force. He was disarmed again, but this time he found himself face first on the ground.

"Three out of five?" Cutter asked?

Aiwren planned to fake to the right and go to the left, but, with a swoosh of the broomstick, Aiwren's sword was hurtling through the air. Cutter had, in a single motion, disarmed Aiwren, buckled the boy's knees, and placed the tip of the broom inches from the boy's throat, pausing for a moment, as his other hand effortlessly caught Aiwren's sword. Aiwren was shocked.

"Do you think you're the only working class boy who wanted to feel important?" Cutter asked.

"No," Aiwren said.

"Up," Cutter said, tossing Aiwren his sword. "This time, loosen your grip and relax your muscles."

"Won't that make it even easier for you to disarm me?" Aiwren asked, getting up.

"Tense muscles move slowly and predictably. Stay relaxed. Stay focussed. Try again."

182

Aiwren took a deep breath, tried to relax his muscles, and fought Cutter again. This time he wasn't so easily disarmed, his wrist rolled with the twisting motion of the broom and the sword remained in his hand. Cutter and Aiwren parried back in forth until moonlight shined into the tent.

"Why do you want to do this?" Cutter asked, sitting on the edge of a table.

Aiwren sat next to Cutter and realized he couldn't answer this question.

Cutter continued, "Glory isn't enough. Glory isn't worth sacrificing family or love or life. When you're bleeding to death on the battlefield, you'll receive little comfort from telling yourself that your name will go down in history, which it probably won't."

Aiwren wondered about all the other soldiers, about how this contradicted what most people believed, about how this sounded so much like something his parents would say.

"I suppose it's difficult to explain," Aiwren said, "and I've never really known for sure what I'm supposed to do, but I suppose I've always wanted to be something more, to be a better version of myself."

"Let me see your sword, boy," Cutter said.

Aiwren reluctantly handed the grouchy old man his sword, worried about what he would do with it. Cutter swung the sword through the air, balanced it on his hand, ran his finger down its edge, and whacked it on the table.

"Tell me, boy," Cutter said, inspecting the blade, "where did you get this?"

"It was my father's," Aiwren said. "He gave it to me before I left for Y-Kewnor."

"The blade is dull, the balance is off, and the iron is brittle," Cutter said, handing Aiwren his sword and walking away. "But it's a good sword, likely far better a sword than you or your father realize. Be careful with it and tell no one of this."

"Tell no one of what?" Aiwren asked.

"That I'm training you, Aiwren Wayde."

Aiwren returned to Leicester's apartment thoroughly exhausted, but thrilled. Leicester and Wanda seemed to be talking about something quite serious when he arrived. They half heartedly greeted him and quickly went off to bed. Aiwren attributed the tension to a lovers' quarrel that wasn't any of his business as he fell asleep to the sound of the indecipherably quiet murmur of the intense late-night conversation Leicester and Wanda were having in the other room.

***

The morning birds chirped, the sun rose over the horizon, and Jocund Plune relaxed in the arms of three prostitutes. After spending hours in the dungeon of the Citadel with the oaf of a moron who had a grudge against him since they were children, Jocund felt he deserved to splurge a little on an exceptionally wonderful night of revelry. The cost of a few prostitutes and enough wine to pickle himself was minimal to Jocund and worth every copper. The time he spent with prostitutes and barkeeps was his favorite. There was no pretense. He knew what they wanted: his money. It was just a business transaction. Jocund closed his eyes and drifted to sleep, exhausted from his most recent transaction. Suddenly the door smashed open and Kewnorian Guardsmen filed into the room.

"Really?!" Jocund said, eyes popping open. "Is all of Allyoshmar conspiring against a good night's sleep?"

"Lord Plune has requested your presence," one of the Guardsmen said.

"That's all?" Jocund asked. "Tell my father that, once I'm out and about for the day, I'll be sure to make an appearance at the Parliamentary Palace."

"Lord Plune instructed me to take you to him immediately, by force if necessary."

"Fine," he said, rolling his eyes with a sigh as he got out of bed, "my sleep has already been disturbed; I may as well visit my father."

The three prostitutes just opening their own eyes looked about the room with confusion, covering themselves bashfully.

"Please don't get up at my expense, ladies," Jocund said, tossing them a bag of coins. "This should take care of my tab and serve as a deposit for this evening, which, will commence as soon as I return."

The prostitutes scooped up the money as Jocund fastened his clothing.

"Uncork the wine posthaste," he said. "I always require a drink after conversing with my dear old father, but, then again, I always require a drink."

Jocund finished dressing and left with the guardsmen, who grabbed his arms as they left so he wouldn't run.

Jocund had been escorted to the Parliamentary Palace before, so he was accustomed to the looks he would receive as guards dragged him to his father's chambers. Occasionally it was a shock that a lordson would be dragged like a criminal, but usually people just shook their heads at how unfortunate it was he had turned out the way he had. Jocund was not surprised, as he entered his father's chambers, that Lord Plune did not appear pleased.

"Do you know why you're here?" Archibald asked?

"I can only assume it's to receive some award or merit," Plune responded, but his father was not amused. "What have I done to displease you this time?"

"You were arrested yesterday for conspiring in the attack on the Citadel," Archibald said, standing up at his desk. "How do you think that looks?"

"The charges were all dismissed," Jocund said. "There is no reason for concern."

Archibald slapped Jocund across the face.

"The charges were dropped at my behest," Archibald said. "My advisors tell me that public opinion of me has, in just one day, become unfavorable. There are some who believe the knight's story. I should have let you rot. "

"But I didn't do it!" Jocund said. "I didn't conspire to do anything but get drunk and laid. You should know that because you sent me to the Citadel that night."

"You think I don't know that, you knave?!" Archibald snapped. "You were supposed to deliver the money and leave without being seen, not end up in the middle of an investigation, accused of conspiracy! If it weren't for your reputation, the people would have assumed that the knight made this up. We do not want anyone poking around in our business. We need to get this attention off of you immediately."

"And how do you propose we do that?"

"You're returning to the guard," Archibald said.

"What?!" Jocund protested.

"In light of the recent attack, we need to show solidarity with the Kewnorians," Archibald said.

"But I've already done my time in the guard," Jocund said, "and it was dreadfully boring."

"Well, we're at war now," Archibald replied.

"You wish for me to die in battle?"

"Dying in battle would be the best thing you've ever done for this family. I'll hear no more words of this. You've already been enlisted."

***

As Rheo had anticipated, his second meeting as a High Knight of the Council was almost entirely spent being scolded. The worst of it came from Sir Allesander, who had clearly decided to hate Rheo. With the exception of Leopold, Allesander was the eldest and most powerful knight on the council. Rheo's injured pride, the loss of Sir Vincent, and wanting to do something but being unable to, sent him into a quiet fury.

After Rheo had been berated by Allesander, he spent the rest of the meeting smoldering as the other knights discussed the news of the day. Sir Ordo told them that the Sima Watusian princess who had been missing for over an annual had recently been spotted in Y-Kewnor. Allesander told him that, if it was true, Archibald Plune would have told him. Sigfried said he had received word from Lees Naglos that Gavlessa was crumbling, the revolution had taken the lives of the royal family, and Princess Teryessa was among those presumed to be dead. T'Ethal worried this might lead to a conflict in the West. Sigfried replied that any conflict could have been avoided if they had intervened. Allesander insisted they needed to focus on improving relations with the Kewnorians and ignore these issues of missing princesses from far away kingdoms. The meeting was concluded with a vote to uphold the status quo. Rheo couldn't wait to leave.

Rheo's frustration surged though his veins as he walked down the street. He had gone to his chambers, but was unable to enter further than his vestibule. The place only reminded him of Sir Vincent. So he left. He wasn't sure where he was going to go, but he had to leave.

Rheo found himself at a pub called "Belver's Brew." It was a dilapidated establishment in a rough part of town near the Guardsman's Smile, but he was hungry and thought that a mead might cool his temper. Heads turned at the sight of his gold armor when he entered, but he took a small table alone near the corner to eat and drink in peace.

There were already several empty plates and many empty mugs on Rheo's table when Jocund Plune entered, laughing nonchalantly, with a prostitute on each arm. Jocund, it seemed, was already too drunk and preoccupied with his own business to notice Rheo in the corner. He ordered a round for everyone in the pub. All of the patrons of the bar, roughnecks and hooligans, cheered and the tone of the establishment quickly changed.

Rheo controlled himself and, though approaching a drunken state, himself, he told himself violence would do no good. Eventually, Jocund went upstairs to check into a room with the two prostitutes he had arrived with and the two more he had met since arriving. Rheo thought, since Jocund had left, there was no longer a risk of losing his temper, but mead and wine had loosened the tongues and fortified the courage of a few of the men in the pub and, intent on picking a fight, they approached.

"Hey," said one of the men, barely able to stand. "Ain't you one of them Knights of the Council?"

"Yes," Rheo smiled, "but I'm afraid I'm off duty right now and wish to enjoy my drink alone, if you don't mind."

"Tell me," said another one of the men, "wut's the difference tween one of you high-an-mighty knights who's off duty and one who's on duty?"

"I don't think there is much of a difference," said the first one. "You know, some blokes don't think any of them knights is worth what we have to pay for em in taxes."

"Well," Rheo said, clenching his fists beneath the table, "we certainly appreciate the support of the community."

"That's all well and good," said a third drunken man, "but suppose a few of them blokes feel they didn't get their money's worth and want a refund."

"Well," said Rheo, really not liking the direction this was going in, but wanting to be the bigger man, "I recommend you write a letter to your district lord."

"Since you're one of them knights," said the first and most brazen of the group, "why don't you just give us our money back here? Maybe one of them gold plates from your armor."

Rheo flashed him a smile and said, "I'm not giving you any of my armor."

"Hey wait," said a fourth man, "this one's the one who just lost his knight daddy in that fire."

Rheo told himself to just keep playing it cool and said, "I'd prefer to enjoy my meal alone, gentlemen."

"I heard the one wut died in the fire is the same one wut started the fire," said the first one. "I heard he went crazy on account a his last knight-son was killed."

The second one leaned in close, pointed his finger at Rheo's nose, and said, "What do you think about that?"

Something popped inside of Rheo's mind and he was suddenly a passenger in his own body. He grabbed the man's shoulders and drove his forehead into the man's nose with as much force as possible, showering the table with blood. Before the man leaning on the table, the instigator in all of this, could react, Rheo had slammed his face onto the table with both hands. As the third man ran in to attack he was met with Rheo's boot squarely in his gut. When he lurched over, Rheo brought a plate down hard against the back of his head dropping him to the floor with the others. The fourth drunk man grabbed a chair and ran in, but Rheo just punched him and he fell.

The bar patrons silently stared at Rheo. The four unconscious men laid on the ground by his feet. Several more men looked ready to attack, but the barkeep yelled for everyone to stop and aimed his crossbow at Rheo's head.

"You're not welcome here," the barkeep said. "Leave the coins for your tab on the table and go."

***

King Noldar was already in his morning conference with Niveous Snew when Sir Truson Everly arrived at the palace. Truson never trusted Snew and every time the greasy little man was around the king, bad things seemed to happen, but, despite their disagreements, Snew had the king's complete trust and Truson was never able to pin any treasonous activities on him, so it didn't look like Snew was going away anytime soon. Snew had just returned and Truson spent the morning waiting for Snew's audience with the king to conclude. It was his responsibility was to ensure that King Noldar didn't take any drastic measures, measures, he was certain, Snew was encouraging him to take.

Finally the throne room doors opened. Truson could tell by Snew's grin that he had the king right where he wanted him. King Noldar followed Snew out of the room. Truson approached him.

"Your Grace, may I beg your audience for a moment?" Truson asked.

The king continued walking and, without looking at Truson, said, "If you can walk and talk."

"Very well," Truson said, keeping up, "I wish to extend to you my regrets over the tragic loss of Teryessa."

"You've already extended your condolences," the king said, not slowing his pace. "Why are you so motivated to express them again, that you inconvenience me by interrupting my day? Do you feel responsible?"

"If I may be completely honest with you, Your Grace," Truson said as he followed the king down a narrow stairwell, "yes, I worry I failed you in my inability to persuade the knights to come to your aid. I also worry that hasty decisions now would only exacerbate the situation."

At a landing at the bottom of the stairs, Noldar stopped, turned to Truson, and said, "Despite, being a knight, your loyalty has always been to me, my daughter, and the people of Lees Naglos. I am not such a fool to overlook your strength of character. Right now I need you to do something for me, though."

"Your Grace, how may I serve you?" Truson asked, surprised by the king's forgiving sentiment.

"You may serve me, Sir Truson," Noldar said, suddenly cold, "by vowing to never speak my daughter's name."

Truson bowed in acceptance of this order, despite his concern that something truly devious was going on.

The king looked into Truson's eyes and said, "Leaving me, my people, and my daughter to die was a decision the council made despite your requests, not because of them; they alone must face the consequences."

Truson wondered what this meant, but the king was walking again. Guards had opened the door to the dungeon. The assassin from Gavlessa was already outside of his cell, being restrained by two guards.

Staring at the king, the assassin said nothing.

"I am Noldar Palidnia of the Palidnia's who once ruled all of this land, who wielded the flaming sword," the king said, handing his robe and crown to a guard. "When my family resigned to Lees Naglos, it was an act of mercy, but the gratitude for this reprieve has expired, and some now wish to rise against me. I have remained patient. For this I've been rewarded with suffering."

Truson didn't understand the king's intentions, but Snew's demented smile made his stomach turn.

"I am going to count to three," Noldar said to the assassin as he handed his crown to Snew. "This is your only chance to confess and tell me who sent you."

Truson had no idea what the king would do, but he hoped the assassin would confess, so they could all relax, so he may speak to the king in private, and they might all begin to repair the damage that had been done.

"One," the king said, but the assassin only grimaced.

The king said, "Two," and the assassin looked up at the king with a smug and fiercely determined face.

"Three."

King Noldar Palidnia reached across his waist for his sword. The assassin's eyes widened as the metal of the blade scraped past the metal of the sheath. Truson knew what was happening and moved towards the king to stop him. He heard himself yell as the blade came down, thick metal sheering through skin and muscle and spine. The assassin's face, still frozen with panic, fell from his body and tumbled to the ground. A moment lingered before the man's headless corpse collapsed and hemorrhaged a pool of red to the stone floor.

Truson was shocked and horrified. He had seen death before, but never an execution carried out with such callous indifference. He looked at Snew, who made no attempt to conceal how pleased he was. King Noldar stared at the body with dissatisfaction and Truson worried this would not be enough for the king.

"Have the Knight Generals prepare their soldiers," Noldar said to Snew, who bowed with a smile. "We're going to war and we won't stop until every Gavlessan is dead and their underground city is reduced to ashes."

***

Breathing was all she could do and every inhaled breath was so tortured that Teryessa swore she would not allow herself to take another, yet, for every exhale held, her lungs would betray her will and her bare, blood and filth-caked chest would raise again, filling her body with air, once more. Weak and disoriented, she didn't know where she was or how she had gotten there. She was in pain and terrified and gratefully slipping away from thought and awareness again. The last thing she was aware of as she, once again faded, was the shackles around her wrists and ankles binding her to blood-dampened, roughly hewn stone.

Steamy hot breath on her skin drew Teryessa from her unconscious state. She smelled the putrid rotting stench. She opened her eyes and, through fuzzy vision, saw Wurm Ahkk-Rhall's long snout twist into a menacing, toothy smile. Everything that had happened to Teryessa, everything he had done to her, came back in a flash. She screamed.

"I'm so glad you're awake, princess," He growled. "I've been so bored waiting."

Teryessa tried to squeeze her eyes shut and realized why her vision was so fuzzy; her left eye was almost completely swollen shut. Partially blind, she whipped about in a frenzy, unable to shake free from her shackles.

"Are you trying to escape, Princess?" Ahkk-Rhall laughed. "What would you even do if you could escape?"

Teryessa thought about the question. She wanted to run or to hide, but knew she'd never be able get very far. She didn't know where she was. She was weak and small compared to this filthy beast. The walls of her situation closed in on her, squeezing out all hope. Fear washed over her in waves, destroying everything she was. The only thing remaining, as the waves of intolerable fear receded, was hatred.

"Let me go and find out," she said between teeth grinding together.

Ahkk-Rhall's reaction was a boisterous laugh as he mounted her once more. Then he stopped, sniffed the air and said, "That will have to wait."

The dragon climbed off the stone table as the walls shook. Teryessa could hear the winds whipping. A thud echoed throughout the cave and Ahkk-Rhall lumbered off towards the sound.

Teryessa could hear Ahkk-Rhall's voice and another voice similar to Ahkk-Rhall's, but she couldn't quite tell what they were saying. The conversation sounded cordial at first. Then she heard the other voice say, "let me see," and she was certain. It was another dragon.

Ahkk-Rhall and the other dragon lumbered into the room Teryessa was bound to the table in.

"Is she alive?" the other dragon asked.

"Yes," said Ahkk-Rhall, "quite."

"Very well, Ahkk-Rhall," said the other dragon, "you have successfully captured the girl. I suppose you expect this to absolve you for your absence in Y-Kewnor. We'll see what the Master says."

"You know, Broch-Isha," said Ahkk-Rhall, "I've been thinking. I never really bought into any of this as much as you or the others. I've never really had much of a proclivity towards camaraderie. Perhaps the girl will just remain with me, after all."

"Ahkk-Rhall!" Broch-Isha, the other dragon, roared. "I would advise you to reconsider and caution you not to deviate from the plan any more than you already have. Our Master wants the girl and I'm here to fetch her."

"And if I should say no?" Ahkk-Rhall asked and Teryessa knew what was about to happen.

Broch-Isha lumbered over to her table. His face peered close to Teryessa's. He had a patch over one eye and was a slightly more pinkish hue than Ahkk-Rhall. She couldn't decide which of the dragons was more terrifying. His claw snapped at the chains holding the shackles on her wrists to the stone table and they broke. As he reached for the shackles at her ankles, Ahkk-Rhall attacked.

The dragons tumbled around the room. This was Teryessa's only opportunity, but she was too terrified to move. She tried to make herself sit up but her body, involuntarily shaking, refused to obey. Her lips trembled and tears flowed from the eye that wasn't swollen shut.

She told herself, if she made the wrong move she would die, but if she did nothing she would die. She closed her eyes, hoping for The Divine Empress to step in and give her guidance in the last minute, but saw only darkness. Then she heard a voice, not The Divine Empress's, but her own.

"Teryessa," she said to herself, "you must never again rely on anybody else. From this point on, you are on your own."

While the dragons were tearing viciously at each other, Teryessa sat up, desperately scanning the room for a way to free herself. Her body was reacting more quickly now. Panic had stepped aside, allowing action to emerge. She quickly took in the details of the room. There was a hatchet, but it was too far to reach. There was a chair within reach, but she would never be able to break the iron shackle with it. Then she realized that, although the shackles were iron, the table was only stone. If she could get one leg free she could reach far enough off the table to reach the hatchet and quickly free the other leg, but she needed something the break the stone that held first shackle. She grabbed the shackle around her left wrist and slammed it into the stone table by her right foot. It only made a small chip, but it made a chip.

Ahkk-Rhall spewed his fiery venom on to Broch-Isha. The flaming gel stuck to Broch-Isha's chest, searing his skin. He lunged in, snapped his enormous jaws closed around Ahkk-Rhall's neck, and whipped the giant beast into the wall of the cave.

"You want to use fire on me, Ahkk-Rhall?" Broch-Isha demanded. "Is that what we're doing now?"

Broch-Isha released his own fire on Ahkk-Rhall, who was picking himself up as stones collapsed on him.

Teryessa's left wrist was bleeding badly, as were the knuckles of her right hand, but she shut the pain out of her mind. There was only one thing that existed: escaping, no matter what. She brought her left wrist down with all of her might and the final piece of stone crumbled the chain to the shackle on her right foot was free from the stone table.

Burnt badly, Ahkk-Rhall whispered for mercy, but Broch-Isha didn't stop until Ahkk-Rhall was charred and bleeding all over, his flesh smoldering and smoking.

"Don't you see?" Broch-Isha said, not noticing the tail slyly creeping up behind him. "This is bigger than you. The Dark One lives and the necromancer is his voice."

It was already too late. The razor-sharp spikes on the back of Ahkk-Rhall's tail ripped across Broch-Isha's throat.

Broch-Isha's eyes widened and he reached for his neck, but blood was already gushing from the mangled pulp that used to be an artery. He dropped to his knees and Ahkk-Rhall leapt on him to viciously finish him.

Teryessa, stretched to grab the hatchet but she couldn't quite reach it. It was leaning against a stool and even with her body entirely off of the stone table with the one remaining chain as taut as possible, it was just beyond her grasp. Ahkk-Rhall approached the table. If she didn't get that hatchet she was dead. She made one final lunge with all of her might She heard the chain snap tight and felt a pop in the ankle she had recently injured in her fall down the stairs to the Dark Gallery. A claw wrapped around her leg, but the handle of the hatchet was already in her hand.

Perhaps, in his frustration and fatigue, Ahkk-Rhall pulled too hard on Teryessa's leg, giving her that extra bit of momentum, but as he pulled her towards him, she, rather than pulling in the opposite direction, went with the flow of the movement and the momentum accelerated. She swung the hatchet with both hands as she flung herself towards him, connecting with the first thing she could, Wurm Ahkk-Rhall's head.

The dragon reeled back, howling in pain and Teryessa made damn sure the hatchet remained in her hands. As the blade popped out of the dragon's skull, she heard the snapping of bones. The dragon collapsed to the floor, where he held his head and wailed.

Teryessa hurried, but it only took her a few hits with the hatchet to break the rocks away, freeing the final chain from the stone table. Naked, holding a bloody hatchet, with a shackle around each ankle and wrist, she stood from the table. Limping on her ankle, she approached Ahkk-Rhall.

"Please. Grant mercy," the dragon moaned.

Teryessa said nothing. All that existed in the world was rage and, wild with fury, she lost herself in a frenzy of hacking and screaming and blood. She wrestled the monster's head still and whacked into the its neck with the hatchet until she reached the fire glands beneath the flesh. Remembering flashes of the precision with which he used fire to torture her, she dove her fingers into the beast and plucked out the sticky orbs as he wailed in pain, but she wasn't done. It took several swings, straddling the beast's back, for her to chop through the bone and sever Ahkk-Rhall's wings and tail.

"Please," the dragon begged. "Please just leave me. I swear, I'll never come after you."

Teryessa said nothing, but raised the hatchet again, for one piece of unfinished business.

"Please, no!" Wurm Ahkk-Rhall pleaded.

Teryessa released a primal scream and swung the hatchet down with all of her might, castrating the dragon with one swing. She stood, dropped the hatched and left him howling and sobbing in misery, to die in a pool of his own blood.

Wurm Ahkk-Rhall's cave was littered with weapons and armor, but she chose to wear the gold armor. To her it symbolized that, despite the pile of the bones of the dragon's victims before her, she was the girl who walked out of that cave and she did so without any help, without any heroes or Divine Empresses or kings or soldiers. She would never need anybody ever again. Daylight bathed her as she stepped out onto the cliff in the Dragonsback Mountains overlooking a city she was certain she could travel to before nightfall. She tossed the fire glands into the cave, where they splattered on the ground, spreading their sticky flammable liquid everywhere, and bursting into flame. She heaved the backpack she had filled with gold coins over her shoulder and limped down the mountain as Wurm Ahkk-Rhall screamed through the torment of being roasted alive by his own fire.

It was already dark by the time Teryessa had arrived at the gates of Orc Doola, but the gatesman let her enter with very little questioning and was kind enough to point her to the closest inn.

The inn was upstairs of a pub, so Teryessa stepped up to the counter between two burly looking guys who had fallen asleep in their ale and, dazed and exhausted, asked for a room.

"Miss," the man who doubled as inn-keep and bar-keep said, "you're covered in blood."

"Thank you," Teryessa said, "I hadn't noticed."

The man behind the counter quickly shuffled around for the key as Teryessa dug into her backpack for a coin.

"Geeze!" said a bar wench, passing by with a tray of empty beer mugs. "Who'd you kill?!"

"A dragon," Teryessa said. "Now may I rent a room or must I answer more questions?"

The man behind the counter slid a key to her and she slid him a coin. She was about to go straight to bed, but decided to see if she could purchase any numbendria, first.

VAYOSH

Vannoria creaked open her sleep-crusted eyes, at first only aware of vague shapes and a discord of garbled sounds, before the blurry room drifted reluctantly into focus. Having no idea where she was or what was going on, her dazed mind grasped desperately through the fuzzy confusion for anything palpable to cobble together some semblance of reality. She was in a bed, in a small room, and it was humid. An old man wiped her forehead with a damp cloth and a cool bead of water raced down her temple. Her numbed limbs and dulled mind left her situation untenable, but, as her disorientation spiraled into a panic that pierced through her lethargy, her eyes widened.

"Easy, teeffah," the old man crooned. "Your fever is breaking, but you still have healing to do. You can call me Mister Uncle. I mean you no harm. Your friend took you to me because you were badly injured."

Vannoria remembered the strange shadowy man, but there were gaps in her memory and pieces that didn't make sense.

"What happened to me?" she asked.

"You had the misfortune of stumbling upon a Balysh-Pah, a Forgotten Place, the last remaining structures built for The Dark One ages ago. They are impregnated with a powerful evil magic. This magic possessed you. Infected you."

Vannoria realized she was covered with bandages and a flood of memories washed over her. She remembered that strange dark room. She remembered feeling angry and cutting at herself, unable to stop. Overwhelmed with terror, she tore at her wrappings with cloth-bound fingers.

Mister Uncle struggled to hold her down. She screamed and fought to free herself. The shadowy man came from out of nowhere and held her arms still. She whipped about until, unable to move her hands anymore, she looked up into his eyes. The shadowy man said nothing, but returned her look with an empty stare.

"I want to see," she demanded.

"Very well, teeffah," Mister Uncle said. "I will remove your bandages, but we must do this carefully."

Vannoria nodded in consent. She looked away and braced herself. The tears welled in her eyes and glided down into the bandages on her face. The Shadowy Man gently held her still while Mister Uncle slowly unwrapped the bandages from her arms, leaving her left hand bandaged. She looked down. Her arms were covered with what appeared to be black ink. They were in strange patterns, symbols she didn't understand.

"What is it?" she asked.

"My people," Mister Uncle said, "know secret magics, lost to most others. When someone suffers from an injury that has been created by evil magic, we use these symbols to protect the person. Your injuries were severe. I have never drawn so many tattoos on one person before. If our friend had found you a moment later, you'd have been too far gone."

"How long must I wear these symbols?" Vannoria asked.

"Teeffah," said Mister Uncle, "they are permanent."

Vannoria crumbled, trembling as her world came crashing down around her.

"What of my hand?" she asked, staring at its bandages, knowing it was must be worse-off than the rest of her.

"A piece of the glass was imbedded in your finger," Mister Uncle said, "the corruption was spreading fast."

"Show me."

Mister Uncle slowly removed the bandage from her left hand. It was marked with the symbols as her right hand was and as her arms were, but on her left hand her index finger was missing from the knuckle down and covered in scabs.

"I had no choice, teeffah," said Mister Uncle.

"May I see a mirror?" she asked after a moment.

Mister Uncle nodded and handed her a small mirror. She looked in the mirror and removed the bandages from her face. Her forehead and cheeks were also covered with the black symbols. She ripped the bandages off her neck and chest, revealing symbols from behind her ears down to her collar bone.

"There is much to understand," Mister Uncle said, standing up, "but for now you should rest. Tomorrow, we will perform a ceremony to help prevent the corruption from returning."

Mister Uncle left the cabin, but the shadowy man remained at her bedside. Vannoria wondered who this man was and why he had captured her. There was something terrifying about him and something spellbinding. It was difficult for her to feel anything. Even her misery was blanketed with the billowy cushions of hopeless defeat. The world was muted.

"Who are you?" Vannoria demanded.

"I do not know," the man said.

"What do you want with me?" she asked, still staring straight ahead, not looking at him.

"I'm going to kill you," he said.

"Why?" she asked, flatly.

"I don't know," he answered, adding, "I exist only to execute my Master's bidding."

"If you're supposed to kill me," she started, "then why would you save me?"

"Because the time wasn't right for you. It was not what my Master wanted."

"I'm going back to sleep," she said. "My name is Vannoria Nillhalla. If your Master requests my slaughter while I'm sleeping, I thought you might like to know the name of your victim."

***

The Nameless Rider watched the Girl close her eyes. When he was certain her eyes were closed, he mouthed her name, Vannoria. It made him think about names and wonder why people had them. It made him wonder why he didn't have one. It made him wonder why she had to die.

The Nameless Rider stepped outside, onto the porch of Mister Uncle's cabin. Below him, other members of Mister Uncle's Family-Clan, hustled through the morning business around their cabins, cooking food, feeding their alligators and tidying up. His own horse was tethered to the bottom of Mister Uncle's cabin. Mister Uncle motioned towards a chair and the Nameless Rider sat. Mister Uncle handed him a mug.

"I'd like to offer you a payment," the Nameless Rider said, "for your help."

Mister Uncle laughed so hard he nearly spit up the contents of his mug.

"Did you come into some coin since the last time we met, old friend?" he asked. "What would a simple man such as myself do with money? Drink your cocoa, rich man."

The Nameless Rider, shaking, looked up from his cocoa and said, "When the time comes, I do not know if I will be able to kill her."

"I am sorry for your burden, for what you were created, beyond your wishes, to be," Mister Uncle said. "There is an old Balysh-Tong word. Vayosh. Path of Lies. To many, this appears to be a bad thing. How can you get where you need to be if the path you are on is lying to you? But there is a Balysh-Tong saying, 'Adheris-a Vayosh.' Stick to the lying path. Do not be so certain where your quest is taking you, old friend."

***

For the third morning in a row, Jocund was woken by men with swords. He was quite certain the world was, in fact, conspiring against a good night's sleep.

The note they delivered was regarding his first assignment back in the Kewnorian Guard and they insisted on escorting him to his father's chambers to discuss the matter in detail. So, again, he was paraded from his room at the inn, across town, to the Parliamentary Palace.

"Perhaps the lavish home I bought you was a waste of money," Archibald said, looking up from his ledger, "since you spend all of your time consorting with prostitutes."

"Well," Jocund said, shaking himself free from the grip of the guardsmen, "Giving up my hope for intelligent company, I've lowered my standards to interesting company, but even that continues to be unnecessarily truncated, along with my sleep, by brutish oafs --no offense to present company-- waving their swords at me, making demands."

"Perhaps the reason you're having trouble keeping intelligent company," Archibald replied, "is because we're all preoccupied with cleaning up your messes in addition to dutifully fulfilling our own obligations."

Archibald waved off the guards and motioned for Jocund to sit. Jocund sat next to an older man in polished armor.

"This," Archibald said, "is General Khoral. He's the man responsible for the entire Kewnorian Guard. He was delighted to hear of you volunteering to serve and has agreed to reinstate you and allow you to resume your rank of lieutenant, which is generous offer considering your unsatisfactory service record."

"Thank you," Jocund said nonchalantly, but his mind raced and, although he was still drunk from previous night, he put the pieces together quickly. Khoral's armor was shiny, but that was normal for a high ranking officer in the Kewnorian Guard. His hands were calloused from hard work, but he wore a large ruby ring that a guardsman wouldn't have been able to afford. Another finger had the marks of where a ring once was. His fingernails had been chewed down the skin. His grey hair was perfectly manicured, but he had dark bags beneath his eyes. Jocund ascertained that this was a soldier who did the bidding of people in power. This obedience had rewarded him well in rank and finance. He had grown too accustomed to living beyond his means, which, now coming to a head, resulted in anxiety and sleepless nights. He was looking to earn the favor of a wealthy lord to solve his financial woes. Khoral was in his father's pocket.

"Lordson Plune, it is a pleasure to have you, once again, in the Kewnorian Guard," he said.

"I suppose that would be Lieutenant Plune," Jocund said. "No need to extend me any kindness. I'm not the one paying you. Of course, that would be the Kewnorian people. Right?"

"Right," General Khoral said, "I have an assignment for you that will win you the respect you deserve."

"I don't know," mused Jocund, "I may already have precisely the amount of respect I deserve."

"Jocund," Archibald said, "will you remember that you are in the presence of a lord and a general."

"Of course, father," Jocund said. "Please forgive my tasteless humor. I am certain that neither a lord nor a general know anything of debasing one's self for money or the shame of involving one's self with those spineless creatures willing to do so."

Archibald fumed and, for Jocund, successfully infuriating his father, made the annoyance of having to wake up early almost worth it. He smiled, sat back, and gave an over exaggerated gesture with his hand for General Khoral to continue.

"As you may know," Khoral began hesitantly, "the princess of Sima Watusia went missing over an annual ago. For quite some time, she was believed to be dead. Because Sima Watusia and Simi Watusia are once again on the verge of war, most people assumed it was the Simi Watusians who had killed her; however, the princess has been seen in Y-Kewnor. If she were to be killed in Y-Kewnor there would be dire political ramifications. With the recent attack and the upcoming election, it would be best if this problem were amended immediately and discretely."

"So, essentially," Jocund said, "anyone who knows about this is going to try to kidnap her so they can collect a reward from the highest bidding Watusian clan. Which Watusia are we bringing her to?"

"We're bringing her home," Khoral said. "King Sima Watus, The Fourteenth, has offered us a reward, which you would be responsible for returning to Y-Kewnor."

"Well," said Jocund, "I'm shocked Sima is willing to part with any wealth that could be spent on that idiotic feud with his cousin across the lake. So I'm to chaperone the spoiled runaway princess back home to daddy? Is that it?"

"Yes," Khoral stuttered, "I was hoping this would be a task you are capable of."

"I'm certain," Archibald said, "even my moronic son is capable of completing this mission."

"Is this an order?" Jocund asked.

He watched as Khoral looked to Archibald for instruction and rolled his eyes when Archibald nodded, yes.

"Yes," Khoral said, "this is an order."

"Splendid," Jocund said, standing. "Being as important as this mission clearly is, I'm sure I'll be afforded the least skilled half wits in the Kewnorian Guard, but, I'd like to pick them myself, so please see to it whatever simpletons you're willing to part with are assembled tomorrow morning so I may form my troop of idiots."

Jocund mockingly saluted Khoral and he left without waiting for an answer. This was so good for everyone, he thought, everyone but him. As Jocund Plune, once again a lieutenant, returned to the prostitutes that were still on the clock, he was glad that he didn't care about anyone.

***

Rheozarccio Rheodo was not at all in a pleasant mood. His head was pounding from his night at Belver's Brew when he charged into the council meeting on a mission.

"They've sent Jocund Plune to bring the Watusian princess back to Sima Watusia" he shouted as he walked in the door, before the meeting had even officially begun. That is an issue involving multiple cities and, therefore, under the jurisdiction of The Divine Empress's Knights. Lord Plune has no right sending his son."

"Well," Leopold said, "It appears as though Sir Rheozarccio has called our meeting to order."

The other High Knights of the Council chuckled at this and turned their attention to the table as Rheo reluctantly took his own seat, continuing to fume.

"You ought to be glad, Sir Rheozarccio," Leopold continued, "Sending the Kewnorian Guard disencumbers our resources and Jocund Plune is, at least for the time being, out of your hair."

"Disencumbers our resources for what?!" Rheo demanded. "Jocund Plune is a louse and a drunkard and a treasonous conspirator and he hasn't been in the guard for annuals."

"This is true," Arowyr said, joyfully, "and, out of shame for his flaws, he has reenlisted to serve the people of Y-Kewnor and earn his repentance."

"The Plunes only do things that serve the Plunes," Rheo retorted. "He's doing this to repair his own reputation and his father's."

"Yes," Allesander snapped, pointedly, "a reputation you wrongfully tarnished."

Leonard, doing his best to calm Rheo and restore reason to the discussion, said, "The Plunes may be serving themselves, and they may be selfish, but the City of Y-Kewnor is served by their selfishness."

"And their careful awareness of their public image," Sigfried added, "is a trait that would benefit us all if you adopted."

"They're duplicitous, greedy, self-serving villains," said Rheo, "of course they're skilled with trickery and deception. I took an oath. An oath I actually take seriously."

T'Ethal slammed his fist on the table and said, "Are you insinuating something about the character of your fellow council members?!"

Leopold, again attempting to establish a more peaceful atmosphere at the council table, said, "Yes, you took an oath to serve, Sir Rheozarccio, to serve The Divine Empress and the people of Allyoshmar, which includes the people of the Watusian Girl, the Plune family, and the people of Y-Kewnor who need to know they can trust the knights... that they can believe in us."

"So that's what you want?," Rheozarccio snapped, "someone to shake hands and smile and look like a hero? Cause I think the people need real heroes not politicians posing as heroes."

"What we want," Leopold continued, ever patient, "is for you to think about the big picture. In the name of The Divine Empress, you're on the High Council, we want you to act like it."

"Unless you'd rather spend your time getting into bar brawls like a common guardsman," Allesander proposed venomously.

"Fine." Rheo said, throwing his hands up in the air, "I'll play your games. What's my first duty?"

"If this young man is so interested in the Kewnorian Guard," Ordo said, "perhaps he ought to be assigned as their liaison. Do I have a second?"

"His knight-father worked with them successfully," T'Ethar said thoughtfully, "I'll second."

"Any objections from Master Rheozarccio?" Leopold asked Rheo.

Rheo shrugged contemptuously. None of these men seemed to show him even the slightest bit of respect. He was certain they were assigning him to some meaningless post just to get him out of their hair, to keep him occupied while they did whatever they wanted and all they wanted was to willfully participate in Y-Kewnor's corrupt political system of bribery, subterfuge, and negligence, but it didn't matter; the vote was unanimous. He would be liaising with the Kewnorian Guard, likely, he thought, with some bureaucrat who spent his time kissing Archibald Plune's ass like everyone else in the damn city.

"By the will of The Divine Empress, it is unanimous," Leopold said. "Report to General Boomswift first thing in the morning. And don't stare."

***

Aiwren woke up that morning sore in ways he had never been before. His muscles ached all over and he was covered in bruises that he didn't even remember getting. He was thrilled. He knew he had dreamt of the Skinless Woman, but the soreness and the thrill of knowing he was getting trained made him forget the dream and think, instead, of how fantastic it was that his body was so sore.

Leicester and Wanda were still sleeping when Aiwren left that morning to rush over to Cutter's tent in the barracks. He hurried through sweeping all day and, looking forward to the end of the day, his chores seemed to take forever.

At lunch, Cutter had all of the young men go through the uniforms that they had been repairing and select one for themselves. Those in the seamsters troop, he said, would not have last pick of the uniforms. The uniforms were basic cloth with thicker leather in some areas to give the illusion of protecting vital organs. Aiwren found one that was the correct length for him, but he didn't quite fill it out. None of the young men in Aiwren's troop quite fit their uniforms. That was how things were though, Aiwren considered. Young men in ill-fitting uniforms would go to war and, more often then not, return in wooden boxes, leaving their blood stained uniforms for the next batch of soldiers to clean, mend, wear, and stain with their own blood. It had been a thousand annuals of peace, but, even in peace, there had been ample excuses to send young men and women off to die.

It was only just nightfall, when Cutter sent everyone home early, telling Aiwren he could leave when he finished sweeping, but as soon as the last tailor left for the night, the attack had already begun. Aiwren brought his broomstick up just in time to block Cutter's blade. Proud of himself for this block, Aiwren failed to block Cutter's hand from punching him in the ribs.

"I just stabbed you in the ribs," Cutter said. "Watch your position. My sword is not your opponent; I am. My sword is just one of my weapons."

This made sense to Aiwren, who, although he was not athletic, had a good sense of his surroundings and was excellent at learning. His view shifted with this new information; he saw the fight differently. He blocked two more attacks of Cutter's sword and sensed his teacher's fist heading towards him.

"When we begin something we possess only our instincts," Cutter said, swinging his sword gracefully. "Then we learn skills and we practice these skills until they, too, become instincts, allowing us to think on our feet and create strategy. But you've a long way to go before that."

Cutter swung hard over his head, exaggerating the movement. Aiwren blocked the swing with his broomstick and the wood snapped in half.

"Now how will you sweep the floor?" Cutter asked. "How will you defend yourself?"

Aiwren held up a short piece of broom in each hand.

"Stop," Cutter said. "Rest."

Aiwren set his broomstick pieces down and asked, "What was I supposed to do? You were attacking me."

"Look at this," Cutter said, handing him his sword, "and tell me about the blade."

Aiwren ran his thumb across Cutter's blade and said, "It's not very sharp."

"But I just sharpened it this morning and I was only sparring against a broomstick," Cutter said.

"I guess it dulls easily," Aiwren said.

"It does," Cutter agreed, "and the damage is only worse when worn against metal, then you also get burrs and chips, which are, of course unavoidable, and I'm not suggesting the purpose of battle is to keep your sword pristine, but you do want your sword to remain sharp for the moment when it counts."

"But I've seen fighters-" Aiwren started.

Cutter cut him off and said, "You've seen morons clanging their blades about with idiotic grandiosity. From the point of view of a general, this is fine because the other army's morons are doing the same thing and the general with the most morons and the greatest strategical advantage is going to win the battle, but what good does that do you?"

"I thought I have to learn skills before I learn strategy." Aiwren said, confused by Cutter's speech.

"Precisely," Cutter said, sheathing his sword. "The most important skill in any martial art, is not the metal you wave about in the air, but your footwork and positioning. I'm not training you to be an infantry man in the Kewnorian Guard. They have their own teachers who are perfectly suitable for instructing on the proper way to walk into a blade in the name of their city."

"What are you training me for?" Aiwren asked.

"Something else," Cutter replied. "Now get up."

Aiwren stood and the lesson in footwork began. At first it was about balance and stance, not just sword fighting stance, but fighting stance for any weapon, feeling his weight pressing down on the earth in a different way. It was awkward at first, being on the balls of his feet rather than back on his heels. Cutter made him shift his balance from one foot to the other over and over again in a way that allowed Aiwren to move more smoothly. Aiwren complained that it was very slow to move this way and Cutter told him that it would be until it became instinctual and that the only way for it to become instinctual was for him to shut his mouth and keep going back and forth from foot to foot. After practicing this for what seemed to Aiwren like eternity, Cutter started shouting out directions for him to move in. At first, given the urge to respond quickly, Aiwren returned to moving in the way he was most comfortable, but as he crossed his left leg over his right, to shuffle to the right, Cutter knocked him over, told him not to cross his legs and to do it the way he had practiced. Aiwren got up and did just that.

Growing exhausted and bored with these drills, Aiwren stopped, and asked how this help him against a sword.

"Tell me," Cutter said, "if we are in a fight, do you want to hit me or my sword? What is the goal?"

"To hit you," Aiwren said.

"Do you think," Cutter continued, "I'm going to intentionally allow you to do so?"

"Well, no." Aiwren replied.

"So what do you do, then?" Cutter asked. "Dull your sword against mine until I change my mind and allow you to strike? No. You must create the opportunity. You must move in a way that not only prevents me from having an opportunity to hit you, but that also creates an opportunity for you to hit me."

Cutter he picked up a broken piece of broomstick, handed it to Aiwren, and drew his sword.

"It is much more difficult to block with a dirk or dagger," Cutter said, "which is why knife fights are so fatal. Use position to defend yourself and to create opportunities for an attack that cannot be blocked."

The two sparred for hours. Understanding the concept, and being forced by Cutter to immediately apply it, Aiwren quickly adopted these new skills. He tripped on his own feet a few times, and, of course, Cutter connected many blows to Aiwren's few, but he could feel himself improving. When they were done sparring, Cutter sat on the table and Aiwren joined him.

"You know so much more than the other swordsmen," Aiwren said, "why become a tailor?"

"Paths change," Cutter said, "go places you never expected. In order to be true to yourself you must be true to the path you are on where ever it leads you."

"Then why return now?" Aiwren asked.

"As I said," Cutter replied, "you must be true to the path you are on. Go home. Sleep. You'll be sore tomorrow."

As Aiwren entered Leicester's apartment he almost ran right into Wanda. Tears were streaming down her cheeks and she looked furious.

"Wanda," Aiwren said, "I didn't see you or Leicester this morning, is everything all right?"

"Oh, everything's marvelous," she said scathingly, "I was just leaving. Apparently some people don't mean it when they say they love you and will be by your side no matter what!"

Aiwren was stunned and confused as Wanda stormed away. Aiwren entered, closing the door behind him, and looked to a bereft Leicester for answers.

"I think the engagement's off, Aiwren," Leicester said. "I have no idea what I did, but she's furious with me. Her temper has been hot ever since the theatre closed and I've been trying to get her to talk about it and she hasn't wanted to. Then, tonight, she starts asking me all these questions in rapid succession. And I guess I answered them wrong because she had an absolute tantrum and wouldn't even tell me why she was angry."

"I'm so sorry, Leicester," Aiwren said. "Do you remember what question set her off?"

"I'm not certain," Leicester said. "She asked me how important being a tailor is to me. And I told her it's very important, one of the most important things in the world."

"Well," Aiwren said. "It may have been that."

"But the only reason being a tailor is so important to me," Leicester replied, "is so that I can have a good career, so that, when I marry her, I can provide for her so that we can start a family and not have to live the way I lived growing up, forever at risk of starvation should the weather not be affable to the next crop. You certainly must understand what I mean."

"I do understand," Aiwren said, "but perhaps she didn't understand that."

"No," Leicester said, "of course she didn't. Her tirade allowed me no opportunity to explain myself."

"Look," Aiwren said, "You're probably more wise about relationships then I am, but I believe you ought to tell her. Be true to the path you are on, where ever it may take you."

"I believe you may be right," Leicester said, "I intend to tell her at once. If I hurry, perhaps I can catch her before she gets home."

In whirl of new found hope in his relationship, Leicester grabbed some of his things and hurried away, thanking Aiwren for his advice as the door closed behind him. Aiwren was alone in Leicester's apartment. He planned on practicing some more, but wanted to sit for a few moments first; however, more exhausted than he realized, he was sound asleep in an instant.

***

The falcon arrived at the Temple of The Divine Empress early that morning. When the young priestess saw the falcon resting on its perch as she stepped in the courtyard, she knew it was urgent. She hurried to get one of the priestesses trained to handle messenger falcons.

When the priestess delivered the note to Sir Truson Everly, he was just sitting down to breakfast with some of the priests and priestesses, since, in Lees Naglos, The Divine Empress's Knights were also housed in the Temple and he had become close friends with some of them. The seal on the scroll remained unbroken. The monogram belonged to Sir Leopold Leonard, the Grand High Knight of the Council. His hand shook as he broke the seal and his heart sank with horror and grief when he learned that the Citadel had been attacked. He left his breakfast without saying a word.

As Truson arrived at the palace, the king was similarly engaged with breakfast as Truson had been when he received the news. The king insisted that Truson join him for breakfast before Truson could tell him about the attack, explaining that he would rather hear bad news on a full stomach. Truson picked through his breakfast with the king, a more extravagant fare than the simple breakfast he normally ate, but the news he was withholding ate at him the entire time.

"The Citadel in Y-Kewnor has been attacked, Your Grace," Truson blurted out. "I received a falcon this morning and reported to you directly. In Lees Naglos, it is only you and I who know. Your Grace, it was dragons. Four of them."

"If only a son could have been born to me as trustworthy, loyal, and dutiful as you," the king said, "thank you for your expediency delivering the message."

"Your Grace, I beg you forgive my candidness," Truson began hesitantly, "but, given these circumstances, I do not believe the time is right for an attack on Gavlessa. I am no priest, but I fear this is a foreboding sign that we may be at risk for descending into a time of darkness, should we neglect this news."

"There is no risk, Truson." King Noldar said. "Dragons are untamed and malevolent beasts, there behavior is unpredictable and destructive, but it's rare. We will proceed with our plans to destroy Gavlessa, plans that will prevent this darkness from spreading."

"Your Grace," Truson began, perhaps too firmly, "if we thin our resources, we will have nothing to contribute should these attacks be a sign of worse things to come."

"We will have no resources to contribute, Sir Truson," the king said, his face reddening and his voice raising, "because it is not my will to contribute any troops to protect other city states, be they Y-Kewnor, or Frins Casicon, or anyone else who stood by as Gavlessa threatened our very existence. Our focus remains on the destruction of those desert barbarians."

"Your Grace," Truson began, "you are a Palidnia, a family long associated with The Divine Empress's Knights, your ancestors were among the first knights to create the order, protectors of not only the people of your kingdom, but protectors of all of Allyoshmar."

"The Divine Empress's Knights?! Protectors?!" The king shouted, leaping to his feet. "Where was this protection for my daughter?! My only daughter?! Where was this protection against the threats from Gavlessa that put me in the position to either give her up or have my entire kingdom enslaved or killed?! The Divine Empress's Knights are protectors of nothing but their own assets. The real threat is the murderous savages of Gavlessa and there's only one person doing anything about it. Me!"

The king took a brief pause and, exhausted, sat back down. Truson, prepared for anything, after hearing Noldar's fury, was momentarily relieved, but still on edge.

"Sir Truson," the king continued, "I understand the misplaced duty you and your fellow knights have, but they are not your family. I want to give you the chance to join those who are, those who have been there for you, those who need you now. If you chose to fight for Lees Naglos, I will offer you the Senior Knight General seat at my round table. My army will be yours to command. I have great respect for the wisdom, skill, and honor of The Divine Empress's Knights and offer the hand of friendship to any who wish to join me."

A silence echoed through the hall where the two men sat. The king picked up his mead and drank. Truson traced his thumb across the silver plate of armor on his forearm.

"And what should happen," Truson began, "to those who decline your offer, Your Grace?"

"Those who refuse," King Noldar said, "shall be choosing allegiance to The Divine Empress's Knights over the kingdom of Less Naglos and therefore treasonous. There is only one punishment for treason and it will be carried out tomorrow morning."

The words hit Truson hard. He could not believe what he had heard. The king was, essentially, declaring war not only on Gavlessa, but also, for all intents and purposes, on The Divine Empress's Knights.

"What of the priests and priestesses?" Truson asked.

"I love The Divine Empress with all of my heart," the king said. "The Temple of The Divine Empress poses no threat against this kingdom. It is a jewel of our city. The priests and priestesses will not be punished."

After the ultimatum the king had given him for the knights, Truson expected the same for the Temple, but the king's words seemed both sincere and fair, which made his ultimatum seem less like the tyranny of a mad man and more like a person who was hurt, but trying, while struggling through pain, to seek justice and safety for himself and for his kingdom in spite of The Divine Empress's Knights refusing to do so. Truson had never been more conflicted. Distant, he thanked the king for his time and left.

Truson had a meeting arranged at the Temple. He was the leader of the Lees Naglos chapter of The Divine Empress's Knights, but he had no jurisdiction over the Temple or its clergy. He may have been inviting mass hysteria, but this was something everyone needed to hear all at once. He first explained the situation in Y-Kewnor. Then refreshed everyone's memory on the events leading up to this decision, so they would have the context necessary to understand why people did what they did. The knights' immediate reactions were strong and divided. The high priest of Lees Naglos insisted, on behalf of the Lees Naglos Temple, that they have time to confer with the Temple of The Divine Empress in Y-Kewnor. The high priestess insisted, on behalf of The Divine Empress, that they confer with the Temple of The Divine Empress in Iclanca, deep in the North, which was, officially, the highest Temple to The Divine Empress in all of Allyoshmar. Truson reminded them that, while the priests and priestesses had the luxury of time, the knights had only until the next morning to make their choice. The high priest and the high priestess agreed that, whatever the knights decided to do, they would remain in the good graces of the Temple, but the Temple, on the other hand, did not want to be associated with either their separation from The Divine Empress's Knights or from Lees Naglos. They were on their own.

The knights debated for hours on the correct course of action, congregating in the first few rows of pews, long after the priests and priestesses left the meeting. They wondered, if they chose Lees Naglos for the time being, if The Divine Empress's Knights would label them as treasonous and not let them return later. Some felt more of an allegiance to the people of Lees Naglos. Some felt more of an allegiance to The Divine Empress's Knights. Some were more afraid of the king. Some were more afraid of The Divine Empress's Knights. If they chose to side with The Divine Empress's Knights, they didn't have much time to devise a plan other than waiting to be slaughtered the following morning. Some suggested they leave immediately. Some actually left. Some decided to stay and fight, resigning themselves to an honorable death defending the Order. Though the knights continued to debate, the time had come for Truson, as their leader, to make a final statement.

"The sun has set," Truson said, turning the attention of the knights, who were arguing amongst themselves in the pews, back to him. "We must now be realistic about our options. If you wish to remain a Divine Empress's Knight, you must leave Lees Naglos at once and to do so as surreptitiously as possible. My suggestion is to head north to Frins Casicon. You will not arrive until nightfall tomorrow, but, if you ride hard, you will be beyond the reach of Lees Naglos before your absence is noticed. I have not commanded you to stay and fight so you will not be punished for cowardice. Those of you who wish to remain behind in the name of The Divine Empress's Knights must already be aware that choosing to do so is choosing to lay down your life. I cannot justly command you to do so, and I ask that you not think contemptuously of your knight-brothers who do not wish to join you. For those of you for whom The Divine Empress's Knights is not the most truthful way to serve The Divine Empress, I grant you clemency from the punishment for abandoning, but I cannot command you to change your allegiance. Each of you has a personal decision to make. Let no knight or king hold sway over you; the decision is between you and The Divine Empress. I, Sir Truson Everly, High Knight in the House of Diligence and knight-shepard of the Lees Naglos Chapter of The Divine Empress's Knights, defer any charge over you and resign from command. Please know I love you all and request you leave me immediately to Commune in silence with The Divine Empress."

Wondering if he had spoken the right words, Truson turned from the knights and knelt before the altar. He heard feet shuffling, but no one spoke. Truson did what he could to absorb the temple, so he might also absorb the gift of wisdom from The Divine Empress. The chapel of the Temple was designed, as were all the chapels of the Temples of The Divine Empress, to represent the great hall of the Palace of Light. On the wall before him was The Source Window, an expansive window with bands of different colored glass swirling in an enormous pattern to represent The Source. When the sun shined through the window, it lit the entire chapel and the expansive white marble room shimmered with color. In front The Source Window, the statue of The Divine Empress towered over the room, more beautiful than any woman imaginable, with a wise lips, kind eyes, and peacefully outstretched arms. In front of the statue of The Divine Empress, a single candle flickered on the white marble altar. The Humility Candle demonstrated how faint and easily extinguishable any light was compared to The Source. As Truson prayed for guidance, the Humility Candle was the brightest object and, in fact, the only source of light.

***

Teryessa awoke, drenched in sweat, her sheets twisted up around her armored body, to find herself in her room in Orc Doola. Lying in bed, she wondered if she would be treated with a hero's welcome for slaying a dragon when she returned to Lees Naglos. She looked upon herself, bruised, cut, filthy, blood-soaked, and she knew she wouldn't; she'd be treated like an anomalous and undesirable aberration; she'd be quickly and quietly married off or locked away in a tower like her mother was; that was what happened to survivors. Remembering the dragons and the necromancer Broch-Isha spoke of, she imagined herself married off to some old nobleman, living a quietly miserable life, waiting for the day the dragons would return for her. Would she welcome the release? She couldn't go home; the life she had known was over; she was being hunted and the only way for her to survive was to keep moving. What had been stripped from her she could never retrieve. Why did this happen to her? Would she always be on the run? What could life offer her now? She needed answers and, based on what she remembered of the two dragons' conversation, she had a good idea of where to start: Y-Kewnor.

Teryessa gathered her things and left. She intended to bathe, since she wanted so badly to scrub the terrible filth from her body, hoping it would make her cleaner, but she couldn't bear to remove her armor, so, without looking in any mirrors, she washed her face in the small basin in the room. On her way out of the inn, she purchased several more bottles of numbendria from the barkeep.

It was important that Teryessa get supplies before she left town. She wasn't certain what she would run into between there and Y-Kewnor. Purchasing food and camping gear wasn't a problem, neither was finding a decent horse. She also purchased a sword, a cross bow and twice as many crossbow bolts as the shop keep said she needed. Anytime anyone asked her where she was going, she said she was heading south to Xcesemtia, in order to mislead any potential robbers.

Orc Doola, or Orc Town, was named after the race that once lived there, but was wiped out during the genocides of the last Palidnian Empire. Orc Doola was repopulated by a small group of humans who enjoyed city life, but, for one reason or another, either preferred or were forced to live on the outskirts of the reach of the great cities of Allyoshmar. Since then, the town had grown a population of people who, considering themselves to be natives of the town, were comfortable with the cold and altitude, and were accustomed to the perils of living on the border of the Wild. It was a small, but important, little hamlet seated in the last valley before the western ridge of the Dragonsback Mountains grew too steep to build any permanent structures.

Four roads led from Orc Doola. The northwest road led diagonally to Frins Casicon. The southwest road led diagonally to Lees Naglos. The southern road led to Gavlessa and, beyond that, to Xcesemtia. The fourth road, the northeast road, was the only known road across the Wild, and required traveling on the only known path across the Dragonsback Mountains. While Era-Mosa was considered the Eastern Wildgate, Orc Doola was called the Western Wildgate. Anyone wishing to travel across the Wild between the Freelands and the Kingdoms of the West, an activity that was becoming less popular, given the recent popularity of travel by boat, had to pass through Orc Doola, so the Orc Doolans made their livings by feeding, renting rooms, and selling goods to travelers.

When the morning's light was still new, Teryessa had already finished her errands and was prepared to leave Orc Doola as she approached the northeast gate, the most heavily fortified gate in the town, the only gate to remain closed at all times... the Western Wildgate. She, on her horse, waited for the gatekeeper.

"G'day, lass." the gatekeeper said. "Traveling cross the Wild, are ya?"

"Yes," said Teryessa, "How much coin do I owe you for the toll?"

"Depends," said the gatekeeper. "How many travelers?"

"Just myself."

"Beggin' your pardon for me off'rin unsolicited advice," the gatekeeper said, "but the Wild ain't no place to be traveling on your lonesome, specially for a pretty young girl. If ya don't know nobody, I could recommend some trustworthy sell-swords. Truth be told, they do give me a percent o their fees for my recommendations, but they is a good ol lot o mates that wouldn't let nothin' happen to ya our there."

Teryessa thought for a moment, wondering if she ought to consider the possibility of sell-swords guiding her. She realized, as she mulled over the idea, that, despite the gatekeeper's recommendation, she couldn't trust these sell-swords. Her hands trembled and froze just thinking about being in close quarters, in the middle of the Wild, with a group of strange men.

"No pardon needed," Teryessa said, keeping her tone even, despite being shaken up. "Thank you for your honesty and advice. But their services won't be necessary. I am quite capable of this journey."

"Furthermore," she added, to make certain this gatekeeper wasn't also participatory in any conspiracies to take advantage of solitary travelers, "I'm perfectly capable of defending myself against any opportunistic robbers seeking easy coin or bed. This sword just slaughtered Wurm Ahkk-Rhall, who was in all likeliness a nuisance no one in this town has been able to eliminate. If a pack of fool brigands value their lives so little that they wish to challenge a dragon slayer, let them. I'll cut them into ribbons and return their heads to whomever sent them my way, before killing him even more slowly and painfully than the rest."

Teryessa did all she could to keep her face cool and her voice even during this bluff that was, perhaps, completely unnecessary; however, on the inside, she was trembling. Necessary or not, the gatekeeper opened the gate for her for just one coin. She was certain he wouldn't send anyone after her, for fear of his own life, but she didn't know if the word would spread that a dragon slayer passed through, which would be verified if anyone when up to Ahkk-Rhall's cave, which they certainly would. She feared that word spreading of a dragon slayer could be dangerous. The word could get back to the other dragons. They would know who she was and which direction she had gone in. They could come after her. Word could get back to Lees Naglos and her father might deduce her identity, go after her, and put himself in danger. A million horrible possibilities raced through her mind as she left Orc Doola. She could not stop imagining these things as she travelled up the thin pass towards the snowy mountains.

The foliage grew sparse as Teryessa approached the timberline and she noticed two lone trees ahead. That was the first time the thought occurred to her that everything was in pairs. She was taken by Prince Grell then by Wurm Ahkk-Rhall. If this was true, and it had to be, then no more tragedies could happen to her. It wasn't as though she decided to believe this. It was just that she had to. Everything had to be in pairs or else something horrible would happen again. If she didn't maintain pairs in everything she did, the it would all fall apart and she would be taken away and brutalized again. Soon, she found herself counting to the steps of the horse. One. Two. One. Two. One. Two. And so on.

Teryessa realized, as she rode from the timberline to the frostline, that revealing her identity to the gate-keep, which she had inadvertently done, jeopardized herself, her kingdom, and her father. She decided she needed to create a new identity. In addition, she realized, by having two names, she also was satisfying the rule of pairs. She chose a name that satisfied the rule of pairs even further, 'Matera,' which meant 'two' in Balysh-Tong. Furthermore, she noted, she was taken from her home on Vari-Matera-a, the night of two moons, which, she was certain, was evidence of the rule of pairs and proof that she had chosen the right name. From that point forward, she would introduce herself as Matera, a warrior from Sima Watusia, one of the twin cities on Twin Lake, which was between two rivers.

Teryessa decided to stop for a break before she reached the frostline to eat lunch and practice her weapons. Riding a horse had been no problem since equestrian training was a noble thing for a young princess to do, she had excelled at it, and was a master rider before she was even the height of a horse's saddle. Weapons, on the other hand, were new to her. Of course, she had snuck the occasional lesson, as a child, from some of her father's Knight Generals who fancied the innocently precocious, curious, and energetic nature she had as a child, but those weren't real lesson and stopped as soon as she got to the age where she was expected to behave as a princess, not a tom boy. So, after eating, she drew her sword and looked for something to chop at, but found very little and wished she had thought of this before she had travelled beyond the timberline.

Finding nothing solid to chop at, Teryessa decided she would simply chop at the air, at imaginary foes. The sword was heavier than she had imagine it would be and it aggravated her injured wrist. She realized that, when she did this as a child, the Knight Generals must have let her use a dagger or some very small blade. She also realized, standing on her feet, that the armor was quite heavy and tiring to move around in. Her injured ankle made it difficult for her to stand for any duration of time. With her arms growing tired, her wrist sore, and her ankle throbbing with pain, Teryessa took a huge swing and found herself slipping and falling to the ground, where she heard her horse whinny with delight.

"Oh, you find that humorous?" she asked, walking over to her horse. "Aren't you just a joker?!"

Standing there, alone on a path in the Dragonsback Mountains, in the Wild, she realized this horse would be her only company, her only companion, her only friend. She was a solid horse, a mountain horse, which were the result of cross breeding the lean and obedient Naglos horses, which were terrible in the mountains, with the untamed and muscular orc horses, which were wonderful in the mountains. She had a grey coat with a short mane and muscular legs leading up to her deep chest. Her eyes were black, soulful, and mischievous. She was clearly a bit more orc horse than Naglos horse, but Teryessa touched her nose to her horse's and couldn't be happier with her choice. Her horse returned the loving gaze, then nipped at her face, whinnying another laugh when Teryessa had to quickly back away to avoid the snapping horse teeth.

"Joker," Teryessa said, "I'll call you Joker."

Joker stomped her foot with glee.

Before heading on the trail again, Teryessa intended to practice her crossbow. She rationed herself to eight practice shots, stacking the bolts, in pairs, in two rows by two columns on the ground. Making mental note that, because of the repetitions of the two rule, eight would be an important number; she must always possess eight bolts in her quiver, no more, no less. She chose a large rock off in the distance as her target, knowing the bolts would likely shatter on impact, but willing to sacrifice them to become more skilled with the weapon. Her first shot sailed high in the air, as she was not prepared for the force the crossbow would exert. Her second shot wasn't any closer to the mark, but she had learned better how to hold the crossbow and was expecting the impact. Her third shot was close to the mark, but did not hit. Her fourth through eighth bolts all hit the rock and shattered. It seemed pretty easy, she thought.

After her lunch and practice break, Teryessa was back on the trail and soon found herself crossing the frost line. Because of the frigid wind, Teryessa had already covered herself in a heavy grey cloak to keep warm, but found out quickly after crossing the frost line that, with the drop in temperature and the snow and ice pelting her face, she was going to need more warmth. She had furs in her saddle bag, but decided to wait until she stopped to camp for the night to fetch them because the trail had become too steep and narrow and she dared not take her eyes from the path even for a moment. She continued on.

She stopped riding before dark because she had found a cave and was afraid riding on the steep and narrow path would be too dangerous in the dark. There was nothing to burn in the cave. There hadn't been any wood for miles. Teryessa wasn't able to warm herself by a fire, but she tucked herself deep into the corner and covered herself with every piece of fur she had bought. Alone, deep in the corner of the cave she tried to sleep, but found it impossible. Being in a cave, all she could think about was Ahkk-Rhall's cave and what had happened to her there. She tried to remind herself that she had destroyed him, but the thought did her no good. In the silence of the cave, with no sound, save the wind blowing forcefully outside, she became lost in her thoughts and she asked herself what she was doing. The whole day she had acted brave and put on a fearless face, but for whom, she wondered. She decided it was herself she was trying to fool into believing she was brave. In the dark of the cave, Teryessa cowered, terrified that every gust of wind was the wing of a dragon. She decided that Matera, her new alter ego, had to be fearless and, while she didn't become instantly fearless, that thought relaxed her enough to remember to drink some numbendria. Soon, doped on the sweet, spicy drink, she drifted off.

FOG OF FATE

Resting in a valley on the Great Sea, mornings in Lees Naglos were often cloaked in a thick soupy mist. That particular morning, Sir Truson Everly could barely see a few feet in front of him as he entered the Temple for breakfast. He wondered how many of his knights left for Frins Casicon. He hoped all of them. He hope those remaining had chosen to betray their oath and live. He hope King Noldar was only bluffing. Much to his dismay, forty knights trickled in to the Temple, each of them keeping to themselves. They all appeared lost in thought, but the dread on their faces failed to reveal whether is was the dread of men about to die or the dread men about to betray their brothers.

Truson watched a young priest whisper something to the high priest and high priestess, who nodded solemnly in return. The young priest approached Truson next and, shaking, told him the king and his men were waiting in the courtyard.

The mist had meandered into the chapel and rolled across the floor from the open door to the courtyard. Truson stopped for a moment to kneel before The Divine Empress and pray for guidance, before walking towards the light of the open door to the courtyard.

At one end of the courtyard, a column-lined outdoor space, for worshippers to gather, stood the white marble steps to the chapel. At the other end, an enormous white pylon housed the gate between the temple and the rest of Lees Naglos. White rocks covered the ground of the courtyard, intersected by a white marble walkway, two hundred paces long, from the pylon to the chapel, representing the path, through the snow, to the the Palace of Light. Truson exited the chapel and stood atop the steps. The king waited in the middle of the courtyard, flanked by his Knight Generals. The king's army lined the pylon wall and the two side walls of the courtyard.

Truson walked down the steps and stopped, waiting for the king to say the first word as The Divine Empress's Knights entered the courtyard from the chapel, but remained on the top of the steps behind him.

"I imagine," King Noldar said, "you have explained to your knight-brothers the terms of my offer."

"I have," said Truson, barely able to speak.

"Well, then," the king declared from halfway across the courtyard, "The Divine Empress's Knights have, time and time again, refused to help in protecting Lees Naglos from real and eminent outside threats, carelessly endangering the lives of all who live here. They then have the audacity to further condemn us by insisting we refrain from protecting ourselves, so we can contribute to an invisible war in Y-Kewnor. They would throw us to the dogs of Gavlessa in order to benefit their popularity in a city on the other side of these lands. Does this seem like a noble order sworn to protect the good people of Allyoshmar? Does this seem like an order sworn to do the bidding of The Divine Empress? I say no. I say The Divine Empress's Knights no longer represent the people of Lees Naglos and no longer represent the Temple of The Divine Empress!"

The king's words rang through out the courtyard, echoing off of the white marble walls and shaking the pillars that lined those walls. Truson looked straight ahead during the speech, much of which seemed to be directed at him. The knights shifted uncomfortably, wondering if they would all be executed immediately.

"But I am, I pray, a loving, reasonable, and merciful king. I know that you, the brave and honorable men before me, stand for what is right and stand for the true will of The Divine Empress. I do not hold you accountable for the actions of politicians in Y-Kewnor. I grant you clemency and I invite you to stand with me, stand with these men beside me, and stand with the good people of Lees Naglos. We are all, born here or not, Palidnians. Take your place in our army; take your place in our family."

Everyone waited, in silence, for someone to make the first move. Truson continued looking forward at the king, unable to move or speak. He could feel everyone's eyes on him: his knight-brothers behind him, all of the soldiers in front of him, and King Noldar, himself. Truson closed his eyes and prayed silently to The Divine Empress that he was making the right choice and that she would protect him. He stepped forward.

Truson could hear the gasps of shock and the sighs of relief. He drew his sword, wondering if an arrow would immediately strike him dead, but, with the king's hand up, insisting no soldier take action, the archers waited. Truson continued breathing and walking. When he was no more than ten paces from the king, he dropped to his knees and rested his sword on the palms of his hands, offering his submission to King Noldar. There, he waited, head down, and prayed for the lives of his knight-brothers, prayed they would join him. Soon he heard the shuffling of feet over the white stones.

"Sir Truson Everly," the king said, "please stand."

Truson stood with his sword laying across his open palms. King Noldar approached him, drawing his own sword. In this moment, the king could cut him down in a flash. King Noldar laid his sword on top of Truson's palms.

Noldar, leaned in and, speaking so quietly that only Truson heard him, said, "I know there are still countless dark days ahead, but your pledge of loyalty is a ray of light through the gloom. You may not be a son I have sired, but you are the son The Divine Empress has granted me, nevertheless."

Truson heard the words, but found himself unable to think of a response. The king spared his life, a base consolation for the nightmare he endured as the conflict between survival and righteousness raged in his heart. He wanted to tell the king to listen to him and stop this insanity, but he said nothing.

Noldar, addressing Truson formally, bellowed, "Sir Truson Everly, I, King Noldar Palidnia, accept you into my Kingdom, into my army, into my family, and into my most esteemed collection of advisors, my Knight Generals. I hereby name you Senior Knight General and Commander of the Royal Army."

Truson's insides swirled. To proceeded any further would break his oath to The Divine Empress, but backing out he would be forfeiting his life.

"I, Sir Truson Everly," Truson said, "accept."

Truson felt dead inside. His emotions made no sense. He could always make sense of his emotions. As with fighting, he as alway able to process his emotions rationally. In this moment, however, he felt lost, but he remained in control of his exterior and he handed the king back his sword, completing the ceremony and officially taking command of the Royal Army.

"The rest of you who have stepped forward to kneel before me," the king said, "please rise and join the ranks of your new brothers in the Royal Army."

Truson turned to see the knights who had joined him. There were probably fifteen of them, fewer than Truson had expected and far fewer than he had hoped. He watched as they hurried to the back of the back of the group of Knight Generals flanking the king.

"To the rest of you," the king said, "I can only assume your position means you are refusing my offer and are, instead, aligning with an organization now considered to be an enemy of this kingdom. Please step forward and face your fate with honor."

Before the knights could react, the high priestess stepped forward, standing in front of the knights.

"Your Grace," the high priestess said, "in the name of The Divine Empress you may not have these men executed within the walls of the Temple. It is known by us all that no blood may be spilt in Her home."

The high priestess's courage served as a touchstone. Soon she was joined by the high priest and what seemed to be all of the priests and priestesses of the Lees Naglos Temple of The Divine Empress.

"Your Grace," the high priest said, with all of his priests and priestesses behind him, standing between the king's soldiers and the knights who refused to pledge allegiance to the king, "we beg for you to reconsider taking arms against the people of your own faith."

The king, clearly furious, but keeping his raging temper in check, said, "Priests and priestesses, my quarrel is not with you or The Divine Empress, to whom I, too, am but a humble servant. I have prayed to Her, begging for a peaceful solution and, when none was given and I was certain this was the only just course of action, I prayed to Her for forgiveness. Please don't think this gives me any pleasure, but I know The Divine Empress is behind me and I will see those who are treasonous punished. Any who stand in my way or stand beside those who do will be considered treasonous, as well. Now, return to your chapel or step forward and meet your fate."

It was the young priest who had alerted Truson to the arrival of the king that morning that stepped forward. Truson didn't even know the boy's name. The young priest, trembling with fear, stepped forward again.

"Young man," the king said, "do not test my patience. I am your king and I command you to turn around and return to your chapel. If you take another step forward it will be your last."

"I serve The Divine Empress." the boy said, barely able to move his chattering teeth, and took another step.

It happened in an instant. There was only one arrow, but it was suddenly sticking out of the young priest's chest, through his white robes, into his heart. Truson Everly was probably the only person there able to hear the twang of the bowstring, isolate the whoosh of the arrow, and watch as the arrow travelled across the courtyard and into its target. Truson's heart shattered, as a thin river of blood trickled towards him along the white marble path.

The high priestess wailed and crumbled to her knees. One by one, the priests and priestesses shuffled back inside, heads hung low with the shame of abandoning the knights, the grief of losing one of their own, and the horror of what they were certain was about to happen. Only the high priestess and the high priest remained in front of the knights. She held tightly to his hand and gave a squeeze, thanking him for standing by her, knowing what it would cost.

The high priest looked at the high priestess, tears in his eyes, and said, "I'm sorry," as he let her hand drop and joined the others inside.

"The others have returned to the chapel, high priestess," Noldar said, walking towards the high priestess, "Will you not join them, so we may conclude our business?"

"I will not," the high priestess said defiantly, summoning all the courage she could to be strong and regal in the name of The Divine Empress.

"Very well," King Noldar said. He stood there for a moment, then turned back to the soldiers with a defeated look on his face. As the king walked towards the Knight Generals, the solders, and the knights that defected, Truson prayed the king would change his mind and allow the knights to go free. The king continued walking, by Truson, through the group of Knight Generals, and towards the pylon.

Just when Truson was nearly certain King Noldar had granted the other knights clemency, the king, without looking, said, "Execute them."

A flurry of arrows raced over Truson's head. The twenty-five knights and the high priestess didn't stand a chance. Within seconds, each of them had been hit by multiple arrows. The knights scrambled to escape. They tried to return to the chapel or hide behind pillars, some even charged towards the soldiers with their swords drawn, only making a few steps before being hit with enough arrows to drop them to the ground, but not the high priestess. The high priestess only held out her arms, welcoming more arrows to hit her. It was the arrow that hit her heart that finally dropped her.

As the arrows stopped flying, the wind shifted and blew the remaining morning mist back out to sea. With the air now crystal clear, Truson looked upon the carnage. There were bodies everywhere. The sight of the white courtyard smeared with blood forever stained Truson's mind. It was a massacre.

One of the Knight Generals asked Truson's permission to return the soldiers to their posts and Truson, lost in his thought, mumbled something and waved permission. The soldiers marched off, and the knights who defected, somberly followed.

Truson, alone in the blood stained courtyard, muttered to himself, "What have I done?"

***

In the center of the Guardsman's Smile, where the crescent of barracks was thickest, there was a practice field. It wasn't lush and green like the Palace Tournament Field, which was only used for picnics and the occasional fair. Instead, it was simply a two hundred square yard gravelly area used for practice by the Kewnorian Guard. The land, originally donated to the Kewnorian Guard by the Plune family hundreds of annuals earlier and named Plune Field, was surrounded by a waist-high split-rail fence, to prevent unmounted horses from escaping into the town should they become spooked during a cavalry exercise. Though the guardsmen would journey to the fields outside of Y-Kewnor for major exercises, Plune Field would house much of the daily training for the Kewnorian Guard that required utilizing troop formations and battlefield strategy, leaving the hand to hand and swordsmanship training to the series of smaller fields, all named for their donors, that were spread out along that eastern crescent of the city. That morning, Plune Field, the Guardsman's Smile, and all of Y-Kewnor were blanketed in a thick fog as Aiwren Wayde stood in a line of new recruits, waiting to find out why he had been ordered to report there.

When Aiwren had arrived at Cutter's tent earlier that morning, two very serious guardsmen waited outside, as though they were guarding it. Inside, there were two more guardsmen guarding the door, while a man he later learned was Sergeant Halibon Hibosi spoke to Cutter.

"I'm telling you, he's not ready," Cutter implored, "none of them are. Their role is to mend and stitch."

"And you know, as well as I do," Halibon said, "in a time of war, even the stitchers have their opportunity to find glory on the battlefield."

"Yes," Cutter argued, "after they've been trained."

"Look," Halibon said, "I haven't come here do debate with you. This order comes from above me. The Kewnorian Guard appreciates your civilian service, but I'm not required to explain Kewnorian Guard orders to you."

Aiwren couldn't believe he had just seen Cutter get pushed around like that. Cutter, Aiwren knew, could cut that man down in a second. He wondered what business this sergeant could possibly want with any of the tailors. He wondered what good they could possibly do.

"Aiwren Wayde," Halibon called, to Aiwren's surprise.

Aiwren slowly raised his hand and said, "That's me."

"I am a superior, Recruit Wayde," Halibon said. "You will afford me the due respect and address me formally."

"Yes, sir." Aiwren replied, completely confused by what title goes to what person. Back in Ribeln there were no 'sirs' or 'lords' or 'misters' or 'lieges.' In Y-Kewnor, he seemed to always get all of the titles wrong and worried that he'd never know what to call anyone.

"You're in the seamsters platoon, yet you've had only one prior day of tailor apprenticeship?" Halibon asked.

"Yes, My Liege." Aiwren said.

"Come with me."

Aiwren followed Halibon to several other tents. Each tent belonged to a trade platoon and each time Halibon selected the least experienced person in his or her trade and ordered them to join him. Soon, Aiwren felt as though he was simply being led on some shameful parade used to show the rest of the guardsmen in the barracks who the least important people were. Eventually, he found himself, along with about forty other recruits lined up against the fence opposite the observation booth on Plune Field.

Halibon had instructed each of the recruits to take their turn to walk across the field and stand before the observation booth. Aiwren wasn't sure what was happening over there because he couldn't see or hear very well and the anxiety of the anticipation made the wait feel eternal.

"Whut trade is you?" a heavy set young man with a soft face more than a head taller than Aiwren asked. "I noticed they was only picking recruits wif trades."

"I noticed, too," said Aiwren. "I'm in the tailor platoon. Are you a blacksmith?"

"Me?" the boy asked, blushing. "Oh, eavens no. I'm a gardener."

"A gardener?!" a voice laughed. It was Roderick Blakely, the guardsman who had punched Aiwren in the gut the other night.

"What good is a gardener?! Perhaps you could slay a dragon with a potato. Actually, you sort of look like a potato. What do you think about that, Potato?"

Roderick and his friends, the rough girl and the muscular boy, laughed. Aiwren thought about saying something, but he wondered if he would get into more trouble if he made a scene. Because of his hesitation, he was too late.

"How do you suppose an army is going to eat without a gardener to feed the troops or feed the animals that feed the troops, you idiot?" a girl snapped. "Do you have even the slightest notion how many wars, not battles, but wars have been lost due to starvation? Perhaps, if there were more gardeners, we'd require fewer gravediggers, which wouldn't be a bad thing since you're all sick little perverts who stink of rot because you bugger with the corpses."

Aiwren didn't know who this girl was, but he thought her response was positively fantastic and couldn't help but laugh out loud. She was petite with dark skin, neck-length black hair combed back tight, an angular but beautiful face, and dark eyes that pierced whomever she was looking at, reminding Aiwren of a hawk.

Roderick, flabbergasted, stammered, "How do you know I'm- Well, what's your trade, girl? Baking cookies?"

"I'm a falconer." the girl said.

"A falconer?!" Roderick said, "I don't see a falcon," but he was interrupted by getting called to the observation booth.

"That was quite humorous," Aiwren said, "I'm Aiwren."

"I'm a funny girl," the girl said. "My name's Serafina T'shona and just to save you the trouble, none of that frilly talk will work if you're fixin' to woo me. You're not my type."

"I wasn't trying to woo you and meant you no disrespect," Aiwren said. "Wait, you think my speech is frilly?"

"Yeah." said 'Potato.' "you sound like one of them lords."

"No." Aiwren insisted, trying to not talk frilly, "I'm not a lord. At all. I'm a dairy farmer. My name's Aiwren."

"Gregory Goodroot," the big lad said, "Pleased ta meet your acquaintances. Wif a name like Goodroot, you know I know me vegetables. That's what me da always says anyway. Why do you s'pose they're interviewing us tradespeople?"

"Because," Serafina said, "they're looking for the worst of the worst, trying to find out who's expendable. They probably want to find out where the dragons live by tying us to the end of a rope, lowering us down into caves, and pulling us back out to see if we've been roasted. If you want my advice, when they call you up there, you better make yourself look useful."

The thought of being bait for a dragon terrified Aiwren. His stomach sank and he hoped Serafina was mistaken about the purpose of this gathering, but he didn't have too long to think about it. He was called up next.

Aiwren found himself standing in front of the observation booth, where, behind a desk, with a quill in one hand and an enormous goblet of wine in the other, sat a man dressed in fine clothes. He was handsomely thin with pale skin, dark wavy hair, and light blue eyes. Aiwren was certain he was a lord. Beside him, stood Halibon.

"Aiwren Wayde? The lord said.

"Yes, My Lord, My Liege." Aiwren replied, not knowing which title to use if the man was both noble and military.

The man rolled his eyes at this and said, "You're a tailor with no experience? What do you do, exactly?"

"I mostly just sweep, My Lord, My Liege." Aiwren replied, immediately regretting how useless he sounded. "I know it doesn't seem like much, but I've only just arrived from Ribeln where I've been working on my family's dairy farm my entire life. So I know a lot about cows and milk, My Lord, My Liege."

"Fascinating. Why are you telling me this, Wayde?"

"Well, My Lord, My Liege, I just wanted you to know I wasn't useless."

"You have a sword," the lord said, "but your records indicate no battle training."

Aiwren thought of Cutter telling him he mustn't tell anybody of the training, but he was also worried that if he didn't say something to sound useful, he'd find himself at the end of a rope face to face with a dragon. He had wanted excitement, but that wasn't at all what he had in mind.

"I can fight." Aiwren said, "I swear I can fight."

The lord whispered something to Halibon, who climbed over the fence and drew his sword. Halibon was only slightly taller than Aiwren and looked to be nearly forty annuals old, but he was quite muscular and appeared as though he'd been in his share of fights.

"First to one point. Halibon, don't kill him."

Aiwren drew his sword. His hand trembled. This was very different from swordplay with his father or the training Cutter had been giving him. This was a real sword fight with a stranger, a cruel stranger. Although the lord instructed Halibon not to kill him, Aiwren knew how things like this happened with men like Halibon... the same way they went with bullies like Roderick and Quinnt.

Standing firmly on the ground, Halibon swung his sword hard. Aiwren wasn't expecting the attack so soon, but he raised his blade to parry it and he nearly lost his balance from the impact on his sword. Then he remembered his stance.

Unlike, Halibon, Aiwren bent his knees, lowering his stance and shifting his weight forward. When he changed how he stood, the way he saw things changed slightly. His eyes felt more open. His breathing changed. He saw things. He noticed Halibon's shoulders tighten and knew he was about to strike again and he guessed it would be in the same spot. Aiwren raised his sword to block.

It felt like forever before Halibon's blade came down on his own and he wondered why the man was moving so slowly. Halibon swung again and, this time, Aiwren merely stepped aside, which reminded Aiwren to move his feet.

The next time Halibon swung, Aiwren predicted it, shuffled to the right of the arcing blade, rather than blocking, and sliced his sword across Halibon's ribs, careful not to do it with too much force. Halibon, expecting the momentum of his sword to be stopped by the impact against Aiwren's, not only got hit in the ribs, but also stumbled forward, nearly falling to the ground.

The lord clapped and Halibon fumed. Aiwren was dismissed and rejoined Serafina and Gregory by the fence, just as shocked as anyone by what he had done.

After all of the recruits had approached the lord, he walked across the field, Halibon by his side.

"If you haven't guessed," the lord said, "you're the worst of the worst. Congratulations. With the state the Kewnorian Guard is in, that's quite an accomplishment. If I call your name, please step forward."

The lord opened his book and started reading names. Aiwren watched, in horror, as young men and women stepped forward, most of them not realizing what horrible death, Aiwren was certain awaited them. He was a little pleased when Roderick and his buddies, Brunff and Kazerra, were called forward, but was sad when he saw Serafina and Gregory called forward. Next, to his dismay, Aiwren's name was called. Horrified, he stepped forward.

"All the rest of you," the lord said, "return to your stations at once and whatever useless busywork you occupy yourselves with ."

The others scurried off, some disappointed some relieved.

"You," the lord said to the remaining group once the others had left, "are the best of the worst of the worst. That's why I've chosen you to be in my platoon."

"Wait," Aiwren heard someone say and turned to see Cutter running on to the field. "Please take me in place of Aiwren Wayde."

"If this is your grandfather, Recruit Wayde," the lord said, "please ask him to return home at once."

"He's not my grandfather, My Lord, My Liege."

"My name is Ulysses James Cutter, former Sergeant Major of the Kewnorian Guard My Liege. I wish to reinstate my service and volunteer for Recruit Wayde's position."

"You can't do that, Cutter!" Halibon said.

"You can't do that, My Liege," the lord corrected. "Sergeant Major Cutter is reinstated and your superior officer, not that I adhere to honorifics, which I was about to address before everyone decided to reenact such histrionic drama. Sergeant Major Ulysses James Cutter, I thank you for volunteering to be in my troop and I accept you. Sergeant Halibon Hibosi, you will suffice as my Sergeant. Everyone else, you are no longer Recruits. You are now Privates, except for Recruit Wayde. Recruit Wayde, because of the circumstances, this platoon has afforded me some leniency in the rules, I am promoting you to Corporal. I hope you'll forgive the absence of the pomp and circumstance usually awarded, but, I don't find it very interesting, which brings me to myself. I am Lieutenant Jocund Plune. I am not a lord, so please don't insult me with my father's foolish title. You may be wondering what perilous mission you have been chosen for. What task was so grandiose that a new platoon be formed to execute it? We, my good men and woman, will be transporting a vacationing princess back to her home, but don't get too excited; the princess is an asshole. So sleep up. We leave from this spot at sunrise. Don't tell a soul."

Aiwren quickly said good-bye to his new friends, Serafina and Gregory, and hurried over to Cutter.

"Permission to refer to you as My Liege, now, My Liege?" Aiwren asked, thrilled to be going on an adventure with his new friends and Cutter.

Cutter, looking bereft, didn't even chuckle at Aiwren's joke, but, instead, lost in his thoughts, walked off without saying a word.

Aiwren, chasing after him, asked, "Is something troubling you, My Liege?"

"Stop calling me that!" Cutter yelled, startling Aiwren with his anger. "I'm sorry. No, nothing's wrong. I'm afraid I don't have it in me to practice tonight and have some affairs to arrange before we leave. I'm sure you'll want to celebrate with your new friends."

Aiwren bowed with complicity, not knowing to adhere to military titles or not, thinking this was a good way to hedge his bets, then ran off to catch up with Serafina and Gregory.

"Don't stay up all night!" Cutter yelled after him, before returning to his worries.

Aiwren found Serafina and Gregory walking together not too far from Plune Field and asked, "Where are you guys going?"

Gregory quickly turned around, saluted Aiwren, and said, "We was headin back to our trade tents, My Liege."

Aiwren burst out laughing. The very thought of someone calling saluting him was positively absurd to him.

"There's no need for that with me," Aiwren said, and it seemed as though nobody in Plune's platoon was going to adhere to any semblance of traditional military hierarchy.

"You know if we don't call you, liege," Serafina said, spinning on her heels, "Halibon will have our asses."

"So how about this," Aiwren said, "around the others I'll be your superior officer, but when we're not, we're just friends. Okay? Besides, isn't a corporal nearly the same thing as a private?"

"I'm pretty sure corporals get punished more if things go shit-shaped," Serafina said, with a sarcastic half smile.

"Naw it's true," Gregory said, adding to the joke, "that's why they call it corporal punishment. Ain't it?"

"I think you need to join me for drinks in celebration of our great adventure," Aiwren announced.

"That sure sounds like an order from from my commanding officer," Serafina said.

"Yup, I was just following orders," Gregory said, overzealously acting innocent, "if you've got a problem you should take it up wif da corporal!"

The three of them burst out laughing, quite certain, since hearing about the simplicity of the mission, and becoming such immediate friends, that their mission was going to be nothing but fun. Aiwren put an arm around each of them and, together, they walked off for a day of drinking and revelry.

At the pub, a hole-in-the wall called, "Belver's Brew," with day-old sausages and tall mugs of watered-down stale beer, the three new friends were too oblivious to criticize, the conversations between Aiwren, Gregory, and Serafina were seamless. In only hours the three of them filled each other in on the details of their lives as though they were old friends catching up after too much time apart. Gregory was from a cabin outside of Norga Doonda, a city nestled in the woods to the north, where his family lived for generations, learning the plants of the great forest called "The Pines," and living off of a small garden on their bit of property. He explained that he'd been in Y-Kewnor for about an annual, but hadn't really become close with anyone because his northern accent made everyone think he was dumb and illiterate. Serafina was Ma-Areshi, which explained her dark complexion and experience training wild birds. She explained that a lot of people in Y-Kewnor assumed she grew up in the swamp, and, although she spent a lot of time there, hunting with her father, she was born in raised in the city of Ma-Aresh and was accustomed to metropolitan life.

Getting their backgrounds out of the way, the three of them spent the rest of the day imagining what their adventure, the princess, and Sima Watusia would be like, making jokes about Roderick, Brunff, and Kazerra, and wondering about their curious leader, Jocund Plune. More savvy with the workings of the city, Serafina explained how Jocund was the son of the wealthiest lord in the city, but a lot of folks suspected him of being involved with the attack, that some even suggested that his own father may have put him up to the attack to remove the delicate situation with The Divine Empress's Knights from the political equation for the upcoming election, and that he had volunteered to reenlist as a means to clear his own name. She went on to say that, when he was in the guard before, he ran away when he was on a mission and, had he not been a lordson, he would have been executed for cowardice. The gossip was fascinating to all three of them and made their upcoming adventure only more exiting. By the time the three of them tumbled out of the bar, they were certain they would have a life-long friendship built upon nothing but good times from that point forward.

When Aiwren finally arrived at Leicester's apartment, completely intoxicated, he was sad Leicester and Wanda weren't there. He reminded himself that Leicester was an engaged man and, even though Aiwren had moved to the same city, things would never be the same. As he laid on the sofa, drifting off to sleep, he cheered himself up by thinking about his new friends and the adventure he was about to embark upon.

***

After the selection of his platoon, Jocund returned to his home. He didn't go visit his father in the Parliamentary Palace because, he was certain, if his father had wanted to see him, he would have sent guardsmen to fetch him unwillingly. He didn't go to a pub or a whore house because he could do that later, and he first wanted to go through his notes and sit with his thoughts, as excruciating as it was. He poured himself a glass of wine and sat at the desk in his office.

In a world of duplicitous subterfuge, which Jocund participated in freely and willingly, the one fiction he couldn't bear was self deception. Jocund hated being alone not out of loneliness, but because, alone, he was forced to drop his games and endure his own brutal honesty; as much as Jocund Plune knew the world hated him, he hated himself even more. The first aspersion he debased himself with was admitting his father didn't love him, that this mission was not intended to clear Jocund's wrongfully marred name, but his father's. His father would politically distance himself from this as much as possible and feed Jocund to the proverbial wolves should anything go awry. The next biting truth he succumbed to was that, despite how hard he tried to be a lazy drunk of a louse, he was, with his cunning manipulations, just like his father, perhaps, unburdened by risk, worse; his father had everything to lose and he had nothing. He opened his journal, the tome within which he kept all of his plans, and turned to the page with his notes from the selection of recruits.

Jocund was pleased with what he saw. He meant it when he told the group of recruits he had chosen they were the best of the worst of the worst, but he was fine with that. Jocund always bet on the lamed horse. He believed being underestimated granted freedom from expectations and freedom was power. Of course, after losing enough, he had put his horse gambling days behind him, but, he thought, switching analogies to cards, something he always won, it didn't matter what assortment of cups and swords and coins and staves he had, the real game wasn't in the cards, but in the players; he was always a step ahead, knowing how to bet even with a busted hand. He also reminded himself that, even if he lost, he always walked away from the card table or the race track to bet another day and he was certain, even if everything went horribly wrong, this little mission would be no different.

After reviewing the notes on his company and glancing at some maps, he walked upstairs to the guest room and knocked on the door. There was no response.

"Do you find your accommodations suitable Your Highness?" Jocund asked, making no attempt to mask the fact that he really didn't care if she was comfortable.

The door opened and the princess stuck her head out into the hallway. It had required some persuading to convince her to willfully return to Sima Watusia. Jocund had made some compromises he hoped wouldn't turn out to be mistakes, but he gambled that having her return with him willingly would be significantly less annoying then having to transport her as a prisoner.

"Yes," she said, politely, "everything is perfectly acceptable. You've been very hospitable. I have already agreed to your terms. You don't have to keep hovering."

"Then you'll be prepared to leave before sunrise?" Jocund asked.

"Yes," the princess exclaimed, exasperated. "I'm not a child or an invalid. I can dress myself and pack my own luggage and ride in a carriage perfectly fine on my own and have been doing so, independently, for some time now."

The princess slammed the door, leaving Jocund alone in the hallway. He really despised this insufferable brat and worried that, if anything went wrong on the journey, it would likely be a result of her stubbornness.

***

Rheozarccio Rheodo walked up the steps with a knot in his stomach about meeting somebody else who would surely hate him. When he knocked on the door, a young guardsman greeted him, escorted him to a study, and invited him to take a seat. A few moments later, the same young guardsman brought him a glass of freshly squeezed yellowberry juice and told him the general would be with him shortly. Rheo, sipping on his yellowberry juice, took the moment to look around the study. Immediately he noticed that the walls were lined with books on dark wooden shelves and piles of scrolls rolled up in stacks inside of bins. From this, he gathered that, unless it was for show, General Boomswift was quite well read. He had heard Boomswift's name a few times from Sir Vincent, but had never met the general in person; however, he did remember that his knight-father had great respect for the general, so Rheo worried, if the general didn't like him, it would be one more way he was a disappointment to his recently deceased knight-father and the name of his house. His thoughts were interrupted by the sound of squeaking.

Rheo spun in his chair to see that the squeaking was the sound of wheels. In the doorway, sitting in some sort of chair on wheels, which had the signature look of an automech from Frins Casicon, was a woman. The woman was older, not decrepitly old, but she was certainly old enough to be his mother. It was difficult to tell the woman's age because her eyes and her smile contained the energy of youth. She wore some sort of floral pattern, but Rheo couldn't tell whether it was a blouse or a dress because she had a quilt over her waist. She used her arms to wheel herself into the room and it was quite impressive how easy she made it look.

Realizing he was staring, Rheo quickly stood.

"You needn't stand out of a misplaced sense of chivalry, custom, or otherwise," the woman said, chuckling to herself. "I never do."

"My lady," Rheo said, "My name is Sir Rheozarccio Rheodo. I have been sent, as the newly assigned liaison to the Kewnorian Guard, to meet with General Boomswift."

"What do you know of General Boomswift?" she asked.

"From reputation," Rheo said, "very little, other than the respect my knight-father had; however, looking around the room, I am imagining someone who's well read."

"Oh," she laughed, "the stuffy intellectual type."

"And," Rheo said, putting the pieces together and trying to be sly, "I'd say she probably makes the best yellowberry juice I have ever had the privilege of tasting."

"Ooh," the woman crooned, "compliments. Now we're talking. General Beatrice Boomswift, at your service, but you can call me Bea, sweetheart."

"The honor is mine," Rheo said, bowing.

"So you've been sent to liaise with me," Bea said. "What did you do to piss off that council of pricks?"

Rheo, taken aback, replied, "Hey, I'm on that council of pricks!"

The two of them laughed as Bea wheeled herself behind her desk, slid on some spectacles that appeared, like her chair, to be of Frins Casicon design. It was clear to Rheo that, in a city that didn't respect him, and a council who despised him, he had found an ally.

"So," Rheo asked, "do you mind leveling with me about the state of the alliance between the Kewnorian Guard and The Divine Empress's Knights?"

"Look," she said, with a grimace and a gesture with the glasses she had just put on her face, "my people won't listen to me. Your people won't listen to you. They paired us up to get us out of their hair."

"My knight-father, Sir Vincent Ackaback," Rheo said, "he was your liaison before me. Did you know him well?"

"You're Vincent's knight-son?!" she asked, shocked. "Yes, of course. I suppose I imagined you younger. You were his only knight-son, that's why you've been promoted at such a young age. I knew Vincent well. He was a finer man than I have ever met."

"So..." Rheo asked, "what do we do?"

"Our jobs," Bea said, shuffling through some papers on her desk, looking for something. "We do our jobs and when we do them so well that we are indispensable, that's when our opinions will suddenly matter. Do you have a protege yet? A knight-son?"

"No," Rheo said, realizing he hadn't thought of that.

"I think it's safe to assume that your council-mates detest you," Bea said, now looking through drawers. "Do you think they were fond of your knight-father?"

"Perhaps Leopold," Rheo said, "but, in general, no."

"No," Bea repeated. "If you were to make a guess about his knight-father? My point is that you are part of a lineage of problems for the council. If something were to happen to you before you found a protege, wouldn't that solve a lot of problems for them, forever?"

"You don't think it's possible that they would-"

"Four days ago someone orchestrated four dragons to incinerate the Citadel" Bea said, placing a small box on her desk and looking up to make a point. "Anything is possible."

"You believe the attack on the Citadel was a cabal?" Rheo asked, shocked to hear someone else might agree with his theory.

"I'm certain of it," Bea replied, sorting through the contents of the small box. "I just don't have proof, but we're going to get it and in order to do so, we need you to live, and a protege will protect you."

"So I'm to pick a knight-son simply to serve as an insurance policy?!" Rheo asked.

"No," Bea replied. "Your protege has to be amazing with an amazing story for people to rally behind. You can't just pick anyone. You have to pick the perfect one."

"Okay," Rheo said, relieved to be working with someone who liked him and was proactive, even if he had no idea what she was planning.

In the bottom of the box she was digging through, Bea found what she was looking for.

"We have much to do," she said, sliding Rheo a spare key to her estate.

***

Teryessa was surrounded by ice, beautiful ice. She was on a path. Fluffy, white snow squished beneath her feet. She knew it was snow because she had seen it once before, when, as a child, she and her father traveled north to visit the breathtaking city, D'Ant-Prol, that was believed to have originally been built for giants. To her left and to her right, stretching over the path, were trees, trees the shape of cherry blossoms, but their trunks and leaves were white and their flowers sparkled like diamonds. As she followed the path over a hill, she saw where the path was heading, the Palace of Light. She ran towards it.

In her hurry, Teryessa slipped on a wet spot and fell, face first onto the ground. With her face in the pristine snow, Teryessa's eyes caught the curiosity that she had slipped on. It was odd. A dark glistening stream of slickness, only about as wide as her finger, tricked down the center of the path. Face still in the snow and unable to make sense of it, she reached out with her finger. And touched the thin stream. It was warm and viscous. As she withdrew her finger to examine the wetness, she knew at once what it was. Blood.

The stream of blood came from the Palace of Light. Although her stomach was turning with dread, she hurried as quickly as she could until she was just outside of the Palace of Light, summoning her courage to enter. She was frightened, but she did.

Inside, Teryessa quickly found the source of the blood. Just inside the great doors there was a giant claret puddle on the palace's crystal floor. She wondered who had bleed there. She called for The Divine Empress, but her voice made no sound. She reached out with her mind to The Divine Empress, but received no response. The Palace of Light was empty.

When Teryessa reached the great hall, from which The Divine Empress took Teryessa to The Source several nights earlier, it was empty. Through the walls, Teryessa saw The Source off in the distance, but it didn't look the same. It didn't swirl and flow peacefully, but instead whipped violently, like the Great Sea during a hurricane. She wondered what had happened and she reached out to touch the clear wall she was looking through. The cold of the wall was reassuring on Teryessa's finger tips, but when she pulled her hand away, she noticed a dark smear on the wall where her index finger had been. She looked at her finger. There was a tiny bead of black liquid oozing from the tip. She looked back up at the wall. There was a small crack, growing from beneath the black smear her finger had left there. She tried to wipe away the smear with the palm of her hand, but it was too late. The crack was spreading.

The crack in the wall of the Palace of Light quickly spread. She could hear the walls creaking and groaning. The palace shook. Teryessa stepped back just as an enormous chunk of the palace's clear wall fell to the ground, narrowly missing her. She looked at the glass-like rubble and saw her own reflection refracted several times in its jagged but reflective surface. There was something different about her face in the reflection. It looked cruel. Twisted. Despite the Palace crumbling around her, Teryessa was mesmerized by this odd reflection of herself. She reached for the the surface and found a hand reaching back. It grabbed her wrist. She struggled to get free, but she just couldn't; this dark version of herself was far too strong. Finally she broke free and ran, dodging pieces of ice and crystal as they plummeted to the ground around her. Looking over her shoulder, she saw, to her horror, the evil reflection of herself emerging from the crystal.

Teryessa ran down the hall, but everything had changed. She couldn't find her way out. Finally, she made it to the foyer where she had entered from, only to see a sight even more terrifying. It was Ahkk-Rhall, except he was entirely made of gold.

Teryessa turned to run away, only to see her twisted reflection, walking towards her, wearing a suit of armor more black than anything she had ever seen, with the exception of that black painting in the Gallery of Nestellishma. She froze in place, too terrified to move, lifting her arms defensively as the twisted reflection drew her sword. The twisted reflection pushed past Teryessa, knocking her to the ground. Trapped in a small vestibule, Teryessa curled up as small as she could become and cowered in the corner as the twisted version of herself sliced the head off of the gold Wurm Ahkk-Rhall, showering the crystal room with blood.

The twisted version of Teryessa, blood soaked, approached. Teryessa, who, shivering, looked up and stuttered, "thank you" to her doppelgänger.

"Don't thank me," the bizarre clone said. "It's just... I want you all to myself."

Backed into the corner there was no way for her to escape as the hands closed around her neck and Teryessa was strangled by her other self.

Teryessa scrambled as she exploded from her dream, flailing her arms about and struggling to catch her breath, as though she had just nearly drowned. Sitting up in her pile of fur, she looked over at Joker, who was already awake and pacing around the cave.

"Doesn't look like you slept very peacefully, either," Teryessa said, "ready to head out?"

Teryessa picked at some food, but couldn't stomach much, so she fed the rest to Joker, who, though nonplussed by Teryessa's depression, was thrilled to be included in breakfast. Teryessa was terrified by her dream, but she held on to the hope that, if she were to vanquish whatever threat there was plotted against her, she might sleep peacefully once again and, if she obeyed the rule of pairs, she could survive long enough to see that happen. If nothing else, she thought, this kept her motivated and moving, and moving kept her occupied and not focussing on what had happened to her. The other thing preventing her mind from wandering was the danger of the journey she was on. She wanted desperately to never think about what had happened to her, even if that meant journeying for the rest of her life.

Perhaps it was due to prolonged exposure to the outdoors, but that morning, Teryessa felt even colder than she had the night before. She hoped the air would warm as the day progressed, but her hopes felt as distant and unlikely as the sun, which was hiding far behind a thick blanket of fog choking the life out of the icy mountain tops and made Joker's every step along the cliffside path a gamble of life and death. It was the wet kind of cold that felt like it was perforating Teryessa's clothes, seeping into her skin, and replacing her blood with its freezing dampness; it was a dark kind of cold, but not as dark or as cold as what was already beneath the princess's skin.

Every horse Teryessa had ever known would have been terrified of the heights at which and the poor visibility through which she was traveling on that mountain pass through the Dragonsback Mountains, but not Joker. Joker, it seemed, couldn't care less. Teryessa wondered would happen if she were to fall off the saddle and plummet down the side of the mountain to her death. Would Joker simply keep on trotting as though nothing had happened? Would anyone care if she died? The answer she gave herself made her want to crumble, to dissolve into infinite indistinguishable particles: no, not a soul would care. The only people who would have cared already believed her to be dead; if she were to perish, their lives would continue unchanged. Perhaps it would be better for everyone if she actually were dead, she thought, since everyone thought she was dead anyway, she was miserable, and her life was a threat to anyone she cared about. She strained her eyes to peer over the cliff, through the seemingly endless depth of fog below her, and wondered how long she would plummet before her body collided with some unforgivably jagged surface and burst into an explosion of bloody pulp. There were other forces at work within Teryessa's mind, however, and one of them was an instinct to survive, an instinct that was changing Teryessa by the moment and inadvertently carving out a home within her soul for other things to dwell. Joker, as though annoyed with the self-destructive machinations of Teryessa's mind, snapped her teeth back at the princess, reminding her to focus on the path rather than the consequences of falling from it; they were in this together.

Eventually, the fog evaporated and, as it dispersed, Teryessa couldn't help but feel as though something was wrong with the world, even more wrong than the day before, but the increasingly tempestuous winds that banished the fog didn't allow much attention to be paid to these nebulous concerns. Instead, the princess was focussed on keeping warm from the convulsions of icy air blasting her with torrents of hail, sleet, and snow that each cut into her like a volley of poisoned arrows and obstructed her view of the path even more than the fog had. She gave up on trying to see the path, put her life in the keep of her aloof horse, and hugged tightly to Joker's neck for warmth, for shielding from the gales of frozen needles, and to help her remain upright against the gales threatening to blow her from the saddle. She felt her lips turning blue and her fingers going numb. Mucus dripped from her nose, freezing to her nostrils like the frozen tears in the corner of her eyes. She knew she had reached the summit of the path.

It was already far past noon when Teryessa and Joker finally found a nook in the side of the mountain to shelter themselves in for a break from the elements and a bit of lunch. Teryessa, appetite diminished by anxiety, exhaustion, and cold, only picked at her food, but Joker was more than willing to eat what the princess couldn't, slobbering up the crackers from her hand and nudging her to fetch more from the saddle bag.

As Joker relaxed, digested her lunch, and rested her eyes for a few minutes, Teryessa pulled out her sword to practice in the tiny cave. Her wrist was still sore and her arms were so fatigued and encumbered by the many layers of armor, fur, and cloak that Teryessa could barely move them, but still, limping on her injured ankle, she made herself swipe around at imaginary enemies until she could barely stand. When her arms were too sore to hold the sword, she knew it was time to return to the cold and continue her journey down the east side of the mountains.

Knowing she had to travel a certain distance and set up camp before dark, the second half of the day passed too rapidly for Teryessa's liking. She felt she was in a race to reach to the eastern foot of the mountains before the sun dipped below the peak of the mountains behind her. When the sun was about two hands from the horizon, knowing that, at one hand she'd have to set up camp, Teryessa did something reckless. She increased her speed.

Throughout the day, the fog and snowy wind prohibited Teryessa from peering over the side of the cliff to accurately gauge her altitude; however, she did notice that, to her left, what was once a cliff, like the one on her right, had become a wall that was steadily growing higher and higher until it vaulted up into the sky beyond what she could see, given the limited visibility. Although this closed her in and made it feel, somehow, more likely that she and Joker would fall from the trail, it was also her only means of measuring her descent, and assured her that the higher the mountain was above her, the closer to the ground she was traveling. The height of the mountain above her created other risks for Teryessa, though, risks she was unaware of when she increased her speed.

It started as a snap. That was the sound Teryessa heard off in the distance, barely audible over the howling of the wind, like a branch innocuously broken over someone's knee, to which Teryessa paid little concern. Shortly after the snap, waiting only through that incalculable moment when time seems to temporarily expand so objects may suspend briefly unrestricted by gravity, the rumbling began. Sounds can be sneaky though; they have a way of easing into existence so a person doesn't really hear them until after they've been audible for some time, until after other explanations like the wind or a buzzing in the ear have been completely exhausted, and, when a person finally is certain they actually hear something and it's actually getting louder and closer, it is often too late to react. When Teryessa first realized she actually heard the rumble she thought she might have heard, her first thought was that it was a dragon. She hugged even more tightly to Joker's neck, gave a kick with her boot, and hurried ahead, focussed only on traveling as quickly as she could without tumbling over the cliff. She wasn't looking above, or to her left, or even ahead of her so she never saw it coming when it hit her.

One moment, Teryessa was seated in Joker's saddle, the next she was flying through the air, certain she was plummeting over the side of the cliff, only hoping she be permitted to die from the fall rather than being scooped up, mid air, by some dragon, but the fall wasn't over the side of the cliff; it was only to the ground on the trail behind her, landing on her back in the ice and snow, but her relief lasted only a moment. Something rocketed towards her face. She rolled out of the way, as a giant triangular sheet of ice easily as tall as she was slammed into the ground, sticking out of the path like an javelin in its target. She scrambled out of the way as several more icy slabs struck the trail.

The cracking sound was unmistakable and must have echoed out for miles. The path was giving way beneath her and Teryessa heard another rumbling from above, a louder rumbling. Those few sheets of ice speeding down the mountain above her had set something immense and unstoppable into motion. It was an avalanche and it was rapidly approaching. The clarity of this understanding struck Teryessa like lightening. She hurried to remount Joker, but as she grabbed on to the saddle to pull herself up, excruciating pain gripped her left shoulder. She looked down and saw blood seeping out from the space between the breastplate and her left pauldron. She didn't know how bad it was, but knew she didn't have time to think about it either. Teryessa grabbed the saddle with her right hand, heaved herself onto Joker with all of her might, and rode off, right as a mountain of snow crashed onto the path where she just had been.

If she was tempted at all to stop or slow down at all, the next crack Teryessa heard immediately changed her mind. She glanced over her bleeding shoulder to see that the section of path where the snow had fallen had broken beneath the crushing weight, separated from the rest of the mountain, and was falling, out of sight, down through the fog and snow. Teryessa rode as hard as Joker would let her. Exhaustion, fear, and blood loss caught up with her and her mind fogged, but she kept riding until all audible evidence of the avalanche were far behind her.

When Teryessa saw the tiny little cave, she knew it might be her only place to camp safely, so she pulled herself from Joker's saddle and crashed to the ground in a heap of ill-fitting gold armor covered in frozen blood. Teryessa sat up and removed the pauldron from her left shoulder. The gash was deep and wide and about the length of her hand from the top of her shoulder down to her chest, and her clothes were soaked with blood, but it looked like the cold and the pressure of the armor over the cut was helping the blood to coagulate. Unfortunately, she had already lost a lot of blood and as much as the gash hurt, what was excruciating was the dislocation of her shoulder. She fumbled with her right hand to pack the wound with more cloth and tighten the pauldron back into position, but everything she did seemed to hurt. Teryessa tried to climb to her feet so she could stumble into the safety of the cave, but her limbs were too heavy and she thought it was amazing how comfortable the snowy rocky ground felt beneath her. She thought, since she was so comfortable, she ought to rest her eyes for a few moments and go the rest of the way into the cave later.

Teryessa, unsure how much time had passed, opened her eyes to the sight of Joker's face. Her horse nudged her to wake her. The sun was setting in the west behind the mountain. Now certain she wouldn't complete her descent from the mountain that night, Teryessa gathered all of her strength to drag herself into the cave, thankful Joker had been there to help her. As soon as she was only a few feet into the cave, Teryessa collapsed and slipped into sleep.

***

Down in the Ma-Areshi swamps, the fog was especially thick that morning. The nearly opaque grey cloud hung low to the ground and condensed where it mingled with the slightly brownish steam rising from the bog as the sun heated things up. This especially murky morning was a perfect time for predators to take advantage of disoriented and unsuspecting prey, so the marsh was active with all manners of swamp life stirring about. The most amazing to Vannoria, who stood barefoot in the mud at the swamp's edge, revealing her glyph-covered body in the loin cloth and bare-midriff shirt customary for the Ma-Areshi women to wear to accommodate for the muggy weather of the area, was the mantarayfly. She had, of course, heard of these little creatures and had even seen illustrations of them in scrolls; however, seeing one herself was both a blessing, because she doubted many people she knew had ever seen one, and a curse, because seeing these strange foreign insects fluttering about from leaf to leaf searching for smaller bugs to eat served as a constant reminder of how far away from home she was and why. She held her hand out and stood as still as she possibly could. After some time, a mantarayfly landed on her hand. It was about as long as her finger, including its tail and it looked very much like the manta-rays she had also seen drawings of, but its wings were as flat as a leaf. The top of its body was a dark purplish grey and its underside was a very light purplish grey. It had a pair of huge red eyes set widely on its head above a pair of mandibles. It felt almost weightless where its six legs touched Vannoria's palm. It looked at her curiously, determined there were no bugs to eat near her hand, and flew off.

"Looks to be there's a slight more vigor in your blood today, teeffah," Vannoria heard, and turned to see Mister Uncle standing behind her. In the distance, behind Mister Uncle, the strange shadowy man was standing on the deck of Mister Uncle's cabin, watching her, as he had been since she told him she was going for a walk.

"Why do you keep calling me teyfah?" Vannoria snapped, wishing this silly old man would just leave her alone to her misery, continuing to gaze out into the swamp.

"Teeffah," Mister Uncle corrected. "It means little one in Ma-Areshi. It is a term of endearment. I apologize if it offends you; I'm a sentimental old man."

Feeling guilty for snapping at the old man, but determined to remain angry, she asked, "Did he send you to fetch me, so I don't wander away or drown myself in the marsh?"

"He'd never ask poor old Mister Uncle to walk all the way down here, a man like that."

"Oh, really?!" said Vannoria. "What manner of man would that be?"

"The type of man who has no notion of how important he is," Mister Uncle said, stepping closer to Vannoria. "The type of man who thinks he ain't worth helping. The type of man who sees all his blessings as curses."

"Right. The type of man who kidnaps young women, has them transformed into disgusting freaks, and then tells them they he's going to kill them," Vannoria said, before facing the swamp again. "Why shouldn't I drown myself?"

"Sure is foggy," Mister Uncle said. "No?"

"Yes," Vannoria replied. "It's foggy."

"You know them, mantarayflies, teeffah," Mister Uncle said, "before they turn into the amazing little hunters they are, they are just ordinary caterpillars, completely indistinguishable from any other caterpillar. They live their caterpillar lives chewing on leaves. But then they go into their cocoons and they come out looking simply magnificent. And they can fly and they can hunt and they care about a whole different pile of concerns then they did as ordinary caterpillars."

"Are you suggesting this was destined to happen to me?" Vannoria asked. "Are you saying this is fate?"

"Do you know what the Ma-Areshi call these soupy fogs, teeffah?" He asked.

Vannoria shrugged her shoulders indifferently.

"We call them the Fogs of Fate," Mister Uncle said. "They're so thick, you can't see through except for glimpses now and then of what's right in front of you. We have choice, but what good does choice do us when we can't see the choices, when it seems as though all directions only lead deeper into the fog. But then, one day, the fog is lifted, the cocoon is gone, and there you are, a beautiful little mantarayfly, teeffah. Fate is just how we deal with the consequences of what we did when we were stumbling around blind."

"So what will I be, then, when the fog lifts." Vannoria asked.

"I don't know, teeffah," Mister Uncle said. "I cannot see through the fog any better than you can. Perhaps we should first focus on healing your wounds. The hunters left before sunrise and should have returned by now."

The Ma-Areshi called their little villages "Communes" and all the people of each Commune, who the Ma-Areshi called a "Family-Clan," really were all related by marriage or by blood and there were hundreds of these Family-Clan Communes scattered across the swamp. In Mister Uncle's Commune there were perhaps two dozen or so little raised cabins, staggered in two concentric semi-circles, each with a alligator or two hitched casually to a leg of its stilts. Behind each cabin, was a garden, each with a crop the residents of that cabin were responsible for tending. The hunting party, which was composed of one person from each cabin, would ride out early in the morning on their alligators and often return only a few sunhands later with enough food for the whole Family-Clan, who, each night, shared the food they grew and caught around a bonfire in the center of the Commune. This was also where they aired grievances, made group decisions, and performed rituals.

As Vannoria and Mister Uncle walked through the center of the Commune, where several Ma-Areshi were stacking fire wood inside the fire pit, Vannoria noticed there was a small stack of dead water foul beyond the fire pit and, beyond that, was a pen. Inside the pen was a wild boar painted with similar patterns to the ones indelibly marked on her body. As Vannoria and Mister Uncle neared the pen, the Ma-Areshi people stopped what they were doing and approached. Even a few of the untethered alligators approached.

"Boars are a great source of life, teeffah," Mister Uncle said, "providing sustenance to both Ma-Areshi and alligators. It is said that long ago, the alligators were invited to a Ma-Areshi feast and have been friends to the Ma-Areshi people ever since."

"Why are you telling me this?" Vannoria asked, looking up from the boar to notice that what appeared to be the entire Family-Clan had congregated around her.

"Because there is something you need to do," Mister Uncle replied, as the Family-Clan made a path for the strange shadowy man to approach with a small wooden box. "The Source doesn't waste, teeffah."

Mister Uncle took the box from the strange shadowy man and handed it to Vannoria. Vannoria had a feeling of dread, but she slowly opened the box. Thankfully she was spared the sight of her own detached left index finger, but the object bundled tightly in leaves could be no other thing. Around her, the Ma-Areshi chanted a terrifying song.

"Teeffah," Mister Uncle said, "this life was once a part of you, but has become corrupted. Now you can no longer use it so you must return it to the earth. You must turn its darkness into life."

Vannoria felt Mister Uncle's hand on her left shoulder and the shadowy man's hand on her right shoulder and she knew what she was supposed to do. She picked up her leaf-wrapped finger from the small wooden box and tossed it into the boar's pen. The boar, a scavenger who would eat anything, quickly gobbled it up without hesitation. Vannoria turned to see a Ma-Areshi woman standing in front of her with her palms out. She handed the woman the small box. The woman bowed and walked away and all of the other Ma-Areshi followed her, never stopping the song they were singing. Mister Uncle nudged Vannoria to follow the Ma-Areshi and she did, with the shadowy man following her and Mister Uncle following him.

The Ma-Areshi procession walked from the boar pen to the fire pit, where they all circled around and Vannoria noticed that the Ma-Areshi woman had taken the box and placed it on the top of the stack of logs. A Ma-Areshi man bowed before Vannoria and handed her a flaming torch. She slowly walked from the ring of people to the fire pit and tossed in the torch. The instant the fire came in contact with the small wooden box, Vannoria heard an awful squeal.

The squealing was coming from the pig pen and the Ma-Areshi were already hurrying over to see for themselves, grabbing spears along the way. Vannoria followed, and was shocked by what she saw inside the pig pen. The boar had changed. The symbols drawn onto its back were glowing a bright red and its eyes were blacker than night. It was viscously rampaging around the pen, thrashing at the wood with its tusks, foaming at the mouth and thirsty for blood. When the first spear struck it, it barely paused. The next Ma-Areshi warrior buried his spear into its back and did his best to hang on, but was whipped

268

from his feet by the supernaturally strong erratic movements of the possessed boar. Two more Ma-Areshi drove their spears into its ribs, keeping their weight back to hold it in place, while the Ma-Areshi who had been thrown by the beast quickly scrambled to his feet and launched himself into the pen and on to the back of the monster.

Mister Uncle pulled a dagger from the rope tied around his waist, held it out to Vannoria, and said, "You must finish the beast, teeffah. Only you."

"I can't do that," Vannoria said, denying the dagger. "I've never slaughtered anything before, not even a chicken. That thing will kill me."

"Do as I say," Mister Uncle said, raising his voice. "You must kill the beast possessed by the evil inside you."

Before she could argue, two of the Ma-Areshi men lifted Vannoria up and threw her in the pen. As soon as she was inside, she saw that all of the Ma-Areshi circled around the pen had their spears pointed, not at the boar, but at her. Mister Uncle tossed the dagger into the pen, the Ma-Areshi on the back of the beast quickly hopped out of the pen, and the two Ma-Areshi holding it down with spears yanked their weapons from the beast. It was Vannoria and the beast boar alone in the pen. It turned to her and Vannoria instantly knew, by the look in its wild eyes, it was her blood it hungered for. There was a dark bond and only one of them was to survive. She dove for the dagger.

A wild boar would be dangerous for a trained hunter to kill with a knife even if it wasn't possessed by dark magic. Vannoria knew this and she held out the dagger as her whole body trembled with the most visceral fear she had ever experienced. In a heartbeat the beast was moving. It was charging for her. She swung at it with the dagger, but it easily knocked her to the ground. Barely able to see through the fog and covered in slippery mud, Vannoria did her best to keep the beast's gnashing teeth away from her. It had tasted her blood in that finger and it wanted more.

Vannoria tried to grab onto it by the neck to hold it back, realizing she must have dropped the dagger when she was knocked to the ground. Her eyes darted around erratically for the dagger but she couldn't see it through the thick fog that seemed to grow even more dense since she was thrown into the pen. The boar's teeth snapped inches away from her face. She let go of the boar with her right hand, trying to hold it back with only her left forearm while feeling around with her right hand for the dagger. As soon as her fingertips touched metal she felt an excruciating pain. The Boar had latched its powerful jaws onto her left forearm. She knew she would have only one chance at this.

With a sudden explosive movement, Vannoria reached hard for the dagger. She felt the hilt, grabbed on tightly, and swung upwards. The tip of the blade plunged into the boar's neck, hitting an artery and showering Vannoria with blood from the possessed boar that was still continuing to wrench at her left arm with its teeth. She pulled out the dagger and stabbed it in again. Blood spraying down on her face blinded Vannoria. She didn't know what else to do. She just kept stabbing and stabbing and stabbing. The beast's jaws relaxed around her arm. With a torrent of blood bursting out of its neck, the beast let go of Vannoria and backed away.

Vannoria wiped the blood from her eyes to see the creature staggering, but shaking off the pain and preparing for another attack. Driven by the beast within her, Vannoria leapt onto the back of the still slightly stunned creature. She wrapped her bleeding left arm around the boar's head and drew the dagger across its throat. The beast stumbled and fell to the ground and Vannoria fell down with it, unable to move, exhausted and still overwhelmed with shock, fear, and panic.

The next thing Vannoria remembered was being lifted from the pit. She felt warm wet stickiness all over her and wondered if she was being lifted because she had been mortally wounded. She remembered she had been badly bitten on the arm and recalled stories of ranchers gored to death by a bull, not realizing a horn had gone through their ribs until they had gotten home and dropped to the ground in a pool of their own blood. She wondered if one of the boar's tusks had gored her and she didn't even realize it, but the world, though spinning and confusing, ebbed into focus. As she was lowered to the ground outside of the pen, she staggered to her feet.

Blood covered Vannoria's body, as she wildly shrugged off the Ma-Areshi who were holding her up, so that she, though hunched over to catch her breath, could stand on her own. When she realized the spears were no longer pointed to her, she dropped the dagger and the Ma-Areshi burst into cheer. Behind her, the beast boar was already being stuck onto a spit to roast over the fire. She said nothing as she walked away from the site of the bloodbath.

Vannoria had been sitting on the steps of Mister Uncle's cabin long enough for the blood to dry before Mister Uncle finally approached her and said, "You did well, teeffah."

"Here to patch me up again?" Vannoria asked without looking up from the ground.

"Perhaps," Mister Uncle said, "perhaps not."

Vannoria held out her left arm for Mister Uncle to examine and said, "that thing nearly ripped my arm off."

"You will be fine," he said. "Let me show you."

Vannoria looked up to see Mister Uncle holding out his hand, palm up. It looked like a normal hand. Then he pointed to a glyph that looked like three squiggly horizontal lines over his heart and covered it with his right hand. After a moment he pulled away his right hand and showed the palm to Vannoria. On his palm were three lines just like there were on his chest, only these three lines were glowing gold. Vannoria was about to ask what it meant, when he grabbed onto her forearm. The pain was instantaneous. Vannoria had been burnt once as a child, when she touched a hot iron stove, but it was nothing like this searing pain. She tried to pry her arm from Mister Uncle's grip, but found herself unable to. Finally, he let go of her arm and she looked to see how badly burnt it was from his burning grip, only to see that the wound had healed. It wasn't completely healed, but it was closed and scabbed over.

"Remove your shirt, teeffah." Mister Uncle said.

Vannoria, stunned, did nothing, not wanting to reveal herself, especially not to a stranger, but Mister Uncle gave her a reassuring nod, and so, glancing around to be sure nobody else was looking, Vannoria unlaced her short shirt to reveal her small firm breasts and the tattoos surrounding them. There, above her left breast, over her heart, was the same tattoo that was over Mister Uncle's heart and, having seen what it was capable of, she knew what the symbol represented. Water. In response to Mister Uncle's encouraging nod, Vannoria held her hand over her heart for a moment then looked at her palm. The glowing mark on her hand vanished almost as soon as it was removed from her chest, but she was certain she had seen it.

"An unintentional side-effect of the magics used to heal you, but it requires time, teeffah," Mister Uncle said to her, "if you wish to learn it."

"What of the other marking?" Vannoria, putting the pieces together quickly, asked. "What do they do?"

"As I said, teeffah, it requires time." Mister Uncle replied with a wink as he stood, before turning and waddling away.

"Wait!" Vannoria exclaimed, not pausing to tie her blouse, but holding it closed with her hands as she leapt to her feet. "What am I?"

Mister Uncle turned to her and said, "Just a foolish young girl who was in the wrong place at the wrong time, but the Family-Clan believes you could become something else. And they may be right, but only time will tell."

Vannoria asked what it was they thought she could become, but it was clear Mister Uncle wasn't going to answer. Despite what had happened to her she felt, for a moment, as though she might be worth something and it had nothing to do with Aiwren's love. Standing on the steps of a witch doctor's cabin, in a far away land, disfigured, almost naked, and covered in blood, it was the first time Vannoria imagined what it would feel like to love herself.

***

He wasn't sure what compelled him when he decided to approach her, but the Nameless Rider found himself inexplicably walking towards the Girl, Vannoria. He crossed paths with the Old Man, who reached up to pat him on the shoulder and he instinctually knew this meant the Old Man was fond of him, but he hadn't the slightest notion why. As he approached Vannoria, she quickly covered herself up, pulling her blouse closed and quickly fumbling to tie the strings, which drew his attention to the fact that, before she had done this, her breasts had been exposed, which made him wonder about clothing. He wondered why some parts of the body were appropriate to expose while others weren't. He also wondered what was beneath

273

his clothing. Was there a body inside, or, if he were to disrobe, would he simply vanish? These brief curiosities quickly evaporated and he realized he was staring at the Girl.

"May I help you?" She asked.

"I just wanted to make sure you were okay," he said.

"Obviously I'm fine," she responded, "no thanks to you. I hope you are as useless at killing me as you are at protecting me."

"The ceremony was vital to your survival."

Rolling her eyes, Vannoria scoffed, "How is it you are certain of so little, yet so certain of the little you are certain of?"

The Nameless Rider gave a confused frown. Her questions made no sense to him. He found himself wondering why she had so many questions. It seemed as though every moment she was awake she was asking one question or another. He wouldn't have minded her questions so much, if they didn't often cause him to ask himself these questions and realize how little he knew. He didn't know why he knew so little and it wasn't until he met her that he realized how little he knew.

"Well, okay, so you were originally supposed to kill, Aiwren," Vannoria started, "but then your mission, from some mysterious instructions, magically changed and your were supposed to kill me, but not until the right moment and you don't know when that is or how you'll even know when that is, but you say you'll protect me until then, even though you did absolutely nothing the very first time I was in danger, danger in the form of a magical boar that didn't seem to disturb you the slightest bit. And none of this strikes you as odd?!"

The Nameless Rider said nothing. This made sense to him, but he hadn't any idea how to explain it to the Girl or why he even should or why people explain things to each other at all anyway. He decided her questions were rhetorical and didn't actually require an answer, so he said nothing, but this seemed to frustrate her even more.

"And what even happened to him?" she asked. "What happened to Aiwren?"

"You were asleep," he said, almost sure she actually wanted him to answer this question, "you fell asleep from bleeding too much. The letter said he left you to go to Y-Kewnor. I rode to Y-Kewnor. I saw him enter the town, but was too late to stop him."

"Letter?!" she exclaimed, with a fury he didn't understand. "Show me!"

The Nameless Rider reached into his pocket and pulled out the letter the Boy had left for Vannoria. She ripped it out of his hands and started reading. After a moment, she looked up. Her eyes were filled with tears.

"Go away!" she screamed. "Leave me!"

Before the Nameless Rider had a chance to walk away, the girl ran away, towards the swamp. He was about to go after her, but a hand on his shoulder stopped him.

"Let her be, old friend," Mister Uncle said.

The old man whistled and his huge white alligator lumbered up to him from the side of his cabin where it was sunning. It was standing in his tall walk so Mister Uncle didn't have to bend to whisper to it. With an understanding look, the enormous alligator scurried after Vannoria.

"I have never known someone so old, understand so little, my friend," the old man said. "Give her time and then talk to her. Be forthcoming. Be honest. Be sympathetic."

"Why must I do these things in order to save her?" the Nameless Rider asked.

"Keeping her alive isn't enough," Mister Uncle said. "She must have a reason to live or the darkness will consume her."

"How is a creature of darkness supposed to help a foolish girl?" the Nameless Rider asked.

Mister Uncle burst out laughing and said, "My dear boy, you really have no idea what you are. Do you?"

The Nameless Rider didn't understand any of this. He watched Mister Uncle return to the fire that was now blazing with the boar roasting on a spit above it.

***

Vannoria stood, again, by the edge of the swamp, but, hoping for some privacy, she walked further from the Commune then she had that morning. She thought about Aiwren. There was no way around it, no confusion. The letter was certainly his writing. She wondered how could it be that, after doing what they did, he could want nothing to do with her. If he didn't want her then, he certainly wouldn't want her now that she was disfigured and covered with marks, which were both his fault; if he hadn't abandoned her, then she wouldn't have gone looking for him and none of this would have happened. He did this to her. He took her hopes and dreams and flesh and body and threw it all away, leaving her with nothing. He destroyed her and she hoped that someday he would pay for what he had done. She didn't love Aiwren Wayde at all, she told herself; she hated him.

Feeling settled in her fury, she wondered what she would do next. She thought about traveling to Y-Kewnor and slitting his throat as she had done with the boar. If she was capable of slaughtering a creature she felt indifferent towards, she would have no problem at all killing someone she hated more than anything else. She wondered what would she do after that. As much as she hated Aiwren, killing him wasn't much to look forward to and would be brief. Was there nothing else for her in this world besides revenge? What else could she hope to do? She couldn't go home, not looking like she did. That place would only remind her how unloved she was. She hated Ribeln, too, and didn't care if she saw the whole town burn to the ground. She thought she might even receive some pleasure from burning it down, herself, hearing the screams of all those who had been cruel to her. Was there any life for her besides rage?

"I can hear you behind me," she said, in response to the footsteps approaching, "I thought I was clear when I told you I wanted to be left alone."

"You didn't tell me how long you wanted to be left alone," the strange shadowy man said, approaching her.

"Usually when a woman tells a man to leave her alone, she means until further notice," Vannoria said, turning to the man. "What do you want?"

"I thought, perhaps," the man said, "you wanted to be comforted because you were feeling sad about the Boy not wanting to be with you."

"You're terrible at comforting people," she said.

"I know," the strange shadowy man said. "I don't think I have ever comforted anyone before and I suppose I was hoping I would have beginner's luck."

Vannoria burst out laughing at this. The very concept of beginner's luck at comforting someone was absurd to her.

"It seems," she said, "you have better beginner's luck at humor, though it's clearly unintentional."

"Well," he said, "you were frowning a moment ago and now you're smiling, so perhaps you my beginner's luck with comforting deserves more credit."

"Clever," she replied to the strange shadowy man, who grew more curious to her the longer she was with him, "at least cleverer than I thought you were. Why is it that, someone so clever knows so little? You don't even know your own name."

"I don't know," strange shadowy man said, "The first thing I remember is riding across the plain to get the Boy. I don't know why I don't know my name. I never thought to wonder what it was until you asked me."

Vannoria thought about the how strange it was that this man knew nothing about himself, that he seemed to have no recollection of his life, that he was just there in the moment. She wondered what it would be like for her, in this moment, if she had no recollection of where she came from. She realized that she would enjoy it more. She realized, if she could forget about the things she had hoped for, the results would be less disappointing. What would she do if that were possible? Who would she be if she could start her life from scratch? She reminded herself that this was impossible for her, but not for this strange man who was going to kill her someday. She decided that, since she forced her one-day killer to know the name of his one-day victim, it made sense for her to know his name.

"Shadow," she said, "that's your name. I know it doesn't sound like a real name, but it will suffice until we find out what your real name is. And it makes sense because you follow me around like my shadow and you dress in dark colors like a shadow. Also, as a child, Shadow was the name of my favorite goat; he, too, followed me everywhere. Of course my father still slaughtered him, but he was my favorite."

"It would be an honor to be named after your favorite dead goat," he replied.

"You should know that just because I gave you a name, doesn't mean I don't hate you," Vannoria said, walking back towards the Commune. "Nor does it mean I won't cut your throat like that pig's if you try to kill me."

Before the sun set, the women of the Commune took Vannoria into a cabin and dressed her in ceremonial clothing. None of them would look her in the eye or speak to her beyond one-word answers or instructions on how to wear the ceremonial garb. One small girl, who's mother was helping Vannoria dress, reached up to touch one of Vannoria's tattoos, but the mother smacked her hand and gave her a look that sent her running from the cabin. After the women removed Vannoria's clothing and washed her with a porofungi, removing all of the blood that had dried onto her skin, she was adorned with a pristine white loin cloth fastened to a belt made of intricate gold plates. Her shirt was also constructed of pristine white fabric and narrow enough that it only just covered her breasts. Over her shoulders was a white cape made of the lightest fabric she had ever felt. When she asked of the cape's origin, an old woman told her it was made by lyffs. Vannoria's long dark hair was combed and fastened into a neat little bun on the back of her head. Finally, a small empty scabbard with ornate gold accents was attached to her belt.

When the women finished with Vannoria they left the room. She had tried to follow them out, but they told her to wait in the cabin. So she waited and it wasn't too long before she heard the drums and the chanting.

The beat of the drumming was rhythmic and unlike any music Vannoria had ever heard and the thunder of the men's voices that accompanied the driving pulse was further accented by the women's voices singing a slightly different melody. She heard bells and other instruments she had never heard before. The sound was powerful and shook her deeply, invigorating her and making her feel powerful. She closed her eyes and felt the music vibrating through her body.

The door opened and Vannoria opened her eyes. It was Shadow, he was dressed in all black as he always was, but his hood was off and it appeared as though he had dragged a comb through his rats nest of long dark hair. He had a broad scar across his face and Vannoria realized that, despite the scar, he was strangely handsome. He told her it was time and she followed him out of the cabin.

Vannoria stepped onto the porch. A path was lit by torches and all of the Ma-Areshi in Mister Uncle's Family stood along the path, their eyes fixed on her. Shadow awkwardly offered Vannoria the crook of his elbow so that he could escort her down the steps, then, even more awkwardly told her, unnecessarily, that he was offering her his elbow to escort her. Nevertheless, Vannoria took Shadow's elbow and allowed him to escort her down the path, through the sea of hundreds of Ma-Areshi, and to the fire, where a chair carved from a single piece of wood was waiting for her beside Mister Uncle. The chanting, drumming, singing, and playing of bizarre instruments continued for the duration of her procession. When she arrived at the chair, Mister Uncle stood and bowed to her.

"You look radiant, teeffah," he said to her with a smile, waiting for her to sit, before sitting to her right.

Mister Uncle gazed upon all the Ma-Areshi who stood before him, and, with a wave of his hand, silenced them.

"This unfortunate girl has withstood torment. Darkness tried to change her into something else, but failed. It required enough magics to kill a hundred men to contain the darkness, but she survived and recovered. She fought the embodiment of the evil within her and triumphed. That evil has been prepared by flame for us to consume so we may share the burden of this darkness, so the evil which cannot be destroyed can be spread so thin that it is rendered impotent to harm her or any of us. Many of you have seen how strong the magic is within this girl, I beg you to share her burden."

Two well built Ma-Areshi men carried a table over to Vannoria, Shadow, and Mister Uncle. On the table was the boar she had killed. The knife she had used to kill it was clamped down between its teeth. Once they set the table down, they bowed before her.

"Sourceresha," they said, remaining by her feet.

"Teeffah," Mister Uncle said, "take the blade, carve the beast and eat the flesh to show the Ma-Areshi you are willing to share the burden of the beast's evil."

Vannoria took the blade from the beast's mouth. It felt different. It was still warm from the fire, but something had changed about it, something Vannoria could not precisely identify. The blade cut through the boar with ease. She pulled out a hunk of meat and ate it. It tasted like any other roasted pork she had had, but she felt something change within her when she ate it. As soon as she swallowed the bite the Ma-Areshi cheered.

Soon the Ma-Areshi were lined up for Vannoria to carve them each a piece of the boar, even the children took part in this ceremony. Each Ma-Areshi knelt before her and opened his or her mouth waiting for their bite of pork. After she fed them, each person said the word, "sourceresha," before standing, bowing again, and walking away. It took a quite some time, but eventually, Vannoria fed meat to all of the Ma-Areshi who had lined up.

"This word, 'sourceresha'" Vannoria asked Mister Uncle, "Is it Ma-Areshi?"

"It is Balysh-Tong, the forgotten language, teeffah," Mister Uncle said. "It is a title of honor that hasn't been given in a thousand annuals. In Ma-Areshi, we say 'majisyenna.' In common tongue, it means 'sorceress.'"

"Did you hear that?" Vannoria asked, turning to Shadow, "They think I'm a sorceress."

Shadow shrugged indifferently and motioned for Vannoria to pay attention in front of her. She turned back to see Mister Uncle kneeling before her.

"Sourceresha." he said, before opening his mouth and waiting for the boar meat.

Shocked and not sure if she should feel honored or awkward, Vannoria carved off a piece of the meat and fed him. He closed his eyes, stood, and sat next to her again, and, helping her extricate her from an awkward social situation, he leaned over to her and said, "I'm still not certain, but I decided to hedge my bets. You have another mouth to feed."

Shadow knelt before Vannoria and waited. Mostly lit from behind by the fire, with an occasional burst of light dancing across his face, Vannoria realized, by looking into his expressionless gaze, there wasn't a soul who understood the worthlessness and loss she was experiencing better than this man kneeling before her. She knew she wanted to say something, but nothing felt right. Finally, after being nudged by Mister Uncle, she sliced Shadow a piece of meat and placed it gently on his tongue.

Once everyone had received a bite of the boar and the remainder of the meat was thrown to the alligators who, unbound by ceremony or ritual, devoured it, bone and all in only a few moments, the real celebration began. Plate upon plate of duck and vegetables were shared by everyone. Vannoria, once she had her fill, milled about the bonfire, meeting the various Ma-Areshi from Mister Uncle's

Commune and several other nearby Communes, who, once they were no longer afraid of her, had thousands of questions about the Forgotten Place, and killing the boar, and befriending Shadow, whom they referred to as "Lonbrajjeau-Kavelons," the "Shadow Rider." As soon as she demonstrated she meant them no harm and wanted to know about their lives, it seemed as though every Ma-Areshi there wanted to get a chance to talk to her or be in her presence. They were a kind and friendly people, the Ma-Areshi, who were more interested in helping one another than they were in spreading gossip or slander. These villagers called themselves a family and, though they were many, she witnessed more familial love between them then she had ever experience in her own small family. Vannoria felt more at home with them than she had ever felt in Ribeln, where her differences always made her feel like an outsider.

Drunk on the gater-wine, the fermented nectar of the swamp blossom, and exhausted from smiling and laughing and dancing around the fire, Vannoria collapsed back in her chair as the bright lights, drums, and a cacophony of joyous voices spun around her, only to feel a tugging on her hand. As she looked down, Vannoria saw the little girl who's mother wouldn't let her touch Vannoria's tattoos earlier that night. Since lines had been crossed, rituals had been conducted, and new relations had been forged in the ceremonial fire, the little girl clambered onto Vannoria's lap, looking up at her with two giant brown saucers peering through the dark curly locks dangling over her face.

"What's your name?" Vannoria asked the little girl.

"Y-Yshaah," replied the little girl.

"What a strong name," Vannoria said.

"Majisyenna, are you going to save my friere?"

"Who's that?" Vannoria asked.

Before the little girl could answer, though, her mother called her and she nimbly climbed down from Vannoria's lap and darted through the sea of people to her mother.

"It means 'her brother' in Ma-Areshi," Mister Uncle said. "He journeyed north but never returned. We've lost several of the Family-Clan's young men this way, teeffah."

"And nobody knows why?" She asked.

"There are only rumors. Terrible rumors of Gavlessans expanding their territory and kidnapping young men as slaves for their blood sports from as far Era-Mosa. And there are even more terrible rumors...rumors of a necromancer."

"And no one will do anything to retrieve them?!"

"Gavlessa is a dangerous place, teeffah. Our people are afraid of the Beast Raiders and of the darkness that flourishes, unrestricted, west of the Realmsend River. If it's true there's a necromancer, we have little hope of stopping the darkness from descending upon us."

That was all Mister Uncle would say though. He excused himself to speak with Shadow. Taking a moment to herself, Vannoria took the dagger from the table and, instinctively knowing where it belonged, slid it into its sheath at her waist. She listened to the music that was even more vivacious than before, watched the energetic dancing around the fire, and absorbed the evening, thinking to herself that, perhaps, she could begin a new life. Perhaps, she could do something to give her life meaning. Perhaps, she could make a difference for these people who helped her. Perhaps, she really had emerged from a cocoon something greater than she was before. Perhaps, she mused, she really could be what the Ma-Areshi believed her to be: a sorceress.

***

Across the land of Allyoshmar, set against a star-scattered sky, a red crescent moon smiled sadistically down upon adventurers across the land who couldn't imagine how far their Vayoshes would diverge from the journeys they expected. On her way to discover the dragons that had been set upon her, a frost-bitten, injured, and unconscious princess dressed in ill-fitting gold armor slowly bled from her shoulder onto the white snow. On the eve of his great adventure to return a princess to her home, a milk boy from the country dreamlessly sweat off the night's ale, drooling onto the sofa where he had passed out. A creature of shadow with no memory, guarding a girl as she slept, reminded himself, as he drifted off to sleep, that his duty was to emotionlessly protect the girl until it was time for her to die and nothing more. A young knight recently thrust into a position of power, slumbered peacefully for the first time in several days, confident his new ally would help him uncover the conspiracy that lead to his mentor's death. The commander of the army of a powerful kingdom, twisted and turned restlessly on the night before leading his men to battle, dreaming nightmares of the shame and horror that his life and position came at the cost of the lives of the brothers he had betrayed. A young girl covered with powerful and indelible marks, feeling special for the first time in her life, dreamt of her new life as a sorceress. A young lordson detested by his own father, lying in his own bed, without the distraction of prostitutes or wine for the first time in a long time, stared at the ceiling, forging a deviously brilliant plan, until he, too, eventually fell asleep. Regardless of their intentions, the Fog of Fate had set upon these slumberers, and, blinded, they had made choices that changed their paths and led them deeper down their Vayoshes.

It had been a day obscured by the fog of fate for many people, but as they slept through a clear night, unaware of where their paths were truly heading, smoke, a distant cousin to fog, was finally dispersing from a cave atop a mountain near Orc Doola, a cave set ablaze with dragon fire by a desperate young woman driven to drastic measures from the torture she endured. Bolts of fine cloth and clothing made from human skin were turned to ash. Piles of gold coins were reduced to yellow puddles solidifying on the rocky ground. A claw, mangled by a hatchet, reached out from beneath a pile of rubble. A stack of rock, avalanched from the cave's roof, tumbled over as the head of a dragon with slits in its throat and a gash in its head burst from below, wailing in agony. Wurm Ahkk-Rhall, mutilated by the princess, pulled himself from the bed of rocks. Wingless and limping along on his chopped up fore and rear claws, he dragged himself from the cave that was intended to be his tomb. He knew he needed to find a safe place to rest. He was in no condition to fight and the other dragons would certainly be on their way when Broch-Isha, the dragon he had killed, did not return. He crawled on charred, bloody claws as far as he could from what was once his cave, tumbling through prickly scrub bushes that scratched bloody lines across his body and over jagged flecks of mountain that tore into his flesh, down the rocky cliff to a large flat landing where he hid himself beneath a pile of stone, squeezing as best as he could into a borough that may have once belonged to a large mountain bear. Laying in the little den, with his head exposed, weak eyes staring intensely at the singular demon moon that was now alone in the night sky, he felt something new. Wurm Ahkk-Rhall, weak heavy eyelids slowly sealing, was changed by the mad engine roaring to life inside of him. He would have his revenge.

PART THREE

THE DRAGONS OF ALLYOSHMAR

GAVLESSA

By the time the coup had completely ended, four days after it had begun, much blood had been spilled and the floors of the castle were littered with bodies. Setting Prince Grell up to murder his father was the easy part; the old man was so cruel to his son, all the prince needed was a nudge. Once the nudge had been given, it was more difficult convincing the prince to wait until the right moment than it was to plant the seed of the notion of murder. Ultimately, the prince ended up acting before all of the preparations had been made, but, after a few hours, the plans were adjusted and the Pitt Fighters were ready to attack.

Not all of the Pitt Fighters were involved in the coup. While the Fradats were eager to erase their debts and become once again free and the Ravusas were eager to fight for a position in the new government, the Vlases, slaves taken during raids, were generally not as skilled in battle and not to be trusted with freedom, so they remained in their cages while the other Pitt Fighters rushed in to

287

battle. This was fine, since the Vlases and the other slaves that had recently been gathered would soon have another use.

The king's guard was strong, but undisciplined, unorganized, and not nearly as strong as the Ravusas, who were the best fighters in Gavlessa and the most dangerous part of the Gavlessan infantry. Those loyal to the king didn't stand a chance. Aiding in the attack on the king's guards, were the prince's guards, but, once the king's army had been slain, the Ravusas turned on them, as well. Most fought back, a few surrendered, but all were killed; it was easier to start fresh than to sort out loyalists. Many of them scattered and hid, as the prince had, so, most of the coup was spent rooting out the prince's loyalists and executing them.

The prince was easy to find; Chancellor Plale actually stumbled upon the young man's still-warm corpse, himself, late in the second day of the coup. Though he couldn't imagine what the prince was doing in the room Plale was certain was his secret, alone. Perhaps the prince had been suspicious and followed him one day, Plale mused. Regardless, the prince was dead and Plale had other duties to perform and, since plans were set into motion prematurely, he had catching up to do. Gavlessa was in his command and in service to his Master, the Master all of Allyoshmar would soon be serving.

Kneeling, he grabbed Soul Stitcher, the razor sharp black dagger laying on the altar, and drew the blade across the scarred palm of his left hand and squeezed the blood onto the stygian surface. As the crimson droplets leaking from his fist splashed on the stone, echoing throughout the dark, silent room, the emptiness from that blackest black of paintings stretched out to envelop everything, gobbling up all light and reflection until everything was manifested with darkness.

"My Master," Plale said solemnly, "Gavlessa is now yours to command, but the princess cannot be found and I'm afraid she may have been lost in the battle."

By the time Plale's seance with his Master had concluded, he was relieved to be forgiven for losing the girl, he was pleased to learn the girl was in the custody of a dragon in the Dragonsback Mountains just southeast of Orc Doola, and he was honored that his Master shared more of his plan with him. His Master informed him there would soon be a battle and that he was to prepare for it, which was exactly what he was doing when he addressed the bloodthirsty men and woman of Gavlessa from the edge of the royal viewing box.

"Gavlessans, for annuals you have known me as your chancellor, your regent to the king, but I have had another role, a role I was forced to keep secret until the time was right. Long ago, we were disconnected from the one true Master, The Great Absence from which everything in existence sprang forth, The Dark One. Gordorah. For many generations the people of Allyoshmar have been unworthy of Him, putting their faith, instead, into a false Goddess, but He has been watching your power grow, a power worthy of Him and He has chosen me to be His mouthpiece, His Dark Vicar. People of Gavlessa, Gordorah is returning and you are his chosen people! Today, we reclaim our own kingdom, but next we shall reclaim all of Allyoshmar! For Gavlessa! And for The Dark One!"

The Gavlessans erupted in cheer from the stands, stomping their feet and clapping their hands rhythmically. Chancellor Plale, the Dark Vicar raised his arms triumphantly in the air and soaked in the adoration.

The next few day were, as Plale had sworn to his Master, dedicated to preparing Gavlessa for war. Though they had always been successful in small raids that relied more upon the mercilessness of individual warriors, Plale knew larger campaigns required more coordination, something the vicious Gavlessan warriors, accustomed to valuing the individual over the community and willing to stab one another in the back for a bit more gold, were not accustomed to. To many Gavlessans, strategy was a sign of weakness and the best way to fight was to charge into battle with no plan at all. In order to decisively win against proper armies, Plale knew their entire means of battle needed to change and this would be difficult since most Gavlessans could neither read nor write. He needed to create a military hierarchy in Gavlessa without diminishing the Gavlessans' bloodlust.

Though the execution of Plale's plan was tricky, the concept was simple: build from the top down. A system that encouraged regular challenges to leadership was no longer beneficial, so he needed to choose those just below him wisely. In most other kingdoms, the fact that he was a divine mouthpiece would have secured his position, but a Gavlessan would cut down another man to be on top even if it meant his own death or damnation. As he drew up his plans, Plale reminded himself that, though born in Gavlessa, it had always been clear he was not like the other Gavlessans. This, he always told himself, was because he was not meant to be a Gavlessan, but to rule them. Unlike him, his people were animals and, with the right reinforcement and punishment, animals could be trained to serve.

The Dark Vicar needed enforcers. His favorite warrior, Ovyrr-Keel, had been slain early in the coup by Prince Grell's slave, who was, it seemed, protecting the princess. Plale had always planned for Ovyrr to be his primary enforcer; the beast of a man was unstoppable in battle, completely loyal to Plale, and, despite his ruthlessness, quite a bit smarter than most Pitt Fighters. He would have been a great asset if he hadn't died; however, because he had died, he would be perfect.

With a small audience invited to the Gallery of Nestellishma and Ovyrr's body lying on the black stone slab before the Black Painting, Plale revealed another secret. He was the necromancer.

Plale had begun experimenting in necromancy when he was just a young probabilitist, absorbing spirit from dead Pitt Fighters to gain insight into the outcome of matches so he could create more lucrative odds, to sway opinions in his favor, and to develop a cache of dark magical abilities with which to protect himself. This necromancy lead to his position as chancellor, which gave him unlimited access to corpses and, therefore, power. It was his skill with necromancy and his thirst for power that eventually led to his ability to commune with Gordorah. Raising the dead was a dangerous and costly spell, but, for the prize of an undead Ovyrr at his side, an unstoppable aberration to loyally do his bidding, it was worth the cost and the risk. He plunged Soul Stitcher, the ancient knife he, since the coup, always wore at his waist, into the warrior's still heart, and began the spell.

The spell seemed to go on for an eternity and, although Plale was old and physically frail, most men would have been ripped apart without the mental fortitude he had. Casting a spell was like a puzzle to Plale and he imagined the pieces of the puzzle to be painted on giant slabs of stone. Not only did he have to figure out what piece went where, but he had to lift the giant blocks and carry them into place. Raising the dead was a much bigger puzzle with heavier and more numerous stones than any other spell he had ever performed. The chanting was a tool, a means for Plale to remain concentrated on what he needed to concentrate on, but the real work was going on inside his mind, which was reaching out and connecting forces and spirits into Ovyrr's body. When the spell was almost finished, Plale pulled Soul Stitcher from Ovyrr's heart, sliced open his own scabbing palm, and squeezed his own blood into the wound to invigorate the warrior's heart with fresh life. This also bound the two of them together.

At first there was nothing, but then, resonating thought the supernatural silence of the Gallery of Nestellishma, Ovyrr's heart beat. Once. Then, again. A minute later there was a third heart beat. Then, slowly, it adopted a slow, steady rhythm. The fighter's heart would never beat at the speed of a living heart, but, its dirge of blood pumping would circulate sustenance and reanimate his body, a body with wounds that would quickly heal, but flesh that would always remain pale, veiny, and necrotic. Ovyrr was, through unnatural means, alive. The aberration opened his eyes, gasped in air, and screamed.

CLEAR WATERS

It was still dark when Aiwren's eyes, accustomed to early mornings, first opened. He was still feeling the effects of the previous night out with his new friends, but excited about the journey about to commence and anxious about arriving late for the departure, so he hurried through his morning routine. He knocked on Leicester's bedroom door to tell his friend about the trip, but there was no answer, so he packed some essentials and hurried out the door without breakfast, into the dark of the streets, towards Plune Field, lost in daydreams about how spectacular this trip would be.

When he arrived at Plune Field, Aiwren was happily surprised to see he was not the first to arrive. Cutter sat on the fence, glowing dimly in the twilight, looking upon the field. As excited as he was, Aiwren sensed that his mentor's mood was somber, so he sat next to his teacher without speaking.

"I've never sired any children or taken a wife," Cutter admitted. "Those opportunities passed me by. There are those serving the greater good, who somehow achieved the balance required to carve accommodations for a family within this bloody life. I could not. After my time in the guard I told myself, if I could throw myself into a trade, I would be able to put my life of battle behind me. Again, I could not. Perhaps I couldn't stand the idea of being the cause of a person being forced to endure a world such as this."

Aiwren listened to Cutter's words, wondering what tragedy had fallen upon Cutter to drive him from the Kewnorian Guard and strip his life of joy. He didn't know what to say, feared saying the wrong thing, and didn't even know if it was his place to say anything at all, but he couldn't stand the idea of someone he cared for feeling the pains of sadness.

"Hold your tongue," Cutter said patiently just as Aiwren was about to speak. "I do not desire sympathy, boy, certainly not yours. I know, to you, this is a holiday countryside excursion to exciting new places and that may be true, but I'm concerned about the grander picture. Relations between kingdoms are strained and Y-Kewnor, itself, appears to be, once again, on the brink of collapse. It's times like this when anything that can go amiss usually does and not one of us is prepared."

Aiwren knew, whatever solution he proposed, his mentor would find it too hastily conceived and not a reflection of a grasping of the situation. To Aiwren, however, the situation simply didn't feel as dire as Cutter was describing and any tragedy could be avoided with proper preparation.

"I know I'm a simple country-boy," Aiwren said slowly, not certain what direction his words were heading, "but these things will either come to pass or they won't. Perhaps, through your training, I can help be a part of preventing them. If they are inevitable, then I will need your training to survive and to help others. Either way, the best course of action is for me to commit to your training and for you to commit to training me."

"So you're a philosopher?!" Cutter said with a regretful chuckle. "Any other advice?"

"Yes," Aiwren said, glad Cutter had invited his advice, "you should train the others in our platoon. The brief time I've spent with you changed the way I look at combat. This mission will be easy and a perfect opportunity to begin the training of a few soldiers in your martial arts."

"No," Cutter said. "You must never tell anyone what you are learning and we'll not discuss this any further. You're friends are arriving."

Aiwren turned. Serafina and Gregory were, indeed, approaching. When he turned back to Cutter, his mentor had already walked away. The conversation was over.

"Your head hurting as much as mine?" Serafina asked.

Aiwren, Serafina, and Gregory burst out in laughter.

"I feel like me brains is being squished out through me nose," Gregory said with a huge smile, "but, despite o that, this is one o the appiest days o me life."

"I couldn't agree with you more, Gregory," Aiwren said and the three shared a few laughs and jokes about the previous night.

The sun was just rising as Aiwren saw Lieutenant Plune stroll onto the field looking as sour as usual. Aiwren rushed over to Plune, thinking a demonstration of his commitment might help relieve his leader's stress.

"Corporal Wayde reporting for duty, My Liege."

"Yes, fantastic," Plune said, "I'm certain I'll never tire of your zeal, Corporal Wayde."

Aiwren wondered why authority figures seemed to always treat him unfairly, but he remembered that this was how Cutter was, and, since then, it had been clear that Cutter actually liked him. Aiwren, was sure Plune would like him, too, if he didn't already. He tried to think of the right thing to say to build the bridge of mutual respect with his lieutenant. He was about to speak when he saw Plune's gaze change.

Aiwren whipped around to see what Plune was looking at. Gregory and Serafina, Cutter, Halibon, Roderick, Brunff, and Kazerra had all dropped to the ground, kneeling before the young couple walking onto the field, which made absolutely no sense to Aiwren. What made even less sense to Aiwren was the way the couple was dressed and their presence on Plune Field.

"Leicester and Wanda?" Aiwren asked, utterly confused. "What on earth are you two doing here?"

"Fool!" Plune hushed. "Kneel, before you make this worse for all of us."

"This confusion is entirely my fault, Lieutenant Plune," Wanda said, raising a hand from the most beautiful flowing gown Aiwren had ever seen in his life, before turning to Aiwren and saying, "I have been dishonest. I was selfish to withhold my identity from you."

"She's the princess!" Leicester, squealed.

"It's true," Wanda said, "I am Princess Wanda Watus of Sima Watusia. Over an annual ago my hand was offered to my distant cousin, in Simi Watusia. Having no intention of allowing politics to make the decisions of my heart for me, I left. I would have returned once my cousin was wed to another, but then I found acting and Leicester and a home in Y-Kewnor. I didn't want to leave, but my identity has been discovered. It's no longer safe for me here; sadly, I must return to my home."

"I'm confused why you're here, though, Aiwren," Princess Wanda said. "We hadn't seen you for days. We left you a note to explain all of this, but I thought you'd be sewing for the army with that awful grouch, Cutter."

As Wanda spoke, Aiwren saw Leicester's eyes bug out of his head and was certain his eyes were probably doing the same thing.

"Sergeant Major, Ulysses James Cutter. Tailor, soldier, and grouch at your service, Your Highness," Cutter said.

"Well," Jocund said, "it appears everyone knows one another. Now, if salutations have concluded, perhaps Corporal Wayde would be obliged to do the princess and her fiancé the honor of carrying their luggage to the carriage so we may be on our way. Or shall I fetch us some tea and picnic sandwiches?"

Aiwren, momentarily dumbstruck, leapt into action, hurrying to fetch the luggage.

"My apologies, dear friend," Leicester said, enjoying himself too much for Aiwren's taste as he handed off the luggage, "I'm afraid they're quite cumbersome."

When Aiwren saw Leicester's face, he realized that, in only moments, his role had changed from friend to steward. He was humiliated.

"Lieutenant Jocund is right," Wanda said. "If we're to leave town unnoticed, we should depart before sunrises."

"Actually," Jocund said, "my urgency is on account of not wanting to miss the parade I've arranged for us."

Upon hearing of a parade, everyone's jaws dropped with shock. Aiwren wondered what could possess his leader to arrange for a parade after insisting they remained secretive about their mission, but less than half a sunhand later, Aiwren had forgotten any misgivings he had, when he found himself walking through the streets in front of Wanda and Leicester's carriage, waving to the thousands of Kewnorians who were cheering for him and his fellow guardsmen. He had also forgotten Cutter's concerns as he soaked in the empty, unearned glory.

***

Not all of Y-Kewnor was awake early enough to watch the parade, but enough that word spread and those who were awake rushed to the street or to their window sills to watch the guardsmen march by, waving and smiling. It had, after all, been a very long time. For the young, they had either never seen a military parade or were too young to remember the last one. For those who were old, it had been a long time since their last Parade of the Guardsmen.

Bea's loyal assistant, Miles, a helpful and kind young guardsman who delighted Bea with his wonderful physique and handsome smile, had wheeled her out onto her balcony to watch the parade go by. She was no older than he was the last time a parade left Y-Kewnor. She could walk then. In fact, she marched in the last Parade of the Guardsmen, marched right out of town on the adventure that cost her legs. She wasn't bitter though. She had grown accustomed to wheeling around and didn't feel insulted by occasional help either. She also didn't get offended by the Kewnorian Guard ushering her off into some useless position, despite her rank and experience. She was confident she would be ready if she was needed again and comfortable with enjoying a life of gardening, cooking, reading, traveling, and playing the role of the eccentric invalid until then. Things worried her, though. She hoped Rheo, her dear late friend's knight-son, would be able to play the role she needed him to play. She also wondered if he would have the foresight to have arranged to receive word of things like this parade and the wisdom to report to her to watch it.

Bea looked down into the street at all of the people mindlessly cheering, ignorant of the history of the Parade of the Guardsmen. Over a thousand annuals earlier, when Y-Kewnor was a new city, recently free from the tyrant king, and the Kewnorian Guard were often sent to help the people in other city states of what would one day be the Freelands, there would be extravagant victory parades when the guardsmen returned from battle. Of course, due to the nature of war, many of the guardsmen never returned. One day, the only guardsmen in the parade returning from battle was a mortally wounded old man, who died in the street before he made it across town. In his dying words, the man cursed the parade, declaring that the reality of the glory of war was a soul crushing disappointment and that a victory parade after that illusion had been dispelled for a soldier, should that soldier even live to march the parade, was disingenuous and cruel. From that day forth, it was decided, the victory parade would become the Parade of the Lone Guardsman, and would be held on the way out of town for battle. Eventually, all history forgotten, the parade became known simply as the Parade of the Guardsmen. She wondered what she would have thought, wheeling down the street in her chair, if the parade had been after her last mission rather than before. On the other hand, she reminded herself, things were kept secret, erased from history, and forgotten after her last mission; there would have been no parade, which would have been fair due to the cost of that victory. There was so much the people cheering down in the street didn't know, that they could never learn. It was a shame to her they had forgotten the things they should have known.

Bea was pleased when Rheo arrived. She reminded herself, watching him hustle into the room, that weaving across town would have been difficult with so many people out in the streets. He didn't look at all surprised to see her already on the balcony when he slid a chair on to the landing and sat next to her.

"It's not right," he said, clearly upset, but controlling his temper. "It's not right for Jocund Plune to get a Parade of the Guardsmen. He is, at best, a scoundrel and, at worst, a traitor. And all for a mission to return some spoiled runaway princess from her carefree life in Y-Kewnor back to her carefree life in Watusia. That's supposed to be a task for The Divine Empress's Knights."

"So the mission is unworthy of glory, yet worthy of your envy?" Bea said. "Could it possibly be the glory, not the mission, you envy?"

"I don't know," said Rheo, with an honesty that surprised and pleased her. "Doesn't something about all of this just feel wrong to you though?"

"Many things feel wrong right now," Bea said, her thoughts at least partially occupied with a long forgotten tragedy and the people she still missed terribly. "We must remain clear headed if we're going to reveal the truth. Let's examine the situation. If anything were to happen to the princess here, in Y-Kewnor, Kewnorian relations with Sima Watusia would suffer. Returning the Princess to Sima Watusia would strengthen relations with Sima Watusia."

"And Bringing the princess to Simi Watusia would strengthen relations with Simi Watusia," Rheo said.

"Right," Bea continued. "So, whether they want to return the girl to her home or give her to her people's enemy, the Kewnorians want all the credit."

"So, which do you think it is?" Rheo asked. "Will they return her home or will this girl be another victim of the Plune family?"

Bea didn't answer the question. The guardsmen in the parade were coming into view and she couldn't be more surprised than she was by the sight of her old dear friend marching along with them.

"Also," Rheo, continued, "even if their intentions are good, the Simi Watusians, and a host of nary-do-wells will likely do everything they can to intercept the girl and use her as a bargaining chip against Sima Watusia. What kind of idiot is Jocund Plune that he would march such a target right through the center of the city?"

"The kind of idiot who has the finest warrior and most honorable man ever to serve the Kewnorian Guard marching with him, despite the fact that he swore he'd never serve again."

Bea pointed to the elderly man joylessly flanking the carriage while he scanned the crowd vigilantly, and said, "That's Ulysses James Cutter and the likes of him simply don't exist anymore. Perhaps they never have. So, now, the more interesting question is what in the name of The Divine Empress could have motivated him to reenlist."

Rheo tilted his head at Cutter's name, indicating it was unfamiliar to him, and rightly so; they had taken measures to keep everything about that mission a secret; those who left the service were forgotten with the fallen. Bea could tell Rheo was curious, she sensed in him the same earnestness of his knight-father, and she was glad for this. She needed that kind of uncompromising idealism in her life again, all of Y-Kewnor did. Of course, she sadly suspected, if he survived what was in store for him, his ideals likely wouldn't. There would be compromises to make, lesser evils to discern, and, like those many annuals ago, everyone involved would likely suffer, but those sorts of things had to happen and, seeing Ulysses marching down the street, gave her hope and made her wonder if some tragic endings weren't endings at all.

"Nothing can done right now," Bea said, postponing the clandestine story, as she was certain Vincent had done, "But we must remain updated on the progress of this mission. It may be more important than anyone realizes."

***

Truson laid awake in his elaborate new quarters, paid for with the blood of his knight-brothers, staring at the ceiling with his stomach twisting in upon itself and his eyes open to prevent the sights of horror. He had always wanted to see the best in people, but was usually a better judge of a person's heart. He wondered what he would have done if he had known for certain what the king was going to do. Could he have made a difference or would he have meaninglessly sacrificed his life only stack one more corpse in the temple courtyard? There was no way to cleanse himself of what had happened the day before. All he could do was try his hardest to protect Lees Naglos and that meant serving a mad and dangerous king. Well before the sun rose Truson gave up on pursuing such agonizingly restless sleep and decided to start his day.

The irony, Truson thought as he dressed himself in the elaborate armor that was gifted to him by the king with a hand-written note thanking him for his loyalty, was that Noldar really did love him and, despite how twisted the king's decision was, Truson still cared about the king. He, too, surely would have lost his mind if faced with the same tragedies. He also thought of little Teryessa, the princess he loved like a sister, how she brightened the spirits of everyone she met. He hoped her death had been swift and had occurred before she suffered the indecencies of the Gavlessan prince. Perhaps, he thought, as he buckled the last iron bracer around his forearm, if she had been allowed to wear this armor, this would have been a different day. That wasn't what had happened though and, in a few sunhands, Truson would have to stand before twenty-thousand soldiers and convince them their broken soulless kingdom was worth dying for. He would also have to numb his heart and focus his mind so he could devise a strategy that required as few of them as possible to do so. Fully dressed, he closed his eyes for a moment, let the still of morning cleanse him, took a deep breath, and opened his eyes again... ready to begin a war.

King Noldar treated his Knight Generals respectfully and, when they planned, they did so at a round table with the king sitting in an ordinary chair just like any other knight. The king did so many things so right, which only made his recent cruelty more tragic. Truson sat to the king's left and Niveous Snew sat to the king's right. The rest of the table was populated by the Knight Generals of the king's army. At any other time they were expected to serve the king and follow Truson's orders unquestioningly, but this forum allowed them to freely express ideas and worries so no stone was left unturned. The king's late wife had always called this a think tank. It was a curious expression, but it caught on. In fact, many of the generals conducted their own think tanks with the officers under their command, to better plan the facilitation of the strategies devised in the king's think tank. This was Truson's first think tank, but he had heard enough about them to understand the format and he was first to propose a controversial idea.

"Gavlessa has spies here, I am certain," Truson said. "Though they are in upheaval, they certainly are already aware that we plan to attack. If we delayed the attack we might be able to root out the infectious traitors."

The king was about to interrupt, to denounce the thought of delaying the war, but Truson held up a finger to show he was not finished and that the king may still like his idea. The king nodded graciously for him to continue.

"But our window of opportunity to attack is small and there is no guarantee that we'd ever be able to successfully identify all of the spies. Our best bet is to race the information to Gavlessa. Of course we won't be able to move an army into position before a single spy on horseback could speed across the desert, but we could give Gavlessa as little time to react to this information as possible."

"How long are you thinking?" a general asked.

"Two suns," Truson replied, and, after a moment of hesitation, he added, "including this sun."

The room exploded with incredulous outbursts. The king asked if it was possible.

"Marching across the desert would require four suns, at least," one general replied.

"We're not marching across the desert," Truson replied. "We're traveling by horse."

"We could get our cavalry to Gavlessa in two suns, certainly, but we've only two thousand of them and that isn't nearly enough to take Gavlessa." a general said.

"We have precisely eighteen hundred cavalry, but could have double that riding around Gavlessa and it still wouldn't breach the walls. No, we're leaving the cavalry behind at first. But we also have another thirteen hundred horses in Lees Naglos and perhaps up to a thousand wagons and carriages. What I'm proposing is that we hitch as many horses as we can to anything with wheels and use them to transport as much of our eighteen thousand infantry as we can fit on them across the desert as quickly as possible. We have this sun to make all the arrangements and the next sun to travel."

"And what of the Gavlessan Beast Raiders?!" A general snapped, outraged. "If the Gavlessans see our infantry with no cavalry, they will certainly send out their Beast Raiders!"

"Precisely," Truson said. "They'll open their front gates to do so. Our archers will be ready as they pass through the choke point and our infantry will be prepared to storm as soon as the Beast Raiders are slain."

"This plan," the king said, "it isn't traditional. Are you certain it will work?"

"No," Truson said, "but I'm certain nothing else will."

***

It only required one full sunhand for Jocund to lead his platoon across the city. By two full hands, Y-Kewnor was already far behind them. Sima Watusia was not very far from Y-Kewnor. Traveling quickly by horse, it could have been reached in only two suns, but they wouldn't be traveling quickly by horse. The Kewnorian Guard refused to spare them enough horses for everyone. In fact, they were only given two horses which were both being used to pull the princess's carriage. Jocund's soldiers had to travel on foot; they were sitting ducks. This concerned Jocund, but not nearly as much as it annoyed him. The way he saw it, there would either be danger or there wouldn't and it didn't really matter whether they went quickly into danger or slowly. On the other hand, he'd have to spend at least four days on the road with an irritating princess and a platoon of idiots, but he had comforted himself with the thought that at least the princess would be sitting comfortably in her carriage the entire trip. So Jocund was quite disappointed when, after only two hands of the sun of traveling, the carriage door opened and the princess poked her head out of the moving carriage.

"What are you doing, princess?" Jocund asked.

"I want to get out," she responded indignantly, as she climbed down from the still-moving carriage.

"Woah," Jocund said, to stop the horses and the whole procession in the middle of the muddy road that divided the expanse of marsh beneath the morning sun. "It seems the princess has to relieve herself already."

"Relieve erself?" Gregory asked, confused.

"He means piss," Serafina whispered to Gregory, "but it ain't right to say piss in front of a princess."

"First of all," the princess said, reaching the ground, "I am not a frail little girl. I know the word piss and I'll let you know when I have to do so. I wish to walk. I'm not an invalid."

Jocund felt the confused eyes of his platoon turn to him for leadership, not knowing what to do or how they should react to this. He saw the princess's fiancé, Leicester, poked his nebbish little head out of the carriage. Jocund knew he needed to establish some ground rules. This was all so absurd to him, but, nevertheless, it was his responsibility; he stepped forward.

"Your Highness," Jocund began, remaining controlled and tactful, "I'm afraid I need to ask you to remain in the carriage."

"Why?!" Princess Wanda demanded. "So I can ride, while the others walk? I detest special treatment of some people simply because they were born into the right family."

"Princess," Jocund replied, pretending not to notice her insinuations about him, "it appears as though your kind and generous heart is momentary eclipsing your reason. May I remind you, the reason for this costly military entourage is because it is unsafe for you to travel? While your thoughts on economics and politics are truly fascinating and while I would love to hear the astounding philosophies a life of pampering has provided you the luxury of pondering, perhaps that conversation would be better conducted over a bottle of wine, safely within the walls of Sima Watusia. For now, however, there are soldiers risking their lives to provide you safe passage who would probably appreciate you not getting them killed slightly more than your hyperbolic but meaningless gestures of self-deprecation."

The princess looked furious. Her face turned bright red and her eyes narrowed. Jocund smiled to himself about her flushed freckly skin only making her green eyes more pronounced and stunning. It would be a very long trip if she was constantly trying to usurp his command. She shot a glare to her puppy dog of a fiancé standing in the doorway of the carriage he was more than happy to ride in, for not speaking on her behalf. When it was clear that she had lost this argument, she stormed back into the carriage and climbed back up, providing Jocund with the irresistible temptation to admire her posterior, which, now that she was looking away for her climb, he did unabashedly; however, as she reached the top rung of the ladder, she shot him a scathing glance and he was certain she had noticed him looking.

"Okay," he commanded. "Time to go."

Jocund knew his decision to conduct the Parade of the Guardsmen would cost them some time, and it remained vital that they made it to Bridgekeep before nightfall, but his stunt that morning, though seen by many as an act of pomp and bravado, would end up playing a vital part of his plan if his timing was just right. He extended his arm to check the sun.

"Let's move!" he shouted as he briskly walked to the front of the procession.

***

Vannoria awoke early that morning, packed her things, and, still wearing her ceremonial clothes, took one last stroll by the edge of the swamp, the swamp that already felt like a home to her. She didn't know how long she had until Shadow would kill her, but she believed him when he said he would and held no grudges against him for something beyond his control or understanding. She felt a distilling calm wash over her soul. For all of her life, Vannoria always knew what was coming next, as though her life had been decided for her, and the one thing she ever yearned for, Aiwren's love, had not only been incontrovertibly unrequited but also unapologetically thrown back in her face as though her affections were some disgusting curse; however, in her return from the edge of death, something within her had been awakened and she had the desire to make decisions for herself, to exercise agency over her own life, if only for its few final suns. She felt Shadow approach her. She didn't need to look. She knew it was him. He was going to try to convince her not to go, to remain in Ma-Aresh and allow whatever suns remained in her life to pass uneventfully until the eventual day when he was supposed to kill her.

"What would you do if you knew your life was about to end?" Vannoria asked, her stare across the swamp clear with resolve, her face relaxed with calm certainty.

"I don't know," he said.

"But you do know," Vannoria replied, "That's all you've known. You've had all these brief little lives, with the singular objective of completing your Master's missions. All these lives but you've never lived."

Shadow didn't respond to this and Vannoria wondered if his silence was indicative of him thinking about what she said or of him having no idea what she was talking about. She stood, gazing across the swamp, taking it in. She only just arrived here but, in knowing she might never see it again, she missed Ma-Aresh and the Ma-Areshi already. She watched as a swamp turkey swam by and, from the opposite shore, a giant alligator silently slipped into the shallow murky water to snatch the fowl from below when it wasn't expecting it. Any moment could be its last.

"I know what I want to do," Vannoria said, wondering if the bird knew how few moments it had, "I want to understand. I want to understand the world. I want to understand this magic that saved my life and why these people think I'm special when nobody has ever thought I was special before."

"You wish to journey to the West, find the Ma-Areshi, and free them," Shadow said, cutting to the chase for her.

"I need to test myself. I need to do something good with my life so I can meaningfully enjoy the precious little of it I have left. Perhaps your Master can find it in his heart to let me live until I do so."

"I cannot promise that, but if that's what you wish, I will accompany you and see to it no harm falls upon you on your journey."

"Except by you," Vannoria said, watching the water stir behind the swamp turkey, sure it would die soon."

"Right," she heard Shadow say, his own voice sounding perhaps a little distant, "except by me."

"Swear to it," Vannoria said, turning to Shadow. "Swear that it will be only be you who cuts me down."

"I swear by my Master," Shadow vowed.

"I don't give a fuck about your Master," Vannoria replied. "Swear by yourself."

"I swear by myself," Shadow apologized.

"Good," Vannoria said, surprisingly comforted to have Shadow by her side. "We should leave soon."

As Vannoria and Shadow stepped away from the shore of the swamp, the giant alligator erupted from beneath the turbid duckweed and fairy-moss speckled muck to consume the large bird with one voracious splash of its jaws, but the swamp turkey, more alert and agile than it appeared, propelling itself from the slough, took to the air and flew.

Slowly and purposefully, taking in all of the reeds, cattails, and sumac she passed, deeply inhaling the sweet smell of the swamp lilacs, trying to capture each bit of insect and animal movement with her glance, Vannoria strolled up the short path through to the clearing by Mister Uncle's cabin, where she saw her small bag already packed and ready to go on Shadow's horse; he must have known any attempt to change her mind would have been inconsequential. Mister Uncle and his Family-Clan were also waiting for her.

Vannoria approached the semicircle of Ma-Areshi around the horse. It wasn't all of them, but it was most. She saw the now familiar faces looking upon her with reverence and an overwhelming tide of emotions welled up inside her as she realized what she really was to them: hope. Y-Yshaah, the little girl Vannoria had met the night before, was in her mama's arms next to Mister Uncle. The little girl scrambled down from her mother's arms. Vannoria knelt and the girl handed her a necklace.

"Thank you, Y-Yshaah," Vannoria said. "Did you make this?"

"Yes, Majisyenna, with dried swampberry seeds," the little girl said.

"It's beautiful," Vannoria said, adorning herself with the swampberry seed necklace and kissing the girl on the forehead. "I'll wear it always."

The girl smiled and bashfully ran over to Mister Uncle. The girl pulled on his hand and he leaned down so she could whisper in his ear. A moment later he smiled with a chuckle.

"It appears as though she has a gift for the Shadow Rider as well, old friend," he said to Shadow.

Shadow hesitated for a bit, his brow furrowed with confusion, before stepping towards the girl. The Ma-Areshi stepped back, except for the girl's mama, who stepped closer and wrapped a protective arm around her daughter. Vannoria watched as the strange man sent to kill her hesitantly crouched down as the girl, freed herself from her mother and cautiously approached. The girl stared curiously at a Shadow, who returned her look, equally curious. She reached her hand out and offered him what appeared to be the tooth of an alligator. It was white, nearly a step-long, and came to a dull point at each end; however it was covered with perfect holes in a pattern of varying sizes along its length. He put out his hands and allowed the girl to hand it to him.

"What is this?" he asked.

"It is an alligator flute, Lonbrajjeau" she said. "Perhaps it will help you remember your name-song."

Vannoria saw that Shadow was about to return the gift and offer some kind of protest, but before he had a chance to, the girl leaned forward, kissed him on the cheek, and ran back to her mother. He clearly didn't know how to react to any of this. Stuck with the flute, he stuffed it in his pocket and stood.

"Teeffah," Mister Uncle said, stepping forward to her, "before you try to explain, I already know where you plan to go and what you plan to do."

"Mister Uncle, you have saved my life. I feel compelled to do something in return," Vannoria said. "My days are limited and I want to be sure that, when I die, I leave behind no unpaid debts."

"You are not yet healed, teeffah, you've never taken a journey before, let alone one as perilous as this, you've learned nothing of your powers, and, if the rumors of a necromancer are true, this journey would be to death, itself," Mister Uncle replied.

Shadow, looking encouraged by Mister Uncle's agreement with his stance on Vannoria's choice to leave, stepped forward. She was so sick of feeling unworthy, of people telling her no. She shot Shadow a look, warning him not to open his mouth and he remained silent.

She turned to the Ma-Areshi and said, "Family, I will be traveling north, along the path your missing brothers journeyed on. I will travel to Gavlessa if I have to, even further, if that's what it takes, to find out what has become of them. If they are alive, I will bring them home to you. If they are not, I will avenge them. I do this in your name, to repay my debt to you, and to earn the title you've given me: Sourceresha."

The Ma-Areshi, staring at her with wonder and awe, solemnly took one another's hands and sang. It was a beautiful song, not as energetic as the music of the ritual the night before, but solemn and moving, a chant that hauntingly echoed across the swamp and brought a tear to Vannoria's eyes and, as she looked over to Mister Uncle for an explanation, she saw he was crying. She threw her arms around him and buried her head in his chest.

"What is that?" she sobbed. "What are they singing."

"It is the hope song, teeffah," he said. "It has been a long time since they sang it last. Please, return to us, little one."

Vannoria and Shadow mounted. She was not thrilled about sharing a saddle with him, but there were no other horses and the alligators would not fair well as far from their swamp as she knew she'd be journeying. Traveling across the marsh, she watched over her shoulder as the Commune grew distant. Soon, it disappeared behind them, as they galloped to the road that paralleled the Realmsend River.

As they neared the Realmsend River road, Vannoria saw an amazing sight to her left. Ma-Aresh. It was far from her, but, because of her injuries and fever, she had no recollection of seeing Y-Kewnor, so this was her first real glimpse of a city and she couldn't believe its size. It wasn't a tall city and it wasn't very shiny and there were no grand palaces, keeps, or towers, but it stretched out for what appeared to be forever. Part of her wished she could go explore it. The world, she realized, was so big.

Realizing it may have been because she knew death was coming for her, she wondered how she could have ever been content to remain on one little farm for her entire life. She knew she'd probably never see that city from the inside and she thought bitterly of all that she could have done with her life and all she could have seen, had she not fallen for Aiwren Wayde. She turned her attention back to the little she would get to see, the mission she was on.

Shadow's horse galloped north, on the Realmsend River Road, and Ma-Aresh was soon behind them. The wide river appeared calm. The land on its opposite shore looked the same as the land on her side. She wondered why it was such a barrier and what was so wild about the Wild on the other side.

Vannoria and Shadow rode all day, not even stopping for lunch, which Shadow skipped and Vannoria attempted to consume while bouncing around on horseback. Soon the marsh around them turned into a plain, not unlike the plains around Ribeln, though, perhaps, not as green. She saw the peaks of the Dragonsback Mountains to appear to grow out of the horizon in front of them, white and jagged. Soon the mountains took their proper shape, scale, and orientation west of Vannoria and Shadow, but there was a new range of mountains in the distance before them, grey, purple, and rocky, the Perdition Mountains.

As the day progressed, the scenery continued to change. By time Vannoria and Shadow had been riding all day and the sun was threatening to set behind the Dragonsback Mountains, the Perdition Mountains had grown nearer and the plains had turned into wooded rolling hills. The Realmsend River still appeared wide and still, but, while the road had been empty for most of the day, they could see wagons and carts traveling to or from Era-Mosa and the areas near the road became more and more populated with little cabins nested in the wooded hills, with plumes of smoke billowing from the stone chimneys of fireplaces and forges. The horse stopped.

"We're close to a city," said Shadow.

"I know," replied Vannoria. "Era-Mosa. They say it's made of iron and was forged, not built. Is that true? Will we be staying there tonight?"

"No," Shadow said. "We'll be entering its southern gate as soon as the sun sets and exiting out its western gate without delay or distraction."

"Why?!" Vannoria demanded. "We've traveled all day and covered a great distance. I've never been to a city before and I would like to see it."

"This is what we're doing," Shadow said, looking over his shoulder to her. "If you want to see the city, then keep your eyes open as we pass through."

He snapped the reins and they continued.

Vannoria fumed the remainder of the way to Era-Mosa, which came upon them suddenly.

It was almost dark when Vannoria and Shadow rode up the hill that was hiding Era-Mosa from their sight. As they neared the top, Vannoria saw the black iron reflecting the setting sun and, in the light of that golden hour, the dull iron looked like glass, a citadel of metal growing from the mountains beside the river. Era-Mosa wasn't built entirely of iron as Vannoria had heard, nor was it a single citadel, as it had appeared to be. It was, however, mostly iron, and the buildings were so tall and built so closely together that they appeared to be one building.

Vannoria, remembered from her lessons that Era-Mosa was an important city-state for two reasons. First, it was the source of the weapons and armor of almost all of the Freelands and most weapons that were made elsewhere got their iron from the mines of Era-Mosa. The other reason why it was important was because it housed the Eastern Wildgate. Until boating became more popular, anybody wishing to travel to Lees Naglos or Frins Casicon, the two western destinations most popular with Freelanders, would have to pass through the Era-Mosa and traverse the Wildgate Bridge in order to get to the Wild, which they had to cross to reach those far away destinations. This one bridge across the Realmsend River was a security measure, built thousands of annuals earlier, to keep out the beasts of the Wild. There was no better place to construct this, than the most fortified city ever built, Era-Mosa, the city of iron.

All the gates to Era-Mosa were fortified, remnants of a time of war, even between the city-states of the Freelands. As darkness fell upon the land, Vannoria and Shadow approached the southern most of these gates.

As they trotted close to the city, Vannoria was surprised to see no guards on duty and that the enormous gate, easily three stories tall, was wide open, with vendors and townspeople casually crossing the open passage. Shadow, she realized, was silent and still as stone, pausing the horse for a moment before entering. The instant they crossed the threshold, Shadow seized in pain, convulsing with a grunt before regaining his composure.

"What was that?" Vannoria asked.

"Nothing," he replied. "Let's keep moving."

The city was overwhelming and amazing to Vannoria, with iron buildings nestled closely together on the narrow cobblestone streets that were, even at night, teeming with activity, but Vannoria's attention shifted to Shadow, who seemed to grow weaker and weaker. She asked him again if anything was wrong, but he insisted for her not to be concerned about anything other than making it to the west side of town.

Another gate vaulted skyward in the distance. They had taken a left earlier, so Vannoria knew it was the western gate, the Wildgate, but she was worried about Shadow. She couldn't see his face, but she knew something was wrong. She, looking over his shoulder, focussed on the gate, but wondered if they should stop somewhere to get help for him. She wondered where they would stop though. She didn't know anyone in this city. She wondered who would help her.

"Don't stop," Shadow muttered weakly, barely audible to her. "You must get out of the city."

"Why?" she asked. "What's wrong?"

Shadow didn't respond. Instead, he slumped over on the horse, nearly falling off.

Responding instinctually, she grabbed around his waist just in time to prevent him collapsing from the horse. Reaching around him, she grabbed the reins without letting go of him and kicked the side of the horse. They were off.

It was almost impossible to keep Shadow on the horse, control the horse, and see in front of her to avoid collision as she sped towards the gate. People dove out of the way, upending carts, and leaving melons, eggs, and iron ore to tumble into the crowded street. She galloped the horse through the gates, but Shadow's condition still did not improve.

She looked up and saw that, before her, stretched from one cliff to another, high above the Realmsend River, was a massive iron bridge. It was floored with heavy wooden slats and had metal arches that spanned its length and appeared to suspend it in place. The arches were tallest at the center of the bridge, soaring high over her head, and covered with strange markings. That was when she felt the warmth.

The heat started subtly, almost unnoticeable, but soon Shadow felt like a fire to Vannoria. She kicked the horse to go faster and faster, but the bouncing toppled Shadow's weight over. The shift in weight shifted the horse's direction. The were galloping closer and closer to the side of the bridge, Shadow's weight was slipping lower and lower, and her grasp on what was now only his cloak was weakening, as she, too, sank to the side of the horse, forced to hold the saddle with her other hand while watching the river race by far below. She thought, for certain, they would both fall to their deaths, but she kept hanging on, hoping the horse would have the sense not to gallop over the edge.

Vannoria made it to the other side of the bridge and Shadow managed to right himself in the saddle before slumping forward. She pulled on the reins of the horse to stop so she could catch her breath, but the beast didn't stop galloping them off into the dark until the bridge, Era-Mosa, and Freelands were far behind them.

As soon as the horse stopped, Shadow fell to the ground and Vannoria screamed and hopped off, after him. It took all of Vannoria's strength for her to roll him over and she nearly screamed from shock when she did. In the moonlight she could see that his eyes were closed and blood was rushing from his nose.

Vannoria acted without thinking. She put her hand to her heart, to that tattooed glyph that looked like water. She pulled her hand away and looked at it. The pattern glowed in gold light. She was about to put her hands to his face, when she immediately stopped. If Shadow died, she realized, she would be free. Would letting him die be the same as murder, she wondered? Would she be able to live with herself, letting him die in her arms? She didn't understand why she didn't want to let him die, but it was too late. The light on her palm was gone.

Vannoria tried again to charge her hand with whatever magics it was those marks contained, but it did no good.

She told herself, if she didn't save him, she would surely die out there. She desperately tried again, but again the mark of light faded.

Vannoria tried one more time. She held her hand on her heart and didn't let go. She felt a warmth in her hand, but she held it still until the warmth turned into a heat unbearable to touch. She pulled her hand away and looked at it. It was glowing with unwavering intensity, glowing like a lantern, brighter than the ghost moon above her head, casting enough light to make the area around her look like day. Then, she grabbed Shadow's face.

Vannoria was somewhere else. It was night, but something was different. The moon was red not blue. She didn't feel like herself. The world felt far away and hazy, like a dream, but she tried hard to focus, to get her bearings. She was crawling on her hands and knees across a muddy, blood-stained field, surrounded by corpses, and she realized she was not motivating the movement; she was a passenger, a passenger in her own body, controlled by someone or something else.

She saw a small puddle of water ahead of her, and, realizing how parched her lips felt, she knew that was where she was crawling. She felt a dull aching in her gut, that sent an agonizing convulsion of pain through her body every time she moved. She saw her hands reaching for the puddle and was shocked to find that they weren't her hands; they were a man's hands. They pulled filthy water to her mouth and the coolness soothed her throat. She looked down into the puddle and, as the ripples subsided, she saw a face reflected in the water. Shadow's face.

There was motion in the water, the reflection of something behind her, behind Shadow, who's eyes she was somehow seeing the world through. She felt herself whipping around and felt her hand reaching for a sword, but it was too late. The blade of an ax was screaming towards her face. Unable to block it, she was instantly cast in darkness.

The darkness felt eternal and infinite around her, but she felt herself moving through it, backwards, away from the ax. In reverse, she passed from the darkness, through a cloud of unimaginable swirling colors, and back to her own body, looking down on Shadow, his face cradled in her hands as he took a breath.

***

When Lieutenant Plune and Wanda argued that morning, Aiwren did his best to not make eye contact with Wanda, for fear that she might look to him to stick up for her in the absence of Leicester, whom Aiwren was certain would get in trouble with her for not sticking up for her. Aiwren slipped over to the far corner of the carriage and stood by Gilmore, who gave him a nod of approval for his decision to avoid any chance of involvement in this argument. Aiwren watched Wanda in this conversation and everything she said made sense to him. He thought of how absurd it was that some people were born to kings and some were born to milkmen and that their entire lives were assumed to be scribed for them based on who they were born to and that didn't feel right to him. Aiwren realized, as he watched Lieutenant Plune and Wanda argue, that it was a lordson and a princess doing the talking, deciding the fate of a platoon of men and women born to paupers and tradesmen, a platoon of men and women who's voices never seemed to be heard, as a princess and lordson decided what was best for them. Soon the procession was moving again and Aiwren put these thoughts behind him.

After the small verbal skirmish between Wanda and Lieutenant Plune, Aiwren was thankful the two of them and Leicester kept to themselves for the rest of the day. Aiwren spent the day walking with Serafina and Gregory, quietly joking about what had happened that morning and how Roderick, Brunff, and Kazerra and had been chumming up with Halibon.

"Wut a pity," Gregory said, "that Halibon didn't quit when Cutter came on board. That way, maybe you would have been made a sergeant and we coulda been corporals."

"There can't be two corporals," Serafina said.

"I know," Gregory admitted. "I jus didn't wanna ave to make Aiwren pick tween my beauty or your brawn."

"Oh, so you're a beauty now?" said Serafina, who was exotically stunning even in the drab Guardsman uniforms they were wearing. "We'll see about that when we get into Bridgekeep. Women love a man in uniform, but find a woman in uniform irresistible."

The three of them laughed loudly enough to get a scowl from Halibon, who seemed to know the joke was at his expense.

Right before they sat down for lunch, Aiwren found himself being whisked behind a tree by Cutter, who instructed Aiwren to follow him to a small field where they ate lunch and practiced. As they returned to the group, Aiwren tried to continue their conversation from that morning, but Cutter was uninterested in talking about anything else and clearly in a surly mood. Aiwren's fighting was rapidly improving though and he could tell, despite Cutter's disposition, his teacher was proud of him.

The group marched on, without occurrence, for the remainder of the day until Bridgekeep was near and the sun was setting. Aiwren and his friends wondered if they'd be staying in Bridgekeep that night. They were tired, so it made sense, but as he saw the little city grow closer, something felt strategically wrong about it to Aiwren.

"So I know we assumed we'd be staying here tonight since the distance works out," Aiwren said, "but doesn't going into a small city like this, with only the few of us to protect Wanda seem like a bad idea?"

"I think you referring to her as anything other than 'princess' seems like a bad idea," Serafina replied.

"I keep forgetting," Aiwren said.

"Well you should probably try harder to remember," Serafina warned. "She and your friend are royalty now."

"Yeah," Gregory added, "there'll be no more consortin' wif the likes o you. Not fer those two. An you have a job ta do now, anyways."

"They're not like that," Aiwren said, forgetting his concern about sleeping in Bridgekeep. "They're terrific. You'll see. And, if anything, them being my friends makes me even more motivated to protect them."

The day had been long. Aiwren's feet were sore and his back was hurting. He was a hard worker, but walking all day with only a brief stop to practice his swordsmanship was exhausting. Soon, he was relieved to find himself, without even a brief explanation to the troop from Lieutenant Plune, heading into Bridgekeep.

Bridgekeep was a small city, not much bigger than Ribeln and only twice as populated, but it was a lot rougher. Despite its smaller size and population, it felt more like a city. It was located where the Y-Kewnor River intersected the main road that travelled across the Freelands. Thousands of annuals earlier, when the city states of the Freelands were kingdoms feuding between one another, trolls used to occupy the space beneath the bridges that crossed what would one day be named the Y-Kewnor River, ambushing travelers to rob, rape, and murder them. Some industrious mercenaries claimed the land around one such bridge, built residences nearby so they could keep the area patrolled and free of trolls, and charged those who wished to cross the bridge a small fee. A small collection of bars and brothels were built to serve this industry, which became a town and, eventually, a small city. Bridgekeep emerged as a city existing not because it was a meaningful destination, but because it was between meaningful destinations and it felt like it.

The streets were line with brothels, bars, and inns containing brothels and bars. Everything was painted brightly to attract customers. Even at night, the streets were filled with vendors and merchants selling food, drunken men stumbling around aimlessly or looking for a fight, and scantily clad prostitutes showing off to drum up business. Aiwren had never seen anything like it.

"How does one choose," Aiwren joked, in awe of the variety.

"There's no choice at all, milkboy," Lieutenant Plune said, putting a surprisingly cheerful hand on Aiwren's shoulder. "There's only one place to go in Bridgekeep. Ptatiana's."

"Ptatiana's?" Aiwren asked. "What is it?"

"A reason to believe in The Divine Empress," Lieutenant Plune marveled. "Come on."

With no more explanation, Jocund was off. It was difficult to follow him, with the carriage, but they managed and eventually arrived in front of a four story building with a picture of a nearly naked woman, holding a pint of ale in one hand and a deck of gambling cards in the other hand painted on the front. The words, "Ptatiana's Tavern," arced over the painting of the woman.

Wanda stormed from the carriage, slapping away Leicester's hand when he tried to help her. She marched over to Plune, who was hitching the horse, with Leicester close behind.

"If you think, this is going to offend my girlish sensibilities, then you're going to be sorely mistaken. I've seen more flesh than this in the dressing room of the theatre."

"You have?!" Leicester and Aiwren both exclaimed, but it was apparently inaudible to Wanda, who was in a state of absolute fury to Plune.

"I've probably shown more, as well," she declared. "That's not what bothers me."

"Please," Plune said, "tell me what bothers you."

She stammered a moment before Lieutenant Plune said, "I sincerely apologize for whatever it is about me that offends you. When you think of what it is, please do let me know so I may correct it posthaste. Until then, I shall be inside this fine establishment, enjoying some spirits, company, and a good night's rest. Wayde, please be certain the princess finds safe lodging. Everyone's tabs this evening will be paid by me, regardless of the cost."

Lieutenant Plune entered Ptatiana's, leaving Aiwren out front, just as flabbergasted as Wanda and Leicester. Gregory and Serafina remained by his side, but everyone else entered the bar, even Cutter, who gave his shoulder a squeeze on his way in.

Aiwren looked at Wanda, Leicester, Gregory, and Serafina, who, he found, were all staring at him, waiting for an answer.

"Well," Aiwren said, "we'll probably be safer inside."

"Yes," said Leicester, "I think we could all use a drink. The carriage ride was dreadfully boring."

Sensing Leicester's statement was unpopular with everyone, himself included, Aiwren changed the subject, introducing Serafina and Gregory to Leicester and Wanda, and ushered them all indoors to the safety of the Ptatiana's just as a pack of roughnecks approached, undoubtably looking for trouble.

By the time they all went inside Cutter, Jocund, and Halibon had already gone up to bed for the night and Roderick, Brunff, and Kazerra made it clear that there was no room for Aiwren and his friends at their booth, so, after securing rooms for himself and the others, Aiwren found a table and ordered his friends a round of pints. They sipped at their beers in silence until Leicester broke the ice, baiting them all into a race to the bottom of their pints, a dare none of them could refuse, and Aiwren immediately felt guilty for secretly resenting his friend all day.

The five of them sat at that table all night, trading stories, learning things about friends, both new and old.

"I'm sorry I withheld my identity." Wanda said, some time into their third or fourth round. "That's probably the worst secret ever."

"It's not so bad," Serafina said, consoling her, "I kept it secret most of my life that it's women I yearn for. Although Ma-Aresh is a city, it's a small city with small minded people and unlike Y-Kewnor, women like me are considered shameful there."

"There's absolutely no shame in who you are, Serafina," Wanda said. "I'm glad you've found a home in Y-Kewnor. With your beauty, I'd wager you have your pick of women there."

"Do I need to worry?" joked Leicester.

"You do, if you don't start speaking up when I look to you for support, darling," Wanda replied.

"I'll take care of you, my princess," joked Serafina.

"I hate being a tailor and I've never told anyone before," said Leicester. "I almost quit and moved back to Ribeln, but then I met Wanda and fell in love, remaining in Y-Kewnor just to be near her and continuing my apprenticeship just so I could take care of her. If I had known she was a princess, I could have quit ages ago."

Leicester's admission softened Wanda's frustration with him. She squeezed his hand and flashed him an adoring smile.

"I'm afraid o dragons; just the thought o one makes me wriggle in me boots," said Gregory. "We've all got secrets, but the big stuff, the things that's in our hearts is ard to hide."

"Aiwren is the worst of all," said Serafina, causing Aiwren to nervously wonder if she somehow knew of his nightmares. "He never told anyone he was such a deadly warrior."

"Aiwren?! Really?!" Leicester exclaimed.

"You didn't know?!" Gregory asked. "I've never seen anything like im. Thas why ol Halibon is such a sour puss. It's on accounta Aiwren beating the pants off im."

Perhaps it was the drinks, or the stress of the day, or the relief of his friendship with Leicester returning to normal, but Aiwren spoke with out thinking and said, "I can train you. It has to be a secret, but I can train you to fight the way I do."

The five of them agreed. They all wanted to learn this exotic style of combat, but, at the moment they were more interested in learning how many drinks they could combat, so Gregory left to fetch another round. As he watched Gregory walk away, Aiwren noticed small group of men in the corner of the inn watching them. They were wearing dark cloaks and deep in the shadows, but there was no mistaking their glances.

"Have any of you noticed that group of brigands in the corner?" Aiwren asked.

"No. Where?" Leicester said, looking around with drunken indiscretion.

"In the corner?" Serafina asked. "I noticed them, too. I think they're watching us."

"You should go tell Jocund, Aiwren," Leicester said.

"I'm sure Lieutenant Plune has this under control," Aiwren said. "He knows what he's doing."

"Jocund's an ass and a drunkard," Wanda said. "You need to go wake him so we can get out of here. Leicester, tell him to go tell Jocund."

"You really should go do it, Aiwren," Leicester said. "I mean it's your responsibility."

Aiwren was bullied into a corner. He wished he hadn't even brought it up. He had no choice but to go tell Jocund. So he told Gregory and Serafina to make sure Wanda and Leicester safely got to their room and then he marched up the stairs and knocked on Lieutenant Plune's door, not knowing what to expect. When nobody answered the door he opened it. The room was filled with several nude women, one which he immediately recognized from the sign as Ptatiana.

"Burning Empress!" Lieutenant Plune exclaimed from beneath a sea of nude women. "Can I never have even the slightest amount of privacy?! Wayde, please tell me you have a wonderful explanation for this."

Some of the nude women cleared off to the side and Aiwren could see Lieutenant Plune sitting on the small bed in the middle of the room.

"My liege," Aiwren said, "there are some dubious characters downstairs. They've been watching us from the corner."

"Dubious characters in brothel and gambling establishment?!" Jocund roared, feigning shock as the women stroking his hair giggled. "My Empress! How is that possible?!"

"I simply thought you might like to know, My Liege" Aiwren protested, "so we may keep the princess safe."

"Thank you, Corporal Wayde," Jocund dismissed, waving a hand at Aiwren. "I have this under control. I suggest you return to the parlor, order another round, and enjoy yourself."

When Aiwren arrived at Wanda and Leicester's room, just down the hall, he found Wanda, Leicester, Serafina, and Gregory all waiting for him.

"So it doesn't look like we're going to get much support from Lieutenant Plune tonight, but he assured me precautions have been taken. Now Lieutenant Plune-"

"What an ass!" shouted Wanda. "That selfish, irresponsible, and entitled little prick is the very embodiment of everything wrong with society!"

"I'd rather not get in between the two of you," Aiwren said, "but I swear I won't let anything happen to you."

Aiwren asked Serafina and Gregory to sleep in Leicester and Wanda's room and told them all he'd guard right outside the door, which he did. The night passed uneventfully as he sat, leaning against their door, with his eyes open.

***

The Nameless Rider heard the fire crackling before he opened his eyes and he wondered if he had failed his mission, returned to his sleep, and was being awakened after some undetermined passage of time, but the pale moon coming into focus above him told him he was still on the same mission. Remembering what happened, he expected to feel some sort of residual pain, but he didn't; that wasn't how things worked for him.

"You got a fire started," he said, sitting up.

"Wait, wait, wait!" Vannoria said, rushing to his side. "Take it easy. Go slow."

"I'm fine," he said, not sure how he knew, but certain he was, as the memory of passing through the city took shape inside his mind.

"You could have fooled me," she said, offering him some water. "I had to use the magics Mister Uncle taught me to save your life."

"You used magics to save me?" he asked, taking a sip. "I thought you were going to kill me. You may have missed a perfect opportunity."

"The timing wasn't right," she said, helping him scoot closer to the fire. "I figured I would save you now and kill you later. That's your strategy. Right? Don't flatter yourself, though. I had the Ma-Areshi to think about. I need your help to free Mister Uncle's Family and it didn't feel right to forsake them in the name of self-preservation."

Looking at Vannoria, part of him wished she had simply let him die, or whatever it was that would happen to him if his body stopped, that way he wouldn't have to kill her later, but this Girl who he was going to kill saved him, allowing him to go on and torturing him with more questions. He wondered what was ethical? He wondered if he had ever considered ethics before that night.

"So," she started, expectantly, "aren't you going to explain what happened?"

He knew the city was protected from him and those glyphs painted on the iron walls were intended to keep him out, but he still didn't know what he was or what the glyphs meant.

"It was magics," he explained, keeping the rest to himself in order to prevent having to explain to her yet again that he didn't have any answers.

"Oh, is that all?!" she snapped flippantly, "Well, that explains everything. No need to worry. It was just magics."

This launched her into a tirade about the ordeal she went through to save him, and he wondered why she was suddenly so concerned about his well being, but the Nameless Rider wasn't really listening. He was, instead, focussed on his surroundings. Someone was coming.

Without worry of trap or ambush, Vannoria, too, noticed and rushed to the grey and gold figure approaching them from up the road. He tried to stop her, but his words were too slow and, a moment later, Vannoria returned leading a grey horse with a gold rider to their camp.

"Some help you are," Vannoria said, but before she could berate him any further, the body fell from the horse.

The rider appeared to be the same age as Vannoria, but she was badly injured. Near her shoulder, blood was caked to her gold armor and her eye was swollen shut.

"Will you please help me remove her armor?!" Vannoria shouted. "I don't know how this stuff works."

The Nameless Rider, speechless, did as he was told, a passenger in his own life, a condition that never seemed to bother him before. He removed the girl's armor. She was filthy beneath the armor and her injuries were even more extensive than they initially appeared to be. In addition to the swollen eye, her shoulder was cut to the bone and badly infected, her wrist was swollen from a terrible sprain, and her ankle was twisted.

"We should go," he said.

"And leave her like this?!" Vannoria retorted incredulously. "Have you lost your mind?! She'll die."

Vannoria's hands, glowing with light, first touched wound on the girl's shoulder. The Nameless Rider knew he was comfortable watching life escape a body, but didn't think he had ever seen life enter a body before. When Vannoria removed her hands, the girl was scarred, but healed. Vannoria moved on to the other wounds. When she was finished she sat back and watched the girl open her eyes.

"Where am I?" she asked.

"Just to the west of Era-Mosa. My name is Vannoria and this is Shadow. You were injured so I healed you. What's your name?"

The girl hesitated for a moment and then said, "Matera," but the Nameless Rider knew she was lying.

"Feel up to any food, Matera?" Vannoria asked.

"I have my own," Matera said defiantly.

"If you have your own food, perhaps you should be on your way," the Nameless Rider said, hoping the girl who's name was clearly not Matera would take this opportunity to extricate herself from Vannoria's doting.

"I agree," the girl said.

"Nonsense," Vannoria said. "I want to make sure you're okay before I let you go anywhere. Where are you heading?"

"I appreciate your help," Matera said, "but my destination is my own business."

"She clearly desires nor needs any assistance," the Nameless Rider said. "We should be on our way."

"Shadow!" Vannoria scolded, then turned to the girl and said, "We're heading to Gavlessa on a mission to free some slaves, it will be perilous, but you're welcome to join us."

Hearing this, the girl softened a little and said, "There's been a coup. It's more dangerous than ever."

"And the slaves?" Vannoria asked.

"Too numerous to count when I was there," the girl said, suddenly looking distant. "I doubt many of them survived."

Matera stood, looking shocked at her ankle's ability to hold her own weight.

"My ankle!" she exclaimed.

"I used magics to heal your wounds," Vannoria replied.

"What are you?" Matera asked.

"I am a sorceress," Vannoria whispered, leaning forward surreptitiously .

"Thank you for healing my injuries, Sorceress. I wish you luck. Perhaps our paths will cross again someday."

Matera quickly dressed herself, mounted her grey horse, and rode off towards Era-Mosa.

After Vannoria scolded the Nameless Rider for being rude, the two of them settled in near the fire. She was clearly exhausted, but she asked him question after question about magics and the Ma-Areshi and the Wild and Gavlessa and his past, but he didn't have answers. He wondered why she seemed more driven than ever to get answers. Eventually, she curled up next to him with her head on his shoulder.

"That girl was so lonely," Vannoria said sleepily. "I suppose I'm glad you didn't die. Goodnight, Shadow."

Hearing these words, the Nameless Rider felt things changing in him. He found himself wanting something. He wanted to be something different. He wanted to tell her, but all he could say was, "Goodnight, Vannoria."

The moment should have been a peaceful one, but as he grabbed a blanket and wrapped it around Vannoria for warmth, he noticed a glyph tattooed to her right forearm. The shape was unmistakable. He knew what it represented.

"The fire tonight," he said, hoping he'd receive a different explanation than the one he feared, "how did you start it?"

She was asleep, but he knew the answer.

***

Teryessa didn't remember waking up that morning or climbing up on Joker's saddle from the cave she had passed out it. Nor did she remember wrapping her hands around the reins and begging her horse to get her to safety. Her recollection only provided her with glimpses of snow and descent and bouncing rapidly across a plain. Her first clear memory of that day wasn't until the night, when she awoke to the sight of a girl close to her face.

After she left the lonesome little couple, she immediately regretted her rudeness, but, upon reconsideration, recalled that the strange hooded man really seemed to be in a hurry to get rid of her, so, although she was thankful the tattooed girl healed her with magics, she was confident her departure was for the best. As she thought more about the situation, she realized that two people who finding her fit perfectly with her rule of pairs and she credited the number two with saving her just as much as she credited the sorceress's magics.

The more pressing issue; however, was her lodging situation for the night. She was invigorated by the sorceress' healing hands, but wanted to get to Era-Mosa and get to sleep as early as possible and it had already been dark for quite some time.

Soon, she saw the iron city erupting from the side of a mountain, spewing its metal bridge across the chasm below. She couldn't remember if she had visited this city in her childhood or not, but ultimately decided it didn't matter; that person was dead and any memories she had of her life before were memories robbed from a corpse.

She crossed the bridge without fear, as Joker trotted beneath the black scaffolding that vaulted up to the sky and seemed to dangle the planks of the bridge beneath it like strings to a marionette, a metallic dragon marionette. Because of her time in the Dragonsback Mountains she doubted heights would ever frighten her again.

Lodging in Era-Mosa was easy to find. She chose an inn right near the bridge. The bed was soft and comfortable and, even with her tortured mind, all it took was a little numbendria to put her to sleep.

AMBUSH

Sitting against that door all night, keeping vigil over his best friend and a princess, Aiwren's mind raced. He though of his changing relationships with Leicester and Wanda and how difficult it had been to balance leadership with his friendship with Gregory and Serafina. He wondered if he even wanted to be a leader, but someone had to be responsible and it appeared as though he was the only person willing and able to do so. Aiwren felt, more than anything, alone. At one point in his sleepless delirium, he imagined a girl with long blonde hair, gold armor, and the most beautiful gold eyes he had ever seen. He imagined her walking down the hall, stopping in front of him, looking down at him, and smiling. She was so beautiful and so good; despite knowing he was only imagining her, he couldn't help but smile back. Then, in a blink, she had vanished.

It was still dark when Lieutenant Plune, much to Aiwren's surprise, crept out of his own room down the hall. Aiwren couldn't imagine what the entitled lordson was up to at such an early hour and was even more surprised when the man, stumbling, tiptoed up to him. Aiwren, not sure what to do, stood to salute. Jocund dismissed the formality with a wave of his hand and put a finger to his mouth to silence Aiwren.

"Don't speak," Jocund whispered in Aiwren's ear. "Please simply nod or shake your head. Understand?"

Aiwren nodded. He smelled the booze on Jocund and wondered what this drunkard could be up to.

"Marvelous. You sleep?"

Aiwren wanted to tell him he hadn't slept because he had to stay up all night doing Jocund's job for him, but instead of speaking, he shook his head.

"Fantastic," Jocund said. "Misery loves company."

Aiwren still had no idea why Jocund had woken so early.

"Listen," whispered Jocund. "We're leaving, but we need to do so silently. Now, who do you suppose is the loudest? Don't answer that. It's the princess. I'll wake everyone else, but I want you to go in there, wake her, and get her to her carriage. Silently. Understand?"

Aiwren nodded his head.

"Superb," said Jocund. "We must leave before sunrise."

After watching Jocund drunkenly tiptoe down the hall and into the next room, Aiwren slipped into Wanda's room, where he saw Wanda and Leicester in the bed and Gregory and Serafina on the floor. He knew, if he made any noise waking her, it would wake the others and they would call for help, so he knew he had to first wake Gregory and Serafina. Aiwren jostled Gregory's shoulder and the large young man opened his groggy eyes. Aiwren put his finger up to his lips. Gregory nodded with understanding and turned to help Aiwren wake Serafina, who drew a dagger on Aiwren as he woke her, but did so silently and sheathed the weapon equally as silent. Aiwren knew Leicester and Wanda would be a problem. Wanda, if woken to a fright, would scream. Leicester had to be the one to do it, so, with Serafina and Gregory silently standing by, Aiwren gave Leicester a shake.

"Is it time to go already?" Leicester asked, failing at an attempt to whisper in response to Aiwren's mimed instructions.

Aiwren quickly covered Leicester's mouth with his hand and whispered, "You need to wake Wanda silently."

Aiwren watched his friend nod and their shared understanding reminded Aiwren of their childhood, when they would plan innocent mischief together. They had come so far. Leicester gently nudged Wanda to wake her and put a finger over his mouth to silence her, but she, surprised, refused to comply, opening her mouth to question his motives. Serafina threw her hand over Wanda's mouth and Gregory held her down, as Aiwren gestured for her to be silent. Sensing the urgency, she acquiesced. Moments later, the group, led by Aiwren, tiptoed out of the little room.

Aiwren knew they needed to leave without being seen. He sent Serafina to scout ahead and clear the way for their departure as they edged down the hallway, towards the stairs. It felt like an eternity on those stairs for Aiwren, certain each little creak would surely wake everyone. In the empty parlor downstairs, Ptatiana winked at the group from behind the bar and put her index finger to her mouth as they exited into the dark of the still-early morning.

Once outside, Aiwren, Gregory, and Serafina helped Leicester and Wanda into the carriage. Up the street, Aiwren spotted a farm wagon approaching, driven by one of the prostitutes from Ptatiana's, a short woman with curly hair and brown eyes. Lieutenant Plune rode beside her, leaning back with his hands casually clasped behind his head and his feet resting on the front board.

"I've decided to grant the princess one of her wishes and allow everyone the privilege of riding," the Lieutenant said as the wagon stopped.

Aiwren still didn't understand Jocund's plan, but he knew it was a time for action not questions. He hurried Leicester and Wanda over to the wagon, where Serafina and Gregory helped them climb in. Aiwren climbed in, himself, and, waiting for Wanda and Leicester to duck beneath a pile of hay, he turned to make sure they still hadn't been spotted. Aiwren watched as Halibon hurried Roderick, Brunff, and Kazerra out the front door of Ptatiana's. Jocund snapped the reins and Cutter, hurrying out the door last, jumped on. Everyone was on-board, ducking out of sight, and heading towards the bridge leading them across the Y-Kewnor River and out of Bridgekeep.

***

Once they were outside of Bridgekeep and Jocund was certain nobody was watching them, he gave a nod to Mable, the buxom prostitute Ptatiana assigned to drive their wagon. Mable gave a double snap of the reins to push the horses pulling the cart to their maximum speed. Jocund loved a working girl. There was something about desperation and a willingness to get one's hands dirty that appealed to him, so much so, he found it difficult to concentrate on his plan or anything other than Mable's heaving, dirt-smudged breasts bouncing up and down as the rickety wagon wobbled down the dirt road.

Once Jocund had reminded himself that, if he didn't keep his wits about him, he'd never see any other woman's breasts ever again, he found it easier to concentrate on the tasks at hand. The beginning stages of Jocund's plan had been set into motion days earlier, when he first put the pieces together and realized something bigger than a delinquent princess was afoot. He knew there was an information leak and that this princess was just one annoying piece in a deviously grand puzzle that he'd have to solve later, should he survive and still find it interesting. He wasn't sure if his father had lead him to slaughter or if he simply wanted to win the election at any cost, but Jocund didn't care. Whomever masterminded this hadn't planned for him, and he had designs of his own. The parade was a shake-down, intended to draw any would-be attackers in Y-Kewnor out into the open. It was also meant to be a spectacle so that those who were plotting against the princess would know that their schemes could not be swept under the rug. He wanted to make his enemies change their plans; it was the best way to make them make a mistake. He noticed they were being followed as soon as they got close to Bridgekeep, but he knew they wouldn't be attacked in Bridgekeep, especially not in Ptatiana's where there witnesses could destroy the secrecy of whatever was going on. The attack would be on the road to Era-Mosa; he, the princess, and his platoon were intended to be ambushed, but Jocund had something else in mind.

"Here," Jocund said, glancing up from the map he was studying. "We'll walk the rest of the way."

Mable pulled the wagon to the side of the road, where it wobbled to a stop.

"Welcome, travelers," he said. "Please disembark with expedience, so we may allow this good lady to return to her business."

The group grumbled a bit, but did as they were told once Cutter barked at them to move. Jocund liked the old man, perhaps, in part, because he was so cantankerous. The retired soldier, who's commanding disposition made him a perfect enforcer, was much more than he appeared to be, but Jocund, an expert in history, as well as every other subject of learning, had a feeling he knew the old geezer's story, knew he was an asset his enemies weren't counting on him having, and looked forward to confirming his hypothesis. The milkboy, who seemed to obey the old man even more reverently than the others, hurried to help everyone else out of the wagon. The boy was also a funny fellow. He was smaller than other young men in the platoon, but he easily defeated Halibon, which was entertaining to Jocund since Halibon irritated him. He was a country boy with a dumb smile permanently affixed to his face, but he was more educated than the rest of his platoon and was, by some twist of fate, friends with the princess. At least, Jocund thought, the milkboy would keep him entertained and serve as a buffer between him and the princess, whom Jocund found to be as irritating as she was beautiful.

"Mable, your company has been an absolute pleasure and your assistance a relief," he said as he climbed down from the wagon, himself. "Hurry back to Bridgekeep before the city awakens for another day of delicious debauchery."

"Yes, m'lord," she said, so wonderfully vacant.

"And do you know what you are to do when you arrive?"

"Yes, m'lord," she assured him. "You an Ptatiana bof went over it a undred times. You sure you don want one more fro in the bushes before I go."

"Sadly, that will have to wait," Jocund said. "Please thank Ptatiana for me."

After telling Jocund that Ptatiana and all the girls would be praying to The Divine Empress that he would be able to thank them, himself, Mable turned the wagon around and headed back to Bridgekeep, leaving Jocund in the middle of nowhere with his platoon of misfits.

"All right, I hope you enjoyed your ride. Let's get moving. Expediency is, from this point forward, essential."

The princess, pulling pieces of straw from her hair, stepped forward and said, "You've ignored our danger, woken us early, abandoned our carriage, and left us stranded in the middle of nowhere. I refuse to march under the command of a spoiled lordson who refuses to respond to these plots against my life with appropriate gravity."

"Plots, Princess?" Jocund said, unsure if he was annoyed by the princess or giddy for the opportunity to put her in her place. "Do you mean the plot to ambush us and kidnap you when we camp tonight where the road narrows between the mountains on our way to Era-Mosa?"

"And how do you know that's their plan?" She snapped, throwing her arms up with frustration.

"Because, Your Highness," Jocund said, exaggerating her title to remind her that this was, after all, all her fault, "the lovely ladies who's company I was keeping last night told me."

He then turned to his troop with a confident smile to ease their concerns and give himself a chuckle and said, "Never trust a prostitute, boys. Unless you're me. And you'll never be me."

"Aren't you just a little bit concerned about being ambushed when we camp tonight?" the princess demanded.

"I would be if we were going through the narrow pass," Jocund replied.

"You imbecile!" the princess snickered, "Everyone knows that's the only way to Era-Mosa."

"Correct, but we're not going to Era-Mosa. We're taking the miner's trails north through the Perdition Mountains."

Jocund had hoped this information would set everyone's mind at ease so they could move on, but the group still looked unsure and this only bolstered the princess's confidence to be defiant.

"Look," he said, "I've spent my life slipping through the fingers of those who would prefer me dead, a streak of enduring I don't wish to be brought to an end on account of the bratty princess of some inbred lake people and their absurd family feuds. Now, if you don't mind, perhaps we can get to the trail head and avoid the brigands due backtrack this way as soon as they realize something is afoot. I think we can all agree we would find their company rather unpleasant."

The princess, flabbergasted, turned to her dopey fiancé with a scathing glance demanding he say something, but he only turned to the milkboy. Jocund raised an eyebrow to the milkboy, daring him to speak, but the boy was silent.

Eventually, the group was moving. The green rolling hills were becoming rockier and Jocund knew the hike would only get more treacherous as they headed into the Perdition Mountains. Marching down the road, Jocund walked ahead of the princess so he didn't have to watch her quietly squabble with her dopey fiancé. He instructed Halibon and his side-kicks to lag a hundred paces behind. He told them it was to protect the group from attacks from the rear, when, in truth, it was because they annoyed him. He also sent the oaf from the North and the Ma-Areshi girl, up ahead to scout so he could observe the relationship between the milkboy and the old man, whom he told to lead the party down the road. He surmised that the old man had been teaching the boy to fight in a way that Kewnorian Guardsmen were not trained to fight. It was interesting to Jocund, who adored puzzles.

As they walked, Jocund's mind wandered. He smiled at the thought of the sell-swords in Ptatiana's waiting for them to leave. He thought of the sight of them hurrying out to the street after getting word the princess was trying to sneak off, only to find a burning carriage and a brigade of Bridgekeep officials arriving to catch them at the scene, with all the prostitutes swearing it was the sell-swords who set it ablaze.

When the sun, high in the sky, just began its descent, the oaf and the Ma-Areshi girl hurried back to the group with news.

"Sah, Plune, sah! There's a rider on the road eading this way," the oaf said.

"Just one?" Jocund asked the large lad as the rest of the platoon gathered.

"Just one, sah," the boy confirmed. "Serafina an me even sneaked past im so's ta make sure e wusn't jist a scout. An e's all alone. Jist im an is orse."

"Should we ambush him and slit his throat so he can't tell anybody where we are?" Brunff asked, emboldened by the odds of eight soldiers against one horseman.

"A lonely traveler, no doubt," Jocund said. "Put your sword away, fool. There's no reason to be alarmed. All we have to do is cordially let the stranger pass, looking as inconspicuous as possible. I don't want you to appear to be soldiers, an objective you can easily accomplish, I'm certain. Let's stop for lunch here and allow the stranger to pass."

The group sat down for lunch by the side of the road, waiting for the stranger to pass. Jocund lackadaisically swigged from his wineskin with tempered nonchalance, as the group, anxious and jumpy did their best to casually eat the lunches Ptatiana's kitchen girls had packed them. Soon, Jocund saw the glint of gold emerging up ahead and, as the sight became more clear, Jocund noticed a detail his idiot scouts had inexplicably missed... the rider was a girl.

***

"I made fire," Vannoria told herself, with glee, over and over again. "I made fire with my hands."

It was her secret. She never had a secret like that before. She was able to do something unique and special. Not only that, but she could heal people, too, and she knew this was only the beginning. She had seen things when she healed Shadow, his past. It was an accident, but she knew, if she could find the right tattoo, she could do it again. She was tapping directly into The Source and channelling it through her body and each tattoo was meant to help direct The Source in a different way. She wasn't sure how she knew any of this, but she did, she understood a connectivity of things that she hadn't a day earlier. She looked at the tattoos on her body and wondered what else she was capable of.

She had woken that morning to the sound of crunching. Shadow was stomping out the last remaining embers of the fire she had magicked into existence the prior evening. When he noticed her eyes were open, he tossed some food at her and tersely instructed her to eat quickly so they could go. She wondered why, after her saving him and after it seemed as though she was chipping through his cold shell, he was being so rude; there was no way he could have known that she had peered, uninvited, into his mind. She saw that he was a man once. It was only a glimpse, but it was more than he knew. She wanted to tell him, but she was afraid she'd upset him.

Vannoria was lost in thought for most of the morning, marveling at the new things she understood, as she rode behind Shadow on his horse. At one point she accidentally released a giggle, thinking again about the wonder of the magics she possessed. Shadow, with one arm, whisked her from the horse and put her on the ground, sliding to the ground, himself, with one motion.

"Look around you," he scolded. "This is not your little farm and his isn't the marsh of the Ma-Areshi. You're on the other side of the river, girl. This is the Wild. Those who aren't careful here die."

Vannoria looked around at the dirt road and the fields of tall grass on either side. It didn't look very different from any unkept fields from her home, except the grass was slightly taller and more of a dead, brownish-yellow color rather than emerald green. Ahead of her, giant snow covered mountains soared into the clouds, but she couldn't tell how far away they were.

"What?!" Vannoria demanded. "I really don't see what you're so worried about. Is grass what I should be so afraid of?!"

"Not the grass, but what lurks within it," he replied. "And you're not focussed."

"Just because I don't have that awful sour look you always have, doesn't mean I can't take care of myself. Who saved you?! Who saved that girl?!"

"You," he said. "You started the fire, too. Did you think I didn't know?!"

"What do you even care?" Vannoria asked. "You're just going to kill me, anyway. And I know you think it's supposed to happen at the right moment, but you haven't done much to make me feel very protected until then. Why don't you just leave me alone!? I'll find the Ma-Areshi slaves on my own and you can come and kill me whenever you have to, but, until then, I'm going to actually live. So follow me or don't. I don't care, but I'm sick of being your little tagalong."

As she said the words, she realized she had giving an ultimatum. Sick of people thinking she was worthless and incapable, she turned on her heels and furiously marched into the tall grass without waiting for Shadow's response. She heard Shadow yell for her to wait, but she didn't care. She had made up her mind. If he wanted to follow, he could follow.

Immediately, she found the grass to be taller than she expected. It was far over her head, but the Dragonsback Mountains, off in the distance, told her what direction she had to go. After a few glances over her shoulder she realized Shadow wasn't coming after her, but she told herself she didn't need the road or Shadow. She was a sorceress.

Vannoria's anger fueled her strides for at least a hand of the sun, but the grass grew even taller. She found, as she pushed her way through, that she could no longer see the Dragonsback Mountains and was unsure if she was still heading in the right direction, but she continued to march.

Suddenly Vannoria had an overwhelming awareness that she was being watched. At first she thought it was Shadow following her, but she couldn't shake a sensation of fear. She looked over her body for a mark capable of washing her fears away, but found nothing. The fire had been so easy to figure out. The tattoo looked like a flame, but most of the tattoos where shapes unfamiliar to Vannoria and, unable to take any action to extinguish her fears, she found herself working into a frenzy. She hurried through the grass, hoping to find a spot where she would be able to see the mountain and at least be certain she was going in the right direction, but found herself increasingly disoriented. She reached for her dagger and realized her hand was shaking. Then she heard a sound that created new depths to her fear, the sound of laughter. At first Vannoria couldn't pinpoint the source of the shrill cackle of deranged, hysterical laughter, but then she grew horribly certain it was coming from behind her, several voices, but they all sounded similarly demented and they were getting closer. She was being pursued.

"I don't think you'll find things quite as humorous when you're roasting!" she called out as she reached for the fire glyph on her right arm and felt the warmth coursing into her mangled left hand, preparing to take a stand.

The running triggered them. Vannoria heard a branch snap behind her and, all manufactured courage replaced with instinct, she bolted. Before she knew what had blindsided her, she felt the impact from her right and was knocked to the ground by something large. As soon as she hit the dirt, she struggled to turn to her back and found herself face to face with a living nightmare.

Long fangs, meant to sink into the neck of their prey and quickly end a life, glistened over Vannoria's face. The creature's head was roughly the same shape as a cat's. It had course fur, with tan and black stripes, pungent with the foul odor of the rotten grime matting it all together. The eyes didn't look like cat eyes though; the beast had eight of them, each one a malevolent, black, lidless orb. Saliva wreaking of death dripped from its teeth. The creature laughed hysterically. As it gnashed its teeth down at Vannoria, she grabbed at its face.

The laughter quickly turned into a howl as the creature, bursting into flames, flung itself from Vannoria and, whimpering, rolled around in the grass to extinguish itself, setting the grass a blaze.

Vannoria quickly got to her feet, preparing for another attack from the now smoldering beast as the fire in the grass spread, but she quickly realized she was surrounded. This was a hunting party.

***

"Stay in the present," Cutter said. "If you can't focus, there is no point in doing this tonight."

Aiwren knew his teacher was right. Once the group settled into an abandoned mining cave to camp for the night, Aiwren followed Cutter out into the wooded mountains near the cave to spar, but Aiwren's mind was elsewhere. He knew he should remain focussed on the mission and on his training, but he could only think about one thing: her, the most beautiful woman he had ever seen.

Aiwren had been thinking of nothing but this woman since the moment he saw her, as though all of his life would forever be bisected by that moment, forever split into two parts that could, from that point forward, only be defined as before and after. The sight of this woman ruined everything he knew and replaced it with something else, not only because she was, to Aiwren, the most exquisite creation The Divine Empress had ever blessed the world with, but also because he had seen her in a vision that very morning. Thinking back on the moment when his path intersected with this strange miraculous woman's, Aiwren could not help feeling this was not only the most important moment in his life, but, perhaps, the most important moment in all of the histories of Allyoshmar. He was smitten.

It was nearly lunchtime when Serafina and Gregory had returned from scouting and told Lieutenant Plune a rider was heading their way. Plune said they should all eat lunch and act as though they weren't trying to save a princess. As soon as he saw the gold of her armor glimmering on the path, he quivered, unable to catch his breath. Serafina, seeing Aiwren tremble, put a hand on his shoulder and told him not to worry. His palpitations were not due to fear of potential battle, but, rather, fear the girl in gold would simply vanish before she arrived, evaporating into the air as dreams often do when one awakens. She didn't evaporate though; the woman in gold armor approached. The conversation between her and Lieutenant Plune was a blur to him. He watched her lips move, but, though mesmerized by their shape as they formed words, he was unable to make sense of her words or anyone else's. Though he prayed to The Divine Empress that he might do nothing but watch her speak for the rest of eternity, the conversation ended and she was on her way.

As the woman in gold armor rode by Aiwren, she turned to him and their eyes met, seemingly freezing the hands of time and isolating the two of them from the rest of the world. Aiwren did everything he could to memorize every detail. Dirt covered the faint bruises that, now healed, gently kissed her lightly tanned skin, making Aiwren wonder who could wish to do anything to mar such perfection. Her blonde hair shimmered as though it was the sun's sole intended target for illumination. Her gold eyes gazed into his and he felt as though, through some unknown magics, they were melting him into a gelatinous pool of mush. Her hands, elegant but scarred, trembled on the reins of her funny grey horse. Aiwren wanted his hands to learn each and every scratch and scab, like a sailor learns the constellations of the night sky, so he may follow them home, because her hands, he felt, must surely be the home to his; they were designed to be intertwined. Her graceful neck arced back, maintaining her gaze upon him as she passed. He had to know who she was.

"Wait!" he yelled, with a voice he had never heard erupting from his mouth, as he leapt to his feet and asked, not knowing if the question had already been posed, "Who are you?"

The girl stopped riding, turned to him, and Aiwren felt her attention was the greatest victory ever won. She didn't answer though.

Instead, she shattered the moment with a crack the reins and quickly galloped off.

Afterwards Lieutenant Plune scolded him for drawing attention to them and for making what was intended to be a forgettable passing into an awkwardly memorable one, but Aiwren barely heard his commander's words and was thrilled the moment was made universally memorable, for he knew it was a moment he could never forget.

The group continued to hike down the road and Aiwren continued to be lost in his thoughts, reliving the sight of the woman over and over again. He wondered who she was and, when he was sent off to scout a trail into the mountains with Serafina and Gregory, he was relieved to learn from his friends that her name was Matera.

"Do you believe in magics?" Aiwren asked as he carelessly heaved a large branch from the trail, clearing the way for the rest of the group.

"I'm Ma-Areshi," Serafina said, ripping a stick off of the branch Aiwren had just removed. "Where I'm from there are many claiming to know magics, especially the Marsh Men who reject city life and live with alligators out in the swamps, but I've never seen any myself."

"Me Ma and Pa always tol me magics is everywhere," Gregory said. "Course I never seen any meself, but they're out there, snatchin children and turning em into ghoulies and such. I ope there's no magics, but I don wanna take no chances neither."

His friends' opinions were not helpful at all to Aiwren, who wanted to know if it was possible for him to be fated to meet a person, if it was possible for two people to be destined to be together and brought into each other's lives by The Divine Empress, Herself.

The group followed Aiwren, Serafina, and Gregory from the road, up the path they had cleared, and into the Perdition Mountains. They hiked along this path until nearly sunset, when they found the mining cave Lieutenant Plune had plotted on his maps and papers and settled in to camp for the night, while Aiwren snuck off with Cutter to half-heartedly practice his fighting.

After Cutter, frustrated by Aiwren's lack of focus, had left the boy to practice on his own, Aiwren continued to go through the paces with his thoughts elsewhere, until he heard a rustling and spun around to see a new visitor.

"Dutifully practicing Master Cutter's training?" Lieutenant Plune asked and, surprised, Aiwren didn't know how to answer.

"You are supposed to be training in secret," the Lieutenant said. "Tell me, Corporal Wayde, remembering your duty to serve me, how long have you been training?"

"Only a few days, My Liege," Aiwren said, knowing, since he had been caught, there was no use in lying.

"Yet," Jocund started, "after even fewer days, you bested a man who is unfortunately considered one of the Kewnorian Guard's finest. To what do you attribute your success?"

"I know I'm not so gifted physically," Aiwren replied. "I think the skills I've learned are simply a better way to fight."

"Indeed," Plune said. "as you demonstrated the other day. I can't help but wonder why you are here, though."

"I'm here to bring Wanda and Leicester- I mean, the princess- to safety."

"I mean the guard, Corporal," Jocund replied. "What are you doing in the Kewnorian Guard?"

"I suppose I'm looking for adventure- well, that, and maybe to prove something. Maybe just to see if I could."

"Well," Plune chuckled, "in my book, you'll find few causes nobler than curiosity. Did you bed a whore last night?"

"No, My Liege," Aiwren said.

"What a pity," Plune replied with a hearty laugh. "That would have been an adventure."

"I suppose I just feel I oughtn't spend my family's coins on prostitutes."

"That's precisely what I spend my family's coins on," Lieutenant Plune said with a sad, bitter smile. "Keep practicing, milkboy. Report to me in the morning. I think you and I are going to be quite useful to one another."

"Yes, My Liege," Aiwren said as he picked up his sword to resume his training.

"One last thing, Corporal," Jocund said, interrupting Aiwren again, "you speak of wasting your family's coins. I assume you're implying they, poor dairy farmers, footed the bill for your move to Y-Kewnor. Doesn't this strike you as odd?"

"I'm very thankful for the sacrifices they've made for me, My Liege," Aiwren replied, evading the question he, himself, had wondered.

"Of course, Corporal Wayde," Lieutenant Plune said. "Of course."

Aiwren watched Lieutenant Plune disappear back into the woods before he resumed his training. He thought his commander's line of questioning had been strange and personal and he wondered what the man who always seemed both calculating and careless could possibly be thinking about him, but he did resume the footwork he had been practicing and his thoughts returned to what was initially distracting him from his training that evening, the girl.

When he returned to the cave where his party had been camping, Leicester asked him where he had been and he lied that he had been scouting, but Serafina and Gregory who valued his drunken offer the previous night to train them to fight as he had been trained, knew what he had been doing and asked him why they weren't included. Remembering his promise, he distantly assured them they'd start soon. He unrolled his Kewnorian Guard issued bedroll and let his body fall into it.

Aiwren laid sleeplessly in the cave, haunted by the woman he had seen that day. Eventually he drifted off into slumber's nebulous abyss and his thoughts turned from the girl of his dreams to the woman of his nightmares.

**

The Nameless Rider, sitting by the fire, staring at the alligator tooth flute the Ma-Areshi child had given him, had been tormented by vexation the entire night. If Vannoria had the ability to set fire with the magics of her hand, then her value to his Master made more sense. Was she to become a foe of his master? Was that why he had to kill her? Or was she meant to become something dark and useful to his Master? He worried she was becoming like him and he hated it. It didn't feel like this girl who laughed and cried and had feelings should be capable of the same monstrosities he was capable of; she needed to be pure. He wondered, as he absently thumbed the flute, why he cared; surely, he had reaped entire villages sometime in his own murky past. The Nameless Rider, so transfixed with thoughts of Vannoria, didn't realize he had brought the flute to his lips to play until the melody crushed his heart and stole his breath with its beauty.

When she finally woke up and they began their journey for the day, Vannoria's giggles taunted him. He knew what she was so happy about. He knew the reason she was rejoicing and the thought of it endowed every fiber of his being with rage. He wondered if being forced to witness this horrible transformation was a punishment from his Master for failing to destroy the boy. He wished he had. He wished he had cut the Boy to the ground for abandoning her and leaving her to be his only prey, a prey that idiotically giggled in the face of the horrors of the cruel world.

He wasn't sure how the argument between he and the Girl had escalated as quickly as it did, but, for a moment, after Vannoria walked away, the Nameless Rider was relieved. Perhaps he would be allowed to slip back into the monotony of having no memories or ideas or feelings, but as soon as she vanished in the grass, fear for her consumed him and he called after her, a call she never answered.

The Nameless Rider rode into the grass after her, but it was thick and high and she was lost to him. Soon he was overwhelmed with a frantic urgency, an urgency he allowed himself to believe was because she was his mission now, a mission he was not allowed to fail.

He saw the smoke before he heard anything and quickly rode in its direction. It was billowing upwards, marring the still blue sky with its black plumes. Then he saw the fire and knew she was in trouble.

The Nameless Rider leapt from his horse without even a glance at what he was leaping into. No fire or beast could frighten him. Only she could, only the fear of losing her. His blade was drawn and, not entirely surprised nor entirely conscious of his actions, he, an objective observer, saw what he was capable of and the blade effortlessly sliced through the first of the beasts.

When the corpse hit the ground, he took in the situation. Fire blazed all around him. Eight beasts remained, with bodies like giant cats and eyes like spiders, laughing as they circled the girl, taunting her. She, in the center, standing on charred earth, surrounded by the laughing cats and the burning grass, swiped out defiantly with her dagger.

The Nameless Rider walked unflinching through the burning grass as the flames licked upon him painlessly. As he cooly sheared the head off another of the beasts, the rest of their group turned their attention to him and one of the beasts made the fatal mistake of lunging to attack. He caught the beast, nearly his size, in mid air. Holding it by its neck, he looked into its eight beady eyes and the beast's laughter turned to whimpers before he had done a thing to harm it; it knew what he was. Before it could whimper too long, he stabbed his blade into he creature's belly and dropped the bloody limp corpse onto the burning field. The others, driven by self-preservation, howled and scampered off, vanishing into the thick grass as the fires extinguished.

The Nameless Rider hurried over to Vannoria, who struggled to stand on wobbly legs. Wishing to save her the shame of asking, he put his arm around her, not to pick her up, but to help her stand. She'd never have to ask.

"Thanks," she said with soot smudged across her face. "I guess I do need your help."

"I shouldn't have been so course with you," the Nameless Rider said, not knowing how to respond to thanks and feeling responsible for her predicament.

"I did use my magics to start the fire last night," she admitted. "but there's something else. When I healed you, I learned things... about The Source, about my magics. Shadow, I think I can help you find out who you are."

"No," he said. "Please. Don't offer again."

"Don't you want to know?" she asked.

"Of course I want to know," he exclaimed.

"Then why won't you let me help you?" she asked. "Why are you so upset about my abilities?"

"Using your magics is too dangerous," he said, wiping the soot from her cheek with his thumb, said, "I don't want you to become like me."

"Why not?" she asked, quietly, grabbing his hand.

"Because I am horrible," he said, somehow unable to free his hand from hers. "And you are perfect."

The girl, looking into his eyes, so close he could taste the sweetness of her breath, whispered, "I don't think you're horrible," and moved even closer.

With their faces nearly touching, the Nameless Rider felt warmth spread all across his body, melting from his stomach into his veins, turning his limbs to lead.

"Look!" she screamed.

The Nameless Rider spun around. The fire had cleared quite a bit of the grass and he could see the corner of an iron cage reflecting in the sun.

The Nameless Rider and Vannoria approached the cage, realizing it was one of several cages arranged in a circle. This was a slave camp. There were also a few abandoned huts made from branches and tall grass. The Nameless Rider pointed to one of the cages at the far side of the encampment. They walked over to it. In its corner was a body. The man's arm had been torn off, most likely by one of those laughing cats, and he was already badly decomposed, but there was no mistaking his features. He was Ma-Areshi.

"This may have been used as a way-station," he said, shaking the cage, "but the iron is too expertly smithed to be the work of Gavlessans."

"Era-Mosa," she said, "but they abolished slavery."

"No, you're right," the Nameless Rider said.

"Something serious is happening," the girl said.

"I'm afraid so," the Nameless Rider replied.

"All the more reason to free those Ma-Areshi," Vannoria said, with a somber resolve the Nameless Rider had not yet seen in her.

***

When Teryessa awoke in Era-Mosa, she felt more rejuvenated than she had in days. It was hard to believe the sorceress had healed her, but the scars that were, the day prior, open wounds served as undeniable evidence. Magics were real. This joy evaporated quickly as she remembered all of the other things that were real. Her encounter only reinforced the fear that, unless she killed all the dragons that were out to get her, she could never be free. She was in the Freelands though, and soon, she hoped, she could find the answers, resolution, and retribution she hoped for, or she could die trying.

It took her the first two hands of the sun to gather her supplies and leave Era-Mosa, but she was confident she could reach Bridgekeep by that evening. Being pampered with the rest and the luxurious stall Teryessa had provided for Joker, the horse was not excited to be back on the road, but once they were galloping down the mountain path she was happy to be moving and Teryessa could tell.

There was a small amount of traffic on the road near Era-Mosa, mostly merchants and farmers that lived just outside of the iron city going in to trade for the day, but the road emptied by the time she had been riding for a sunhand, and, though it was hilly and rocky and twisted with switchbacks and turns, she galloped Joker hard, closing her eyes to feel the sun on her face and the breeze from travel in her hair on that still and cloudless day as she silently counted the beat of Joker's hooves. One. Two. One. Two.

Teryessa had slowed Joker's gallop to trot at highsun with the intent of finding a secluded place to practice and eat, when she came across a small band of travelers. She had just come around a switchback and she saw them eating their lunch off to the side of the road. The first thing she did was count them. There were eleven, a number that, to her terror, didn't work at all. Even if she included herself, there were twelve which could be divided into two groups of six, but six was made of two groups of three and three was terrible. Three was all wrong. Three was disastrous. She knew she had to stop. If she didn't, they would surely attack her from behind as soon as she passed.

"Good highsun, traveller," one of the men said. He seemed to be the group's spokesman.

"Good highsun," Teryessa replied, halting Joker.

"What gives you purpose to ride on this glorious day?"

"My name is Matera," Teryessa said, hoping the courage she had created for her alter ego would surface, "I'm journeying to Bridgekeep for business."

"What is your business in Bridgekeep?" the man asked.

"My business is my business and none of yours," Teryessa replied, feeling a bit of the Matera confidence.

"My apologies," the man said. "If you are in need of bed or meal, I suggest, Ptatiana's."

Teryessa worried for a moment that Matera had overstepped herself making her too memorable to this group of travelers. She knew she needed to justify the defensiveness and put them at ease so they'd forget her as soon as she passed. She had to tell them something.

"It's my rudeness that requires apology. I'm a sell-sword from Sima Watusia. One never knows who one may trust."

Though she intended to put them at ease, Teryessa noticed an especially nervous woman in the party glancing up and down the road and she realized she had met her before. She recognized Princess Wanda's freckles, red hair, and green eyes immediately. The two of them were both young girls when Teryessa and her father journeyed to Sima Watusia on a diplomatic trip that meant nothing to Teryessa at the time, other than the rare opportunity to play with another little girl. Princess Wanda didn't seem to recognize Teryessa, but Teryessa barely recognized herself. Teryessa marveled at the impossible odds of two princesses passing each other in the middle of nowhere, but her numbers set her mind at ease. The rule of pairs worked and reassured Teryessa until she remembered she said she was from Sima Watusia. Saying they were from the same kingdom could make her memorable and then, perhaps, Wanda would realize how she knew Teryessa. She knew she had to bid them farewell and trot Joker away.

It was as though she had been struck, the sensation Teryessa experienced when she noticed the young man. She trembled with fear of an awe more powerful than the horrors of a dragon and more amazing than any magics she could ever imagine. He was so simple, so pure, so vulnerable. The way he looked at her made her feel as though she could raise her blade to cut off his head and he would do nothing to stop her, that she could stab him through the heart and his damned smile wouldn't change even as the blood poured from his mouth. She wanted to run. She wanted to gallop off as fast as Joker could take her, anything to break the connection with this young man in front of her, the young man who clearly had a powerful strength that defied his average stature, the young man who's wise eyes she could look into forever, the young man who's weathered hands she could imagine holding her, the young man who, she could tell, would see her for who she was rather than what she was. She had never been more terrified in her life.

As she rode past him, Teryessa found herself unable to look away from the young man, just as he, too, failed to break eye contact. She turned her head so much, she feared she would fall from her saddle and feared, even more, that he would catch her. She hated him for existing, hated him for being there and ruining her numbness with momentary hope for things that could never be. Just as she was about to be free from her trance, he called to her.

With a voice cool and strong, like a gently rumbling thunder shower soothing the scorched land on a hot Lees Naglos summer night, he asked her who she was. She wanted to say she was whomever he wanted her to be. She wanted to say she was his destruction, the one thing that could infect his soul and ruin him. She wanted to say that she was a lost princess who was hurting very badly inside and needed something to believe in more than anyone has ever needed anything. Instead, she said nothing. She could no longer be there. He was killing her.

Teryessa, tears steaming from the beauty that she knew in an instant shined in this young man's soul, summoned all of her courage to become Matera as much as she possibly could in that tragically perfect moment and, secretly praying that Joker would refuse to oblige her command, she cracked the reins, leaving the strange haunting man behind her in a cloud of dust.

Teryessa couldn't stop thinking about what happened. She knew feelings like that were dangerous. She knew she must actually become Matera. She had to turn off her vulnerabilities and purge every weakness from her system. She had to eliminate the princess in her and forget she was a daughter. She had to murder the girl named Teryessa, a task that rapist princes, sadistic dragons, and icy mountains had all failed to accomplish. She had to become as heartless as those who hurt her. As she approached Bridgekeep, Teryessa wiped away her tears, drank deeply from her last bottle of numbendria, and let her feelings slide away as Matera grew stronger.

High on numbendria, she vacantly rode into Bridgekeep, a small city painted with bright gaudy colors like the tapestries and murals in the palace of Gavlessa. Perhaps it was random, perhaps it was because the place had been suggested by the man leading that troop, or perhaps something else was at work, but Teryessa found herself hitching Joker in front of a building covered with a painting of a nude woman. Tired and ready for sleep, she grabbed her backpack from Joker's saddle bag at a place called Ptatiana's.

Teryessa noticed the commotion before she even entered. Several men, whom she presumed were the representatives of what ever law and order this tawdry town had to offer, circled what appeared to be the burnt ruins of a carriage, scribbling notes and drawings onto parchment scrolls. Several others were keeping people away from the scene, while scribes, kept distant by the Bridgekeep soldiers, scribbled down their own notes to document the event.

"What happened?" she found herself asking a woman who must have been a prostitute sitting on the railing in front of Ptatiana's.

"Some blokes wuz settin' fire to that carriage," the woman said, looking traumatized, "but when they wuz caught by the marshals, instead o jus givin up, they locked themselves in the carriage an let themselves burn to death. I ain't never seen nothing so orrible in all me life."

"To whom did the carriage belong?" Teryessa asked, unmoved by the description of the scene or the feelings of the obviously distraught prostitute.

"Some folks is saying it belonged ta some princess," the woman said, "but now they can't find er so nobody knows."

The woman wasn't helpful to Teryessa at all, so she headed inside, desiring to pass by without further conversation with anybody other than the clerk to get herself a room for the night, but, as soon as she entered Ptatiana's, she knew she wouldn't be so lucky.

"You, girl," a marshal said. "You came in to town from the west, did you see any travelers on the road?"

Part of Teryessa wanted to lie so she might extricate herself from the situation as quickly as possible, but the numbendria flowed through her veins and she heard her own voice, or perhaps Matera's voice, say, "Just outside of town. I saw a party. They were eating lunch at the side of the road. Eleven of them."

"Is that all?"

"Yes."

"If we have any further questions we'll find you."

"Certainly," she replied, cooly. "If you've nothing further to ask, I'd like to go to bed."

Teryessa paid for a room and a few more bottles of numbendria and headed up the stairs with a key in her hand. As she reached her floor, a sight stopped her dead in her tracks, ejected Matera from her body, and pierced the numbendria coursing through her veins.

Sitting on the floor, with his back against the door, she saw the young man. The young man who had shaken her up and sent her

361

world crashing down around her, the young man with the wise eyes and the goofy smile who stared at her and asked her who she was. The hallway was dark so she thought her mind had deceived her, but she swore she saw him sitting there and, to make matters worse, he, with that stupid grin, looked up at her. Taken aback, she acted without thinking. She looked down, at what was certainly a trick, and smiled. A noise distracted her. She turned to see two prostitutes arguing down the hall and, when she looked back to the door, the young man had vanished.

Teryessa stumbled into her room, flopping down into the bed with her armor still on, but she couldn't sleep and she couldn't stop thinking about that young man.

*****

Bea was a light sleeper, but it wasn't nightmares or ghost pains from where her legs used to be that kept her awake. For her, it was an over abundance of energy that denied her sleep. Since growing older, she usually went to bed late and rose early. Perhaps it was an effort to stave off aging, but it also could have been due to the fact that she was a woman with unsinkable spirit forced to spend her days in a chair. Whatever it was, she was immediately alert when her assistant knocked on her bedroom door.

"Come in, Miles," she said, sitting up, trusting him not to bother her with nonsense and expecting him to inform her of anything important no matter what the hour.

Grabbing her glasses, she clearly saw Miles enter, silhouetted by the soft moonlight coming through the window.

"General Boomswift, My Liege" Miles said, coolly and competently, the result of annuals of serving her. "We've received word from Bridgekeep. The princess and the party escorting her have gone missing. They vanished this morning and never arrived in Era-Mosa. The road between the two cities is clear. A group of mercenaries made a failed assassination attempt early this sun, then killed themselves to avoid capture."

"Very well," Bea said, concerned that the sell-swords hadn't given themselves up or put up a fight. "Fetch Sir Rheozarccio and prepare my carriage. We're going to Bridgekeep."

SIEGE

Truson Everly didn't bother to have his men set up a long-term camp.
He didn't expect a protracted siege in this battle. However it was going
to end, he knew it wouldn't be too much longer than a day, perhaps
two days, and he knew his men would have very little opportunity to
reap the benefits of a place to sleep. There were a few tents here and
there to perform field triage to any injured men who might be able to
return to battle, but the little camp was sparse and temporary with
just enough fires for the eighteen thousand infantry men to stay warm
through the cold desert night while waiting for the order to move in
and attack Gavlessa, the order he was to give. He had sent the horses
back as soon as they arrived the previous day, so the cavalry could
arrive as reinforcements halfway through the day, exhausting almost
all of the resources at his disposal. This was an all or nothing tactic
and he knew it.

Standing atop a small dune, Truson watched the twisted metal
and sand spires erupting from the ground, waiting for some sign. It
was likely the Gavlessans already knew they were there and were
waiting to see what he was going to do. He hoped it would appear as
though this was only the first wave of the attack. He had taken great
measures to conceal their numbers, but he was worried the Gavlessans

would attack that night. If they did, he had enough men there to dispatch of what would have been the first wave of a preemptive attack from the barbarians, but he would lose many men in the process, jeopardizing the next stages of his plan. He had to wait until sunrise, not for the element of surprise, for that would come into play when the Gavlessans rushed out to defend their city against an army larger than it appeared to be. The reason for waiting until day was simply so his men wouldn't be at a disadvantage against beastly men accustomed to seeing in the dark. So, when the sun first illuminated the desert, creating silhouettes of those horrible towers, he sounded the attack, not by giving a command, but by drawing his sword and sprinting towards the giant gate, himself.

As he ran, he heard a footsteps behind him, men loyal to him, loyal to Lees Naglos, some former Divine Empress's Knights, some soldiers in the Royal Army, following his lead, five hundred men charging in like barbarians against barbarians. As he ran, he carefully watched the gate, hoping his bold attack would lure out the enemy. Behind him, he heard his own army's trumpets sound. The battle had begun.

When he was only three hundred paces away, he watched the gates open. Dozens of men, Gavlessan Beast Raiders, on the backs of armored dunebeasts, poured from the mouth of the cave. Truson sheathed his sword and pulled his bow from his back. It was time to put the precision of his skills to the test. While running he nocked an arrow and let it fly, all in one smooth motion. The arrow sailed steadily, racing over the sand, never wobbling or shaking, its velocity increasing until it found its home, driving down to the feathers in the eye of one of the barbarians with enough force to rip him from his saddle. Truson nocked another arrow, repeating these direct hits five times before he was within melee range of the Gavlessans. A rider was closing on him, but still he nocked another arrow.

The man on the dunebeast thundering towards Truson swung a ball and chain wildly over his head. Everly's arrow sailed by as the giant iron ball raced towards his face, but Truson had already drawn his sword again, was ducking adeptly from the unwieldy weapon, and was slicing through the leg of the beast. The arrow hit its intended target, knocking another rider from his dunebeast. The raider who had swung at Truson tumbled from his saddle when his dunebeast, now missing a leg, crashed to the ground.

Truson, deflecting attacks from all around, watched the Gavlessans close the gate to prepare another attack. Truson knew he had to dispatch of Gavlessa's first wave with only the five hundred men who charged in with him, but his men weren't as skilled as he was, the Beast Raiders were brutal, and Truson wasn't certain how many soldiers from his initial charge into battle would survive.

Soon the first wave of Gavlessans had been slain. Unfortunately, it was at the cost of far too many of his men. Returning to his camp with fewer than one hundred able bodied survivors, dragging close to a hundred injured, he knew he needed to adjust his plan. Something felt off; Truson had a feeling he had overlooked something, that his plan had a fatal flaw.

***

The Nameless Rider rode through the night, allowing Vannoria to sleep on the back of his horse. He had told her it was so they could take full advantage of him not requiring sleep so they could find the Ma-Areshi as quickly as possible, but this was only partially true. He was also avoiding stillness, avoiding the quiet of night that would provide his mind with an opportunity to wander, avoiding any chance he would get close to the girl; however, sharing a horse, he was almost constantly preoccupied by her closeness to him and his only reprieves from this were the moments his mind wandered. He was supposed to be freeing slaves, a mission not assigned by his Master, but he felt like a slave himself, tortured by the confusion of what he felt.

In those moments when his mind wandered, he was consumed with questions. What was he? Who was his Master? Why couldn't he recall any of his deeds? He thought of the vision he had while recovering from his passage through Era-Mosa. It was just a brief moment, but he remembered crawling. He remembered hearing something behind him and turning around to see an ax racing towards him. He wondered if that ax had caused the scar on his face; it should have split his head in half. In this vision, he felt different; it was a vision from before he became what he had become. He was a man once. Did his Master offer him power in exchange for his humanity and the vow of his service? What if he didn't want to serve anymore? The Nameless Rider wondered if any of his questions would ever be answered and he was terrified that they would be.

The Nameless Rider also thought of the Girl, Vannoria. He liked to think of her first as "the Girl," so the sound of her name in his mind would be a blissful surprise, opening like a blooming flower kissing his lips as he silently mouthed the syllables. To the Nameless Rider, no word more sacred had ever been uttered by man or Master or whatever manner of beast he was.

Despite his wandering mind, the Nameless Rider's body continued to obey what he deemed to be the proper path and, riding up into the Dragonsback Mountains by sunset, he was making good time. Most would never dare ride along the edge of that precipice in the dead of night, not even in the foothills, but the Nameless Rider knew his steed needed no sunlight to safely navigate their path and he feared no cliff, whether it was in the foothills, where gnarly scrub pines twisted into the cracks, or whether it was above the timberline, where the jagged peaks of ice vaulted up, into the moonlight, ahead.

When the sun finally rose behind him, illuminating the snowy blanket with the first light of day, he was neither relieved nor overjoyed. This light meant the Girl would awaken soon. He was certain she would destroy him, but what was especially terrifying to the Nameless Rider was that, knowing he must either kill her or perish, he welcomed his own demise.

As Vannoria stirred, a stirring he learned was a preamble to her opening her eyes, she murmured a good morning to him and it felt as though all the heat from the rising sun had waited until that moment to bathe him in its warmth. She was awake.

***

There was no sunlight piercing through the shade of the cave to wake Aiwren from his nightmares. Although, the thrill of adventure had kept thoughts of the Skinless Woman so distant from his mind that he had almost forgotten all about her, his nightmares returned that night with a such fury that they seemed to will themselves back into existence to remind him he'd never be free from their bloody grasp. He saw Serafina and Gregory and Leicester drowning in the bloody pond, with waves of red crashing down upon their faces, gurgling in their mouths, and pulling them under. He had rushed in after them, only to find himself in the gory crimson grip of the Skinless Woman. The demoness pressed him beneath the surface where darkness waited to consume him and, spraying villainous globs of bile onto his face as she spoke, told him it was all his fault.

"What's your fault?" Leicester laughed, standing over Aiwren.

Wanda, Gregory, and Serafina were also standing above Aiwren, sharing a laugh at his expense, ignorant of the toll Aiwren's nightmares had on him. Aiwren's heart couldn't hold them accountable for their jokes and he was simply relieved to see them alive and not treading for life in that horrible pond. Quick to remove focus and unburden his friends with concern, he convincingly laughed at himself.

"It's my fault for choosing this adventure," Aiwren teased back. "I had the most awful dream I was stuck with the lot of you forever."

"I'm afraid naughtmares come true," said Gregory. "Cause we'll be by your side till the end."

Aiwren laughed at this remark and gave his friend a squeeze on the arm as he helped him to his feet, but the joke only magnified his concerns. He worried they would be with him till the end and that, as the Skinless Woman said, that end would be his fault. Aiwren wondered why he had been cursed with those dreams. He also realized how tired he had become, his mind worn thin by a lifetime of keeping out the darkness. He feared what awaited him, should his will to survive erode completely.

"You've been having nightmares quite a bit on this adventure," Cutter, whom Aiwren had not noticed sitting nearby, prodded somberly. "Anything you want to tell us?"

"No," joked Aiwren, afraid his teacher would see through his facade. "I'm simply a homesick baby."

"Everyone finished with hugs and merriment?" Lieutenant Plune asked, entering the cave.

Aiwren did his best to get everyone moving, pulling away from his friends and mentally isolating himself from their jokes and laughter. Judging by Lieutenant Plune's disposition, things were far more perilous then the rest of the group imagined them to be. Aiwren knew he needed to protect his friends, not joke with them. He swore he was not going to let anything happen to them. He swore he would not let his nightmare come true.

The party was on their feet and continuing their hike along the miners' pass through the Perdition Mountains and, soon into their day, Aiwren found the terrain changing from hilly forest with an increasing number of large rocks and boulders, to a steep climb up a wooded mountain. Although it felt like a sudden change, Aiwren remembered from his geography that he had been on an increasingly steep incline ever since he crossed the Y-Kewnor River in Bridgekeep and that even the occasional boulders he saw in the Indigo Forest were the beginnings of this mountain, a mountain that, once an abstract notion he studied in school, was very real and beneath his aching feet. He sadly wished he could have appreciated the marvel of actually being in a place he once studied, but that was a long time ago and Aiwren knew his days of wide-eyed wonder were coming to an end.

"Walk with me," Cutter said, hiking up next to him. "I think we should talk."

Aiwren, wondering what he did wrong, slowed his pace so he and his mentor could speak in private.

"I've seen shadows I haven't seen in quite some time and I fear my unfinished business is returning for closure," Cutter said.

"Shadows?" Aiwren asked.

"Contingency plans must be kept secret because, if revealed, they'd be jettisoned as soon as they appeared unnecessary."

"Is that why you didn't want me to tell anybody about my training?" Aiwren asked. "Lieutenant Plune guessed that you'd been training me, but I didn't give him any details."

"Silence," Cutter commanded. "Many annuals ago, I was made a part of such a contingency. I was a poor farm boy, like yourself, when I was chosen."

"Chosen for what?" Aiwren asked, receiving a sharp glance for interrupting.

"There were others," Cutter continued. "Three of us received the training together, but there were more. We had our superficial lives; two of us became guardsmen and one was a knight, but secretly we were a clandestine group. We were taught the mysteries of Allyoshmar and the forgotten martial arts were only the beginning."

"This group," Aiwren asked, "what were you called?"

"We were the Order of the Crystal Blade," Cutter said. "a group named for the swords we wielded, swords that, when used properly, harnessed the power of The Source, itself."

"Does this mean-"

"There is no Crystal Order," Cutter said. "Not anymore."

"What happened?"

"There was a new generation of pupils. One was a girl with power none of us had ever seen before. We were deceived by one of our own, tricked into aiding in a plot to use that girl to conquer all of Allyoshmar. In the end, the plot was thwarted, but the girl and most of the Order perished. Those who survived, destroyed the remaining Crystal Swords, dissolved the Order, and made a solemn vow never to speak of it again, to kill the legend."

Aiwren wanted to know more, to learn about the Order and the girl, but Lieutenant Plune approached and Aiwren knew the conversation was over.

"A word, gentlemen?" Plune interrupted, appearing from seemingly nowhere.

"Shall I fetch Halibon, My Liege?" Aiwren asked.

"Halibon is an ass," Lieutenant Plune replied dismissively. "Nobody will benefit from his participation in our conversation."

"You have our attention, Lieutenant Plune," Cutter said, immediately changing his demeanor from suspicious concern to dutiful attention.

"We'll reach the end of the mountains by this evening," Plune said, "returning from the wilderness of the mountains to the well-travelled road south of Twin Lake that links Sima Watusia to Simi Watusia, eliminating our element of surprise. If we're lucky, my scheme has given us enough of a head start to reach Sima Watusia without incident; however, I'm rarely lucky. If we're going to be attacked by whomever is after the princess, that's where it's going to be."

"Forgive me, sir," Aiwren said, "but you've kept your plans and information to yourself this entire time. Why share with us now?"

"The privilege of my interest in your thoughts isn't enough without knowledge of my motives, Corporal Wayde?!" Jocund asked, once again assuming his aloof persona.

Aiwren was certain Lieutenant Plune knew far more than he was telling him, just as he knew Cutter knew more than he was telling him, but he also knew he had no moral authority to judge either of these men for their secrets; after all, he had his own secrets. He understood that there was nothing anyone could do to help him with his own secrets and so he gave both men the benefit of the doubt regarding theirs and, although the thought that what they were hiding might be as foreboding as what he was, he did his best not to think about it and he decided the way he could best help them all was to make certain his dreams didn't become a liability.

The miners' pass eventually leveled out as a canyon cutting through the mountains with entrances and paths to the entrances of mines long ago exhausted of their iron along both sides of the path. It was an empty road, but Aiwren could imagine how busy it must have been hundreds of annuals earlier. Men had come and gone, leaving the mountain barren, using its contents to build cities and wage wars. It was a sad place. Aiwren, now having seen it with his own eyes, wondered if whomever named the Perdition Mountains somehow knew what they would become. It was here, in this dismal valley cut into the side of the mountain by men, that Aiwren and his traveling companions stopped to eat lunch, the last bits of the food Ptatiana had prepared for them. Sitting there, off to the side, watching Cutter and Lieutenant Plune each eating alone, while Serafina, Gregory, Leicester, and Wanda laughed and goofed around, discarding bits of bread in an impromptu food fight, wasting the last of their food and leaving evidence behind that they had been there. Aiwren noticed Halibon, Roderick, Brunff, and Kazerra brooding joylessly off to the side, bullies that had, at some point in the journey, become outcasts. He wanted to go sit with them offer a hand of friendship; he didn't feel up to his friends' fun and games, nor did he want to meditate with Plune or Cutter on the horrors that were most certainly around the corner, so he might as well have made the effort, but he did nothing; he was too preoccupied with thoughts of the Order of the Crystal Blade, the powerful girl in the story, and what Bonishara had told him. He knew he should tell Cutter about his dreams, but was afraid that, if he did, Cutter would no longer trust him with the training.

***

Plale watched the battle from his rusty metal tower, a location he had claimed as his own once he took control of the underground city. At a glance, it appeared as though he was losing the battle, but he smiled confidently. Everything was going according to plan. With his aberration, Ovyrr-Keel, dutifully by his side, he soaked in the sight of all that death, a banquet waiting to be feasted upon.

One of his generals, a man selected for the job as a reward for killing many of the king's warriors, entered the small room atop the tower.

"My Vicar," the man said, "our men are being slaughtered out there. What orders would you like me to command on your behalf?"

"Those aren't our men, General," Plale said. "All life belongs to Gordorah, loaned to our corpses for exactly the duration He wishes."

"Yes, My Vicar. What would you wish me to do?"

"Send more," Plale said, eyeing the sun, "but not too many. Just enough to continue to keep them occupied."

"But, Your Holiness, we're losing most of them."

"Their lives don't matter. It is what they are dying for that matters. We will win this battle and Lees Naglos will fall tonight, now have faith in our Master and do His bidding."

The general nodded and hurried off.

"How do we stand on our project, my most faithful servant?" Plale asked Ovyrr-Keel without looking at him, continuing to watch the battle below.

"The balance of the slaves we were expecting arrived before the attack. They are in their cages and the machine is ready for your inspection."

Plale was excited to witness the machine. The idea was a result of his connection to Gordorah and he had been watching its progress and was looking forward to its completion since he drafted it.

The machine was built in the arena of the Pitt Stadium. A hole had been dug into the earth. Above the hole, four sets of scaffolding had been erected, each set holding up a massive stone wheel. The stone wheels were each twenty paces tall and were carved so the four of them interlocked perfectly. There was also a black stone altar in the hole in the ground. Finally, all of this was located directly beneath the bridge that spanned the arena.

Plale approached the altar and swiped Soul Stitcher across his hand. His blood dripped into the black stone and he closed his eyes. When he opened his eyes the markings chiseled into the stone wheels glowed. He focussed his energy again and the wheels turned, slowly at first, but the speed of their rotation quickly increased. It required his energy to start the machine, but soon the machine would become a source of energy for him to defeat any who stood in the way of his Master. Plale gave a nod to one of his guards who was above the machine, on the bridge. The guard, who had a slave with him, gave the slave a shove.

The slave fell from the bridge into the machine's wheels, screaming until he was ground through the machine and all that could be heard was the crunching of his bones. A pulpy red stream oozed from the bottom of the machine into the hole in the ground. It would require the blood of many slaves to fill that hole, but Plale had thought about this in advance and had been gathering slaves from all over for the last annual, overloading the cells beneath the Pitt Stadium.

"Bring them forth!" he ordered. "Feed the machine."

As Plale walked away, guards began the procession of slaves onto that narrow bridge. It would take all night and into the next day, but soon Plale would have enough power to continue his plan. Soon, there would be an undead army marching to his command. There was no one who could stop him.

***

When Vannoria awoke the sun was already rising. She had, clutching Shadow and sleeping soundly the entire time, rode through the night. The first thing she noticed was how bright and white everything was. The very next thing she noticed was that, despite being bundled in a blanket close to Shadow, she was freezing. As her eyes, looking down, focused on her surroundings, she screamed with terror. Below her was a seemingly endless, white abyss. She grabbed tightly to Shadow, afraid she would fall, until she gathered her wits and realized she was riding on Shadow's horse on a snowy cliff. She was never one to be afraid of heights, but she had never seen such heights before. She was above the clouds.

"Why are you grabbing so tightly?" Shadow asked.

"Because I'm frightened, you ass!" she screamed, burying her head into his back.

"What's frightening you?" he asked.

"The cliff!" she exclaimed.

"As long as we remain on it we'll be perfectly safe."

"Well it's scary to look at!" she screamed above the howling wind, whipping a flurry of snow everywhere.

"So don't look."

Frustrated with Shadow's innocently and obliviously callous response, Vannoria buried her head inside the blankets, where, hidden from the icy dangerous world atop the path through the Dragonsback Mountains, she embraced what had become her new favorite past-time, looking at her tattoos, tracing them with her finger and guessing what they could mean, guessing what abilities they could grant her. She noticed one on the inside of her left wrist that looked like an eye. It must grant her the ability to see something, she thought, wondering what it allowed her to see. Another one, she noticed, inspecting her forearm, looked like a shield. She felt certain she knew what this one did, it was clearly a rune of protection. She thought about using it then, considering the perils of traveling so high above the ground, but she reconsidered, reasoning that a shield would do very little at this height. She wondered if she had wings tattoos so she could fly like the mantarayfly Mister Uncle had compared her to.

She missed Mister Uncle. She hoped she could free the Ma-Areshi quickly, so she could return to him and his Family-Clan, her Family-Clan. She knew there was a chance she'd never see him again. Living on borrowed time and traveling with a man who seemed to be death, itself, constantly reminded her that every moment could be her last. Ever since the incident at Era-Mosa she realized, when the time came for Shadow to take her life, she would not be able to fight him, even if she had the ability to kill him, herself. And she found herself, once again, thinking about who his Master could possibly be that they would be so cruel to make him do such horrible things. She didn't need a tattoo with magics to see his heart. He was good, and brave, and noble, and strong. These feelings welling up inside of her made her realize she felt more alive than she had ever felt, even if she was balancing on the cusp of death. She poked her head out of the blanket, held on to the strange dark horse with her legs, and stretched out her arms, breathing in the icy air and welcoming whatever was next for her.

"I thought you were afraid," Shadow said. "What are you doing?"

"I'm flying," Vannoria replied with a smile bigger than she had ever smiled before. "You should try it."

"I don't think we can fly," he said.

"We can do anything," she replied. "We're magical."

Then, Shadow did something that shocked Vannoria. He stretched out his arms like hers and, although she couldn't see his face, she would have bet her life he was smiling, too, and her smile grew even wider.

The day passed uneventfully on that snowy path for them. Vannoria even cackled with glee as they vaulted over a seemingly uncrossable chasm created by a recent avalanche. Shadow had asked her if she was ready and she told him she was, even if it all ended right there. It didn't end right there, the horse leapt over the abyss and neither of them were certain that, in that moment, they weren't actually flying.

Afterwards, Vannoria decided they should name the horse. Shadow told her, since she like naming things so much, she was welcome to, but she insisted they name him together.

"Something that's up in the sky," she said.

"Birds," he replied.

"You can't name a horse, 'bird,' you ninny!"

"See?" he said. "I'm terrible with names, Valorie."

"No, you're terrible with jokes," she laughed.

"How about rainbow, then?" he asked.

"Now you're just intentionally being obtuse."

"What about moon?"

She knew Shadow was just joking, but the name seemed to fit, since the horse was so mysterious.

"Darkmoon!" she exclaimed. "I love it!"

"What do you think, Darkmoon?" Shadow asked the horse. "Is that a suitable name?"

The horse, Darkmoon, for the first time either of them could recall, whinnied, a sign that there was something there, that the horse was a living thing.

The remainder of the day passed quickly and Darkmoon seemed to be traveling even faster than usual. As the sun set, the snow receded behind them, and they were surrounded by trees once again, Vannoria clung tightly to Shadow once more. This time it wasn't out of fear or even cold. She clung to Shadow simply because it felt good. The light of fires and candles glowed in the distance before them and soon they were standing on a cliff looking over the city of Orc Doola.

"There are inns here, with beds," Shadow said, looking over the edge, his hood billowing in the wind. "If you like, I can meet you on the other side of the city in the morning."

"No," Vannoria said, simply but decisively. "I want you to come with me."

"These cities of men," he said, "they're protected from creatures like me by ancient magics. You've seen what they can do."

"Yes," she started, not sure how much of what she was thinking she would actually have the courage to say. "But I have magics, too. I think I can shield you from their harm. Will you let me try?"

Vannoria held her breath, waiting for his response.

"If you wish," he said. "You may try."

Vannoria touched the tattoo that looked like a shield with the palm of her hand. She held it until it burned her, until the pain was unbearable. Then, she turned to Shadow and held out her hand. He hesitated a moment, then took it. She grabbed his hand with her other hand, afraid it wouldn't work and the magics wouldn't hold. She held his hand tightly and felt the energy flowing into him.

Vannoria, hooded, did all the talking at the inn, while Shadow tethered Darkmoon to a hitch. She ordered one room, telling Shadow it was in case the magical protection faded during the night. Her hand trembled as the skeleton key clicked into the lock. When the door opened she gasped at the sight of a bed, realizing how much she had missed this comfort. She flung herself on it and laughed wildly, as though it was the first time she had ever seen a bed. Then, without warning or thought or even a moment of preamble, she leapt to her feet, threw her arms around Shadow and hugged him, burying her tattooed face into his giant chest. He was cold at first, but, as it had when she cast her magics on him, she felt the warmth spreading. There was life in him. It was a different sort of life, but it was life and it was special to her, more special than any life she had ever known.

"Shadow," she said, noticing the tattoo of the eye on her wrist as she clung to him, "let me help you."

Without saying a word, he broke away from her and walked over to the window, looking down at the street below. Vannoria, feeling exposed and rejected, but, more than anything else, concerned for this man, joined him.

"I've never been on a second floor before," she said, gazing out the window, herself. "I suppose it isn't so impressive after being as high as we were today."

Shadow said nothing and the silence was tearing Vannoria apart. She never knew silence like this. She never knew a need for words more than this. She felt things. She had not said anything out loud, but she had at least admitted it to herself.

"I think I should leave," Shadow said.

"Why?!" Vannoria asked. "What are you afraid of?!"

"Falling," he said, turning to her.

"So don't look," she said, closing his eyes tenderly with her hand, feeling herself being drawn closer to him.

Vannoria reached for Shadow's hood with both of her hands and lifted it off of his head, bringing her face close to his, allowing them both to be equally bathed in the moonlight spilling upon them through the window. She wanted to move closer, still. She wanted to bring her lips to his. She wanted to touch him. She wanted so many things so badly, but she resisted.

"Okay," he said.

Vannoria reached for the tattoo on her wrist, the eye. She had no hesitation or doubt. She knew what that glyph meant.

The instant Vannoria touched Shadow's temple with her glowing hand, darkness crashed down upon her like a wave, crushing her, smothering her with emptiness. Then she felt Shadow's presence. There were no sights or sounds but she knew she was with him. Etherial, they pulsed rhythmically together, entwining. They were one. In the distance she heard a heart slowly beating, one reluctant heart for the two of them to share, as they slowly slipped into a singular supine body.

Vannoria felt a sudden pain in her chest and her eye opened, but she was no longer in the inn in Orc Doola. It was a dark room, dimly lit with torches mounted to its black walls. It looked familiar, but the pain in her chest was too distracting for her to realize why it looked so familiar. She looked at her chest. It was a man's chest, Shadow's chest. There was a black knife sticking into it. She was terrified. Shadow was terrified. She felt for her face, remembering, from memories that weren't her own, being struck by an ax.

"You were dead," a malevolent voice crackled, "but I've resurrected you to do my bidding."

"Who are you?" Vannoria heard herself ask.

"I'm the necromancer," the man said, his face hidden within a hood. "I'm your Master."

The hooded man ripped the knife from Vannoria's chest and she felt light surge up around her, rocketing her through a void. Spinning and spiraling wildly through an ever brightening emptiness, she felt herself splitting from Shadow. The tactile world squeezed itself back into existence until she was, once again, in the little inn in Orc Doola, where Shadow stood in front of her, trembling.

"I am a monster," he said, refusing to look up. "I've always thought so, but now I've seen it."

"What we saw was what happened to you," Vannoria said, searching to meet his eyes with hers, to grant him the acceptance only true love can grant. "It wasn't who you are. I've already seen everything I need to see about who you are."

When Shadow, reluctant and shameful, finally relented his gaze to Vannoria's, his eyes, so close to hers, so deep, so soulful, so beautifully pained, she could no longer resist her urges. She knew what she felt and she knew he felt it, too. Raw and exposed to one another, there was nothing left to hide. In the inn in Orc Doola, Vannoria and Shadow kissed deeply and passionately. For a moment, they felt the darkness of the world could never corrupt them. They were flying.

***

Rheozarccio had been woken late the previous night to the sound of knocking on his door in the Citadel. A young guardsman told him General Boomswift asked for him, that he should pack for a trip, and that the general's carriage would arrive shortly. He didn't know what this was about, but he was excited to share with her what he had pieced together at the library the previous day. He packed quickly and, when he reached the steps of the Citadel, he saw, under the moonlight on an otherwise empty street, a carriage ornamented with bronze was waiting for him.

"Where are we going?" Rheo asked as he entered.

"Bridgekeep," Bea said, looking wide awake, but not the least bit cheerful, "the Watusian princess is missing."

Bea quickly got Rheo up to speed on what she knew, telling him that, for political reasons, they'd have to conduct interviews with potential witnesses in the name of The Divine Empress's Knights rather than the Kewnorian Guard. Then, she told him to rest and Rheo eventually fell asleep on the tufted leather seat inside the carriage.

They approached Bridgekeep just as the sun was rising and Rheo awoke feeling rested and ready for the day.

"I spent the day at the library yesterday," Rheo said. "The librarian, she helped me find some books, and I pieced some things together about the Citadel attack."

"Such as?" she asked, gesturing him to continue.

"I don't know how accurate it is, but, there's an account of the battle to overthrow Argratosius that described fire in the sky. I didn't think much of it at first, but the palace... It's charred at the top."

"Fire is often used in battle."

"Fire that melts stone? It was Dragons, Bea. Dragons helped us win that war."

"Are you suggesting benevolent dragons?"

"That's absurd, but you see how this raises questions."

"We'll have to think about all of this more later, but we're arriving so we should pause these questions and turn our attention to the princess problem for the moment. This is Ptatiana's. Where she was last seen."

Rheo fell easily into his role of representative of The Divine Empress's Knights, even if it was an unofficial role. In Bridgekeep, while the people may not have liked The Divine Empress's Knights any more than the people did in Y-Kewnor, at least they feared them more. The officials for the town quickly updated Rheo on their investigation. There were several witnesses to the sell-swords burning themselves alive, but their stories smelled fishy to Rheo. The whole stunt was clearly a ruse, and Rheo was determined to get to the bottom of what happened, so, after interviewing every single one of Ptatiana's prostitutes, Rheo hoped that the one person who possibly saw Jocund, his platoon, and the princess after the attack would be helpful.

The first thing Rheo noticed about the girl as she entered was that she was wearing the gold armor of a High Knight of the Council. At first he thought this was some sort of insult directed towards him, but inspecting its condition, thinking of how much coin a suit of armor like this would cost, and realizing she had no idea what she was wearing, he decided no insult was intended, but he still wondered how she acquired such armor and the brooding look on her face only increased his attention.

"What is it you want from me?" she asked, making no attempt to conceal her contempt. "I already answered all of your questions last night."

"Forgive me," he said, courteously. "I understand you answered some questions to the Bridgekeep Marshals, but I'm a representative of The Divine Empress's Knights."

"What a joke!" she scoffed.

"I understand some have an unfavorable opinion of the knights. I apologize for whatever grievances you may have."

"The Divine Empress is the joke," the girl bitterly clarified. "I have no grievances with the fools who believe she actually cares about our suffering."

Rheo had never heard contempt for The Divine Empress before. Clearly this girl was insane. He was certain The Divine Empress cared. If she hadn't cared, then how would he have been blessed with the abilities he had been blessed with? He worried that it would be difficult to get sensible information from the girl.

"Let's start from the top," he said. "Your name?"

"Matera," she snapped.

"I see," he replied, refusing to acknowledge her disdain. "And what is the purpose of your travel, Matera?"

"I'm journeying to Y-Kewnor," she sighed.

"Forgive me," he replied, sensing her deflection. "I understand Y-Kewnor is your destination, but I don't seem to have any notes on the purpose of this travel."

"Good Sir Knight, I don't see the relevance to this missing princess, unless you suspect I'm involved."

"Not at all," said Rheo. "Just trying to glean a context to your point of view. You mentioned a princess though and I don't recall anyone saying the missing party included a princess."

"Everyone knows this is about the Watusian princess," she answered dismissively. "Plus, when I saw them on the road, it was clear she was fancy, that she had spent her life being bathed by a nurse, that she was doted upon but lonely, and that she was weak."

Rheo thought about this girl's words. She clearly seemed to have something against princesses, but he suspected something else was afoot and he wondered why it seemed that recently something else was always afoot.

"I saw them all at the side of the road and they were eating lunch and that's all I know."

The girl, Matera, whom Rheo doubted was really named Matera, stood to leave, clearly disliking the questions. He knew he needed to calm her down if he was going to get any useful information out of her, he stood to put a soothing hand on her shoulder, but the girl, appearing to sense the movement as an attack, drew her sword and held it out defensively. It was a good sword, but she was holding all wrong, as one might hold a fire poker.

"Relax," he said. "I only wish to help this princess."

"What if this princess doesn't want your help?" she said, swiping out at him. "What if everyone who says they're only trying to help ends up hurting her?"

Rheo knew he had to diffuse the situation promptly. He knocked the sword out of the girl's hand and held her still. She struggled wildly, but he continued to hold her.

"Calm yourself!" he shouted. "I mean you no harm."

When she stopped struggling, he let go.

Picking up her sword, he asked, "Why would someone with so little skill have such a finely crafted blade."

"Would you rather I be defenseless?!" she seethed.

"I would rather you learned how to use the thing so you don't get yourself into unnecessary trouble waving it around like a fool at anyone who asks you a few questions."

She pouted indignantly and threw her nose up. Beneath the filth and scabs was a beautiful complexion and perfect white teeth. She wasn't the ruffian she appeared to be.

"Look," he said, patiently, "You don't need to worry. I'm guessing you're a lady from some court who, betrothed to some horrible man, took flight before her wedding."

"It's a little late for that."

"Well, whatever the case, Y-Kewnor is a big place. It'd be easy to become a new person there. Let me help."

"Why?" she demanded. "Why would you help me?"

"Because I see something in you," he said, and he did; he saw a resiliency and determination.

"What?" she prodded. "What do you see?"

"I see someone who was tired of waiting for a hero to rescue her so she became one and rescued herself, which is exactly what The Divine Empress's Knights need right now."

"What would that entail?" she asked hesitantly.

"Learning to actually use this thing, for starters," he said, handing her back her sword. "After that... protecting the people, killing dragons."

As soon as he said the words, he saw her gaze narrow.

"What would I have to do?" She asked.

"Go to the Citadel, stay out of trouble, and don't pick any fights until I return this evening."

"I will do as you say," she said, "but if this is a trick, I swear, I'll slit your throat."

"Very well," he replied with a smile. "I'll see you this evening, Matera."

The girl sheathed her sword and headed towards the door, but then, stopped, turned around, and said, "The princess and her entourage were about to head into the mountains."

"How do you know this?" Rheo asked.

"Because the young men looked nervous when I approached and they kept glancing over their shoulders, towards Bridgekeep. If you're afraid of what's before you and afraid of what's behind you, you have no choice but to change your path."

Rheo thanked the girl and she left, leaving him happy that he was right about her and wrong about Jocund.

Boomswift wheeled in from the adjoining room where she had been monitoring the interviews.

"Her?" She asked.

"Her," Rheo said.

"And what of Jocund?" Bea asked.

"He's fooled us all," Rheo replied. "I hope his plan works."

***

The road from Sima Watusia to Simi Watusia was a busy road and Jocund had no intention of camping there. He had wished his party could have made it straight through to their destination before sunset, but, as the sun submerged, the group had only begun their descent from the miners' pass. Exhausted and cranky, Jocund knew they'd never be able to complete their journey that night. He needed to find them a safe place to camp.

The princess, whom Jocund preferred when she was in her carriage all day, had spent most of the day laughing and joking with her idiot fiancé, the oaf from the North, and the Ma-Areshi girl, her confidence clearly boosted from her proximity to the home she hadn't yet realized had changed without her. She only took breaks from her horse-play to harangue Jocund about the litany of decisions she felt he was making incorrectly. He looked forward to completing this mission, but he knew this last part of the journey was the most dangerous.

"The sun is setting, Lordson Plune," the princess said to Jocund, who knew she accentuated the title on purpose just to irritate him and he cursed that damned milkboy for the terrible job he was doing as an intermediary.

"I thank thee for graciously sharing you wisdom with me, Princess," he said. "Please, dost thou know the color of the grass as well? If it be, I pray thee tell."

"You may find yourself to be humorous, Lordson. You may think yourself above it all, but really you're just rude and inconsiderate."

"Well, fortunately, you've only to endure the burden of tolerating me a little while longer. Was there a purpose to this conversation or were you merely bored and seeking amusement at my expense?"

"As much as it pains me to suggest we protract our time together, everyone is exhausted and we need to camp for the night."

"Thank you, I'm aware, Princess. We'll set up camp posthaste as soon as I find the proper location."

"Proper location?!" she scoffed. "We need to set up camp so we can get an early start tomorrow."

"Look, we'll stop to camp as soon as we find a place that's safe and secure, unless you prefer the men who have been following us since lunch to come and take you when you sleep, take turns raping you, and drop your corpse at the feet of the Simi Watusian King to collect their reward."

The princess was silent, but Jocund's outburst piqued the attention of the milkboy, who hurried over, and Jocund wondered where the damned boy was when the princess approached him in the first place.

"Yes," Jocund said, completely exasperated. "We're being followed. We've been followed since lunch. At first I wasn't certain, but then I heard the song of a red breasted robin, a bird that doesn't live this far north. I once met an Auptherenese prostitute who went by the name of Robin. Her breasts weren't red, but they were enormous. Completely unforgettable. The girl could sing, too. Learned all the songs of her namesake bird, probably part of her bit, but her favorite was the red breasted robin because it reminded her of her home in Auptherenon. At any rate, I heard that song and it doesn't belong here. I'm certain it was a band of thieves communicating, likely Auptherenese, themselves."

"So you know we're being followed because of a singing prostitute?" the milkboy asked.

"Yes," Jocund said. "Well that and because I saw them. So, if you could be a little more on your toes and if you could possibly keep your eyes open for a safe place to fortify ourselves, then that would just be marvelous."

It was the oaf that found the place. He was scouting the path and, like an idiot, started yelling that he had found something. When Jocund and his party caught up to him, at first all Jocund could see was a few out of place stones, but he realized they were more than just a few stones. There was an old field stone wall, dilapidated and forgotten, about one hundred paces from the path.

"Thems are field stones, Me Liege," the oaf said. "Unless me eyes is lying, that's a wall. This is a property line. At least it used to be."

"We mustn't enter," the princess said. "It isn't safe."

"Oh no?!" Jocund asked, not wanting the princess to ruin a good chance at a safe place to barricade themselves. "And why, pray tell, isn't it safe."

"That stone wall," said the princess in a somber tone, completely absent of jabs or instigation, "it's the property line of Old Watusia. Every child around here knows of it and not a soul dares enter. Most who have entered have never returned and those who have returned from a night in Old Watusia have never been the same. This place is haunted."

"Haunted?!" scoffed Jocund, not believing what he was hearing. "There's no such thing as a haunted town. You lake people really are quite primitive."

"No!" she protested. "It's true. Long ago, before there was a Sima or a Simi Watusia, there was only one Watusia, a small fishing kingdom on a lake, but people started vanishing. One morning, the king, himself, was murdered. He was found by the town crier early in the morning... skinned alive."

"Skinned alive?" the fool milkboy asked.

"No," said Jocund. "It's just a story."

"It's not just a story!" the princess protested. "The killer was one of the king's own twin sons, Simi. When he was confronted by his brother, Sima, he ran off into the woods. Soon, more people started mysteriously dying. They say the king, with his dying breath, cursed the land. Sima knew he couldn't stay, so he and his people abandoned the kingdom, travelled to the western shore of what is now called Twin Lake, and founded a new Watusia. His brother, Simi, meanwhile, had founded a Watusia of his own on the eastern shore of the lake. The two kingdoms have been at war ever since, each claiming to be the rightful Watusia."

"Of course," Jocund said, "I'd wager the Simi Watusians tell a different version of the story. Either way, kingdoms all have miraculous little tales regarding their origin and they're all based very little on fact, but I have some facts for you. Cursed or not, this village is our best chance at barricading ourselves from an unknown number of brigands who most certainly do not have friendly intentions. Furthermore, I'm not asking. I'm commanding my platoon to march into this town and the princess, should she wish to be protected, will follow. Now let's move before it gets dark and all manners of unnatural things come out to spook us."

The group was tentative, but they followed Jocund, who had little patience for superstition, a trick powerful men used to control the people, no more realistic or helpful than The Divine Empress. There was so much manipulation in the world. He wondered how one could even dream of being an honest man, surrounded by such mendacity? He, at least, he told himself, was honest about his knavery. Jocund, immune to the fear of what he deemed to be make-believe, casually stepped over the fieldstone wall in the woods, leading his platoon and the princess into Old Watusia, brazenly daring peril's grasp.

Old Watusia was in ruins. In most places, all that remained of the structures was a footprint of stones not much taller than the grass, only a trace of what would have once been a house or barn, eroded by annuals of neglect. Of course no one was paying these ruins much attention as they blindly stumbled over them, transfixed on the sight at the center of the town before them, the Old Watusia House, the one structure still standing, nestled in the woods and overgrown with vines, patiently waiting for someone to cross its threshold. It looked more like a fortress than a home. It was three stories tall and built of a grey, moss-covered stones. Jocund judged, by the utilitarian architecture, that it was approximately two thousand annuals old; there were a few buildings from that era scattered throughout Y-Kewnor, remnants of Argratos. Jocund also knew Old Watusia fell about the same time Argratos did, though his knowledge of the history was based more on facts than folk-lore. One perturbing detail to him, however, was the house's condition; it was far too good to have withstood a thousand annuals of neglect and the rest of Old Watusia was in far too great a state of disrepair for that duration of time; the stories and numbers didn't match.

"This place gives me the willies," the oaf said.

"Well, ladies and gentlemen," Jocund said, swallowing the lump he didn't realize was in his throat, "welcome to this evening's quarters. You may feel apprehension due to its uncomely appearance and the good princess's fairytales, but I assure you, we're safer in there then we are out here and, should you seek further motivation than not having your throat slit by sell-swords in the middle of the night, perhaps this house will provide us all with answers to life's mysteries."

Inside the large wooden door, an enormous foyer, plain and empty, vaulted up through all three stories of the house. At the far end there was an arch to the left, an arch to the right, and a stone staircase in the middle, which led to the mezzanine and the balcony overlooking the hall, each jutting out from the wall, the balcony more than the mezzanine, a tapering that eventually led to one singular point at the top of the room, from which an enormous iron chandelier hung by a thick chain. Jocund ordered his men to seal the door and start a fire. It was growing darker and he wanted the place secured before there was no light to see what they were doing.

"There, you see?!" Jocund said once the fire was burning. "Not a single ghost or ghoul or skinless king. Let's make sure the rest of the house is secure and then get some sleep. Princess, you wait here."

"I will do no such thing," the princess said. "I'm not going to wait here to be kidnapped or haunted or murdered."

"You want a room?!" Jocund asked. "Fine. Milkboy, take some logs and a torch and see to it the princess and her fiancé are safely secured in a room."

The milkboy, Jocund noticed, looked terrified, but he began picking up some of the wood they had dragged inside. Jocund laughed to himself at how country folk were so much more inclined to believe in nonsense like ghosts. The milkboy was one of those types who wanted to please people, which was why he was so good at following orders; unfortunately, the types who wanted to please people also tended to believe people. Despite the milkboy being smarter than the others, he was no less gullible, a trait Jocund made note of, should he be required to exploit it at a later time, knowing that, even with the Old Watusia House secured, they weren't out of the woods yet, figuratively or literally.

Once the milkboy left with the princess and her fiancé to find them safe quarters, Jocund sent the rest of the group off to accomplish their tasks, taking the opportunity to pick the old man's mind and see if his hypothesis about him was correct. He wasn't sure why he wanted to know for certain about the old man's past, but, always seeing life as a game, it was important to him to learn the nature of all the pieces on the board. He waited until they had cleared the archway and nobody was earshot.

"So," he started casually, continuing to walk, "twenty annuals out of the guard and then you decide to return."

The old man grumble in vague agreement.

"That makes me rather fortunate you ended up in my platoon," Jocund continued, pressing for more of a reaction, "given your background."

"And what background would that be?" the old man asked calmly, letting Jocund know he'd have to press harder.

"Your experience, of course, but I suppose a warrior of your caliber wouldn't have much interest in the dull daily life of a soldier during these annuals of peace. I suppose someone like you would want to wait for something really exciting to happen before signing up again."

"I signed up to protect the boy who you strong-armed into this mission before he was ready; my past has nothing to do with this," said the man casually, but firmly.

"So you reenlisted to protect a boy assigned the routine task of accompanying a princess to her home?" Jocund asked dubiously.

"Are you suggesting, Lordson," the old man said, "that there is nothing to this mission beyond its face value?"

"This is about more than guard duty," Jocund said. "We both know it."

"Oh?" asked the old man, his casual tone betrayed by his shaking hand on the torch. "What do you think is really going on then?"

"Well, correct me if I'm wrong," Jocund said, matching the old man's casual tone as they walked down the cold, dark, stone hallway, "but, in a millennia of peace, there was an incident, twenty annuals ago. They say a dragon was involved, and only one man returned, a knight. All records have been redacted from the histories, but I'd bet there were more survivors and I think you're one of them."

Suddenly, the old man dropped his torch, grabbed Jocund by his lapels, and crushed him into the wall.

"You know nothing, boy!" the old man growled. "Those weren't just hapless victims; they were my friends. They made sacrifices you couldn't even imagine, never claiming even a mote of credit, so spineless parasites like you and your father could sleep well at night, safe from an evil you can't possibly imagine."

"But we aren't safe, are we?" Jocund asked softly, accustomed to ignoring insults and bodily harm, focused on the information he was getting. "The evil has returned."

"No," Cutter said, softening his grip. "The evil was never vanquished. It's been biding its time, manipulating those with a thirst for power, and now it's making its move."

"The evil," Jocund said, "does it have a name?"

The old man, exhibiting a fear Jocund had never seen in him looked over his shoulders, then whispered, "Gordorah," and, though the old man's breath was light, the torch Jocund was holding flickered with the word. Then, they heard a scream. Cutter let go of Jocund, drew his sword, and ran towards the foyer. Jocund drew his rapier and followed.

When Jocund arrived in the foyer, only steps behind Cutter, he found the old man rushing to the large front door; it was wide open. Other than that, the room was empty.

"Get that closed!" Jocund commanded, rushing to the door, himself.

As Jocund arrived at the door he saw several fires off in the distance. It was, he was certain, the brigands that had been following them. It appeared as though they had set up camp. They were probably closer than their fires, he figured, waiting for the right moment, which would be soon if they didn't get that door shut.

"What of Brunff and Kazerra?" Halibon asked, rushing into the room with the gravedigger's boy. "Where are they?"

"Outdoors, no doubt!" Jocund said. "An open door usually means someone's exited! Now let's get this closed. I'll not have all our throats slit on account of two soldiers afraid of a scary story!"

"Me Liege!" the oaf said, as the door finally groaned into place and Halibon hesitantly secured the jam. "Aye think aye found them."

"Where?!" Jocund snapped, turning around, certain he hadn't seen them in the room.

The oaf, his face absent of all color was pointing his finger like a damned fool. Jocund hurried towards the oaf to tell him this wasn't the time for his idiot antics, but as he stepped closer he felt a drip on his head. He felt his hair with his hand. It was warm and wet. When he looked at his hand he saw it was red. He looked up. Above him, covered with blood, two bodies dangled from the chandelier. Brunff and Kazerra were dead.

"Where's their skin?" the Ma-Areshi girl asked.

Jocund realized the two bodies skewered onto the chandelier were completely skinless.

Overwhelmed, but thinking on his feet, Jocund said, "Make sure the princess doesn't come in here and see this."

"See what?" the princess asked, standing at the bottom of the stairs, but before Jocund could think of a lie, she released a blood curdling scream.

"Listen!" Jocund shouted above the commotion in the foyer. "I think brigands may have somehow entered this castle. We need to keep the princess safe and find whomever did this."

"Wut if it's a wut?" the oaf senselessly asked, completely confusing Jocund with his question and his damned northern accent.

"What?!" Jocund demanded.

"Wut if it's a wut wut did this not a who, sah? They was skinned... Like the king o' old Watusia."

"Look." Jocund said, exhausted. "We can't go out there and we can't just sit around and wait for what, or whomever did this to attack again. Milkboy, please take the princess back to her quarters, where she'll be safe while the rest of us do out best to figure this out."

The milkboy never responded. He wasn't in the room.

***

Teryessa had no interest in being one of The Divine Empress's Knights, but it was an opportunity, an opportunity for her to learn the skills she needed to exact her revenge on the dragons and free herself from their grasp. The man who offered her this opportunity was well built, but stocky; however, it appeared as though he was once muscular. She remembered from her childhood that the knights were often a little on the heavy side, no doubt the result of rigorous training while young, transitioning into lethargy as they matured. The knight who offered her the opportunity to become a knight reminded her of every knight she had ever known. Over-confident, opinionated, and judgmental, but she saw something else, too. She noticed a rage, simmering below his surface. This was probably the range of emotion, she figured, full of himself until the moment he didn't get his way, then it would be a temper tantrum. This was fine. She would know what to expect, and knew how to behave around men such as this, men like her father. At least this one would actually teach her to use a sword and not treat her like a little princess. She decided she would play the game and become a knight as long as it was useful to her.

As she rode from Bridgekeep to Y-Kewnor, Teryessa had a strange sense of loneliness or emptiness. She couldn't decide which it was. The night before she had dreamt of the ice castle again and, again, The Divine Empress was missing, but that reflection of herself had been there to slay the dragon and then turn on her. She blamed her discomfort on the dream, but something told her it wasn't only the dream that was bothering her and she couldn't help doing what she had sworn only the previous day she'd never do; she thought of that dumb boy with his stupid, charming smile, standing like an idiot at the side of the road. She wondered why she was thinking of him, but she also wondered if he was thinking of her, too. For a fleeting moment she wondered if she should turn around. There wasn't a doubt in her heart that, if she wanted to, she could find him. She thought about forsaking her adventure and following that awful boy, but it was too late. The die had been cast; this new version of her was to be forged with iron. She would use the knight and his generous offer, become a warrior, and exact her revenge. She snapped the reins and Joker galloped ahead, never stopping for meal or rest. She was traveling south next to a river and the glint of a giant city emerged on the horizon, growing from the earth; it was like Lees Naglos, but completely different. She was approaching Y-Kewnor.

Teryessa had instructions of where to go when she arrived in Y-Kewnor; she was to go to a building called the Citadel. She would wait for the knight, Rheozarccio Rheodo to return and provide her with quarters, stables, and clothing. She was also given a note from the knight, which she was to hand deliver to some other knights, some sort of council and she realized she didn't really understand very much about The Divine Empress's Knights for someone who was so obsessed with it as a child, but, then again, it wasn't hierarchies or councils that interested her; it was stories of adventure and heroism and hope.

There were security checkpoints at the gates to Y-Kewnor. They were run by men wearing similar uniforms to the men she saw on the road to Bridgekeep and, for a moment, she swore the man approaching her was that ridiculous boy she had seen by the side of the road. Her eyes were playing tricks on her. This man was almost a head taller and probably twice as heavy. He asked her a few questions, vaguely wondering if she came in peace, as though some idiot would ever, severely outnumbered, admit to ill intent. After giving him some equally vague but reassuring answers, the man, whom Teryessa learned was a Kewnorian Guardsman, granted her passage into the city.

Y-Kewnor was a bustling metropolis, just like Lees Naglos and, while both cities were round, the buildings within Y-Kewnor were mostly square, grey blocks and not as elegant in shape or color as the buildings in Lees Naglos. The people also looked different; they seemed stockier, but also more angular, they weren't as graceful. They moved faster, too, hurrying about, everyone looking so busy. Between the security checkpoint and the frenzied pace of the town, Teryessa wondered if they were preparing for war. There was one building, tall and white, that stood out to Teryessa, and she knew it had to be the Citadel. As she trotted closer, weaving Joker between the well fed but overworked cart horses, she noticed the top of the Citadel was charred. As a man on a horse quickly trotted by her, she snapped the reins to catch up to him.

"Sir," she said, barely getting his attention, "that building, the Citadel. Has it always been charred?"

"What kind of idiot girl are you?!" the man snapped, "That's from the attack."

"Attack?!"

"Yes," he scoffed as though she were the simplest fool he had ever met. "You know, the dragons?!"

Then he snapped his own reins to hurry away from any further questions, but Teryessa was too shocked to ask any, even if he had provided her the opportunity. She remembered the dragon, Broch-Isha, mention Y-Kewnor. This recent attack on the Citadel must have been what he was referring to, but she couldn't figure out how it all connected. One thing was clear, though; if she wanted to find out, if she wanted to be free from their talons forever, if she wanted to avenge herself... then she was going in the right direction.

Teryessa's blood immediately simmered at the sight of the knights at the Citadel, when she thought of someone she hadn't thought of since this nightmare began, Truson Everly. He was a young knight when she was just a girl and was one of her favorite persons in the kingdom. Lionara used to tease that Teryessa wanted her father to arrange a marriage for her with this handsome knight, but it wasn't true; although she was smitten by Truson, she didn't want to marry him, she wanted to be him. She imagined that how she felt about Truson was the same way a girl would feel about an older brother. For a moment, after hitching Joker to a post, Teryessa indulged briefly in a happy thought, imagining, as she walked up the steps to the front entrance of the Citadel, how proud Truson Everly would be of her.

Once inside, Teryessa realized almost everyone was staring at her. She wondered if they had guessed her identity and wondered how that could even be possible. Her head was on a swivel, whipping around at all the eyes in that grand, white, stone lobby focussed on her. She could have sworn, in that moment, she would have been able to hear a pin drop. She continued across the marble tiles, beneath a monochromatic fresco on the ceiling depicting some sort of battle in whites and blacks and various tones of grey, to the singular splash of color in the room other than her, a gold reception desk.

"What do you think you're doing, miss?" a thin man in silver armor working behind the desk looked up to hiss at her. "Is your intention to mock The Divine Empress's Knights, the knights who have stood up for rotten waifs like you for thousands of annuals?!"

"What?!" Teryessa asked, truly shocked. "I was sent here by a knight, Sir Rheozarccio Rheodo. I'm afraid I have no idea what you're talking about."

"And he let you walk in here, wearing that armor? Figures, with him. He hasn't been right since the attack."

"This?!" Teryessa asked, pointing to her armor. "A woman isn't allowed to wear armor?!"

"Not gold armor."

"Why not?" she asked.

"Gold is one of the sacred colors. Only a High Knight of the Council can wear gold armor."

"Well, I had no idea," Teryessa said defensively, though, the sacred colors did sound familiar to her, once he had mentioned them.

"Now you do," the man said. "And if you want my advice, you'll be careful associating with Rheodo. Since becoming a High Knight of the Council, he's made enemies."

"Well, I'm to deliver a message for him to the council, so, if you don't mind directing me to their chambers and sparing me your advice on what I ought to wear and with whom I ought to associate, I'd be most grateful."

Moments later, Teryessa found herself climbing a spiral staircase, counting the stairs in twos so the building wouldn't collapse around her. She had become so engrossed in her counting that she walked past the correct floor without realizing it. There was only one door. She knocked.

"Enter!" a voice called from within and she did.

Standing in an entryway, Teryessa saw an older gentleman in gold armor, just like hers, sitting alone at a long table furiously scribing something onto a scroll.

"I'm afraid you've already missed the Grand High Knight," the man said without looking up. "He had some disciplinary measures to administer immediately after today's council meeting."

"From what I understand, I may be here on behalf of the High Knight of the Council due to receive said discipline," Teryessa said, "I've been sent by Sir Rheozarccio Rheodo with a message."

The old man scribbling at the table looked up and the expression on his face could not have been more surprised. It appeared as though he had been struck by lightening, as though some spell had manifested his body.

"Yes, indeed," he said, pulling on a pair of gloves as he rose to his feet. "What a coincidence."

"I already know I'm wearing the wrong color," Teryessa said, going through the motion of apologizing, "so I'm sorry if I'm offending you, but I found this and have no other armor or clothing."

"I completely understand," the man said. "I'm on the council with Sir Rheodo and would be happy to be of service."

Teryessa told the man she didn't want to interrupt his work and just had to deliver a message, but the old man told her he was finished, snatched the note from her hand, and quickly ushered her down a few more flights of stairs.

The room the old man brought her to was almost identical to the one he had been writing in, save a few small differences. He offered her a chair at a long table like the one upstairs, and sat on the edge of the table to read the note as she devoured an apple from a fruit bowl.

"So you met Sir Rheodo being questioned by him as a potential witness to something he was investigating... Without the blessings of the council, no doubt."

Finishing the apple, Teryessa said, "I was on my way to Y-Kewnor from Sima Watusia and saw some princess he was looking for on the side of the road."

"Yes, the missing princess," the old man chuckled. "Young Sir Rheodo sees conspiracy everywhere he looks, but missing princesses do seem to be reoccurring problem as of late. It appears as though Rheodo may have found at least one of them. No?"

"Well, he hasn't found her yet," Teryessa said, feeling that something wasn't right, but careful not to give away her suspicions, "but with the information I gave him, she should be easier to find."

"Indeed," he said, tapping the note against edge of the table. "You practically handed her to us. But enough of politics and princesses. Your journey must have exhausted you."

"Yes," Teryessa said, carefully sticking to her story, anxious for an excuse to leave the presence of this man who seemed to be probing her for answers, "I am quite tired, Sir Knight."

"Of course. I hope Sir Rheodo doesn't mind if I have the pleasure of entertaining you this evening."

"Perhaps I should just retire to Sir Rheodo's quarters as he instructed."

"Nonsense," he insisted. "Tell me, are you fond of numbendria? I happen to have a cask of the most potent blend the Wasteland has to offer, imported to me as a gift from a C'ar-Ifan Chief I've been friends with since we were both much younger."

The offer of numbendria was an offer Teryessa couldn't refuse. She had recently run out and was craving that bland emptiness more than anything she could imagine. Before she could say no, the old man poured some into a small glass, the thick golden syrup oozing from the cask. She could imagine its spicy sweetness on her tongue. She reached for the glass.

"There you go," he said, as she swallowed the liquid. "Enjoy your sleep, princess. It is likely the last peace you'll ever have."

Teryessa tried to leap to her feet, to run or fight, but her lugubrious muscles disobeyed and she found herself remaining in the chair. Her eyes grew heavy. Her vision blurred and narrowed until all that existed was darkness.

***

"You know she's not who she says she is," Bea said to Rheo after a long moment of silence.

"She was lying about her identity," he replied "of that I'm certain."

"Good," Bea replied, watching Rheo return to his silence, wondering if she was doing the right thing. "Then you are, no doubt, working to put the pieces together to expose her true identity."

"I am," he defended dutifully, slamming his fist into the table with frustration in a manner that reminded her of Sir Vincent Ackaback, "but that's all there ever seems to be lately, pieces of information that lead nowhere."

"Easy," she soothed. "Pieces are a good thing."

"I know I chose right," he said, "I don't know who she is and I know she's a liability, but I also know she's the only one I could have chosen. There's something about her."

"Then you probably know more than most," Bea said, knowing answers weren't enough, Rheo had to come to the conclusions, himself; he had to grow if he was to become what she needed him to become.

Rheo walked over to the window, staring at the Bridgekeep street below them. He was so confident and strong in so many ways. He was sincere and kind-hearted and even had the look a city could rally behind, especially if he lost a few pounds, but he had shortcomings. His physical prowess, looks, and charm, had made life easy for him. He never had to learn how to think or scrap his way out of a problem, but, for someone who had lived his life by the book, his recent behavior showed great promise for his potential to break away from convention. Just as he was confident in who he chose, so was she confident in her choice of him. She wheeled up next to him and, together, they watched the girl, who's true identity Bea had already solved, pack up her horse and ride off.

"She's quite a skilled rider," Bea said, pointedly, "for someone who doesn't know how to pack a saddle bag."

"She does seem quite comfortable on a horse," Rheo mused. "What Watusian would ride a mountain horse though, and one with such strong Orc horse traits? She acquired that horse recently, from Orc Doola most likely; that saddle is barely broken in. Managing a stubborn horse like that so quickly, she isn't a good rider; she's an expert rider."

"Who, as you said," Bea urged, "recently bought that horse in Orc Doola, wearing armor that doesn't belong to her, armed with weapons she doesn't know how to wield."

"Her skin, hair, and eyes aren't Watusian either," Rheo said. "They're western and high-born."

Rheo, turning from the window, all the pieces of this tiny little puzzle clicking into place in his mind, said, "I've just chosen the presumably dead princess of Lees Naglos as my knight-son, but you already knew that."

"Never!" Bea joked.

"How did you know?"

"Her eyes," Bea said, suddenly saddened. "I knew her mother and I'd recognize those eyes anywhere."

"You seem to know everyone, Bea." Rheo said, proud of himself and oblivious to Bea's sudden sadness. "Perhaps you're the mastermind at the center of this conspiracy."

She wanted to admit to him what she knew, but there was so much to tell and so much she, herself, didn't understand, and there wasn't the time, because she saw something truly alarming out the window.

"That man," she said to Rheo, pointing out a hunched over elderly looking man with a black cloak pulled high over his face, hobbling over to a horse, "Have you seen him before? Quickly, Rheo! Yes or no?"

"Yes, he was here when we arrived. Right there. Why?"

"We have to go. The princess is in grave danger."

Bea and Rheo moved quickly down the hall, and Bea didn't resist when he threw her over his shoulders and grabbed her chair with his free hand so they could quickly descend the flight of stairs in Ptatiana's. He had offered to go after the man alone, but she, knowing what the man really was, refused to let him. Trusting her, he did his best to help her along and she didn't put up a fight when he lifted her into their carriage without asking. The fate of that girl and perhaps all of Allyoshmar depended on them responding quickly. Miles snapped the reins and they were off, in pursuit of the man in pursuit of a different princess than they had come to Bridgekeep looking for.

The carriage rocked and creaked as it bounced over the uneven road west out of Bridgekeep. Miles pushed it as fast as the horses could go, much faster than any carriage was designed to travel. Bea could hear the wood splintering and cracking and she hoped they would catch the beast before the carriage broke apart.

"This man," Rheo said, shouting over the clacking of the carriage, "who is he?"

"That's no man," she said, "that beast is the bastard who took my legs. He's a dragon."

"A dragon?!"

"Yes," she said, "he looks injured, but that only makes him more dangerous, so let's hope you're as fine a swordsman as Vincent said you are."

Bea watched as Rheo drew his sword, checking the blade in the same manner Vincent would have. Although he looked nothing like his knight-father, the way they moved and acted was strikingly similar.

"He's not flying," Bea said. "Something must have happened to his wings and I'd wager it was our princess."

Soon, the man on the horse was in sight and they were closing on him, but he noticed the carriage and snapped his reins, speeding up. Bea knew they'd never catch him like this and she cursed herself and cursed her legs and cursed the dragon for taking them, but then Rheo sprang into action. He threw open the door to the carriage as it sped over the gravel and grabbed on to the top, kicking his legs up to where Miles was sitting and then heaving the rest of his body after them. Looking out the open door, Bea saw Rheo leap onto the right rear horse of the four horses pulling the carriage. He kicked out the cotter pin holding the horse's yoke to the carriage and quickly cut the leather straps with his sword, kicking the side of the horse and speeding off after the dragon, leaving the carriage behind in a cloud of dust.

Moments later, they passed Rheo's horse galloping off into the field next to the road, but no Rheo was in sight. Then she saw the other horse, again riderless, galloping towards them, obviously spooked. The carriage slowed down and she saw Miles leaping from the top and drawing his own blade before they even came to a stop, leaving Bea to lower her wheelchair from the carriage, herself. As the dust settled, she saw the man, the beast in disguise, cowering on the ground, pleading at the tip of Rheo's blade, with Miles standing by, ready to join the battle. Rheo raised his blade over his head.

"Wait!" Bea screamed. "Stop."

"Thank you. Thank you. A thousand times thank you, kind lady," the beast groveled. "I don't know why this mad man has attacked me."

"Save your breath, Ahkk-Rhall," Bea said, "I know who you are. Have you already forgotten me? I suppose old women don't interest you as much as girls. You have changed, but I could never forget you."

"The soldieress," he said, his tone different, "you were always one of my favorites. It's a pity we didn't have more time together, but perhaps fate has brought us a new opportunity to play."

Bea remained cool, her younger self, the one he maimed, despite her bravery, would have been shaking now, urinating herself at the sight of her mutilator, but age had given her distance and time to think about this moment. She sat calmly.

"Go ahead," she said, "reveal yourself. We all know what you are."

"I'm afraid that form is under repair at the moment, my sweet soldieress," he said, showing her his deformed hands. "This one isn't in optimum shape either. Would you slay a defenseless creature?"

"No," she said. "But I'd make an exception for you, were it not for the fact that I need something and you're going to give it to me."

"Why were your after that girl?" Rheo shouted.

"Soldieress," Ahkk-Rhall said, "perhaps you could tell this fool to silence himself, so the adults may speak without interruption."

"Why were you after that girl?" Rheo demanded.

"The princess?" he said. "I have my motives. The soldieress knows my pleasures. Perhaps you should ask her. If it's the girl's safety that concerns you, perhaps you should be less concerned with why I'm after her and more concerned with who else is after her."

"You know something." Bea said.

"I know a lot of things," Ahkk-Rhall replied. "Perhaps we can arrange something."

"Who's after her?" Bea demanded.

"Dragons," he replied casually.

"Who are the dragons? Where are they?" she asked.

"Everywhere," he said, "right beneath your noses. But now I've already given you something. If you want more questions answered, you'll have to do something for me."

"What would you have us do?" Rheo asked. "Let you go?!"

"Goodness, no," he replied. "I want you to save the princess. I have big plans for her."

***

The castle was almost empty and Noldar was fine with that. He enjoyed the solitude and wanted every possible resource sent to Gavlessa to destroy those barbarians once and for all. The horses returned had left with the cavalry before sunset, so he was certain they'd arrive on the battlefield before the next morning. It was an all or nothing strategy, but Truson was right; there was no other move. All alone in his throne room, he sat and stewed, allowing the anger and hatred to simmer just beneath the surface until his solitude was interrupted by the sound of one man clapping.

"Very well done," Niveous Snew said, strolling into the throne room. "You couldn't have been more predictable."

"Snew, what's the meaning of this?" Noldar shouted.

"The meaning is that this is the end of the line for you, Your Grace."

Noldar stood to draw his sword, but Gavlessan barbarians rushed into the room with their swords drawn before he could unsheathe it.

"Bring him to the dungeon," Snew said, "For now."

***

It was already late when Aiwren found a safe room for Wanda and Leicester. It was a bedroom once. The door and furniture were still intact, but everything inside the room was covered with white sheets. The moon beams piercing the utilitarian balistraria cast the white sheets and cold grey stones in such an abundance of crimson light that it appeared as though the entire room was ablaze, but the air, so cold Aiwren could see his own breath, made a liar of the room's appearance. Aiwren and Leicester made quick work of breaking apart the table and chairs to start a fire in the fireplace while Wanda, who had offered to help with the fire, attached the removed sheets to the curtain rods that had long ago discarded their moth-eaten curtains into rotting piles on the floor, but even with the curtains hanging over those ominous red arrow slits, the fire still paled in comparison to the full demon moon light.

"Do you really think we're safe here?" Leicester asked Aiwren surreptitiously.

"All we have to do is make it until the morning," Aiwren said, unsure, himself. "Thieves and brigands aren't interested in attacking face to face in broad daylight. If we keep them out tonight, they'll have no recourse but to give up and go after a more winnable bounty."

"I know," said Leicester, "this is their final chance to capture Wanda and I'm concerned fleeting opportunity may cause them to be more brazen."

"If they attack, we'll give fight," Aiwren said, "and I swear, my dearest friend, I will allow no harm to fall on you or Wanda. You have my word."

Leicester grabbed Aiwren's shoulder and gave a squeeze. "In my heart, I have always known you were special. It is a comfort beyond words to have such a hero as one's own best friend. I only hope I may one day invent some way to fully express my thanks."

"I'm no hero," Aiwren said, "but for whatever I've done, your friendship is more than a sufficient reward. Just be sure to invite me to your fancy royal wedding."

"Invite you to my wedding?!" Leicester laughed, "Royal or not, I insist you serve as my groomsponsor."

"It would be an honor," Aiwren said, touching his best friend's cheek as he stood.

Before he left the room, Aiwren instructed Leicester and Wanda to slide the heaviest furniture in front of the door. He was determined to be sure they were safe. Although he didn't express his fear, he was worried, as Leicester was, that the thieves on their trail would, knowing it was their final opportunity, attack that night. He fully intended to hold watch in front of their door, but he knew it was his duty to check in with Lieutenant Plune first and to see for himself that the main entrance was fortified. He headed back the way he came.

For some reason the hallway appeared longer on the way back. There were some turns along the way, but Aiwren didn't recall the walk to Leicester and Wanda's room being such a labyrinth, which left no explanation for why, after walking for what he felt was twice as long as it ought to have been, Aiwren still hadn't found the main hallway to the foyer where his platoon was waiting for him. Not wanting to panic, he took a deep breath and continued to walk down the windowless hallway, his way lit only by his torch. Eventually he found a set of stairs.

Aiwren didn't recall ascending a flight of stairs to this hallway, but he was tired and not thinking clearly and he doubted his memory. He didn't recall much of his way here, so he assumed he simply had been too distracted by his concerns to have paid full attention to his way.

"Some hero," he thought, "defeated by a hallway."

As he pondered the stairs, a scream from below made his mind for him. He worried that there had been an attack and he hurried down the stairs to another unfamiliar hallway.

"Hello?" he called hesitantly, holding the torch as far in front of himself as he could. "Is everyone okay?"

There was no response, so he continued walking, but, as he rounded yet another unfamiliar corner, he swore he saw a wisp of motion disappear around the corner up ahead.

"Hello?" he called, uncertain of who was ahead of him.

Whomever it was said nothing, nor did they wait for him as he rounded the next corner, but up ahead he was certain he saw a figure disappearing around yet another corner and he followed trepidatiously, waving his torch in front of him, wandering deeper and deeper into the inexplicably vast house, both terrified and mesmerized, certain there was something familiar about all of this but unable to specify what was so recognizable about such an abnormal situation since nothing about his surroundings was familiar to him at all. The corridor was dark and narrow, constructed with rectangular stones, fitted together so tightly that, although he could see their seams, the mortar was nothing but a thin grid stretching down the length of the hall, outlining each grim block.

"Come to me," a voice whispered from what felt to Aiwren like just over his shoulder.

Aiwren spun around to find the source of the sound, but saw nothing. Waving his torch frantically, as though he meant to douse the hall with the light of the fire, all he saw was the hallway, which somehow appeared both narrower and longer than it had a moment earlier. He kept walking into the unknown, feeling horrifyingly certain he'd felt this way before.

Finally, as he turned another corner, now having completely lost track of his direction, Aiwren saw, up ahead, a sight that shook him to his core. At the end of the hallway, standing by another turn, facing him, was a woman in a long red gown.

"Aiwren," he heard her say, but her lips never moved.

He was transfixed by the sight of the woman in the red gown. The curves of her body tingled his desires, and made him want all the things he didn't want to want.

She continued around the next corner, moving as smoothly as the silk of her red dress. The long, red train swept tantalizingly across the floor behind her, like an obedient pool of blood following her wherever she went. Her focus strait ahead, she ignored him in a manner that invited him to pursue with the same compliant devotion as the train of her dress. There really was no other choice. After what felt like an eternity, he finally reached that corner where he saw her standing, hoping she'd be there, waiting for him with her crimson lips, to let him take her right there in the hall of this strange enormous house. She was gone, but there was light, a sliver of light up ahead, razor thin across the floor, the light that escapes from that small space beneath a door.

As Aiwren reached the door, he hesitated before reaching for the handle. It was a wooden door. Plain, but smooth and new looking. There was a key hole, through which light was cast upon Aiwren's sweating hands. Also, there was a plaque that said one word: "Gallery."

Aiwren crouched down low and peered through the keyhole. He could see very little. The room, he could tell, was lit by torches, but his vision though the keyhole was limited to what was right in front of him and what was right in front of him was all he was interested in. Standing only ten feet from the door, with her back to him, was the woman in the red gown. Her slender fingers reached behind her, nimbly grabbed the black lace of her bodice and tugged sensually, unfolding the bow gracefully into her hand. Her bodice fell to the floor. She watched over her shoulder as it fell, watched it fall in a way that made Aiwren momentarily certain she wanted him to watch. Her eyes glanced too close to the keyhole for Aiwren's comfort and he quickly darted off to the side and held his breath, nervous the woman would hear his heart that felt as though it would burst from his chest. After a moment, he glanced into the keyhole again. The woman was gone. He stood and found himself involuntarily turning the door knob.

The Gallery was a long room, wider than the corridor, but narrow for a room of its length. Along the sides of the room were buckets, at least ten on each side. The buckets were all knee high and sitting below pumps with long wooden handles jutting out of the wall. Slow heavy drops dripped from each pump into its respective over-flowing bucket. It looked like some sort of utility well, but it was strange that it was so far from the kitchen. Beyond the buckets and pumps was another door. A dark door. A closed door. The woman's red bodice was lying in a pile on the smooth stone floor in front of the door. Aiwren knew he mustn't enter; he was terrified of what waited within, but he felt an overwhelming urge to grab the handle and twist.

The room beyond the door was filled with steam. Through the steam, Aiwren could see a large bath that had eroded and crumbled over time into the spring that was the source of its water, so, although the back wall of the pool was still intact, the side near him had dissolved away and the floor tiles had crumbled, leaving a muddy patch that slipped into the dark depths of the spring. The steam, Aiwren discovered, was coming from the water, itself. He peered through the dense fog and saw the woman in the red gown standing at the near end of this decaying bath. She smiled at him and let her dress slip down over her flesh and onto the muddy ground. The steam was increasingly opaque and the torches on the walls were dim, so Aiwren strained to see the details of her nude figure.

416

Aiwren wasn't sure how it happened, but water was seeping into his boots. Although he couldn't remember taking a step, he was standing ankle deep in the spring with the soles of his feet in the mud and he didn't care at all. The water was warm and comforting and the sight of the woman, her pale skin and dark red hair, had been irresistible; he had to see her again.

"Aiwren," the voice said seductively, "I've removed everything for you. Will you join me in the bath?"

"In the bath," Aiwren repeated, realizing he was now up to his waist in the pool. Silhouetted by the flickering torchlight, he saw the figure of the woman. She was in profile, arching her back and rolling her neck with pleasure, the outline of her body glistening and backlit in crimson, her dangerous curves defined by a hazy red corona. Then, in a flicker of the torches, she vanished.

Aiwren, chest-deep in water, tried to speak, but he couldn't. He looked around frantically for the woman. He waded further, to where the floor of the pool had crumbled apart completely, creating a hole down into the spring below and forcing Aiwren to tread the water that had just gone from chest high to unimaginably deep.

Aiwren bobbed close to the surface, his wet clothes heavy on his body. Water splashed into his mouth and he was surprised by how briny it was, but there was something wrong about how metallic it tasted. He spit into his hand. It was red. He was swimming in blood. He splashed frantically to swim to the edge, to escape what he realized was his worst nightmare coming to life, knowing what would come next, when he suddenly felt a pressure around his ankle and saw the room rocket up away from him, his world instantly darkening in the depths. He had been pulled beneath.

Like the steam above, the clouds of thick blood swirling in the water obscured Aiwren's view as he fought to get to the surface, choking him as he fought for air. The vortex of blood twisted and spiraled, obediently orbiting its master. She wasn't wearing the red gown any longer when she pulled Aiwren deeper into the bloody water and wrapped her strong legs around his waist. She wasn't wearing anything at all, not even her own skin. Heart pounding as the torch light above grew more and more distant, Aiwren fought to escape but she was brutally entwined with him, tearing at him, squeezing him, dragging him deeper and deeper into the darkness. He felt her skinless flesh sliding slimily against his skin as she writhed, grabbing at him with her sinewy hands. Aiwren knew he should keep fighting, he knew he needed air, but, eventually, with the light from the torches above almost too distant to reach him, he relented. He looked into her black eyes as she grabbed his face and breathed into his mouth, submitting to her long wild tongue that forced its way through his lips. The world faded for Aiwren as the Skinless Woman dragged him down, filling him with both terror and pleasure, and he begged for death's sweet release.

***

The stone wheels, turning autonomously, had mashed victim upon victim into a pulpy human sludge that dripped down into the hole dug into the bottom of the cavernous arena that was once used for pitt fighting, but had recently been converted into a mechanized pantheon intended for purposes that were even more insidious than it was originally designed for. By the middle of the night, when the bloody pool was knee deep, representing the hundreds of men who's lives were viciously extinguished as they were fed into the ravenous machine, Plale was woken from his restful meditation in the ancient Temple of Gordorah by Ovyrr-Keel, who informed him that although the sacrifices would continue as he had instructed, the preparations were complete; Plale could begin his spell.

Plale knew what he was doing and, as he strode down the dark hallways of the Gavlessan palace, he thought of the annuals of planning that he had dedicated to the destiny he was about to fulfill. A grotesque grin spread maliciously across his burned disfigured face, mutilating any remaining appearance of humanity.

It was a holy place that he had built and Plale knew it. The enormous room was humming with the energy of his one true Master, Gordorah, energy that he had facilitated and would soon control on behalf of his Master. The Pitt Stadium seats were empty, but Plale's guards, his soldiers, the Army of Gordorah ushered the slaves into a single file line leading from their increasingly unpopulated cages to the middle of that thin bridge over the arena, where they were pushed over the edge, one at a time, into the hungry wheels of the machine, where the gears shredded them into the pool of blood below. With liquid human lapping and bubbling against it, no sacrifice would be required upon the black stone altar erected in the pool; it was there to focus Plale and channel life energy through him and out into the world. As he stood at the edge of the pool the room silenced, the soldiers stopped throwing men over and the screams of the most recent victim soon were silenced by the machine as it turned him to soup.

One of his generals stood by the pool, waiting for him. Plale approached the man, but said nothing. He stared at him a long moment and as soon as Plale stepped away, he heard Ovyrr's sword crunch through the man's chest and the man's body fall to the ground. He didn't need to look; Ovyrr, Plale's dutiful aberration, didn't make mistakes.

Plale stepped down into the pool and the blood grew still. The smell of death filled his nostrils, intoxicating him with life and power. When he arrived at the altar, he held his breath, drew Soul Stitcher, and slid the knife's blade across his palm. He squeezed his fist and a glob of his blood dripped from his hand above the stone altar. The drop splattered against the smooth black surface with an explosion of percussive silence rippling forth from that singular point, radiating outward like a shockwave. A moment of emptiness suspended obediently, devoid of sound or motion. Plale exhaled and the blood touching the altar changed to black, a black that spread across the pool.

"Rise," he hissed almost silently, before bellowing a command that echoed enough to shake the walls. "Rise!"

The corpse of the general Ovyrr had, only moments earlier, killed, slowly opened his eyes; they were blacker than night. He heaved himself from the ground, a gaping hole still gushing warm blood from the spot where his heart once was. Plale felt the general's presence near him, but he also felt the presence of more, so many more. He felt the presence of his death savage army rising from the desert sand where they had been slain the previous day. He felt that the princess his Master needed was within his grasp. He felt his forces closing on another princess, one of lesser importance, who's demise would eliminate the possibility of the Freelands coordinating any sort of effort to defend themselves. He felt Y-Kewnor crumbling from within. He felt his Master's strength growing and, as the Mouth of Gordorah, he roared a sinister laugh.

POOLS OF BLOOD

Truson Everly knew battles weren't meant to be fought at night. He also knew the sun setting would only bolster the Gavlessans' resolve, emblazon their vicious retaliations, and disadvantage his own men with low morale and the inability to fight as well as their enemies in the dark of night. The siege was not supposed to last this long. At some point, he had planned, the enemy would fully engage in warfare, leaving their gate unprotected, and that was when he would signal the archers to begin their volley and the cavalry to ride onto the battlefield. He hoped the savage Gavlessans would abandon strategy and send forth their men before nightfall, but they didn't. Meanwhile, Truson's army, unequipped with the supplies to deal with a lengthy siege, grew tired and, as the night grew darker, each platoon returned with fewer and fewer men.

Truson didn't lead the charge of every attack, needing time to strategize, take stock, and rest, but, feeling a leader should never ask his soldiers to do anything he wouldn't do, he was on the battlefield more than anyone else in his army. There were a few tents set up for the wounded that had the greatest chance of surviving their injuries, a single tent for Truson to meet with his generals, and a pile of fallen men that grew larger while the cavalry and the archers waited for the right moment to attack; however, when everything went wrong, Truson was in the thick of the battle. Silhouetted in crimson and illuminated only by the terrifying light of the full red moon, a boated sack of blood ready to burst, Truson hacked his blade with careless exhaustion into the neck of a Gavlessan. This platoon was exhausted and he felt as though the Gavlessans would send a fresh group of warriors at any moment. He knew he needed to retreat and send in a fresh platoon, but, close to the gate, he held out, desperately hoping this attack might turn the protracted battle back to his favor. He waited too long.

It wasn't the sound of the stone gate grinding open to send forth more Gavlessans that Truson Everly heard, it was the whoosh of a silence. He felt the silence slam against him like the crest of a wave and pass through him like a cold breeze through a curtain, chilling his insides in the most unnatural way. Truson's head swiveled in an attempt to focus his blurring vision on something concrete and anchor himself against the disorientation threatening to sweep his mind away. The survivors of his current platoon spun around frantically, similarly confused. Truson focussed on returning to the ability to reason that earned him his nickname, the mathematician, but it didn't do him any good. The darkness enveloped him.

Lost in nothingness, Truson thought, again, about how it wasn't right for men to fight at night. It wasn't right to have to choose between the king who treated him like a son and the knights who treated him like a brother. It wasn't right for knights to be massacred for treason without a trial. It wasn't right that all he could see, when he closed his eyes, was the high priestess bleeding to death on white marble tiles. It wasn't right that he turned his back on The Divine Empress and invited these evil magics into Allyoshmar.

The first thing Truson was aware of as he returned from his thoughts to reality was a scream. It was one of his men, but by the time he turned, it was too late for him to help the soldier. The Gavlessan he had just killed had thrust his enormous jagged sword through the man's body. The Gavlessan, whom Truson had previously presumed to be dead, looked up at him with eyes filled with blackness, a lifeless corpse possessed with evil magics standing before Truson. Another scream turned Truson's attention to another of his men being slaughtered by two corpses, muscles twitching and jerking from the unnatural speed and strength they possessed in place of life, ripping the man's limbs from his body. Truson turned back to the first corpse, and sliced its head from its body completely, a task he had left incomplete the first time he had killed him, but was grabbed from behind. As Truson swung around to free himself, he saw another of his soldiers have his head ripped from his body. He knew, if he didn't get out of there, he'd share a similar fate. The corpses all around him, the Gavlessans he had sacrificed many of his own soldiers to kill, were rising. Beneath the demon moon, the dead returned to kill and, as the sun rose, Truson hacked his way through a sea of corpses. The death savages had risen.

***

Noldar was, as any was any king, a child once, a little boy as frightened by the dark as he was curious about what lurked within it. Annuals before he would be burdened with the responsibilities of the crown, he had assigned himself the task of patrolling the dungeons for monsters. With one shaking hand holding a lantern and the other gripping the tiny sword he had been trained to use since he could walk, Noldar, young and round, would creep from his family's protection in the palace, down into the dungeons below that had been abandoned for generations in exchange for proper humane prisons, dungeons Noldar was certain contained monsters. Although he would always reply to the knights who kindly asked him how his hunting went with feigned disappointment, part of him was always relieved he found nothing, for he was, in his gut, certain something lurked beneath.

Many annuals later, King Noldar, a broken man, captured in a coup he ought to have seen coming, waiting for execution, found himself in the dungeon once more.

Though mostly abandoned for generations, the slime on the walls seemed to preserve the stench of death and decay. Of course he had been to the dungeon since his childhood; he had, only days earlier, executed a man there; but he hadn't been down there alone for a very long time. Stripped of his clothing, his large soft body, covered in cuts and bruises from his attackers, hinted that he was once muscular, a chubby boy who grew into an athletic young man who grew into a chubby old man. He was certain what was next for him was only death, most likely cruel death at the hands of Snew, the backstabbing traitor living in his palace the entire time. He welcomed death. With his daughter gone and no chance for revenge, there was nothing left to live for. If he had known he and his daughter would both end up dead and Lees Naglos would fall, he never would have sent her away. If he had known his wife was in danger, those many nightmare-filled annuals ago, he never would have left her side. It seemed as though his actions, no matter what he did to protect those he cared about, were inconsequential. Every imagined scenario led to his suffering. He was cursed and, at the moment, shackled in the middle of a cell.

Early in the morning, before the sun had cast out the red moon, King Noldar heard the cell door open, certain it meant his demise. If they cut off his head now, it could be on a spike before the people of his kingdom awoke. He made no attempt to look at his attacker. It would have done no good.

The attack never came though; instead, an unidentifiable, but familiar female voice said, "do you remember what you were looking for down here?"

"If you've come to kill me, get it over with," he growled. "I've no desire to speak with traitors."

"Do you remember what you were looking for down here?"

"I was looking for nothing. I was locked down here."

"When you were a child, you were fat and clumsy and down here looking for something."

"Who are you?!" Noldar demanded, trying to turn to see this mysterious woman.

"Me?!" she asked. "I'm your liberator. Here to free you from both the shackles at your wrists and the shackles around your heart. I'm here to make you king."

"I am king," he exclaimed.

She laughed cruelly and said, "You told yourself you were looking for monsters, but you weren't"

"Oh really?!" Noldar sneered, certain he remembered his own childhood better than this woman, even if she could read his mind. "What was I really looking for then?"

"The Sword of Palidnia," she replied.

The shackles at Noldar's wrists snapped open. He quickly turned around to see the woman who freed him, but he was alone in the cell and the door was wide open.

"Where have you gone?!" he screamed, but his call went unanswered.

His sword waited for him on the cold dungeon floor, beside the blood-stained table where his clothes and armor were haphazardly piled. Naked, he crept to them, once again frightened yet mesmerized, as he was a child. He reached for the sword. It wasn't the small blade he wielded as a child; it was his father's sword. As he reached for his clothes, he noticed a tattered dust-cloaked banner clinging to the wall. His family coat of arms. The Flaming Sword of Justice. Noldar Palidnia, king of Lees Naglos, heir to the Flaming Sword, knew what he must do.

***

Aiwren awoke in the back room of the Gallery, close to the pool, naked in the cold mud where the stone floor had relented to the water and earth just as he had to the woman in the red gown, the Skinless Woman. The sun had not yet risen and, even if it had, its light would have no way to reach this chamber buried deep in the ground. Shivering, Aiwren slipped gradually from sleep, exhausted from what felt like the truest nightmare he had ever had, but, as he took in his surroundings, he realized it was no dream. The sight of the woman skinless in the water, writhing against him, flashed in his mind's eye and nausea spun the room around him. Erupting to his hands and knees, he tried to make himself puke, putting his finger down his throat for aid, but he could only gag out a few painfully dry heaves. He reached his hands into the water to take a drink, but threw it when he saw it was black like ink.

"I've been admiring you from afar for quite some time now, Aiwren Wayde and I must say you did not disappoint me."

Aiwren whipped around to see the source of the voice. The Skinless Woman, wearing her red gown and her skin, once again, stood behind Aiwren. He admitted her beauty to himself, mesmerized by her flawless, alabaster skin, her thick, raven hair, and her full, red lips, but something about her inhuman presence siphoned away his strength and injected him with overwhelming and paralyzing dread. Reality warped towards the inextricable, rippling, dream-like haze enveloping her and Aiwren, terrified, yet unable to escape the overwhelming pull, shuddered on the floor, pulling his feet close to his nude, grime-covered body.

She crouched down next to him, looked in his eyes and, with a contained fury, hissed, "When the time comes for you to cower in fear from me, you will know."

Then, as she stroked his face with her hand, in a tone as close to kind as a mockingbeast sounds to its prey, she cooed, "But none of that is necessary. I have chosen you and now you are nearly ready."

"Ready for what?" Aiwren asked.

"Ready to rise," she whispered, so close her lips brushed against his ear.

Aiwren's eyes opened. He was not in the back room of the Gallery, nor was he with the Skinless Woman. He was lying on the floor of a corridor, fully dressed, and he couldn't tell what was real and what wasn't. In the distance, Aiwren heard a clanging. It sounded familiar, but he couldn't place it; his mind was still foggy as he used the wall of the hallway, which wasn't quite as narrow as he remembered it being, to stand up, gripping the stones and trying to make sense of the world. Then, Aiwren heard the unmistakable sound of screams.

Aiwren's vision suddenly focussed as he sprang into action, hoping it would not be too late. The halls were less confusing. He ran towards the stairs leading to the foyer, where he was certain the noise was coming from. He wasn't thinking about what had happened or worrying about his own safety. He was running. It was reactionary. Instinctual. His vision narrowed, not in a foggy dream-like manner, but in a manner that centered his attention, isolating what was right in front of him from a meaningless world. He reached for his sword.

Bursting forth from the narrow containment of the stairwell into the vastness of the foyer was disorienting. Aiwren's body, primed to react to something physical, stalled for a moment as he took in the scene. The melee was spread across the vast room and the floor was littered with bodies. Aiwren's eyes scanned through the battle, to see if his friends were still standing, still fighting. A glint of steel caught his attention. A spear rocketed through the air. Aiwren screamed, but the spear plunged into flesh; the body was already falling.

***

Beatrice Boomswift could usually sleep in a moving carriage, soothed by the repetitive motion, but, as she travelled to Y-Kewnor that night, she couldn't shut her eyes for more than a moment without being overwhelmed by a torrent of thoughts, questions, and concerns. Occasionally stealing a glance at Rheo, she noticed his restlessness, as well, and her thoughts turned to pacifying him, encouraging him with words that everything would be okay, but those reassurances were lies, lies in a world of lies compounded by lies, lies she had participated in disseminating. She wanted to tell him the truth, but she didn't think it would put his mind at ease at all and the truth she kept secret could tear Y-Kewnor apart; it could tear all of Allyoshmar apart. Finding Teryessa and learning of a plot against this princess from the dragon who took Bea's own legs, left little room for any possibility other than the situation being convoluted and quite relevant to her secret, but, for the time being, there were immediate goals and the big picture would have to wait to be addressed. Teryessa had to be saved, and this would have to be accomplished without letting Rheo know the secret, at least for the time being. She needed to keep Rheo on task.

"There's nothing we can do until we return to Y-Kewnor," she said to Rheo after a length of silence as ominous as the red moonlight illuminating them, unsure if he was even listening.

"I know," he replied, his gaze fixed outside the window. "I'm anxious about Jocund."

"I thought you said you were wrong about him," she said, hoping she could focus Rheo on what could be done.

"Yes, I may have been," he admitted, still looking out the window, his brevity and absence indicative of remorse.

"But that's not what's troubling you," Bea probed.

"I'm worried about what's waiting for him and the Watusian princess. Is it a dragon? This all seems so related. We should have sent help."

"Sent help from where?" she asked. "Your knights?!"

"So you, too, speak of my order contemptuously?" he snapped. "Thank you for the small bit of honesty."

"I make no secret of --nor apologies for-- my contempt for what the knights have become, but that is only because I've had the privilege of knowing its finest," she said. "Had we somehow sent troops to Jocund's aid it would have given away his position. Stealth is his greatest ally. Right now the enemy is fractured searching for him."

"And then there's that," Rheo said pointedly, looking at her, his trust in her clearly waning for the first time since they had met.

"Who is the enemy? Everything seems to be constructed in subterfuge and lies and I am expected to stop an enemy I can't even identify."

"Well we know it isn't the Watusians," Bea replied, fearfully certain she already knew sting-puller's motives, "neither of them."

"No," Rheo said, relaxing his guard. "It's someone motivated to entrench the Watusians in their ongoing feud. But why?""

Rheo's attention turned, once more, to the window and Bea wondered why staring off in this manner helped him think. She closed her eyes and tried to calculate scenarios, a task she knew was impossible against a force with plans set into motion thousands of annuals in advance. She wondered how she could compete with that, what a cripple old woman could possibly to to stop this?

"Water!" Rheo suddenly exclaimed. "The boats. The Kewnorian fleet is Watusian-made! If the Watusian feud escalates, they'll refuse to build our ships."

"Someone's trying to cripple our navy," Bea marveled, "someone planning a naval attack."

"But who?!" Rheo demanded. "And what of the attack on the Citadel?! Are we to presume, after a thousand annuals of peace, there are coincidentally two unknown enemies of Y-Kewnor?! The only alternative is the terrifying possibility that none of this is a coincidence."

"I don't know," Beatrice lied, "but we are disadvantaged with the onus of having to face these collusions at a time when the people of Y-Kewnor are most splintered, the morale is lowest, and the politics are most unstable. And I fear that isn't coincidental either."

"I know," Rheo said, with a sadness Beatrice couldn't identify. "If Jocund perishes we'll make him a martyr."

"And if he succeeds?" Beatrice asked and, looking upon her protege, this window to the secret glories of her past. She recognized his sadness. It was the look of a warrior succumbing to the realization that he would not be playing a glorious role in this story.

"If he succeeds, we'll make him a hero," Rheo said, the rising sun illuminating him in hazy light. "He'll deserve it."

***

Jocund never liked ghost stories as a child and he took great pleasure in describing to other children how the stories keeping them well behaved or indoors on Vari-Matera-a were nothing but lies to keep them under control, but that night, confronted with unknown factors for the first time in his life, Jocund felt lost. He was certain there was no Divine Empress looking out for anyone, especially not for him, so, in the face of the brutal and apparently supernatural murder of two of his troops, he faced not only the responsibility of keeping his platoon safe from what was unknown, but also the grim realization that the world was even bleaker than he imagined. His mind froze, unable to act or speak or even process the situation coherently. Then, his instincts took over and he regained his ability to do what he did best.

He had a plan, but he knew he didn't have long. If the attack was not supernatural, then the enemy was already inside the old castle. If the attack was supernatural, then the enemy outside would soon arrive to exploit the confusion. His mind raced, creating dozens of potential scenarios. His best chance was to be unpredictable. If the horrible shitty world was going to deliver nothing but chaos into his life, then he was going to create some chaos of his own. Noticing all of the eyes of his platoon looking to him, he regained his composure.

"When I was a boy I was the object of derision," he said. "The greatest perpetrator was a giant ass named Rheo. There was a game we would play at school called dodge the ball. As you can imagine, I was always picked last for athletic teams and Rheo was always either picked first or a captain, himself, but one day, I suggested Rheo and I each be a captain, that each captain would chose twenty teammates, and that I would let Rheo chose his twenty first. Of course, he picked the most athletic students and I was left with the weaklings."

"How'd you win?" the dear, kind oaf asked him.

"Oh, we lost," Jocund said. "We lost terribly, but each time someone was struck out by the ball, they would be sent indoors. Since only my team, the losers, were being sent inside, we took turns pissing in their water flasks with nobody to stop us or say anything when the winners returned from the game."

Jocund felt everyone's hopes pinned on his every word. He knew they needed hope, but all he had to give was truth.

"I don't know if the milkboy has been skinned like these two, or if he has decided to take a midnight stroll, or if he is simply off sleeping somewhere, dreaming of whatever fairy tales his absent little mind dreams of. While your hearts may tell you we should immediately go looking for him, we have a problem that is exceedingly more eminent. We have been attacked. By whom or what I cannot say, but we have every reason to believe the attacks will continue and will soon only be exacerbated by attacks from the cut throats waiting for an opportunity outside. I have no desire to let them take the princess without putting up a fight. Now we could count on the door to protect us until morning, but sensing our weakness, I doubt those thieves would relent at the rise of the sun. Furthermore, I doubt anyone is coming to our aid. We are on our own. Fortifying the door will only delay the inevitable intrusion from those camped outside and will do nothing to protect us from any potential dangers within."

The group took Jocund's news as well as he imagined they would. They were frightened, but didn't quiver. They, too, knew how dire things were; he could read it on their faces, but they stood strong, looking to him, not for lies or miracles, but for something to do, for a way to make their final moments count, seven people waiting for him to tell them how to make a stand.

"Halibon, Roderick, Cutter, Serafina, Gregory, Leicester, and Princess Wanda. Not a soul intended for any of us to survive this journey. We were, each of us, even you, Princess, a sacrifice. They presumed us to be too feeble, too inexperienced, too old, too cowardly to make it ten feet outside of Y-Kewnor, but we have, because I'm a resourceful little prick with a strong will to live, but my guile has fallen short of bringing us safely to our destination and now, with the finish line in sight, we must fight. We may be outnumbered, my friends, but let's piss in their water. Shall we?"

The group stared bleakly at him, silent, exhausted. Jocund's speech didn't instill the fool hearty morale in the group he had hoped it would, but this wasn't a group of naive heroes hungry for a brawl and some glory. Wanda stepped forward first.

"I'm no warrior, but if I'm unwilling to protect myself it would be shameful to ask any of you to do so," she said. "Hand me a weapon, Lieutenant Plune, and tell me you have a plan."

"I do," he said. "The campfires in the woods. What proper ranger would create such an unnecessarily large campfire? These are thieves from a city, most likely Bridgekeep. They're accustomed to barroom brawls and stabbing someone from behind in a dark alley. We retreat to the back of the room. Put archers in the mezzanine. Open the doors and let them carelessly pass through a choke point. This will help us thin their numbers. Some will certainly pass through. Every archer is paired with a swordsman. Roderick, take position on left front mezzanine. Halibon, defend him. Serafina, you're our best archer, so you'll be at the rear left mezzanine with Gregory defending you. Wanda, I want you far from the door; you'll be at the rear right mezzanine. Leicester, your future wife's life is in your hands. Cutter, you'll be defending me at the front right mezzanine. Swordsmen, you may be tempted to rush in to battle as soon as it appears to be a fair fight. Ignore this impulse. We don't want a fair fight. We want to live another day and worry about honor tomorrow."

Without even a word of disagreement or doubtful glance, Jocund's group sprang into action. Roderick was no archer and neither was he so he took a crossbow for himself and handed one to the gravedigger's son. It would take longer to load a bolt than it would to nock an arrow, but a crossbow would be more accurate at this range. The princess took a bow. He didn't know what skills she had, if any, but as long as she added to the volley and didn't hit any of them, it would be helpful. He counted on Serafina the most, hoping her sight was as good as a falconer's vision ought to be.

Jocund, silently waiting in the dark, with his crossbow pointing at the door from the mezzanine, focussed on the details around him. He heard the morningbird song and he knew the sun would soon rise and the enemy's eyes would be adjusted to the light, making him and his platoon more difficult to see in the dark recesses of the foyer. As the dark of the empty doorway warmed into purple early morning light, he heard the footsteps. He closed his eyes. Listened. Counted. There were at least forty of them and they were big, but they walked carelessly, snapping leaves and twigs beneath their feet. The first brigand stepped in the door, his sword drawn, waving a lantern. Jocund took aim, but, before he could fire, an arrow plunged deep into the man's skull, swiftly and silently dropping him to the ground. Jocund smiled, thinking his plan might actually work. He squeezed the trigger, firing a bolt into the next cutthroat to walk in the door. The bolt sliced into the man's neck, showering the area with blood from the artery it shredded, but not before the man could howl in pain. Knowing they were being attacked, the rest of the brigands rushed in and Jocund knew this was where things were going to get tricky.

***

The first light of day eased into the room of the inn in Orc Doola, softly and gently, but the Nameless Rider kept his eyes shut so he wouldn't be disappointed, so he wouldn't have to learn that it was all a construct of his mind. He wanted to keep reality at bay and remain in this world regardless of whether or not it was true, but his mind could not keep all things out and had no power against the sensation of something brushing against his lips. He opened his eyes.

He wondered how this could be real. His eyes were open and yet, like a dream, she was staring right back at him, her eyes twinkling with affectionate mischief and something else. He felt her skin against his. All over their bodies their skin was touching. Before this, he wasn't even sure if he had skin beneath his clothing, but to have skin and a body and have so much of it in direct contact with so much of hers was bliss. He was real. He was real and for the first time he could remember, he was certain he was alive. He did feel things. He did want things. Even if his feelings and desires were limited to that moment of blissful awakening, he would have bet he experienced those feelings and desires just as much as any man ever.

Let his Master punish him, he thought. He didn't care. This girl, this tattoo'd magical woman nuzzling her chin into the softest part of his neck... She was his light. She was illuminating and warm and more alive than any creature he had ever seen and she was teaching him how to be alive, too. He would do anything for her. He would follow her anywhere.

"Shadow?" she asked, "Do you believe in fate?"

"I don't think so," he said. "If there was fate, then I would be unnecessary. Why send some creature to kill someone at a certain time if that person is going to die at that time no matter what, regardless of what actions you take?"

"Oh," she said with a glum tone.

"That's a good thing," he said. "Nothing is set. There are rules created by people who want things a certain way, but if some unnatural creature and a beautiful girl were ever to meet and decide being together was more important than anything else, then they could break all the rules and disobey all the people who wanted things to be a certain way. They could write their own story."

"What would happen in this story?" she asked. "What would the unnatural creature do?"

"He'd go wherever the girl went. He'd feel more and more alive every day he spent with her. He would smile. He would laugh. He would forget he had lived lives he'd forgotten and he'd never forget a moment of his life with her."

"And how would the story end?" she asked.

"It wouldn't end," he said.

"All stories end," she replied.

"A good rule to break." he said.

She smiled at him with her mouth so close to his that he could feel her breath as she traced the scar on his face with the tip of her finger.

It wasn't until he stepped outdoors that The Nameless Rider fully realized how different he felt. He inhaled the cool mountain air deeply and wondered if he had ever breathed before. His skin felt awake. His awareness surged with details of the world around him and opinions of those details. The sun was brighter. As they rode down the mountains, towards Gavlessa, her body felt different against his than it did the day earlier. Her embrace was unabashed and he wanted nothing more than to be close to her. Shadow didn't need any memories to know this was the greatest morning of his life.

Soon the mountains transformed into high desert, with gnarled little juniper trees and the occasional tongue plant. The squirrels scurrying away had been replaced by lizards scurrying away as they traveled. It wasn't hot, but it was still early in the day.

By the time it had gotten warmer, the Nameless Rider and Vannoria were sitting in the shade of a cantilevered rock, eating lunch. Shadow didn't even realize he was eating until he was halfway through the sandwich Vannoria had purchased for them in Orc Doola. He was hungry and so he ate and eating made him feel less hungry. It was amazing. He thought of Mister Uncle's stew and decided that it was his second favorite food, other than the sandwich he was eating. Vannoria asked him what he was thinking about so seriously and he was hesitant, but decided to tell her, to tell her everything from that point on. She laughed and kissed him and said that, when they returned to Ma-Aresh, she would insist Mister Uncle prepare a stew for them as their reward. Their rest was over too soon and, nearly forgetting why they were journeying, they continued on.

Shortly after their lunch, The Nameless Rider and Vannoria had their first view of Gavlessa. The dune they stood atop gave them a view of the rusty metal spires of the underground city off in the distance. Even from far away the Nameless Rider could tell something was wrong.

"There's a battle." she said.

"Yes," he said. "Perhaps we ought to turn around."

"That's absurd!" she said. "If someone is attacking Gavlessa, this could be the opportunity we need to free the slaves. The enemy of my enemy is my friend. We should help them."

"And what if they don't want our help?"

"If they don't want our help then they will need it for they would be fools. Now give me a kiss and let's find whomever is in charge."

On the back of Darkmoon, the Nameless Rider turned around and kissed Vannoria. He snapped the reins and the two of them rode off, with the hot sun beating down on them, across the cactusia-pocked sands of the Great Desert, towards the west side of Gavlessa, where there seemed to be some sort of make-shift encampment.

Not even a sunhand later, the Nameless Rider and Vannoria saw a group of men on horseback approaching. Vannoria waved her arm high in the air and shouted to greet them, but the salutation went unreturned. She asked if they had seen her, but the Nameless a Rider knew they had. They were still just dark dots on the vast brown expanse, but he knew they were going to be a problem.

"They're going to attack us. Aren't they?" she asked.

"Yes," he responded.

"Are they Gavlessan?" she asked.

"No," he said, unsure of how he even knew what a Gavlessan looked like. "I believe they are the enemy of our enemy."

"Then we mustn't kill them," she declared. "We simply have to explain to them that we're on the same side."

The men rode faster towards them. the Nameless Rider could see there were ten of them and their swords were already drawn. It didn't appear as though they were in the mood to listen to any explaining.

"We mustn't kill them," she repeated sternly.

"Ho!" one of the men yelled.

"Trust me," Vannoria whispered to the Nameless Rider, not giving him an opportunity to question her.

The Nameless Rider brought Darkmoon to a halt and Vannoria was already sliding off the side of the saddle and walking towards the men. The Nameless Rider wasn't thrilled with the ease with which she cast herself into peril, but he slowly dismounted, himself, and caught up with her, making sure not to move too quickly.

"Perhaps, in the future we could discuss before we act," he suggested calmly, knowing he could and would end all these men in an instant, should they be any threat to Vannoria.

"My name is Vannoria and this is Shadow," she called out. "We come in peace and wish to speak with your leader."

"What is your business, girl?" one of the men asked.

"I hate being called that," Vannoria whispered.

"But you are a girl," the Nameless Rider whispered, utterly confused, especially since he was quite certain of her gender.

"It's disrespectful to say it with that tone, to use my gender as an insult, insinuating weakness and naïveté, to imply that I'm defined only by my gender," she whispered to him before returning her attention to the men on horseback. "My business is to speak with your leader, which you will kindly arrange posthaste."

The man leapt from his horse and approached. As the other men hopped down from their horses, the Nameless Rider knew he would probably have to go against Vannoria's wishes and kill all these men to keep her safe, but Vannoria's hand coldly stopped his as he reached for his sword. He reluctantly let his sword slide back into its sheath.

"What did you say, girl?" the man asked threateningly.

The blast of fire exploded from Vannoria's palms, too brief and cool to seriously injure the man, but powerful enough to knock him all the way back to the horses. The other men rushed in to battle. The Nameless Rider just watched it all, grinning.

***

Once upon a time, Aiwren was a boy who didn't feel like he fit in with any of the other children. He was a thinker. A dreamer. Most of the children couldn't see beyond their fate in Ribeln and their aspirations were limited to securing their place in the social structure of that small-minded community, but Aiwren dreamed of adventure and, until he met his best friend, he dreamed alone. Leicester was like Aiwren. He excelled in school and imagined grand stories. Together, the boys would play out great battles, the two of them pretending to slay dragons and giants with the sticks they waved around like swords, rescuing imaginary princesses from trees their minds had transformed into towers, slaying the beasts everyone else saw as piles of hay, and defending their castle, an ordinary dairy barn, from a siege of orcs. Aiwren never would have thought that, once day, he and his best friend would defend a real princess from a real siege in a real castle and that the cost would not be imaginary.

Wanda was firing a bow at the cutthroats who were entering through the door. Leicester was positioned with her to protect her from any swordsman who succeeded in climbing the stairs to their position on the mezzanine. Jocund's strategy, Aiwren realized, was to retreat to the mezzanine of the foyer, and allow the enemy to enter through the door, turning it into the perfect choke point. It was a wonderful plan, and seemed to be working to even the odds. Wanda was a terrible shot and she and Leicester were furthest from the door, so the enemy mostly ignored the arrows sailing far over their heads, splintering against the stone wall over the door or landing anemically at their feet; she wasn't a threat. Leicester had little to defend, but he stood by dutifully, holding his sword as though it was a stick from his childhood.

The plan was working. The bodies were stacking up, but everything changed almost immediately when Aiwren entered the foyer. It was almost as though things were patiently waiting to go wrong until he arrived and it all started when Wanda didn't miss.

Aiwren had emerged from a hallway on the first floor of the foyer. First he saw Lieutenant Plune almost right above the door, up in the mezzanine with his crossbow, firing down on the invading force. Behind him, Cutter defended a small spiral staircase, deftly slicing apart any who were missed by arrows and attempted to climb up to the mezzanine. Above the door on the opposite side, he saw Roderick firing a crossbow in a similar fashion, with Halibon there to defend him. He heard an arrow whoosh by over his head and assumed Serafina and Gregory were directly above him. Then, his eyes turned to Wanda and Leicester. They were up in the rear right corner of the mezzanine with Wanda firing a bow and Leicester standing by with his sword, mostly owing to Wanda's poor aim, until Wanda didn't miss. Her arrow went into the shoulder of a burly bearded man, with bag of spears slung over his shoulder like a quiver of arrows. He didn't seem to be in much pain from the arrow, which went into his chest just below his collar bone, but he was burning with fury when he turned to face her and launched a spear at her with with all of his might.

"No!" Aiwren screamed, but the sound he heard wasn't coming from his voice.

Leicester screamed as he dove towards Wanda. For a moment, it appeared to Aiwren as though his friend had successfully saved her life, knocking her out of the path of the massive spear, but time collapsed and Aiwren's world was ripped apart when he witness the cost of Leicester's bravery. The spear slowly wobbled through the air as Leicester and Wanda slowly tumbled towards the ground in a surreal fraction of a moment expanded beyond recognition while Aiwren was frozen in one place. The spear struck Leicester, rocketing time back into its normal progression as it ripped through his gut and exited out his back leaving a trail of blood in the air before it shattered against the back wall and Leicester collapsed onto Wanda, quickly drenching her in his own blood and bile.

Aiwren couldn't see them behind the mezzanine railing, but he heard Wanda release a scream of horror, a wail of agony he knew would haunt him for the rest of his life.

He turned back to the burly bearded man who smiled smugly as he ripped Wanda's arrow from his chest and let loose a spear towards Roderick, exploding the gravedigger's head on contact. In retrospect, Aiwren would swear to himself that his actions were out of necessity; the bearded man was a threat; but in his heart, in the place housing the things he couldn't bear to admit, Aiwren knew it was fury pushing him across the foyer and forcing him to draw his blade.

"Aiwren, No!" he thought he heard someone yell, but the voice was muffled by the fog rolling over his mind and he really didn't care what anyone yelled.

The sword was heavy in his hand as the blood-soaked stone floor of the foyer raced by beneath Aiwren's feet. He saw the man raise a spear to throw at him, but he easily dodged the javelin as the man reached for another.

The man had grabbed the spear just in time to thrust it towards Aiwren, but Aiwren slashed at the man's left hand and easily knocked the spear away; he had been trained for this. What he hadn't been trained for was murder, but, fueled by rage, that part came easily. He plunged his sword into the large man's heart. The man opened his mouth to gasp for air and Aiwren twisted his blade to ensure the pierced heart would never beat again. He pulled the sword out and the man fell. A blade flashed through the air and Aiwren immediately felt pain in his ribs. He realized he was severely out numbered.

Aiwren, did his best to hold his ground, but the arrows that were once systematically killing the intruders had stopped. As more brigands rushed in the door, Aiwren heard his platoon coming to his aid. He knew he had ruined the plan, but he was determined not to see any more of his friends fall. He wouldn't be the cause of their deaths; he raised his sword and charged into the fray.

***

In only a few hands of the sun, Truson's siege on Gavlessa had turned from bad to nightmare. Now it was all Truson and his men could do to keep the damned corpses at bay around the little camp they had set up. It was a relentless and seemingly inexhaustible force. To make matters worse, even his own slain men had risen to attack him. It didn't seem as though there was an end in sight, but still, he sent his soldiers out in waves to defend the camp so the others could rest, volunteering himself more than anybody else. If there was a way to win he had to find it; if there was no way to win, he would die trying to protect his troops.

Alone, Truson walked the perimeter, a barricade he and his men had quickly assembled with overturned carts, carriages, and anything else they could find to keep the death savages away. It was a close patrol, intended only to kill any of the rotting beasts that had gotten too near; there were other patrols out on horseback to slay as many as possible, but he was exhausted from too many rides and hoped he could catch his breath cleaning up the edges of the barricade and, hopefully, with a rested mind, come up with a plan. Unfortunately for Truson, his exhaustion, the heat of the sun, and a desperately wandering mind made him careless.

Focussed and rested, he would have heard the feet in the sand far before they were close enough to attack. With a brief flash of his blade, he would have sliced the head from the death savage, but he was slow and unfocused. He turned and drew his sword, but it wasn't until the other sword was already speeding towards his head. Metal clanged against metal. With his sword held horizontally over his head, the other blade slid down, deflected from his skull onto his left shoulder. It bit in deep; the dull blade ripped through the muscle and his left arm went limp, his right hand barely able to keep a grip on the handle of his sword. His eyes focussed on his attacker as he felt the warm blood flowing from the wound and he wondered if this was how it was going to end for him.

The creature's black, vacant eyes gleamed with the desperate viciousness of a wild animal. It growled and gnashed its teeth at him. Truson pushed through the pain and kicked the creature in the gut to create some distance so he could raise his sword again. With his left arm dead on his side, he swung his sword one-handed, knowing he had one chance before the blood loss would make him too weak to defend himself.

Truson's blade wildly cleaved into the top of the beast's pate, but the creature was unfazed and Truson's sword was stuck, wedged into the skull. As the ghoul swung at him again, Truson let go of his sword, dove towards the undead thing, and they both tumbled to the ground. Black, foamy bubbles gurgled from its mouth as it chomped at the air, trying to bite Truson. The death savage's blade smacked into Truson's back wildly, clanging against his armor. He got to his knees to pin the monster down and ripped his blade from its head. Without enough room to properly swing, he hammered at the undead assailant with the pomme of his sword, mashing in the skull until the creature stopped moving and all that was left of its head was black pulpy mush. Exhausted and bleeding to death, he rolled off of the once-again dead Gavlessan and crawled back towards the entrance to his barricaded camp.

Truson opened his eyes. The pain in his shoulder wasn't so sharp, but he knew the dull throbbing pain and the fact that he couldn't move his left arm was not a good sign. His arm was bandaged, but the bandage was already a deep crimson. He sat up in the cot, still groggy. He was in his tent, the tent he had intended to be a strategy tent, the tent he had little use for since the dead rose to attack and the only strategy employed was trying not to get killed. In front of him stood stood a soldier who's eyebrows and hair had been singed down to nothing.

"Sir," the man said, "there are people who wish to speak with you."

Truson wondered who could possibly wish to speak with him. Was it an ambassador for the Gavlessans, there to accept the surrender he probably would have given? Was it a representative of his own men, there to revolt against him and execute him for leading them into certain death? Either way, he feared it wouldn't be good news and wondered if good news was even possible anymore.

"It is a man and a girl," the soldier said. "They say they want to help."

"If they want to die at the hands of those beasts, let them," Truson said, trying to assemble his armor.

"Sir, they insisted they speak with you at once," the soldier replied.

"Did you tell them I'm rather busy?" Truson asked, tightening a strap with his teeth.

"They didn't exactly take no for an answer."

"I don't have time for this," Truson proclaimed, lifting himself to his feet. "Give them a merciful beating and send them home. They'll thank you when they live to see another day."

"We already tried that, sir," the soldier said shamefully. "It didn't go very well."

"Light of the Empress?!" Truson grunted. "Who are these relentless meddlers?!"

"My name is Vannoria," Truson heard a voice say behind him and he whipped around to see the speaker.

Standing behind Truson was a young girl and a hooded man. The girl wore a thin white loin cloth and a small midriff top. Strange black markings covered her dark skin. The hooded man's face was barely visible in the shadows and Truson found he could not look at the man without fear rising in the pit of his stomach.

"Get these people out of here!" Truson shouted, shocked his soldiers would allow two strangers into the strategic center of his failing campaign against Gavlessa.

Soldiers rushed towards the strangers and a few more troops hurried into the tent to help.

The girl raised her hand and said, "If you'd prefer not to be roasted alive, I'd suggest you not take another step. If you'd like to win this battle, I'd suggest you listen to what I have to say."

The soldier with the burnt eyebrows and hair said, "Sir, the girl is a necromancer."

"I am no necromancer," the girl corrected, "but there is a necromancer in Gavlessa and he is responsible for raising the undead army that is plaguing you.

She held up a glowing palm and approached. Truson was too mesmerized to move. She put her glowing hand on his injured shoulder. Her touch was icy fire. He screamed in pain, but held his hand out to stop any of his troops from approaching. A moment later she removed her hands. His shoulder tingled even after her hands were gone. He ripped apart the bandage to see that the gash in his shoulder had become a scar.

"Light of the Empress!" he gasped, having seen priests and priestesses heal minor wounds before, but nothing like this. "How did you do that?"

"I'm a sorceress," she said plainly.

Tears flowed down Truson Everly's cheek. He had abandoned The Divine Empress and her knights, but She, perfect and merciful, repaid him not with punishment, but with forgiveness and hope.

"How many of my men can you heal?" he asked. "Enough to overpower those unholy things and win this war?"

"No," she said. "As long as the necromancer lives, the army of death savages will only continue to regenerate. I am the only one capable of stopping him. A very kind man saved my life. His people are prisoners in Gavlessa and I'm here to free them. I ask you to trust me. To risk your life and the life of your men to get me and my friend inside. If you do this, I will destroy the necromancer, his army will fall and you will win this war, but you must trust me."

Truson trembled in awe. The Divine Empress was asking him to risk his life and the lives of his men on the slimmest of chances. She was asking for faith.

"Will you pray with me?" he asked.

The girl nodded, lifted his chin with gentle kindness, and said "I think we'll both need strength."

Together, Truson and the sorceress knelt, lowering their heads before his blood-soaked cot. He heard the clanging of armor and knew his troops were also kneeling. He had an idea for how to get the girl into Gavlessa, but it was unclear. He prayed for focus, for clarity, and for courage.

***

Teryessa was once again in the Palace of Light. Once again The Divine Empress was absent as the place disintegrated above her and, once again, her dark fractured self emerged from the rubble to save her from Wurm Ahkk-Rhall only to turn on her once the dragon was slain. Teryessa cowered in fear as the hands grabbed her neck.

"Why are you doing this?" She asked.

"Because you are weak," her demented self replied.

"I'm trying," she pleaded, unsuccessfully trying to pry the hands from her throat. "I'm trying to be strong."

Her shadow self never relented and the crumbling palace faded into darkness as she felt herself slipping and growing weaker. The darkness, in turn, faded into the light of a room, as Teryessa woke from the nightmare of sleep, only to find herself in the nightmare of her life.

Teryessa's eyes first focussed on the ceiling. It was high above her head and gold, gold like Ahkk-Rhall wore, gold like she wore. Having been in this situation before, the panic fell upon her immediately, crushing down on her chest and preventing her from breathing. She gasped for air as though she was drowning, as though she was being choked by the terrifying version of herself from her dreams.

"Relax," said a voice with a perversion of calmness that only terrified her more. "Struggling will do no good."

Then she saw his face. It was the old man who claimed to be friends with Rheozarccio, the old man who was supposed to help her. She had been fooled again. She hated everything. She hated the world. She hated men and monsters and her own body. She felt his hands sliding over her skin, their touch like poison seeping into her flesh as they unbuckled her armor. She struggled to get away from the venomous fingers, but there was no escape and soon she was nude, completely exposed, stripped of her armor, the flimsy gold foil she had pretended would protect her.

"You must have so many questions," he said.

Teryessa refused to speak. She refused to give him the pleasure of a response. She was determined not to howl in agony when he did what she was certain he was about to do. She would not cry. Ever again. She clenched her teeth.

"Aren't you going to ask what kind of monster I am?"

She watched emotionlessly as he removed his clothing. She didn't flinch when he howled from the pain of the transformation, but when the dragon he had become stared at her, she bit down on her lip, defiantly refusing to make a sound, so hard a bead of blood dripped from her mouth.

"I see my true form does not impress you," he snarled in a new voice. "It is, no doubt, the result of a lackluster experience. I apologize for Ahkk-Rhall's behavior. I assure you, we are just as displeased as you, and I promise, despite my urges and how delicious you look, your presence has not been carefully orchestrated over the past twenty annuals for my pleasure."

The dragon sat back on his haunches and stroked her hair roughly with his long fore claw, brought his mouth close to her ear, sniffed deeply, then whispered, "You do have to die though and I'd be remiss if I didn't admit I'm really going to enjoy this."

"Just kill me," she said, barely able to keep her dread under control.

"Oh, I can't just kill you," he laughed, reaching for some sort of jar. "It's important to my Master that you die in just the right way at just the right moment."

The dragon opened the jar and, with the hook of his claw, scooped out a massive glob of the dark grease within it.

"Because you're special," he said as he smeared it across her naked abdomen. "You're a sacrifice."

"A sacrifice for what?!" she demanded, wincing as he anointed her with the thick oil that burned and tingled on her skin, making her flesh feel both hot and cold at the same time, oil that smelled sweet, spicy and putrid.

"A sacrifice to create a great power," he replied, sealing the jar and returning it to its shelf, "so my Master, the one true Master, can once again rule."

Teryessa, certain the end was near, welcomed death.

"It will take some time for the ointment to saturate your skin and the vapors to fill your lungs," the dragon said, shrinking before her eyes, transforming, once again, into a man. "In the mean time, I have a meeting with the High Council I must attend. It seems your new friend, Rheozarccio has become a burr beneath their saddle to be extracted. Pity."

***

Jocund had hated Halibon from the moment the man was assigned to his platoon. He was a bully and precisely the type of sycophantic coward the Kewnorian Guard and Y-Kewnor loved to mislabel as a hero and hoist into a position of power. Jocund never felt guilty for taking advantage of his position and openly ridiculing the man, who had little intelligence and a big chip on his shoulder. Jocund had required no justification for this mockery, but if he had, he probably would have chalked it up to performing his civic duty. He had told himself, should anything go wrong on this journey, Halibon was expendable. It was callous, but that was how Jocund viewed the world.

Jocund's plan had been going well until he heard the footsteps bounding up the hallway behind him. He turned to look. It was Aiwren, the milkboy he had presumed to be dead, rushing into the first floor of the foyer of that horrible old castle in the woods. The glance was a distraction. The boy ran in from the furthest corner of the room from him. If he heard it and looked, he was certain the others did as well. It was most likely this brief distraction that caused him to miss the large man with the beard and the spears. It was also most likely this distraction that caused Leicester and Princess Wanda to not notice the spear heading towards them until it was too late, a spear traveling so slowly even the two of them could have easily avoided it. This also distracted Roderick from noticing the spear heading towards him until it was too late and caused Serafina, who's aim with a bow was superb, to miss the shot that could have at least saved Roderick.

Aiwren, the milkboy whom Jocund hoped would be of the greatest use on this journey, ruined everything.

To make matters worse, the stupid boy rushed towards the door to engage the invaders in a melee that prevented any of them from having a clear shot. At this point, the proper strategy would have been to maintain the plan regardless of how many of their arrows the milkboy accidentally took, but Serafina and Gregory rushed in and Jocund knew his plan had just been jettisoned in favor of their emotions for the milkboy. He had no choice; he looked to Cutter, who also knew the boy had screwed it all up, and the two of them hurried down the stairs with their swords drawn.

Jocund was, by no means, a swordsman, but he was nimbler and better at avoiding a blade then any of them. He was also not bound to deadly things like honor, so his strategy in battle was to focus his skill and attention on not getting his head cut off while stabbing anyone who's back was to him. He had been told this was roguish and cowardly, but, by making all the easy kills, he freed up the better swordsman to engage with other enemies. From a strategic point of view, his way was more efficient.

Jocund rushed in and, as he ran towards the fray, he saw a swordsman with a patch over one eye running towards him with his sword over his head. Although Jocund knew this swordsman could easily defeat him, he ran faster because he knew he didn't stand a chance if the battle got too spread out; he had to keep things clustered. Serafina was already clanging swords with a lean and ill-looking brigand who, most likely picked up some disease from not choosing his whores carefully enough. The man's back was to him. As he charged towards his one-eyed attacker, he rammed his sword into the sick man's back, pulling it out just in time to dodge the eye-patched attacker's sword.

"I had him!" Serafina shouted.

"Good for you!" Jocund replied, dodging his attacker's blade again.

When Jocund's sword slipped between the ribs of the tall muscular woman Gregory was fighting, dropping her to the ground, Gregory looked confused for a moment, but Jocund winked at him and the young man shrugged, turning his attention to another attacker, while Jocund barely missed another swipe of the sword. He noticed that the brigands, though unexceptionally skilled, were exceptionally dedicated. The tides had changed, they were clearly losing, yet they continued to attack with no consideration for their own safety. This made no sense to Jocund, but he raised his blade to block another attack from the big guy he had been keeping at bay.

Unfortunately, Jocund's tactic had gotten the attention of his attackers. He heard one shout some words he didn't understand, most likely a code they had created for their gang, and noticed several eyes turn to him. His success and survival in battle required going unnoticed; this was not good. A blade raced towards him from the right, he arced his body to avoid it, but it put him off balance. He saw the blade racing towards him from his left.

That was when Halibon surprised him by leaping in from out of nowhere. Jocund saw the blade exit through the middle of Halibon's back, between plates of armor, and he knew he was dead. With his dying breath, Halibon drove his own sword into his attacker's ribs, holding him there, twisting until he was certain they'd both go to the grave.

Jocund didn't shout, but he gritted his teeth and swung his sword up to slash his surprised first attacker across the throat. The blood came fast, a red mist spraying Jocund's face. Jocund raised his blade to swipe at the brigand who had attacked him from the right, but Aiwren had already killed the man.

Soon, all of their attackers in the foyer were dead. Not one of them had escaped. Not one of them even tried to flee, even when they were clearly losing. Jocund had only a brief opportunity to make a mental note of this before his rage overtook him.

Jocund had no control over his impulse. His hand dropped the sword and balled up into a fist as he charged. He felt the anger and adrenaline surging through his body. Before Aiwren had a chance to react, Jocund dove towards him, tackling him to the ground and punching him as hard as he could in the face. Tears were streaming down Aiwren's face, but tears were streaming down Jocund's face as well.

"Where the fuck were you!?" Jocund screamed, punching the boy again.

Jocund grabbed Aiwren's throat before the boy had a chance to answer.

"You killed them. You killed Halibon and Roderick and Leicester. They were mine to keep safe just as I kept you safe and you killed them! You were supposed to be here!"

The boy grew distant. Through the fog of fury, Jocund could feel himself being pulled away. He fought to get back to the boy and choke the rest of the careless idiotic life out of him, but the hands holding him back were too many and too strong.

"Stop!" someone wailed.

Jocund turned to see the princess standing a few paces away, looking like a ghost in her pale dress soaked in her lover's blood, red splashes staining her face.

"Stop," she said more calmly.

Still held in Gregory's grip, Jocund watched Aiwren, now sobbing, crawl over to Wanda.

"Please, tell me he's okay," Aiwren wailed. "Please, tell me it's a wound that will heal."

"Leicester's dead," Wanda said coldly, her fury contained within the poise she was raised to emote.

Aiwren screamed.

"Get up," Wanda said to him. "Stand!"

Aiwren staggered to his feet and, contorting his face with torment, stood before Wanda unable to look her in the eyes.

"Where were you, Aiwren?" she asked.

The boy stammered, then said, "I was lost."

"Yet, when screams were heard, the rest of us found our way back to this room," she said. "Give me your hands."

Aiwren stammered, confused and aching. Jocund wondered what the princess was going to do. If she had killed him for deserting them Jocund would have made no effort to stop her.

"Give me your hands," she commanded and, sobbing so hard he could barely stand, he did.

Wanda took Aiwren's hands and held them against her own face, smearing them with blood.

"That is your best friend's blood on your hands. That's Leicester's blood. You have no idea how much he loved you, how highly he regarded you as a hero. You have no idea how meaningless my life will be without him."

"I was lost." Aiwren protested, choking back tears.

"Perhaps you should have remained lost," she said.

Aiwren crumbled back to his knees, but Jocund, having regained his composure, took stock of the situation. Gregory, Serafina, Wanda, Aiwren, and he had all survived. Cutter had a bad cut across his leg, but it was an injury the old warrior could certainly survive. Leicester, Roderick, and Halibon were dead.

Having let go of Jocund, Gregory went to the door. The oaf was smarter than he looked, Jocund admitted to himself.

"Ey," he said. "There's one more o dem thieves out there."

Jocund hurried to the door, snatching his sword up from the ground on the way, assuming he'd have to go stab it into the heart of some injured brigand attempting to crawl away. What he saw was very different.

There was one man outside, an enormous beast of a man. He wasn't crawling or injured. Nor was he attempting to escape. He was walking right towards them. The man was unarmed and holding one hand in front of his eye as he calmly strutted towards the huge front doors.

"Wut's that bloke doing?" Gregory asked.

"I have no idea," said Jocund, "but these brigands have some kind of death wish and I'm happy to fulfill it."

"My Empress!" Cutter exclaimed with horror.

"What?" Serafina asked.

"Take the princess and keep her safe," Cutter said. "It was a privilege to serve you, but not you must run."

"What are you talking about?!" Jocund asked, thoroughly confused by the old man's sudden gravity, but it was too late; Cutter, with an injured leg and his sword raised over his head, was running towards the man.

Even from the distance he was watching from, Jocund recognized the spark of realization in the body language of the man approaching the castle. As soon as he saw Cutter, he, too started running, not away from, but towards him.

As the man ran towards Cutter, something changed. It was subtle at first, too subtle to identify, but to his horror, Jocund quickly realized what was happening. The man's strides grew longer and longer. His legs and arms lengthened and grew until his clothing burst at the seams, his chest expanding until the suit of armor he was wearing popped off like a button. His face and neck contorted and distorted as a long tail whipped from his spine and huge wings violently ripped through his back, spilling his human flesh to the ground. Cutter dove to the side, rolling out of the way just in time to avoid the blast of fire erupting towards him from the mouth of the dragon.

It all happened so fast. Jocund was so stunned he nearly missed Aiwren charging after Cutter. He grabbed the boy and, with Gregory's help, dragged him back inside, where Wanda and Serafina were already sealing the massive door.

"I have to help him," Aiwren insisted. "I have failed you all. My life is forfeit."

"You have to help Wanda!" Jocund screamed. "You have to help Serafina and Gregory. If you want to lay down your life then do so doing something useful. Now pull your head out of your ass, stop trying to act how you think a hero is supposed to act, and actually be a hero!"

Wanda, Serafina, and Gregory dropped the brace into the door. The thud of the heavy wood told Jocund that Cutter's fate was sealed. All their fates were sealed. Aiwren nodded reluctant consent and the five of them ran towards the back of the room, towards the hallway Aiwren had emerged from earlier.

As they exited the foyer, Jocund heard the door burst open behind them. It sounded like kindling. Twigs.

***

Noldor, freed from his shackles and his cell, charged through the halls, fueled with fury, and possessed with the will to avenge everything that had ever been taken from him, his wife, his daughter, his throne, his power. He was fortified by the rage burning quietly in his gut his entire life. He wanted to destroy and thirsted for nothing less than all of the blood of any who had ever or would ever stand in his way.

Noldar was an imposing man and none of the Gavlessans patrolling the halls of the castle stood a chance against him on their own. He had been taken by surprise in the throne room. He was outnumbered and distracted by his own woe, but now his enemies where spread out, few in number, and it was his turn to spread his woe to others. The first Gavlessan he saw was a large man who must have assumed the king to be weak, having seen him captured in the throne room, but Noldar was anything but weak and he cleaved the man in half at the waist without slowing his steady pace down the corridor or making even the slightest move to defend himself.

The second Gavlessan, holding his post at the intersection of two hallways with back to the king, barely had a chance to react before the massive sword crushed in his head, bursting bits of brain and skull on to the emotionless face of the king. The king hoped these Gavlessans would be grieved by widows and children, hoped their loss would be too much to bear, hoped there was some way of spreading the pain to make as many people suffer as much as possible.

Ahead was a door. Beyond it, Noldar knew, if Snew had any sense, he'd post a guard. He knew this, but he didn't care. His massive boot easily leveled the door, snapping the pins and cracking the wood from its hinges, flattening a Gavlessan guard beneath it. The man struggled to crawl out from beneath the door, but Noldar walked over the door and crushed the man's head with his large foot as he walked by. The Gavlessans had earned a reputation of being merciless. It wasn't weakness preventing him from matching this cruelty all these annuals; it was restraint, restraint which he no longer had the desire to exhibit.

The final portal to the throne room had no door. Its stone archway was only protected by two red velvet curtains pinned back decoratively. A guard flanked each side. Before they even knew he was there, King Noldar crammed his sword through the middle of the curtain on the right side, through the curtain and through the man standing on the other side of it. When the man crumpled to the ground, leaving a smear of even darker crimson on the fabric, the other guard jumped in to face Noldar. The king deftly sheared the man's sword hand from his body and, with blood spraying all over him from the handless stump, he grabbed the back of the shocked handless man's head and shoved his sword up, through the bottom of his chin, and out the top of his head.

King Noldar Palidnia, having dispatched of every Gavlessan he had encountered in a matter of only moments, walked to the center of the throne room, blood dripping from his father's sword, the sword that was once his grandfather's, the sword that was once, long ago, the sword of a tyrant.

"Well done, my king," Snew said from the throne, nonplussed by the sight of the carnage. "You have performed exceptionally."

"Are you not frightened that I am about to do the same to you?" the king asked.

"Oh, yes," Snew quipped, "positively terrified."

The slimy little man stood and walked towards the king, raising his hands to show he was unarmed.

"You have been a traitor of the worst kind, Snew." The king accused. "You have been here, by my side, a trusted colleague for all these annuals, the whole time plotting to betray me. I vow your death will be the most prolonged and painful."

"Ah, yes," Snew said, "vows and threats, the hallmark of royalty."

"You have observed what I am capable of, seen my wrath," Noldar said. "I assure you, the feeble crew of barbarians you ambushed me with last night will not be coming to your aid. There is no point in stalling."

"You've no doubt dispatched of the small group Gavlessans I brought with me," Snew said, walking over to one of the palace windows. "I have no desire to delay the inevitable, other than to savor the expression on your face when I show you what I've done."

"What have you done?" Noldar asked.

"Come," Snew said, with a grand gesture of his hand towards the window. "See for yourself."

King Noldar Palidnia slowly approached the window, with every step feeling his stomach drop deeper and deeper, twisting inside his belly, while his heart beat so hard he thought it would explode. Nothing could have prepared him for the sight he saw outside of his window. Lees Naglos, his city, his kingdom, was burning. His people, like children to him, were most certainly lost to the raging fire. He screamed and fell to his knees, clutching his chest.

"Heart problems, Your Grace?" Snew hissed venomously.

"How..." the king muttered weakly, barely able to complete the sentence, "could you?"

"How could I?!" Snew laughed incredulously. "Do you mean morally, as in how could I ethically make the decision to roast your people alive, my king? Or do you mean physically, as in how was I capable of accomplishing such a thorough massacre in just one night?"

From his knees, the king stared out the window unable to speak. The flames from the fires flickered in his eyes brighter, it seemed, even than the sun.

"It was easy," said Snew.

Noldar turned from the burning buildings to look at Snew, gripping his sword tightly as he rose, but Snew was waiting for him and had one more surprise left to reveal.

"If you haven't put the pieces together, Your Grace," Snew boasted, "I am not what I seem to be."

Before King Noldar's eyes, Snew changed. The man's clothes ripped from his body as he grew in size and shape. Claws replaced his fingers. A tail whipped back and forth. Wings dripping with blood unfolded to block out the light. Saliva dripped from his massive fangs. He was a dragon.

***

The carriage had barely stopped when Rheo flung the door open and heaved himself out and onto the street, bursting into a sprint as soon as his feet touched the cobble stones of the plaza before the Citadel. Behind him, knights encircled the carriage, on Beatrice Boomswift's command, to arrest Grell Ahkk-Rhall, the dragon in human form tethered to the back, but Rheo didn't have time to oversee the foul beast being brought into custody; he had a princess to save.

His heart pounded and he threw one heavy foot in front of the other, bounding up the front steps of the great white tower with the blackened top, ignoring the greetings of the knights who paused their daily business to salute him half-heartedly. Sweat trickled down his brow as he raced up the seemingly countless stairs. He could feel a pain in his sides, he wondered if too many pickled sausages had finally damaged his heart. His mind had raced for the duration of the seemingly eternal journey back to Y-Kewnor from Bridgekeep and he thought, once he was finally able to take action, the anxiety would dissolve, but it remained in his mind.

Rheozarccio Rheodo, nearly tore the door to his quarters off its hinges as he rushed inside, hoping he would see the sullen and damaged girl sitting at his table eating his food, but his world collapsed when she wasn't. Instead, he found the entire council standing in his parlor, waiting for him to arrive.

"Sir Rheodo," Sir Leopold Leonard, the Grand High Knight of the Council scolded gravely, "it appears as though you have some explaining to do."

Rheo had many things to explain to them, but he knew time was of the essence and he didn't have time to get involved with politics at the moment.

"Your behavior is an outrage!" Sir Allesander Montgomery cried. "I demand this insolent boy be relieved of his duty and thrown behind bars until he can be properly court-martialed!"

"Yes!" Rheo said, "Fine. I absolutely accept your request to court-martial me and I'll happily turn myself in at the end of the day, but there is a crisis of collusion going on right now and I mustn't be jailed until it is resolved. Someone of importance is in peril and the fate of Allyoshmar may hang in the balance of their safety!"

"I assume you are going to suggest, without sufficient evidence, that another of our esteemed colleagues is plotting against us," Sir T'Ethal La-al boomed with a contemptuous laugh. "Is it another lordson this time? Or, perhaps, a high priest?!"

"I'm saying there are dragons among us, hiding in plain sight as members of the community and I know their next intended target!" Rheo shouted.

"Who, prey tell, is this target?" Sir Arowyr Malegon asked, waving his gloved hand dismissively in the air. "And what makes you think she is in peril?"

"I cannot give her identity," Rheo replied, "nor can I tell you how I know."

"Rheo," Leopold said, "your behavior has been erratic and highly suspicious. You have arrested a lordson, started a bar fight, taken leave without notice to investigate something that wasn't your business, and now you are asking us to ignore our better judgement to jail you and trust you as you tear apart our city in search of a dragon who is threatening the life of a person you refuse to identify."

"I realize how it looks." Rheo said, "but something is happening General Boomswift and I saw it-"

"Boomswift is behind this?!" Allesander exclaimed. "I thought you said she would keep him out of our hair, Ordo!"

"She is a great leader and was a friend to Sir Vincent," Sir Ordo Ollycanterer said. "I thought it would make things better. It appears as though I was mistaken."

"Sir Rheozarccio," Sir Leopold said, "this may be difficult for you to believe, but we're not against you. Losing Sir Vincent has been hard on all of us, but I think I may have underestimated the toll the loss would have on your spirit and mind. I fear you may be a danger to yourself and others, Rheo."

"Look," Rheo said, feeling the walls closing in around him, "Boomswift was leaving town. I had only a moment to decide to go with her. I didn't leave with insubordinate intent, but to strengthen my relationship with her and, therefore our relationship with the

Kewnorian Guard. I never would have imagined what we would find or how it would relate to the attack on the Citadel, but I would be doing the council, the city, The Divine Empress, and the memory of my knight-father an unforgivable disservice by ignoring it or by failing to connect the seemingly disparate parts. Please, just give me today. I have information and I'll tell you everything, but I need today."

"I say we give him a day," said Arowyr Malegon.

"Don't be absurd, Arowyr!" Allesander snapped. "The boy has clearly lost his mind; you're just too humble to recognize fault in anyone. Humility, the virtue of your house, has blinded you!"

"I wish I could," Leopold said to Rheo. "I wish I could trust you, but I'm afraid you leave me no choice."

Rheo looked at the six men and wondered if he would be willing to fight them. Would he be able to raise his sword against his own brothers? Would he survive if he did? As much as they frustrated him, they were his brothers and he vowed them his allegiance. Could he break his vow and betray that trust? He had only one more chance to resolve this peaceably.

"I have taken a dragon as my prisoner," Rheo said. "He is injured, but alive and locked in the dungeon of the Citadel under the protection of knights I trust and General Beatrice Boomswift, herself. He is proof. He is my evidence. His name is Grell Ahkk-Rhall and he is willing to provide us with all the information we need about the attack on the Citadel in exchange for a stay of execution."

BLOODY HANDS

Aiwren stumbled down the rumbling corridor in a daze, his world crumbling down around him. He made little effort to dodge the debris and chunks of ancient stone bombarding him from above as Serafina dragged him by his hand through the corridor. His mind raced manically without direction, leaping from the horror of seeing a dragon, to the rage of suspecting the Skinless Woman had planned this tragedy, to the hopelessness of the certainty that Cutter was dead, to the grief of knowing that Leicester was dead, to the guilt that these deaths were his fault. The only thing that wasn't really crossing his mind was survival. He couldn't get to that point in his mind; he couldn't even feel his limbs.

Serafina continued to hold his hand. He was slowing her down. She should have left him, he thought. It would serve him right for inviting this disaster. But she didn't. She squeezed tightly. What a heart, she had. It would be a lucky woman, whomever she fell in love with, he thought, for he could imagine a life for her, a life of heroism and fiery passion, of always sticking up for the little guys and the big oafs of the world, fearlessly squaring off with anyone who would pick on the weak. She would go on to have great friends. Gregory, who was pushing Aiwren from behind, would be her friend till the end. Gregory would use his knowledge of plants and his deceptively sharp mind to become an herbalist after this journey was over. He would be Serafina's bridesponsor at her wedding and she the groomsponsor at his. He would have a lovely fat wife and lovely fat children who would all grow up calling Serafina their Auntie. He could imagine a life for them after this day, but not one for himself.

The rumbling grew closer, the chunks of rock were grew larger, and the hallway grew hotter as the dragon approached them, booming from behind as its body ripped through the hallway, breaking the ancient stones apart like a sausage bursting from its skin on a fire, yet they continued running, running with no destination or hope of exiting this castle with their lives. The place was cursed. It was a tomb. The beast would follow them to a dead end and melt their flesh from their bodies, turning them to cinder, as he doubtlessly had already done to Cutter. There was no escape from this nightmare, Aiwren thought, not even for Gregory and Serafina.

"Wait!" Jocund said. "Every one stop. Quiet. Listen."

The group stopped in the middle of the hallway.

"I don't hear anything," Wanda said.

"Exactly," Jocund replied.

"You don't s'pose that dragon gave up an went ome?" asked Gregory, bleakly.

"No," said Jocund. "Dragons may look like beasts, but they're just as smart as any of us. He's hunting. Waiting for us to make a move."

"What do we do?" Wanda asked.

"I suggest we walk quietly," Jocund said, "find some stairs, go up to the second level, and then back track to the mezzanine and out the front door."

Aiwren agreed with Jocund's plan. They were all set to continue on when Aiwren caught Gregory's face out of the corner of his eye. He was frozen with fear.

"What?" Aiwren asked. "What is it?"

"I can't move my legs," Gregory said, his voice trembling and his body quivering, "I was just running and I was plenty afraid o wuts after us, but I adn't really thought none 'bout the reality of it. That's a- that's a- I don' wanna be scared, but I can't breathe and I'm tellin me legs move, but they ain't listenin' and ave I mentioned that dragons is wut I'm scared of more than anything in the ole world and my legs. What if he catches me."

"Gregory," Serafina said, "I know you're scared."

"I'm trying to be brave," he said, tears streaming.

"We know you are," Aiwren said.

"You are brave," added Wanda.

"You can do this," Serafina said.

"We're going home," Jocund said.

Gregory turned to Aiwren. He knew he was the last bit of reassurance his friend needed, but he didn't know if they'd make it out of there.

"As long as we're all together, we're going to be all right," Aiwren said as convincingly as he could.

Gregory gave a small smile and a nod. He slowly put one foot in front of the other, breaking the paralysis caused by his fear, when the hall lit up.

Aiwren saw a small bright orange square quickly growing larger as it blasted towards him and the explosion of fire engulfed the hallway. He saw Gregory look over his shoulder, then, unable to move, himself, Aiwren saw Gregory leap towards him. He felt the impact of the large young man's body against his. As he hit the ground, he saw

Serafina tackle Lieutenant Plune and Wanda similarly. Gregory's face, with squinting eyes bracing for pain, was close to his as Aiwren felt the powerful wave of unimaginable heat surge by, lapping all over his skin and enveloping body, his body that was, thanks to Gregory, shielded from the fire.

As quickly as it had come, the fire was gone, and Gregory opened his eyes. For a brief moment, Aiwren thought that everything might be okay. They they would, perhaps, all survive this after all, but Gregory's confused look quickly stole this belief from Aiwren.

"I thought there'd be more," Gregory said, before freezing vacantly and ultimately.

Aiwren pulled himself from beneath Gregory's huge body, slipping out to the side so the young man was lying face first on the cool stone ground. Gregory's clothes were completely incinerated from his backside. His skin was charred and black in some areas and red and raw and bleeding in others. His spine and the back of his skull were completely exposed to the air. Blood was flowing fast from the areas that hadn't been instantly cauterize by the dragon's fire.

"Gregory!" Aiwren screamed.

Wanda screamed in horror at the sight.

"Fucking shit!" Serafina choked, clenching back tears.

Aiwren rolled the large young man onto his roasted backside, but when he saw Gregory's face, he knew Gregory was gone. He screamed again as Jocund covered Gregory with his cape and put a hand on Aiwren's shoulder.

"Come on." Jocund said, somberly, before helping Wanda to her feet and hobbling down the hallway, with one boot on and one boot melted from his charred black foot.

Serafina lifted Aiwren to his feet. She was badly burnt and her clothes, that standard issue Guardsman's uniform, had crumbled, leaving only charred tatters that barely covered her. Her once thick dark straight hair was singed and speckled with ash. Her skin was slick with sweat and blood and grime. She was in no condition to help, but she put her arm around Aiwren and they helped each other down the hallway towards Jocund and Wanda.

"We'll grieve when this is over," she said. "For now, we need to get out of here."

"He's toying with us," said Aiwren, "the dragon. He wants to kill us one at a time."

"I know," she said. "We need to do what Jocund said. We need to get upstairs and then double back to the mezzanine in the foyer."

Aiwren and Serafina caught up with Wanda and Jocund and the four of them found a stairwell to the second floor. For a moment, Aiwren thought about going down the stairs instead, wondering if he would be able to find that strange room, but something inside of him told him that, although this castle would likely crumble, that room would always be there. He wondered how he could possibly think of that room. How could he long for it?! He shook the thoughts from his head and followed the others up the stairs.

***

Vannoria clung tightly to Shadow on the back of Darkmoon as they galloped across the desert. Shadow had been quiet ever since the plans had been made back in Truson Everly's tent. She could feel Truson staring at her. She wondered what he felt as they galloped across the hot desert sand, wondered how he was able to incorporate anything that happened, tragedy or miracle, into his belief in The Divine Empress, into his belief that things happened for reasons. She didn't know about The Divine Empress, but she believed in reasons.

She felt a connection to the world that she couldn't put into words, but had felt growing inside of her; she felt The Source; she felt the power. It felt as though everything that had ever happened was leading her to this moment. She could feel Shadow's concerns and wished she could reassure him, somehow let him know they were going to be okay.

"This used to be a tower," Truson Everly said, hopping from his horse near a pile of metal shards in an otherwise featureless expanse of sand. "The Gavlessans use these towers to channel the smoke from their fires out of their city, but they also double as lookout posts. This one was destroyed a very long time ago. I knew there was no way to get an army down this small hole, but-"

"But we don't need an army," Vannoria said.

"Are you sure you don't want me to go with you?"

"I'm certain," Vannoria replied. "You'll be needed to lead your troops in through the main entrance the moment the death savages are weakened."

Truson reluctantly agreed. He seemed like a good man to Vannoria. Intelligent and sensitive and kind, he wasn't at all what she had ever imagined a general to be like. She wondered why his heart felt so heavy to her, but then she realized everyone's heart felt heavy to her. She wondered if hearts were always so heavy and she had simply never noticed before.

"May The Divine Empress protect you," he said as he nimbly swung onto his horse.

"And you, as well," she called out as Truson galloped off, leaving her and Shadow alone in the middle of the desert.

"Vannoria," Shadow said, somberly, crouching by the hole, peering down into it, "I have been by your side for every step of your journey. Is there nothing I can say to change your mind, to convince you not to climb down this hole?"

"Shadow," she said, "this is what we come to do. There are people down there who need us."

"Have you considered that this necromancer could be my creator, that he could be my Master? What if this is the moment I was saving you for? What if my Master intends for you to die today? Have you considered that?"

"The necromancer who created you, did so long ago," Vannoria said, crouching next to him. "We know this."

"But what if this necromancer is my Master now?"

"Shadow," Vannoria said, holding her dear Shadow's scarred face in her hands. "Your heart is your Master now."

"There's nothing more important to me in this world than you are," he replied, holding on to her hands tightly.

"Then let's survive this," she said, hopefully, giving his hands a reassuring squeeze. "Let's free those Ma-Areshi and end this war and live together forever. Okay?"

"I'm frightened," Shadow said.

"Me, too," Vannoria replied, wanting to say so much more, wanting to make sure he knew how happy he made her, wanting him to know she felt she had never lived until she met him, but the words 'I love you' would have fallen leagues short of these feelings. "But we can do this. Together, nothing can stop us."

Together, Vannoria and Shadow descended into that hole in the ground, leaving Darkmoon and the desert and the sky behind them, as they climbed into the inky abyss. Twenty or so paces beneath the surface, where the light still cast its beams through the cracks and onto some of the broken rocks and metal, Vannoria and Shadow wiggled their way down to the abandoned stairwell that once vaulted high above the desert. They continued down the stairs, which were, despite the grotesque and sinewy look of Gavlessan architecture, stable. They followed those stairs deep into the darkness, twisting and twisting as the corkscrewed into the earth. Finally they came to a landing.

Vannoria looked both ways before entering the corridor, but it looked like it had been abandoned for quite a long time. In the dark, Vannoria remembered a tattoo on her right shoulder that looked like the sun. She wasn't sure how she remembered, but she knew it was there. She held it with her left hand until her palm glowed intensely. She held extended her arm and lit their path with the light from her hand. Increasingly more in control of her power, she felt The Source flow through her. She understood it.

"Don't waste your power," Shadow said, "I don't require light to see and can lead the way, if you like."

"It's okay," Vannoria replied. "The power isn't coming from me; and it's more abundant than I could ever use."

Eventually, a light gleamed up ahead. Vannoria relaxed her arm, let the energy dissolve, and the light from her hand dimmed until it disappeared completely. She and Shadow approached the irregular shafts of light slipping between the boards meant to seal the end of hallway.

Looking through the cracks between boards, Vannoria and Shadow stared into the belly of the beast. Beyond the boards, a catwalk spiraled up to the top of a room so vast, all of Ribeln could have fit in its base and could have been stacked upon itself many times up to its rocky dome. Below them, a single bridge, thin and made of rope and wooden planks, stretched across the enormous space. Men and women who appeared to be from all parts of the world, including

Ma-Aresh, lined up on this bridge. They were kept in single file by Gavlessan guards, forcing them to move forward until they reached the center of the bridge. At the center of the bridge, Vannoria saw the guards push the men and women over the edge one at a time, but they weren't simply falling to the ground. They were being fed into four enormous stone wheels that crushed them into a pulp that drained into a pool of blood beneath it. Is was so distant, but so horrifying and Vannoria wondered if the sight was even more disturbing from her perspective because, from high above, she could see the scale of the operation.

Vannoria's emotions overwhelmed her. She stepped away from the grotesque sight and vomited on the floor of the hallway, tears streaming down her face. She wondered how anyone could be capable of such an unspeakably evil act.

"We have to stop them," she said, choking on her tears, when Shadow put a hand on her back. "We have to stop them."

"I know," he said.

A moment later Shadow kicked the boards out. It was relatively quiet compared to the grinding and the screaming below, but not quiet enough to go completely undetected. Several guards rushed along the catwalk towards them from both directions.

"Thoughts?" Shadow asked, referring to the guards, as he and Vannoria stepped out onto the stone catwalk high above the horrors below.

"I'll take the ones on the right," she said.

Vannoria could feel the comfort of Shadow's back against hers as she reached her hand to touch her own bare skin. She could hear his blade being drawn from its sheath as she channeled the energy of The Source into her hand through the tattoo that could only mean one thing: fire.

She thrust her hand toward the Gavlessan guards running her way. She could feel the energy course through her fingers as fire burst from her hand, dropping the men to the ground where they stood. She turned around to see Shadow, already wiping the blood from his sword, a pile of bodies laying at his feet.

***

The catwalk was narrow and the oncoming Gavlessan guards ran perilously close to the edge with no concern for their own lives. As they grew closer, the Nameless Rider, who lead the way in front of Vannoria, realized the guards weren't concerned for their lives because they were already dead. These were death savages. The twitching dead men approached quickly, but the Nameless Rider found himself lost in thought. He wondered how Vannoria, the only person with a life to risk, could risk it so easily.

Against his sword, the procession of corpses stood no chance; they were cut down easily and they fell from the ledge like stones, spattering upon the rocks below. The Nameless Rider had cleared the path all the way to a set of stairs, but, as they arrived, he realized that the wave of living dead attacking them was seemingly endless and he knew, if they went into the stairwell, they'd leave themselves vulnerable to attack from behind.

"Go!" Vannoria shouted, seeming to read his apprehension. "I'll take any who attack from behind."

The Nameless Rider found himself faced with a dilemma. Should he continue protecting her at all costs or should he do as she said?

"Trust me," she said, answering the question not through magics, but through a connection so strong that their hearts were synchronized.

He went down the stairs and, as he cut into the rotting flesh of his attackers, hacking them to piles of mush beneath his feet, Vannoria incinerated any guards or death savages who attacked them from behind. He shook is head in awe as her fire crackled behind him. He felt the warmth from her flame and he sliced through the last corpse at bottom of the stairs.

The level the Nameless Rider and Vannoria were on extended beyond the giant arena below and deep into the earth where there were cages as far as they could see. From these cages, living guards ushered a procession of prisoners over to the bridge. As the Nameless Rider and Vannoria approached, the prisoners joined in the attack.

On the thin bridge, two guards pushed a prisoner out of the way as they charged towards the Nameless Rider and Vannoria. The prisoner tumbled over the edge but hung onto the rope, dangling over the horrible death machine below. The Nameless Rider saw Vannoria sprint towards the dangling man and towards the two Gavlessan guards. He saw the fire explode from the tips of her fingers as he followed her onto the bridge. Vannoria grabbed the man's hand just as his fingers could no longer hold on to the rope and the Nameless Rider helped her pull him onto the bridge. The man was Ma-Areshi.

"Your markings," the man said, touching her face.

"Mister Uncle sent me, my brother," Vannoria said, touching the man's face gently. "You are safe now."

Another wave of the living dead charged towards the thin bridge, the corpses of the guards and prisoners who had just died. The Nameless Rider helped the Ma-Areshi man to his feet and ran towards the edge of the bridge, but there were too many corpses on the landing where the prisoners had just revolted against the guards. It wasn't safe. He turned around to see if they could escape off the other side of the bridge, but a swarm of guards clotted that side, running towards them. There was only one way out.

"Hold on to the rope," the Nameless Rider said as he hacked into the rope with his sword, adding, "tightly."

The first rope came free easily and several death savages tumbled down from the bridge, but the living guards held on as they hurried towards him. He grabbed on with his left hand and gave one final swing of his sword. The bridge hesitated to fall for a moment, as though it didn't realize it had been cut, but then the Nameless Rider felt the boards beneath his feet fall away. Then, he, too, fell.

As soon the Nameless Rider cut the rope, the remaining death savages on the bridge lost their rigid balance and plummeted over the edge. The guards, who were already close to them, hung on for a moment longer, but as soon as the boards buckled, they, too, fell, leaving the Nameless Rider on the bridge with Vannoria and the Ma-Areshi man as it arced downwards.

As the bridge raced towards the ground, the Nameless Rider looked up to see Vannoria pull the Ma-Areshi man off and then leap off, herself, into the pool of blood below. Confident that they had landed safely, he, too, let go, rolling safely to the ground at the bottom of the arena before the pendulous motion of the bridge could crush him into the stone wall.

The Nameless Rider sprang to his feet, at first unable to see the Ma-Areshi man or Vannoria. Then he heard a scream and he spun around. Vannoria was up to her waist in the pool of dark blood, her white clothing stained red and black, her hair slicked back with crimson dripping down her face. She screamed, but not from pain. Standing in the pool with her was a thin man dressed in black, the necromancer; he had slit the throat of the Ma-Areshi man.

The Nameless Rider hurried towards her, but the guards swarmed in and blocked his path before he could reach her and from the other direction, the necromancer's dead army closed in on him. Surrounded by death savages, his concern wasn't for himself; he thought only of Vannoria, who seemed stuck in one spot in the middle of the pool of blood, as the necromancer, letting the Ma-Areshi man's dead body slip beneath the surface, approached her.

The Nameless Rider felt a wave of emotion rush over him. He felt a strength he had never felt before. He felt power rush up as a scream, climbing out of his mouth from deep within his body. It didn't matter what happened to him; he would save her. He hacked his way through the sea of guards and reanimated corpses, an unstoppable juggernaut, not feeling a single one of the blades piercing his flesh.

***

Rheozarccio knew, given his brief but tumultuous track record with them, he should have been pleased with the reprieve granted to him by the council. He also knew he shouldn't be too relieved, though, because he knew would be held accountable, the scapegoat for all their recent troubles, if he failed, but he was only concerned with finding Princess Teryessa. Those men up in his room accusing him of insubordination worried about politics while a girl's life was in jeopardy and an unknown threat was upon the people of Y-Kewnor and perhaps all of Allyoshmar. Things would be different the next day no matter what the outcome, but, for the moment, his attention was singular and compulsively driven. He had to find the girl and he had only one lead. The door to the dungeon below the Citadel burst open as Rheo barged into the room.

"Out," he commanded.

The knights he had posted there, friends from the days before he was burdened with the weight of his responsibilities, hurried from the room. Were they afraid of him, in his urgent state, or just relieved to extricate themselves from the proximity of a dragon? It didn't matter, he thought, they were cowards who didn't understand duty or sacrifice.

"You, too," he said to General Boomswift. "I need to speak with the dragon alone."

He liked the general. Even though the secrets she kept infuriated him, she was kind and wise and important to Y-Kewnor, even if the city didn't realize it. If his plans failed they would need her, so he needed her to be far from him and uninvolved with the situation.

"I know what you're doing, Rheo," she said, "and you need to be careful. As strong and imposing as dragons are physically, they are just as dangerous without their claws and fire. They can get into your head and this one, Wurm Ahkk-Rhall, is perhaps the deadliest of them all."

After a moment of Rheo not answering her, she said, "I'll go, for the sake of plausible deniability, but you need to be careful."

Bea wheeled herself out and Rheo walked up to the cell Ahkk-Rhall calmly sat in. When Rheo heard the door latch behind Bea, he sat on a stool in front of the cell.

"Where's the Princess?" Rheo asked. "I know you know more than you're telling me."

"What an adorably naive understatement," the dragon, still in human form, responded. "Asking for my help finding her is, essentially, asking me to perform the one task I asked you to perform in exchange for the information you desire. Does that seem like a fair deal to you?"

"Considering what you've done, I wouldn't hope for fairness," Rheo declared with righteous indignation, "there's no torture imaginable to balance your deeds."

"Do you know why I'm here, be hind these bars," Ahkk-Rhall asked.

"Because I put you there."

"I'm here because this is precisely where I want to be. I'm here because I need to speak with Teryessa. You may think I'm horrible, and I realize my taste in recreation may not suite everyone's palate, but those you seek have slain entire cities, wiped out generations. If you want to stop them from what they have planned, then I suggest you adopt a more cooperative attitude, stop wasting my time, and go find the princess; she's the only one I'll confide my secrets to."

"Look," Rheo said, "if you want the princess, you're going to have to give me a little more information."

"Well," said the dragon, "this renegotiation of our terms will require a few more concessions on your part."

"Like what?"

"Oh, nothing too extravagant," he replied. "I assume you'll not allow me a scroll and quill, so if you send in a scribe, I'll dictate a list, but we can worry about that later. Are you familiar with Na'Akrakro-manasa-visu?"

"What are you talking about?" Rheo asked. "What does that have to do with anything? Just tell me where she is."

"Young master, Rheodo, you're preparing to enter the world of politics; you really need to learn your Balysh-Tong," Ahkk-Rhall said. "Speaking the old language really is a hallmark of culture, but I suppose you had enough difficulty learning the modern tongue. What language did you grew up speaking? Xcesemtian?"

"Mind your own business, dragon," Rheo said, leaping to his feet. "You know nothing about me."

"Ah, yes," the dragon said patronizingly as he approached the edge of the cell. "Nobody gets outraged like a peasant who has risen above a life of shoveling shit or what ever it was your filthy little people do."

Rheo grabbed Ahkk-Rhall by his collar and pulled him close, slamming the foul creature against the bars.

"Such violence," the wurm declared, feigning shock. "Was that how your father demonstrated his love?"

"If you speak of my family again I'll break your spine, Wurm," Rheo screamed, slamming his prisoner against the bars even harder, holding him so close that he could taste the foul breath.

"It's amazing to me the abuses from a loved one you humans will endure and justify," the dragon casually pointed out, "while casting judgement upon those who you do not understand."

Rheo let go of Wurm Ahkk-Rhall, for fear that he would actually kill the beast. He hated it, but he knew he needed him if he was going to find the princess and get the information he needed from the monster. He slumped back onto his stool.

"Na'Akrakro-manasa-visu," the dragon said, returning to his own stool, "literally means hand rot vision. And it doesn't mean you're vision is declining as mine unfortunately is in my old age. It is a necromancy spell in which a hole is rotted through one's hand. When the hand is held to one's eye, it allows one to communicate over vast distances by sharing one's sight to the necromancer who cast the spell. This is not to be confused with Na'Akrakro-morte-visu, in which a necromancer, through killing a person, sees all that they have seen. Dead men may not talk but, if you're a necromancer, they certainly do show."

"Enough!" Rheo demanded, tired of the dragon's mind games. "What does this have to do with the princess?"

"Oh, nothing," the Ahkk-Rhall replied. "Please forgive my tangential thoughts. I have no idea where your princess is. With so many dragons dispersed among the citizens of Y-Kewnor, it's difficult to say which."

"There are dragons in Y-Kewnor?!" Rheo asked, shocked at the mere suggestion, a suggestion that defied all he had ever learned about dragons, especially their frequency.

"You don't think The Divine Empress's Knights overthrew King Argratosius alone, do you? Or that the corruption in your organization is a new plight?! Although, I suppose you didn't notice the dragon in your esteemed High Council, so perhaps this is news to you."

"Lies!" Rheo shouted, horrified by the suggestion of dragons in the High Council, despite the dragon corroborating his theory about dragons aiding in the destruction of Argratos. "There is no way The Divine Empress would allow that!"

"Allow it?!" Ahkk-Rhall laughed. "She condoned it!"

Rheo stood. It felt as though he had just been struck. Then, it made sense. He bolted from the dungeon.

"Lovely discussion, Sir Rheodo," Wurm Ahkk-Rhall called out with a sickening grin. "Lovely."

Ever since Rheozarccio Rheodo accepted his seat on the High Council there was one man doing everything he could to discredit him and Rheo ran as fast as he could to that man's chambers, replaying key events in his mind, thinking of how this man did everything he could to turn attention away from any investigation of the attack on the Citadel. Without bothering to knock, Rheo kicked Sir Allesander Montgomery's door in.

"What is the meaning of this, boy?" Allesander demanded, leaping from his chair in outrage.

"Show me your hands!" Rheo demanded to a flabbergasted Allesander. "Show me your hands!"

Allesander held out his hands. They were old, but not rotting. No Na'Akrakro-manasa-visu spell had been cast on him. Allesander Montgomery hadn't been communicating with a necromancer. He wasn't the dragon.

***

The fumes quickly went to Teryessa's head after the Dragon left. Time lost all meaning. Light turned to darkness. All colors turned to black. She could no longer feel the table beneath her or the shackles around her wrists. She floated in a vast abyss of nothingness. Flashes of images swam across the darkness, little portraits floating like flotsam and jetsam in the sea of nothing. In one portrait, she saw her father looking out the window of his palace, at Lees Naglos; it was burning. In another portrait she saw Truson Everly in mid-battle, swinging his sword in front of the gates of Gavlessa, surrounded by rotting corpses. She looked high above her and saw, a portrait of the tattooed woman who had saved her life, staring down from a catwalk made of stone. Another portrait was of the boy she saw, the boy who's name she didn't know, but about whom she couldn't stop thinking. He was running down a stone hallway from a dragon with three of the others she had seen him with. Finally she saw a portrait of a small dark room. There was a girl in the room standing before an altar, looking at a portrait on the wall. It looked so familiar.

Teryessa seemed to gravitate towards this portrait as she floated across the void closer and closer, until she could see that the girl in the portrait was her and she suddenly remembered that room. She remembered everything about it. She remembered that Prince Grell would soon burst through the door and try to kill her, but the fool girl she was looking at was still looking at the painting on the wall of the small, dark room. The painting wasn't how she remembered it, though. In her memory the painting was just darkness, but, in this version, eyes emerged from the darkness, her eyes.

The girl reach out towards the painting and at the same time, Teryessa felt a light touch upon her face.

"Grell is coming, Teryessa," she said to girl in the portrait staring at the painting. "When he finds you he is going to kill you. Do you want that?"

"No," the girl who looked a lot like her said, "No."

"Then kill him," Teryessa instructed, seeing the dagger on the altar, the blade made of cool smooth darkness that she wanted to touch.

"I'm defenseless," her pathetic, weaker self replied.

"The altar," Teryessa replied patiently, watching the girl pick up the knife.

Teryessa heard the door open, but she didn't take her eyes off of the girl. She watched, mouth watering as the tip of the dagger pierced the girl's fingertip. She licked her lips as the single drop of blood fell onto the black altar. As the girl fought off Prince Grell, Teryessa fixated on that drop of blood. She felt it seep into her skin. She felt herself melt into and out of the previous version of herself. Finally, she felt time stop as she walked into the portrait that was now as big as life.

As she entered the portrait, her surroundings became even more real. She looked towards the door, where Wurm Ahkk-Rhall was frozen in place, drawing his sword, thinly disguised as the Gold Knight. She raised her eyebrow and watched him vanish. She looked down at Prince Grell, who was on top of her other self, captured in the moment when he was pushing the dark knife towards her throat, but he was no longer a threat to her. She burned through him with her eyes until he vaporized into nothing. She was alone in the room with her former self. She knelt, picked the child up, and carried her to the altar, laying her out on its glossy surface.

"Who are you?" the girl asked, allowing Teryessa to remove the dagger from her hands.

"I'm you," Teryessa said, "just not yet."

"You look different," the girl said, trying to sit up.

Teryessa stroked the girl's cheek, soothing her back to the altar, and lovingly said, "You're weak."

The girl acquiesced, laying back down for Teryessa, and asked, "What are you doing here?"

"Saving you," cooed Teryessa.

"Oh," she sighed with relief. "How?"

"With blood," replied Teryessa as she plunged the black dagger into the girl's chest.

Teryessa's eyes opened as she returned to the table in the Citadel that she had been fastened to. The reality of the room locked into place and she shuddered, not because of the dream she had just had or her current situation, but because she knew she was not alone and she was glad.

The door opened and the old man entered. She knew his name, not the name he went by as a human, but his real name.

"Well," he said, dropping his clothing to the ground and returning to his true form, his bat-like wings stretching out to fill the room, smoke wafting from his nostrils, "Are you ready?"

She was.

***

It was quiet on the second floor and slightly brighter, with the light from the windows in the rooms along the corridor casting long terrifying shadows in their path. Aiwren had thought, momentarily, about leaping from one of those windows. The height might not kill them, but with broken legs, they'd be easy targets. They slowly tiptoed down the hallway, back towards the foyer.

Aiwren's body was numb, but he felt his insides falling apart, crumbling into despair. He knew he had to keep his body moving, that he had to keep his mind from the crippling guilt, shame, and hopelessness, so he did his best to continue putting one foot in front of the other. The ground appeared normal, but Aiwren knew, beneath the surface, it was damaged by the dragon squeezing through the hallway below. It could collapse at any moment, just like him.

As he put his foot down, Aiwren felt a sudden shift. He heard rocks tumble below. Lieutenant Plune, who was leading the way, threw his arm up to signal for everyone to halt, but Aiwren was already frozen. Jocund slowly started walking again, carefully staying close to the wall, where the floor would be more structurally sound, and signaled for the group to follow. He watched Wanda slowly follow after Jocund, but found he could not move. The loose stone beneath his feet told him it was his step that caused the shifting below and that one more false step could send them all plummeting down to the first floor in a pile of rubble or, worse, alert the dragon to their position.

Aiwren felt a hand on his shoulder. It was Serafina. She gave his shoulder a squeeze. He turned to look at her and, although they all knew better than to speak, her expression encouraged him to continue. He took the next step. Nobody fell through the floor.

They continued walking down the hall that seemed to stretch out forever. He could see, in the distance, the light coming from the foyer. Part of him wanted to bolt, to run for it, to gamble that their feet could move faster than the stones could fall, but it was still too distant.

He heard another shifting of rocks coming from in front of him. It was either Jocund or Wanda who had taken the false step. They froze as they heard stones tumbling beneath them. Aiwren braced himself through the silence. He held his breath, certain the loud beating of his heart would trigger an avalanche.

Suddenly, Aiwren heard a loud bang and more rocks crashed down below them. At first, he hoped it was just a collapse, prayed that, in a moment, things would settle again and they'd be able to continue. Then he heard the scratching. It was the scratching of metal against stone. The dragon had found them and was digging up to them from the hallway below. For a moment, Aiwren was hopeful that the floor was too thick for the dragon to burrow his way up, but then he heard a loud bang from the impact of a dragon on the other side of the stones beneath his feet. Aiwren heard rocks falling the two more loud crashes in rapid succession. They all knew what this meant.

"Run!" Lieutenant Plune screamed.

As Aiwren ran, he felt the floor wobble and give. He heard a scream from behind him and quickly turned to see Serafina disappear, slipping down into the rocks. He turned around and, without thinking, dove for her.

The stones had settled a bit and Serafina was hanging on to the edge by the tips of her fingers. Aiwren, on his belly, inched his way towards her, reaching his hand as far as he could, as she grunted and panted, trying to pull herself up.

"I'm almost there!" he yelled. "Don't let go."

Aiwren's fingertips extended. He could feel the skin of her hand. He felt the rocks sliding down beneath him, but he was already touching her. He only needed a few more inches to be able to wrap one of his hands around her wrist. She looked over her shoulder down at the ground below her and shrieked.

"Don't look down!" Aiwren called out. "Look at me!"

Serafina's head turned back to Aiwren as he stretched as long as he could and inched forward again. Her brow furrowed as she gritted her teeth. Aiwren's hand was on her wrist. It was slippery with sweat, but he grabbed tightly. As soon as he could reach, he grabbed her wrist with his other hand as well. With two hands, he was able to lift her up. Rocks crumbled beneath him and he felt himself sliding into the hole in the floor. Lieutenant Plune and Wanda grabbed his feet just in the nick of time, dragging him away from the hole as Serafina's arm wrapped around his neck. Serafina, her chest now on the crumbling stones of the floor, wiggled to safety on her belly.

"Thanks," she said, her feet still dangling over the hole. "For a moment, I thought my story had ended."

Suddenly, Serafina's eyes widened, and before she could scream, she was ripped from Aiwren's arms with a force he had never felt before. He saw the large mouth clamp violently down on her ankle, immediately crushing all the bones. Even if it hadn't happened so explosively fast, there was no way Aiwren could have held on to her. The dragon was too strong. Serafina disappeared into the hole again.

Aiwren scrambled to the edge, hoping to see her holding on with her fingers again, but the dragon had pulled her down below. He whipped her body against the wall of the corridor and Aiwren saw her head explode against the stones, but the dragon continued lashing her body against the walls and the floor, gruesomely painting the area with Serafina's blood. Aiwren screamed in horror. The dragon looked up, dropping Serafina's limp body from his mouth, and stared directly into Aiwren's eyes.

"Run!" Aiwren shouted, as the dragon leapt towards him.

Lieutenant Plune had already pulled Wanda away and started running and Aiwren hurried to catch up with them. Unable to resist the fear-driven glance over his shoulder, Aiwren saw the dragon burst through the floor and scramble to get his footing. Aiwren ran as fast as he could.

When Aiwren reached the mezzanine of the foyer, Jocund and Wanda were already hurrying down a staircase. He heard the dragon charging down the hallway behind him as he ran towards the stairs, but he nearly stopped running completely as he passed Leicester's body, lying in a pool of blood with his eyes closed. Jocund and Wanda were near to door, but what was the point of escape? They'd just get murdered by the beast in front of the castle rather than within it.

Aiwren continued running, hurrying down the stairs, himself, as he heard the dragon bound from the hallway onto the mezzanine. As Aiwren emerged from the stairs, he saw the pile of log-sized splinters that used to be the huge front door. The light of the outside world was no longer a beacon of hope. A typhoon of air whooshed about the room as the dragon floated down to the ground behind him. Aiwren watched Lieutenant Plune and Wanda run into the clearing in front of the Old Watusia House, but he stopped running. He knew what he had to do. He thought of Leicester, turned to the dragon, certain he would die, and drew his sword.

**

Vannoria wrapped tightly around the rope of the bridge with both of her hands as Shadow severed the first cable. She felt the twist of fear rising in her stomach when the first rope went slack, sending the death savages down to the rocky ground below. Shadow's swung his sword again. She felt the tug on the tension of the rope she was holding and wondered if it had worked, but she soon felt the ground slipping from beneath her and her stomach rising up. The first thought she had as her free fall began was that she was going to vomit, but, when the rope went taut, that was quickly replaced with the paralyzing fear of crashing into the wall she was quickly swinging towards. Overcoming her panic and thinking quickly, she grabbed the Ma-Areshi man by the foot and pulled, sending him tumbling down past her. Without waiting to watch where he fell, she let go of the rope, herself. She watched Shadow rise up above her as she plummeted towards the ground. She saw him holding on with one hand as she passed by him in mid air.

Vannoria felt the surface give when she made contact and wondered if her body had splattered against the stones, but soon she realized the wetness was blood and it wasn't her own. She had landed in the dark pool.

Vannoria felt her face scrape across the rocky bottom, but she pushed herself towards the surface, not knowing the blood's depth. She scrambled to her feet, relieved she could stand, but the relief was short-lived as the visceral response to standing in a pool of blood washed over her like the thick syrupy liquid that was dripping from her face. The pool was almost black and something about its magic felt familiar. She found her footing and took in her surroundings.

Standing in front of Vannoria was a man with an evil energy surrounding him, the likes of which she had never seen and had only felt once before, it was the darkness she had felt in that room with the dark mirror. Up to his waist in the liquid gore, he was thin and wore all black. He drew back a hood to reveal the burns on his old, withered skin. A sickening smile spread across his scarred face with malice and delight. It was the necromancer.

Vannoria's first impulse was to find Shadow. She saw he had landed, but he was far away and there were guards between them.

The Ma-Areshi man took longer than she did to adjust to the fall, but, as he reoriented, his reaction to the blood was less controlled. He panicked and, as he scrambled to the edge, unaware of the dangers of his surroundings, the necromancer easily grabbed him and sliced across his throat with a dark knife. The necromancer let go of the man's body and it sank to the bottom of the blood.

Vannoria screamed with rage and thrust her fingers towards the necromancer, sending a burst of fire directly towards him, but the flame never reached him; it sputtered out in the space between them.

"A girl with a bit of magic," he said. "You'll be wonderful fuel for my machine, though I may just consume you, myself."

Vannoria tried to send another ball of fire towards him but this time nothing happened at all. She held her hand against the fire glyph tattooed on her skin. Her hand glowed as it was supposed to, but, just as she was about to release the fire, the necromancer swatted his hand and she felt the power escape, as though he had simply knocked it from her hand. She tried to reach for more power, but found she was suddenly unable to move at all.

"We wouldn't want you to waste any of that power," the necromancer said. "I'm going to need that."

"Vannoria!" Vannoria heard Shadow yell as he battled Gavlessans, both living and undead. "I'm coming."

The necromancer glanced over to Shadow, himself and said, "Oh, this is interesting. What is your name, girl?"

"I am the sorceress," Vannoria said, her eyes on Shadow as he fought to free herself.

"The sorceress," the necromancer laughed. "You're a child who's been given a sword and believes she's a warrior. Sure the blade will cut, but is it really wise to allow a child to play with sharp objects?"

Vannoria said nothing, continuing to watch Shadow cut down the guards, but behind him she saw the death savages closing in.

"Little girl," the necromancer said, "I'm a necromancer; your wraith will not be able to save you. There's no hope of you winning, but if you pledge yourself to me, I will spare you on account of your usefulness."

"Never!" she swore.

"We'll see how brazen you are when you lapdog has fallen," he said, turning his attention to the battle, where Shadow was cut twice more by the death savages's blades.

"Shadow!" she screamed, the sight of his injuries too heartbreaking for her to watch. "Go! Leave me!"

"Never!" he shouted, continuing to fight, to put one foot in front of the other, inching closer and closer to her, regardless of how many times he was struck.

"Ovyrr Keel," the necromancer said, "destroy him."

Vannoria screamed a warning as she saw an enormous undead warrior, a grotesque abomination cleave his way through the death savages.

***

King Noldar Palidnia stood in shock as he looked upon the dragon, the beast that, through all of these annuals, sat in his council, disguised as a man named Niveous Snew. He wondered how he could have been so blind. He wondered how dragons could walk among people for so long without detection, how, in all of these annuals, there had not been one slip up or even the briefest reveal of his true nature.

"One might think it would be awful for me to keep my human form for so long, hiding my true self," the beast snarled, "but, while I can't speak for my brothers, personally I found the deception to be one of the most rewarding aspects of my charade."

"What are you?" Noldar stammered.

"I think it's clear what I am, Your Grace," he laughed. "Although, I must be honest with you, there was one person who saw through my disguise, but I couldn't have that, now could I?"

"No," the king said, feeling the blood flush from his body and his limbs grow weak.

"Yes," the dragon smiled. "Do you know who it was?"

"No!" Noldar screamed.

"Yes," he gloated. "Say her name."

Noldar couldn't believe what he was hearing. He didn't want to. The thought of that foul beast's claws on her, ripped him apart. He swore he would never say her name, never hear it or think it ever again, but in that moment the only thing Noldar could imagine was his wife.

"Alice," he moaned with a trembling voice.

"Alice," the monster confirmed. "You see, she and I had met before. She was supposed to be a gift to me, but she didn't want to be my gift and so she fought me. She almost killed me, too. She was strong. I liked that. You can only imagine my surprise when you brought her here, waving what should have been mine right under my nose. At first, I was certain she would recognize me, but she didn't, not at first. Unfortunately, she did eventually see me for what I really am. I didn't know how I was going to isolate her from you and finish what I had started, but that night, that Vari-Matera-a those many annuals ago, you gave me a gift, you helped me by locking her up in that tower. Can you see it out the window? I left it standing for you."

Noldar did see the tower out the window. It was in a far wing of the palace. He had not been there since he discovered his wife missing those many annuals ago. Nobody had been there.

"I flew up to her window," he continued. "She was expecting me, but I was not caught off guard as I had been the first time she and I fought. This time, I killed her."

"No," whispered Noldar, barely able to stand.

"Yes," Snew insisted, "When I was done I roasted her until there was nothing left of her but a pile of ash, which I swept into the fireplace before flying to your side to help you host your Vari-Matera-a celebration, her blood still on my tongue. You didn't listen to her, but you must have guessed something like this happened. Why else would you have been so determined to blame her, if you didn't know that her death was entirely your fault?"

The words ripped out the final scraps of a soul clinging to the inside of King Noldar's heart. The remaining vacuum was immediately filled with hate and rage and madness. Noldar could feel his limbs again, feel the blood surging through them, pumping through his veins like magma. His head pounded. His cold hands tightened into a fist around the handle of his sword. The world narrowed until all that existed was the dragon standing proudly in front of him. Anger consumed him and vanquished everything in the world except for the desire to kill.

Raising his sword, he charged towards the dragon.

***

Jocund could hear the beating of the foul beast's wings as he ran towards what was once the door to the Old Watusia House, he could feel the heat of fire and smell the sulfuric stench of the dragons rotting and smoldering breath and he imagined the milkboy, who was trailing behind had probably been instantly incinerated when the monster burst into the foyer. He then did something that surprised even himself; he grabbed the princess by the hand and he shoved her in front of him so that he would be a barrier should the dragon release his fire.

As he ran, he saw his life flash before his eyes. He wondered if his father would finally be proud of him or if the cruel man would only shake his head in disappointment that Jocund had failed to bring them honor even in his death. He wondered, for an instant, if he had been wrong for his entire life, if, upon dying, he really would go to The Source and join his mother in The Divine Empress's loving embrace. He missed his mother. He had worked so hard to callous himself against loss, but in that moment before what he was certain would be his death, he found himself wanting to call out to her. She had ruined their family by dying too young, but he forgave her and wanted nothing more than for her to hold him.

He didn't call out for his mother though; instead, Jocund simply yelled for the princess to run, even though they both were already running as fast as they could. Perhaps the encouragement helped or perhaps it was just the force of him slingshotting her in front of him, but it seemed like the princess sped up a little as they ran from the building, its foyer now clouding with the dark smoke from the dragon's lungs. The daylight served as little encouragement, for he knew such a beast was not bound by darkness, but, instead, cast darkness wherever he flew. His heart sank even more as he and the princess sprinted past Cutter's body, with its entrails strewn about the yard. He wondered if he would have done anything different with his life, had he really understood that such powerful evils capable of doing that to a man existed. If there was any hope at all, it was that he and the princess could reach the woods and cleverly sneak their way to the safety of the princess's kingdom, but those hopes, too, were soon crushed, as Jocund saw another troop of brigands charging from the forest.

Jocund, certain his fate was sealed, stopped running, morbidly curious about who would reach him first to end his life, the dragon or the troop of cutthroats. The princess, too, stopped. With nothing else to do, he grabbed her hand tightly.

"Sorry," he said, unable to think of anything else.

"You did your best," she said, graciously, the true nature of her strength and nobility revealing itself in that bleakest moment.

The words barely had an instant to resonate, as Jocund turned to see how close the dragon was. Much to his surprise, he saw Aiwren emerge into the pool of daylight just inside the door. He expected to see the milkboy run through the door, only to burst into flames from the dragon's fire, but Aiwren stopped running, turned towards the dragon, and drew his sword.

Jocund wanted to yell for the fool boy to run. He wanted to yell that he took back his harsh words and that honor was not worth him throwing his life away, but this would do no good and Jocund knew it; they were all dead. He decided to let the boy die fighting, rooting for the boy to get in at least one good slash of his sword on the dragon before being burnt to a crisp.

A thin stream of fire from the beast's mouth engulfed Aiwren's sword, causing him to drop the red-hot metal. With no way to defend himself, the enormous creature grabbed Aiwren with one claw and threw him against the wall of the foyer. Jocund watched the boy fall limply to the ground, leaving a smear of blood from his head on the stone wall. They were all dead.

***

Teryessa was small. She had long thin arms and slender legs with little muscle. Although she was strong for her size she would have stood no chance, physically, against something as powerful as a dragon. She knew this. She also knew she was bound to the table which would have made it impossible for her to fight even a human of her own size. Still, she knew the story that her mother fought a dragon and she wondered.

She also wondered about what she had just seen. How was it possible for her to look upon herself in a previous moment of her life? How was it possible for her, in his moment, to be the voice she had heard back in that room? None of this made sense to Teryessa, who, while trying to put together the pieces of her life, was also writhing in excruciating pain. She wondered why her body hurt so much. Wide-eyed, her mind raced as the dragon approached and, most of all, she wondered why she felt as though this was the moment she was waiting for.

"You're going to drink my blood, aren't you?" Teryessa asked.

"Yes," said the dragon, "it's part of the ritual. Things like me aren't born, we are made."

"And now you hope to use my blood to create something new?" she asked. "Something new of yourself, I assume."

"The dragons are waiting for their leader to rise, to give them the signal to come forth from where they've been hiding and set the world on fire," he said, "I will be that leader, I will be the Hand of Gordorah, I will be Tiamatera, the Destroyer."

"No!" Teryessa screamed. "I won't let you. I have killed one dragon; I will gladly kill another."

The dragon roared with laughter and said, "You fancy yourself a dragon slayer, little girl? You think you killed Ahkk-Rhall? The fool beast isn't dead! He's trapped like a rat in the Citadel."

"No," she said, certain she had killed Ahkk-Rhall.

"But don't worry," he continued. "He's been a liability for far too long. I will destroy him as soon as I'm through with you."

Moving like lightening, the dragon's head darted towards Teryessa. Like a cobra striking, his fangs dove into the flesh of her forearm. She screamed from the burning pain. She felt his cold reptilian lips curl around her arm. She felt a suction so strong, she worried he would drain all of her blood in one monstrous gulp. She felt the burning of his saliva melting her skin. It was excruciating. Then, she felt another burning. Ignited in the pit of her stomach, she felt it spread through her body and explode in her mind like a lightning storm. She felt the rage burning through her like a fever.

The dragon gagged and backed away from her, leaving her arm blistered and bleeding.

"No! This isn't right! Something is wrong!" he grunted, wincing in pain as moved closer to Teryessa's face to inspect her. "What have you done? What are you?"

Teryessa, remembering how Ahkk-Rhall had killed Broch-Isha, attacked the dragon with the only part of her body she could move, her head. Her mouth clamped down on the soft patch of skin just below the dragon's jaw. The taste of his skin was rancid, but she squeezed her teeth around the mound of flesh, thrashing her head like a mad dog, refusing to let go. Then, something popped.

An eruption of fire exploded from the neck of the dragon with enough force to knock her back to the table. She had crushed one of his fire glands. She could taste the bitter liquid burning in her mouth, feel it searing her lips and melting into her tongue and throat. She could feel the skin all over her nude body sizzling painfully. She could hear the dragon howling in pain on the floor and could hear the raspy sound of air gurgling through blood as he tried to catch his breath. Screaming in pain, herself, she reached for her face and realized the leather shackles had burned to a crisp, easily disintegrating with her movement.

Teryessa opened her eyes just in time to see an explosion blow a huge chunk of flesh out of the dragon's neck, beneath his chin. Blood sizzled as it gushed from the wound and down his charred neck, blistered and glowing like hot coals. One side of his face was melted by his own fire, the eyeball oozing from the socket. His arms raced towards her as he bellowed out a furious roar, shaking the room. She rolled out of the way and onto the floor as his massive claws instantly reduced the huge table to shards. He was going to kill her.

***

The Nameless Rider never knew fear, not that he could recall, until the moment when, surrounded by Gavlessan Guards and death savages and unable to reach her, he saw Vannoria frozen by the necromancer's magic. He didn't know how he knew she was paralyzed, but he did. No matter what happened to him, the only thing that mattered was her, so he did what he did best, did what he always knew he was created to do: destroy. He cut down enemies with a power and fury that surprised even him. He knew every motion he had ever made, every life he ever ended felt effortless compared to that moment. He knew there were at least two swords already wedged into his back, one to the hilt, and there were countless slashes covering the rest of his body that never bled, but took their toll, nevertheless. He was getting closer and, for a moment, thought he would succeed, until he saw the beast.

It was a man once, but it no longer was. The thing was huge; it was easily a head taller than the Nameless Rider and built of grotesquely over defined muscles. One of its arms appeared to be stitched to its body. It had the black eyes of a ghoul, but there was thought inside, consciousness, a desire to kill even stronger the Nameless Rider's.

The enormous man-monster walked towards the Nameless Rider slowly, dragging an enormous battle ax. As it approached the Gavlessans that were between it and the Nameless Rider, it gave a swing of its hand and sent the men sailing into the stone wall where they splattered to their deaths. When it was close enough, it heaved the ax over its shoulder and swung it towards the Nameless Rider with all of its might.

The Nameless Rider had plenty of time to see the giant blade arcing towards him, but rather than duck, he raised his sword, his dark sword he knew would never break, to block it. The ax crushed into the Nameless Rider's sword, sending a shower of sparks up into the air and, although the Nameless Rider could see that the unknown material of his sword chipped the giant ax, he felt the force of the blow ripple through his body as his feet slid across the ground, dragging though the gravel. He would not be able to overwhelm this opponent with force.

The Nameless Rider looked over at Vannoria. He saw her scream in pain. He knew the necromancer was hurting her and he knew that he needed to help her. With his sword raised over his head, he charged in towards the giant beast.

Chopping into the monster with his sword was like chopping into wood, its dense undead muscles were like the fibers of a tree and the Nameless Rider found that, although he easily struck the massive arm of the creature, his blade was stuck for a moment in the tough flesh. The giant grabbed him with one hand and whipped him to the ground as though he was weightless and the Nameless Rider barely rolled out of the way in time to avoid the giant ax screaming into the ground like a guillotine. He knew he had to get rid of that ax. He climbed to his feet and prepared for the next attack.

When the ax rocketed towards him again, the Nameless Rider was ready. Rather than blocking the ax at its blade, he risked getting stuck, stepped forward and put all of his strength into blocking it at the handle. As the thick roughly hewn tree limb holding the giant head of the ax plowed into the shiny black metal, the Nameless Rider heard a snap. Then he heard a deep whooshing sound as the head of the ax, freed from its handle, rocketed away, crashing into the huge stone machine in the center of the room, but he didn't have a chance to inspect the damage before the huge monster's booted foot kicked him squarely in the chest and sent him hurtling through the air as well.

The Nameless Rider was vaguely aware of Vannoria's screams as he unclouded his head and picked himself up off the ground, realizing he, too, had crashed into the same wheel of the machine the ax had struck, causing it to wobble as it rotated. The moment of disorientation was just enough time for the giant ghoul to get to him.

500

The beast lifted him up over its head and threw him against another wheel of the machine.

The Nameless Rider felt every bit of this impact, as he slammed against the leg of the bloody stone wheel. Climbing to his feet, the Nameless Rider raised his sword for the next attack.

This time the giant beast charged him, nothing could have prepared him for the force of the collision. In an instant he was crushed against the stone wheel's leg. He heard snapping as he felt himself falling backwards, through the leg of the wheel. On the ground, he rolled away as the wheel fell with an earthquake of a thud and then toppled over onto the beast. The beast lifted the stone wheel, climbed out from beneath it, and rose to its feet.

The Nameless Rider used the slight head start he had getting to his feet to charge the giant ghoul, but when he stuck it, the beast locked its arms around the Nameless Rider's body, squeezed, and lifted him off the ground. Despite the pressure, the Nameless Rider kept fighting. He smashed the beast's face with his forehead repeatedly, but it seemed to have no effect on the monster.

When the Nameless Rider was almost gone, weakened from the pressure of the monster's arms around him, he heard the worst scream he could possibly imagine. Vannoria. His eyes popped open and he sprang back to life, grabbing the beasts head and lifting with all of his might. The creature howled and the Nameless Rider didn't know if it was with pain or fury or just base instinct, but he kept lifting.

The Nameless Rider felt the giant ghoul crush him into another of the machine's giant legs. It was the first wheel he had been smashed into, so its leg was already cracked and it broke easily, freeing its wheel. He heard the wheel roll away and crash into a far wall. Huge rocks plummeted down from above. He felt the rubble crashing down on him and gouging his flesh, but the Nameless Rider kept lifting and the beast stumbled into the pool of blood.

When the beast, roaring madly, fell to its knees, the Nameless Rider's feet touched the ground, the slick mud on the bottom of the bloody pool. He dug his heels in deep and lifted with all of his might. Vertebrae dislocated, crunching and crackling beneath the beast's thick, muscular neck, but, screaming in agony, the beast survived the pressure until the Nameless Rider, arching his back with enough force to uproot a tree, gave one final pull. Bones snapped, flesh ripped apart jaggedly, and the Nameless Rider tore the beasts head from its body. A geyser of dark, gelatinous, putrid blood erupted from the giant ghoul's headless neck and it slumped over. The Nameless Rider dropped the beast's hideous decapitated head into the pool of blood.

The Nameless Rider could barely stand and his vision was blurry, but he could see Vannoria and the necromancer. With all the energy he had, he raised his sword to strike down the necromancer, who made little effort to run. Then he felt a slight stabbing pain in his ribs. He looked down to watch the necromancer pull a small black knife from his side. Blood, black as night, flowed from the wound and the Nameless Rider felt the most excruciating pain imaginable surge through his body. He looked at Vannoria and felt, not cursed, but lucky. In the end, he was glad he couldn't remember all those previous lives and missions, because the one life he could remember, the only one that mattered to him, was almost entirely filled with her. He knew he was dying, but was determined to save the Girl.

He grasped the alter to steady himself so that he could stand just long enough to kill the necromancer. She screamed his name and he tried again to stand, but, as the necromancer's hand plunged down, he felt a surge of pain burn in his back and weakness overtook his body. She screamed again.

"I'm sorry," he said, devastated that he had failed her and that they would not share an eternity together.

The Nameless Rider looked upon Vannoria with loving, sorrowful eyes for as long as he could, until everything vanished, not into darkness, but light.

***

Allesander Montgomery had several knight-sons and they all quickly came to their knight-father's aid, rushing into the room as Rheo held his sword towards the elderly night.

"Allesander Montgomery isn't a dragon, Rheo," Leopold Leonard said, entering the room through a path between knights pointing their swords at Rheo.

"I know," said Rheo, keeping his sword raised to defend himself from the other knights, knowing Allesander could command them to attack him at any moment.

"Give me your sword, Rheo," Leopold, the High Knight of the Council, said to Rheo, firmly.

Rheo handed Leopold his sword. The other knights moved towards him, but Leopold raised his hand for them to stop. Rheo watched as the knights apprehensively lowered their weapons. After Allesander shot them a look, the knights left. Once the three men were alone, Leopold spoke.

"The two of you loathe each other, which doesn't particularly concern me, because quite frankly, I'm not very fond of either of you and I'm too old to pretend I like people I don't. Of the entire council we can only be certain three knights aren't a dragon and all of them are in this room. Whomever it is, their entire service to The Divine Empress and Y-Kewnor has been a charade, so what we know of character and motivation we must assume to be lies that we must disregard. We can't base our assumptions upon who we believe behaves guiltily."

"Ahkk-Rhall said dragons have been in Y-Kewnor for ages," Rheo said, hoping to provide more information for the three of them to solve the riddle.

"The only knights of the council from Y-Kewnor are in this room," Allesander said dismissively. "Can we really trust the lying tongue of a dragon?! Perhaps the three of us should confer with the dragon to see what it thinks we should do."

"The dragon will only speak to the girl."

"This is absurd!" Allesander shouted. "Conferring with a dragon to rescue a girl, so the dragon will identify the other dragon?! If we find the girl, we won't need her to speak to the dragon on our behalf; we will have already discovered the dragon. What good would that do us? Why would we do that?!"

"Because there are more," Rheo shouted, "hiding in plain sight, waiting for the right moment to strike. They are organized and have an ability to communicate with a necromancer through a diseased hand."

"A necromancer?! A diseased hand?!" Allesander scoffed. "Perhaps we ought to just line up all of the knights and ask them to show us their hands."

"For the moment we only need to be concerned with the council," Leopold said, ignoring Allesander's outburst and removing his gloves to show his own hands. "On the council, who's hands can you recall seeing recently?"

"I recall T'Ethal La-al's hands," Rheo said, removing his own gloves. "When I joined, I remember how large his hands looked. There was no wound."

"Good," Leopold said, "So T'Ethal is not the dragon. Anybody else?"

"I recall Ordo Ollycanterer's hands," Allesander said. "He always removed his gloves from those chubby little mits to reach for more ale at meetings. It isn't him."

"That leaves only Sigfried Illanto and Arowyr Malegon. Can either of you recall either of their hands?"

Rheo could not remember seeing either of their hands and Allesander looked as though he couldn't either.

"Okay," Leopold said. "What do we know of them?"

"Sigfried is from Les Naglos and Arowyr is from Era-Mosa," Allesander said, "Sigfried has been very vocal in trying to sway the council to involve the knights in the affairs of the West. Perhaps entrenching us in war is part of their plan."

Rheo didn't think it was Sigfried. He recalled a council meeting and Arowyr making some small gesture with his hands. He didn't remember seeing a wound, but he did recall that the man's hands were gloved."

"Arowyr," Rheo said. "He never removes his gloves."

"Nonsense," Allesander replied. "You can't base your judgement on hands you admittedly have not seen and besides, he spoke up for you when I suggested we throw you in the dungeon. He suggested we send you to Boomswift."

"He suggested my partnership with Beatrice because I was determined to figure out who was behind the attack on the Citadel when everyone else was willing to sweep it under the rug," Rheo said.

"That makes sense," Leopold said. "He likely argued for your freedom because it would be easier to kill you if you weren't in the dungeon."

Rheo didn't wait around for permission or a plan. He grabbed his sword from Leopold and bolted from Allesander's chambers. By the time he made it to the hallway, he feared he was already too late. There was panic in the corridor as people ran towards the stairs, shouting that the Citadel was, once again, on fire. Rheo smelled the smoke in the corridor, but he already knew where it was coming from.

Rheo joined the swarm of panicking knights rushing to the stairwell, but the stairs were clogged by the droves of knights trying to descend as he was trying to go up, so Rheo worked his way through the crowd, pushing against a sea of fearful men. As the cloud of smoke thickened, he was overcome with memories of the night his knight-father died. Rheo felt his mind split between the present and that fateful night. Each step was torment, reminding him he wasn't fast enough. His tortured mind burned with the fear he would again be too late.

Eventually Rheo made it to Arowyr's floor of the Citadel. The floor had already evacuated and was filled with so much smoke he could hardly see. He covered his mouth with his arm and headed towards Arowyr's door.

***

When Aiwren was young, he was climbing in the rafters of the barn one snowy day, when he slipped on a patch of ice that had formed over night on a damp wooden beam. He crashed to the ground and hit his head on a stone. He remembered how his mother had reacted to even the smallest of his bumps and scratches and he knew he was not allowed to climb in the rafters. So, with the wind knocked out of him and afraid to frighten his mother, he laid there, freezing cold, with the cut on the back of his head bleeding into the snow for what felt like an eternity, until his father, standing above him, backlit by the bright winter sun beaming into the barn, offered him a hand. Aiwren, having heard of boys falling and breaking their necks, was certain he was paralyzed and, laying on his back, unable to catch his breath, cried to his father that he couldn't move.

Aiwren's father, always so calm, said, "There are going to be times in life, when you're certain all is lost. In those moments, it's more important than ever to look within yourself and find a reason to get up."

Then, his father bent down, with a ray of sun directly illuminating his kind face, and picked him up.

The ground was cold and Aiwren felt a warm sticky wetness on his face. It was blood, his blood, matting his hair to the back of his head. For a moment, he thought he was in that snowy barn of his childhood. When he remembered he wasn't in that barn and he wasn't a child, a wave of hopelessness and loss consumed him. He could not get up. He remembered his father's sword being destroyed by the dragon, he remembered being struck and hitting the wall hard, and, once again, he was certain he was paralyzed, if not physically, then emotionally; having lost so much, there was no reason to go on. He thought of his parents, who didn't even know he was on this adventure, finding out he had been killed. Then, he thought of his father, standing above him, offering him his hand. His parents had kept him safe for so long, preserved him, and he realized that his reason for wanting to travel to Y-Kewnor, his reason for signing up for this crazy adventure wasn't for the excitement; it was to be worthy of the care of his parents; it was to make the right choices in the grandest way possible; it was to matter. He also knew that, at that very moment, a dragon was about kill a princess and his commanding officer, and he wasn't about to let that happen.

The first thing Aiwren saw when he opened his eyes was the hilt of his father's sword, the sword the dragon had melted with a stream of fire, but even from far away, his father was there to pick him up once more. The iron blade of the sword had been melted away, but beneath it was another blade, the true blade, the crystal blade that was revealed when the metal shell had been destroyed. Aiwren reached for it.

When Aiwren picked up his sword, the light streaming through the facets of the thin, clear blade produced a resplendent twinkle that seemed to amplify the light and project it out with brilliant beams in a multitude of colors. It was light in Aiwren's hand and, as he slid his thumb across it, he found it to be sharper than anything he had ever felt. Aiwren climbed to his feet.

The dragon was already outside the Old Watusia House and slowly approaching Lieutenant Plune and Wanda. Beyond them, he could see more brigands were closing in. He knew he might die, but having remembered his family, Aiwren was more concerned with the intent of his actions than their outcome.

"Leave them alone!" he demanded, approaching the dragon.

The dragon turned its head to see Aiwren and, in the light of day, Aiwren understood the scale of the beast, immediately wishing he'd considered a surprise attack. It was too late to change tactics though, the dragon was preparing to finish him. He knew he had to act fast. He raised the crystal sword and sprinted towards the dragon.

The dragon, shockingly perceptive and blazingly fast, seemed to expect Aiwren's charge and blew another thin stream of fire towards the boy, but the crystal sword didn't melt and the fire bounced off harmlessly. His hands didn't even feel warm.

Realizing the crystal sword protected him from the dragon's fire, Aiwren focussed on the dragon's fore-claws and mouth. He didn't expect the massive barbed tail racing towards his head.

Aiwren brought the sword up just in time to protect his head from the spikes on the dragon's tail, but the force of the impact launched him into the air, flipping head over feet and landing on his belly. He was face to face with the corpse of his mentor, Cutter. The man's guts were spread out and Aiwren could imagine the monster grabbing Cutter by the stomach with his teeth and shaking the man until his body ripped apart. Cutter's still eyes reminded Aiwren of his lessons.

As he ran back towards the immense beast, Cutter's lessons flashed in Aiwren's mind. Considering the dragon had four means of attacking him, Aiwren realized he had to treat this like fighting two men. Even if he blocked every attack, the impact was enough to kill him. To win this fight, he'd have to focus on evading attacks and positioning himself for the right counter attack. When the next strike came, Aiwren was ready.

Aiwren expected the dragon's tail rocketing towards him and, ducking as the enormous spiked mound of veiny grey flesh screamed by over his head, he sliced up with the crystal sword. The dragon howled. The tail was moving far too fast for Aiwren to get a clean enough strike to sever the end completely, but he made a deep gash to let the dragon know that he, too, could cut.

"You brutally murdered my friends," Aiwren said, maintaining equal distance in relation to the beast.

"You say this as though it matters," the dragon laughed, circling Aiwren, forcing him to move and change directions to maintain position, "as though a few humans make any difference in the grand scale of things."

"They mattered to me," Aiwren said, keeping his blade raised like a sight, making sure his footing was correct, watching for any opportunities to strike.

"You fight well, human," the dragon said, suddenly changing directions and swiping at Aiwren with its claw.

Aiwren avoided the claw, but was too slow to counter the attack. He knew he had to rethink the enemy. He focused on trying to find the beast's weakness. He thought about his friends. Gregory was burnt, an attack from a distance. The beast grabbed Serafina with its mouth when she was defenseless. If Cutter had been armed when it grabbed his stomach than he would have decapitated the beast. Against Aiwren, it had attacked first with fire them with its tail. The dragon, Aiwren realized, though powerful, was driven by self-preservation.

"I see your little mind working, human," the dragon hissed. "It's charming, but pointless. Time for you to put down your toy sword."

The dragon was strong and fast and smart, so it would be protecting its most vulnerable areas with these assets. It was built like a beast, but it didn't lead with its head in an attack like a beast does. Aiwren thought of trying to bait it to attack with its head, but the move was too risky. He circled away from the tail slowly.

As Aiwren had hoped, the dragon rocketed its tail towards him. He ducked like before, but, rather than swiping at the barb of the tail as it sailed by, he rolled towards the base of the tail, positioning himself behind the beast, but far from any vital targets. Then, he leapt.

The dragon's back was nearly as tall as he was, but it sloped down to the tail, so Aiwren landed just far enough onto the spiny festering flesh to get purchase with his feet and grab on to one of the thin spikes coming out of the beast's spine. He scrambled higher and higher on the beast. It shook and roared beneath him, and Aiwren realized the enormous wings were beating down upon the air and giving the huge monster lift off the ground. If Aiwren wasn't fast enough, then, even if he succeeded, he'd be crushed when the dragon fell to the earth. Aiwren could see he was already at least forty paces off the ground. The dragon arced its head back towards him and released a blast of fire that swirled about Aiwren in the storm created by the dragon's beating wings. It wasn't meant to burn him, just to knock him off, but Aiwren didn't let go. As the dragon gained even more altitude, Aiwren inched his way up the back to its neck. So high above the ground that the castle looked tiny, he wrapped his legs and his free arm around the neck and inched further. Finally he got to the dragon's throat. Had he raised his sword to strike it down, he surely would have been flung from the beast, so he held the dragon's head with his left arm and sawed steadily at the beast's throat with his sword.

The crystal blade went between the haphazard metal plates and through the grimy flesh easily, blood oozed between Aiwren's fingers as the dragon screamed with horror. The thick artery, buried in the gore of the dragon's neck, burst as the edge of the blade bit into it. The blood oozing from the wound immediately gushed as the dragon quickly plummeted from the sky, leaving a trail of red streaking behind it.

Aiwren clung tightly to the dying monster as it dropped from the air, hoping its wings would slow the fall and its body would soften his landing, but they were higher than Aiwren had calculated. The wind was fierce and the ground quickly raced towards him.

Aiwren heard the thud and the explosion of the enormous beast compacting in upon itself before he felt it. He heard bones snapping and ribs collapsing from the pressure, wondering which of them were his. He heard the splattering of blood and organs, but just as he realized that the soup of viscera he was swimming in didn't belong to him, the beast exploded in a giant ball of fire. He could feel his leather armor disintegrate from the syrupy heat sticking to him, but he also felt the crystal sword's steady coolness spreading through his body.

It had taken all of Aiwren's strength for him to climb to his feet. Completely naked and covered with ash and blood, he stepped from the fire of the burning dragon's carcass and collapsed to his knees.

The brigands, unmoved by the death of the dragon, charged towards Jocund and Wanda. Aiwren, using the sword as a crutch, forced himself to his feet, pain surging through his legs as they took the weight of his body. He raised the blade over his head and, stripped of his armor, screaming through the pain, he stumbled towards his remaining friends to defend them, only to collapse back to the ground after a few steps.

Aiwren tried his hardest to move, but his body would not obey. He scratched his way across the ground towards them, but soon, even that was too difficult. He was only vaguely aware of what was happening, when he saw a platoon of soldiers emerge from the woods. Their red hair and ruddy complexions told Aiwren these were Watusians, but he didn't know if they were there to help or take Wanda for themselves. His eyes closed. The last thing Aiwren heard as the din of the battle faded and he slipped from consciousness, was the voice in his mind.

"See?" she cooed. "I knew you had it in you."

***

Teryessa scrambled across the floor, rolling out of the way just as the giant beast's tail crashed down to the ground, shattering the wooden floorboards, chipping away the stone beneath it. She stumbled to her feet just enough to dive over the bannister into the sitting area of the Citadel apartment, narrowly avoiding the sputtering barrage of flames blasting against the wall, crashing to the hard ground, and crawling behind a wooden sitting bench. Peering out from behind the bench, she saw the dragon, half-blinded and bleeding badly, leap onto the bannister.

"You can't hide for long, girl!" the dragon roared. "You think wood will protect you? Metal? Stone?!"

Teryessa held her breath, praying that the dragon wouldn't find her. The voice in her head kept talking, but she was too terrified to listen.

"You know I was going to grant you a relatively peaceful death," the beast bellowed, "but now I can't wait to invent new ways to make you suffer!"

Suddenly the bench Teryessa was hiding behind burst into flames from the dragon's fire. She had to run. Across the room she saw her crossbow. Without a second thought, she went for it.

The whole time she was running, a lethal blast of dragon's fire followed closely, destroying the wall behind her, forcing her to run faster and faster. She could feel the heat on her back, feel the skin on her shoulders blistering. She leapt for the crossbow and the quiver, grabbing them just as the table they were sitting on burst into flames.

"A crossbow?!" the dragon laughed. "You think you can defeat me with a crossbow?!"

Dark smoke filled the large room, refracting and clouding both the shards of sunlight from windows and the light of the burning furniture. Benches, tables, and chairs were in flames. The stones the dragon had charred were pocked from his blasts and red hot. Teryessa struggled to see where she was going. She hoped the dragon was suffering a similar limited visibility. She snuck behind a large vase to load her cross bow. Her nerves fortified her strength, making it easier for her to cock the string, but she struggled to fit the bolt into its slot with her trembling hands. Then, in a silence underscored only by the crackling of the fires, she dropped the bolt and the sound seemed to ring out. She knew the he would hear her, but she fumbled for another bolt.

Suddenly, the dragon's face, disfigured by its own fire, furiously roared up next to her, saliva dripping from his enormous fangs and melted lips. Screaming and nearly dropping the crossbow, she backed deeper into the corner, behind the vase, but the dragon shattered the vase with its massive tail.

"Nowhere to go, Princess," the dragon said, wrapping his tail around her body.

Teryessa pulled the trigger. The string suddenly released its tension into a thin piece of wood traveling a very short distance. A crossbow bolt could not stop a beast the size of a dragon, but a calculated hit could take away the beast's remaining fire power. The bolt buried itself into the dragon's neck, but nothing happened. The dragon, furious, grabbed at the bolt, ripping it from his neck and a stream of liquid fire burst from the puncture. The dragon screamed in agony, scratching at the wound, only screaming louder as the fire burned the flesh from its claws.

Howling with fury and pain, he ripped the crossbow from her hands with his burnt, bloody claws. Suddenly unarmed, she ducked just in time for the huge barbed mound at the end of his tail to race over her head and crash into the wall. The stones crumbled and a shaft of light from outside poured into the burning, smoke-filled room. She dove away as the tail crashed down.

Across the room, Teryessa's eyes spotted the sword Rheozarccio said she was too unskilled to wield, but she looked beyond it and saw the door to the hallway. Across the room may as well have been a thousand paces away, but she knew she needed to try to escape. Picking herself up off the ground, she bolted. For a moment she thought she was actually going to make it, but she tripped as she scrambled up the steps to the foyer, landing on her stomach only feet from the door. Knowing the dragon was upon her, she reached out and grabbed the only thing she could and raised her arms to defend herself when the dragon pounced.

Teryessa felt the impact, but the crushing blow she was expecting never arrived. She opened her eyes. The dragon clutched at the sword driven deep in his chest. She let go of the hilt and he rolled to his back, writhing in pain. She looked at the door, but backing out felt impossible. There was only one way this could end.

Princess Teryessa leapt onto the belly of the dragon, straddling his enormous hemorrhaging chest with her bare bloody legs. He whipped his tail frantically, but she dodged the first two swings and caught end of the tail, pinning the massive lump of skin at the end under her arm. After giving the sword a good twist, she pulled it from the dragon's chest. Continuing to hold the end of the dragon's tail under her arm she hacked at the base of his tail with the sword. He slashed at her with his claws, but the lethargic attempt with the mangled claws did little more than scratch her body, the body she no longer cared about. He gnashed at her with his teeth, but she kicked him in the throat and pinned his head to the ground, cramming her big toe into the wound in his neck. Teryessa's arms were so tired she could barely hold the sword, but, with one more swing, she severed the massive bludgeoning whip of a tail before letting the bloody piece of iron fall to the ground.

Exhausted and driven mad with rage and panic, Teryessa faced the dragon. She looked at his cruel face, now begging for mercy. Making her hand as narrow as possible, she forced her fingers into the hole the sword had made in the beast's chest, fishing around until she found what she was looking for.

"You said Ahkk-Rhall survived me," she said, consumed with rage, covered with blood, and grasping the beating organ inside the monster's chest. "I won't make that mistake again."

"My Master," the dragon said, suddenly quiet, staring off vacantly into the burning room. "I was never intended to be Tiamatera. I was the sacrifice!"

"I know," Teryessa said with a voice that wasn't hers, as she yanked the heart from the dragon with her bare hand.

***

Vannoria raised her hand to try again to send a surge of flames towards the necromancer, but this time she felt the painful fire coursing through her own body. She screamed in pain and tried to release the magics back to The Source, but she could not. She couldn't even move. She was paralyzed. The necromancer was squeezing his mangled hand and she could feel the power crushing her body. All she could do was scream in pain.

She watched as Shadow was crushed into a wheel of the giant machine by the beast of a man attacking him and saw as the wheel fell from machine and onto the huge creature, only to have the creature lift himself up and grab Shadow.

The necromancer squeezed his hand again. Vannoria screamed even more loudly, as she felt her ribs breaking and her spine compressing. She screamed until the pain was so great it took her breath away.

Shadow reached for the giant's head, began lifting and, with a tear trickling from her eye, she tried, once again, to control the energy and free herself, but, once again, she could do nothing as she watched Shadow, in the beasts deadly grasp, smashed into another giant stone wheel.

The wheel broke free and smashed into the wall, but Vannoria was unable to do a thing as stone rained down from above, splashing into the blood around her. The beast stumbled into the pool with Shadow holding tightly to its head. When the beast fell to its knees and Shadow ripped its head from its body, she saw, in the cruel darkness of that cave city, what appeared to be a glimmer of hope. When he stepped forward, barely standing, with his sword raised, she thought they would see another day together. She thought she would see his sword race down upon the necromancer, freeing her from his magics and that she would run to him and leap in his arms and kiss him and never let him out of her sight ever again. She thought for a moment that the two of them actually could live forever.

The necromancer, didn't seem to see Shadow coming towards him; the cruel man's eyes were locked on her, but when Shadow was only a breath from cutting the man down, the necromancer turned. Vannoria saw Shadow's eyes widen before she noticed the small black blade the necromancer had plunged into her lover's body. She drowned her shock in hope that it could still be all right, by telling herself that it was just a tiny knife, but her hope evaporated when she saw dread wash over Shadow's face.

The necromancer allowed Shadow to slump onto the black stone altar. As soon as he touched the altar, it seemed that whatever was happening to Shadow was happening more quickly. His sword dropped into the pool of blood. He gripped the edge of the stone with hands that immediately seemed older and more frail. His mouth open wide to dryly rasp for air.

Vannoria struggled to move, but could feel only the slightest budging from the necromancer's magic as she looked into Shadow's eyes and watched them age.

"Shadow!" she screamed, feeling her heart start to tear itself out of her body.

The necromancer who had watched all of this with glee, joyfully thrust his knife into Shadow's back. Vannoria screamed with horror as she saw the flesh flake away from Shadow's fingers, crumbling into the pool of blood. She lost her breath completely when the skin on his arms dried until they were wafer thin, peeling off to leave only bone. His clothing hung loosely on his shrinking frame.

The lips Vannoria had kissed with more love than she had ever known, dissolved from his face as he breathed, "I'm sorry," leaving behind only a skull while the whispered syllables still echoed.

"And now," the necromancer said, "you will become what you were always meant to become. Dust."

Suddenly, Shadow's skeleton turned to ash, which glided down lightly to the pool of blood, white specks floating on its nearly black surface, and Vannoria's heart, like Shadow's body, crumbled.

With a fury, she never knew was imaginable, Vannoria screamed so loudly, it shook the underground city, sending more stones down to the bloody pool and the arena floor. She felt the magic holding her snap like strands of thread. She gritted her teeth and clenched her fists, squeezing whatever it was connecting her to The Source so violently, it felt as though her tiny body would explode. Then, all at once, the remaining stone wheels shattered like broken glass. Her hands trembled.

The necromancer looked up at her with shock, unsuccessfully attempting to bind her again.

Vannoria, consumed with anger, took a step forward, as bubbles rose to the surface of the bloody pool. They were slow at first, but with every step towards the necromancer, she felt them intensify. The blood was boiling.

The expression on his face turning to terror, the necromancer struggled to flee the bloody pool, but Vannoria continued to approach. He called for help from the remaining guards in the room, but Vannoria narrowed her eyes and they burst into flame before they could reach her.

Vannoria raised her hand to burn the necromancer with fire, but he stabbed her in the hand to defend himself. The dagger was called Soul Stitcher. She knew its name as soon as it pierced her flesh. She knew everything about it. She knew everything about the necromancer and his magics. Trembling, he pulled Soul Stitcher from her hand and was about to stab her again, when she grabbed his face with her hands and focussed.

"Fool," he said, concentrating to repel her magic, "you cannot destroy the Mouth of Gordorah!"

"Watch me," she said, as he burst into flame, the pool of blood igniting behind her.

The necromancer screamed until his head, burnt to a crisp, crumbled between Vannoria's palms.

She gasped for air, only to have the wind knocked out of her again as the reality of her loss dealt her a devastating blow. She reached into the pool, as though she might grab Shadow by the collar, pull him from the depths, and hold him once again, but the dust that was Shadow only slipped through her fingers.

Vannoria grabbed the necromancer's Soul Stitcher. She knew his spells and knew there was a way to reanimate the dead. She swiped at her hand with Soul Stitcher and squeezed the blood from the gash in her palm onto the pile of Shadow's clothing, she touched her healing tattoo until her hand was so bright, she could no longer look at it. She felt the life energy the necromancer had collected in the pool surging into her body. She pressed her glowing hands onto the pile of dust and expelled everything. But nothing happened. Shadow was gone. Vannoria fell to her knees and howled.

***

King Noldar Palidnia had let go of any concerns for his own well being when fury drove him to charge towards the dragon with his sword raised. All he cared about was making Snew pay for what he had taken from him, all the annuals of happiness that could have been, but never were, his wife, his daughter, and his kingdom.

Although he was a large man, Noldar was physically no match for the dragon. Snew casually waited as Noldar drew close, then, at the last instant, nonchalantly lashed his tail out at the king, sending him crashing into a wall.

"So quick to rise to action," Snew said as he slowly approached the king, "so hasty in your decisions. I often wondered why I was tasked with infiltrating the most impulsive and shockingly dim of targets."

"Go ahead," Noldar said, staggering to his feet. "Boast about your bloody coup."

"Coup?!" The dragon sneered. "From your shadow I have raised an empire and rendered all of Allyoshmar incapable of defending itself. And now, I'm afraid, you're no longer useful."

Snew, reared back, inhaled deeply, and exhaled a cloud of fire towards the king. Noldar, acting quickly, dove out of the way. The fire missed Noldar, but scorched the stone wall of the throne room. Holding his side, Noldar struggled to get away. He wasn't afraid for his life, since it was, he decided, already forfeit, but he was determined to take this dragon with him when he died. He was determined that his final act would be one of vengeance.

The next burst of flames erupted right in front of Noldar and he barely stopped in time to avoid being roasted. The dragon missed him, but one of the giant tapestries of the throne room went up in flames, quickly spreading to the thick wooden beams high above, and Noldar could feel the heat charring his skin.

Across the room, Noldar saw a glimmer of hope. Sitting beside his throne was an enormous shield. He knew the metal wouldn't protect him for long against the dragon's fire, but he didn't need it to. If he could get that shield, he could get close enough to the dragon to strike, even though he would certainly die in the process. He narrowed his eyes and bolted, ignoring the fire chasing after his feet as he sprinted across the room.

Noldar was nearly at throne when he stumbled, unaccustomed to running even for brief durations. He skidded across the floor, but, determined, scrambled quickly to his throne, reaching next to it to grab his shield and hold it in front of him as his hand tightened around his sword, preparing to head into the fire.

Suddenly the shield was ripped from Noldar's hand. In one swift violent motion, Snew grabbed at it so ferociously that it sailed across the throne room, clanging uselessly to the ground. Snew was so close. Noldar swung out with his sword. He felt an impact and heard the piercing of flesh.

Snew, standing above the king, smiled. King Noldar looked down. The dragon's tail pinned him against the throne, the giant barb piercing into the center of his chest. Feeling his life fade, the king stared around his throne room. He watched as the tapestry telling the story of the epoch of peace in Lees Naglos turned to ash. He watched as flames devoured the tapestry documenting the peace treaty between Palidnia and Frins Casicon as the two cities built the canals that brought water and abundance to his lands. Finally, Noldar saw the tapestry of his ancestor holding the Flaming Sword of Justice over his head as the fire ignited the fabric.

King Noldar Palidnia, a man who recently lost the little faith once had, closed his eyes and prayed. Sitting on his throne with the barb of a dragon through his chest, the king didn't pray to The Divine Empress, nor did he pray for mercy or protection. Gasping for air as the world faded, King Noldar prayed to his ancestors. He prayed for merciless justice. Noldar swore he would do whatever was required for justice to be reaped, as Snew, smiling with delight, released an explosion of fire upon him.

The heat of the fire was consuming. All fabric the king was wearing was instantly incinerated. He could feel his hair singe and his skin blister. The metal of his armor did its best to stand up to the heat, but it was soon red-hot and melting into Noldar's already charred flesh.

"You're robust, King Noldar," said Snew, when he stopped to inspect his work, "but you know what they say. Given enough heat, anyone can burn."

Snew released another burst of fire on Noldar, even hotter than the last one. The king could feel the pain giving way to painlessness as the brightness of the fire gave way to the darkness of the nothing waiting for him and silence swelled around him. Then, through the darkness, the king saw light.

King Noldar Palidnia opened his eyes to see the throne room. He looked down and saw that his own body was in flame. The dragon was walking away, leaving him for dead. King Noldar wasn't dead though and, as the flames died, leaving behind charred crispy flesh, the king reached for his sword and stood. As he slowly walked towards the dragon, the king could feel the burnt soot that used to be his skin flake off, leaving behind only raw flesh.

"You are a tenacious little nuisance," Snew said.

Suddenly there was a flicker was on the hilt of the king's sword, and it quickly turned into a small flame that spread up the length of his blade until the entire sword seemed to be made of fire.

"This is impossible," Snew said, his jaw dropping as he slowly backed away from the king. "That sword is a myth. We tried to find it for thousands of annuals. How could it be that it was beneath our noses the entire time."

Noldar said nothing, but continued to walk towards Snew, the flaming sword in his hand.

"You have something powerful in your hands, Your Grace," Snew said. "I see now how it eluded us, but there is so much you don't understand of the larger picture. You're still out of your league. Let me help you."

The king still said nothing and continued to approach the dragon, who continued to step back cautiously.

"Fool!" Snew shouted, as he backed into the burning tapestry of Noldar's ancestors. "You can't kill me with fire. I'm a dragon."

"Given enough heat," Noldar said, in a new voice, crackling like a fire surging from the breath of a bellow, "anyone can burn."

Noldar's unblinking lidless eyes, stared directly into Snew's as he plunged the flaming sword into the beast's chest. The burning blade easily pierced the dragon's moldy scales and melted into the flesh below. Snew screamed.

"Stupid and impulsive as always, Your Highness," the dragon whispered. "Don't you see? We've already won. I was wasn't fighting for Gavlessa; I was building an army for the one true Master and it appears as though I've accomplished my task."

Noldar, uninterested in Snew's words, turned the blade.

"Your daughter..." the Snew whispered.

King Noldar paused to hear what the beast would say of his daughter, but it was too late. The dragon was dead.

***

Truson Everly was at the front of the attack on Gavlessa. The death savages hadn't dropped to the ground, but after he heard the huge explosion of sound from within the city, he noticed the new corpses were no longer rising from the dead. Calculating that this was the best opportunity he was going to have, he led the charge through the gates, fighting his way through the underground city, to the giant arena that the necromancer had used as his base of operations. Depositing other platoons to fight at various points along the way, he and his small squad, all former knights who had defected with him to pledge their allegiance to King Noldar, hurried to the arena, avoiding avalanches of stone, Gavlessans defending their home, and death savages roaming the streets, hoping they might bring the Empress's light to the heart of darkness.

As Truson and his twelve former knights charged into the arena, they were shocked to find the place almost entirely empty. The ground was littered with corpses that would forever be still. In the center of the enormous room, surrounded by piles of rubble, was dark pool. It was blood, Truson realized, to his horror. There was a dark altar off to one side, within it.

In the middle of the pool, Truson saw a ripple. He raised his sword and approached the edge, wondering what horrible monster he was about to sacrifice his life to protect the world from. He noticed a heap of clothing on top of the altar and the body of a thin, headless man leaning against it. A figure emerged from beneath the surface. He couldn't tell what it was, but it was bloody and holding black sword. Truson gave his men an encouraging nod.

The blood flowed down, back into the pool, revealing a woman's body. It was Vannoria, the sorceress, retrieving a black sword from the depths of the blood.

"The necromancer is dead," she said, eyeing the headless corpse.

"Here," Truson said, hurrying to the edge, removing his cape and handing it to her so she could wipe the gore from her face and body.

She took the cape and used it to wipe the blood from the sword before handing it back to him. She gently took a sheath from the pile of clothing on the altar and slung it over her back.

"Your friend?" Truson asked.

"Gone," she said, sliding the sword into the sheath on her back. "He's gone."

"I'm sorry," Truson said.

She seemed to ignore him, as she examined a black knife for a moment, then slipped it into her belt.

"What you've done," Truson said, feeling how distant she was, "because of you, we won."

"Won what?" Vannoria asked. "That man was the only happiness I've ever known."

"Then you've made a great sacrifice," Truson replied, squeezing her shoulder encouragingly, "It is a miracle."

"Miracle?!" she asked, removing his hand from her arm.

"I thought all hope was lost," Truson admitted to the girl. "I had lost my faith, but The Divine Empress, our merciful Creator, she sent me you and your friend and now I know She was watching over me. She gave me a second chance"

"I've felt the reaches of The Source," she said, walking away as Truson's men stepped aside to let the blood-covered woman pass. "Your Divine Empress is either absent or cruel."

"What will do next, Vannoria?" Truson asked.

"Vannoria's dead," she replied without looking back.

***

When Rheo kicked the door in, the cloud of smoke and the wave of heat nearly knocked him from his feet, but the sight he saw when the smoke cleared and his eyes adjusted was even more unsettling. Only feet from the door, leaning upon the steps to the vestibule, was an enormous dragon. Princess Teryessa, completely nude and covered with blood, straddled the dragon's corpse with her right hand raised over her head. Rheo could have sworn he saw the heart in her hand, beat its final beat. She crushed the heart and, with an insanity fixed in her eyes, screamed as she ripped apart the dragon's carcass with her bare hands.

Rheo could only imagine what the girl had been through to drive her to this maddened state, but he knew, if he didn't get her out of there, she would die from the smoke and the fire. He called to her, but she didn't seem to hear him.

Rheo ran into the room, narrowly avoiding a collapsing beam as he charged towards the girl, determined to save her no matter the cost. The fires licked up around her as he approached. He could see, even through the blood and ash, that her skin was blistering and burning.

Rheo stumbled over the massive head of the dead dragon and reached for Teryessa's shoulders, but she gave a swing at him with her elbow and continued tearing apart the dragon's corpse, bloodying her face as she used her teeth to rip through tendons. He called her name again and held her arms down tightly to her side. She twisted and squirmed, but he was much stronger than she was and, after she snapped at him a few times with her mouth, her body became still within his arms.

"You're okay," he said, "but we have to go."

"What's the point?!" she screamed, struggling again to free herself from his grasp.

"I don't know!" he screamed back.

"They'll never stop! The darkness is everywhere!" she wailed, then, suddenly frail, cried, "I'll never be free."

Finally, Rheo had the grip he needed around the scrappy princess's body. He clasped his hands under her arms and, as she squirmed and flailed and sobbed, he dragged her from the wreckage, collapsing for a moment in the hallway, where she passed out.

As he had with his knight-father, Rheo threw Teryessa over his shoulder, carried her from the Citadel, and laid her down in the same spot where Vincent Ackaback had died.

***

Disbelief was too casual a term for Jocund to describe his reaction to what Aiwren did. In just a few days, Jocund had gone from believing dragons were either imaginary or extinct, to being accused of colluding with them, to watching his platoon massacred by one, to watching a simple milkboy destroy one. Most people wouldn't have the presence of mind to macro-examine their perspective in the heat of battle, but most people didn't have Jocund's mind and, as quickly as things were happening around him, Jocund's mind was always faster. He noted, equally, that the brigands closing in on the princess and himself seemed completely nonplussed by the sight of the dragon. They were supposedly thieves; he couldn't help but wonder how it was they were so unaffected by the sight of a dragon. He wondered about the suicidal manner in which the brigands attacked the Old Watusia House. He wondered what could possibly motivate a brigand to attack with such disregard for personal safety. Finally, as Aiwren collapsed to the ground, Jocund wondered what he was going to do about the suicidal brigands closing in on him, but luck, it seemed, had granted him another day, when the Watusians charged from the forest.

Although brigands were severely outnumbered by the army of Watusians led by the princess's father, Jocund knew he and the princess weren't yet safe. Though outnumbered, the brigands were dedicated to killing the princess, so Jocund had to kill a few of them, himself, as he guarded her. Princess Wanda had also picked up a sword and was doing her best to defend herself, while exhibiting the wisdom not to unnecessarily endanger herself or anyone else by diving into the fray. She was made of tougher and smarter stuff than Jocund had originally suspected.

When the battle was nearly over, King Sima Watus, The Fourteenth, a burly red-haired man who was surprisingly young for a king, hurried over to the princess and picked her up in his arms.

"Wanda, my favorite little bird," the man said tenderly, "I cannot tell you how overjoyed I am to see you. The thought of losing you like I lost your mother-"

"You didn't lose me," the princess said with ice and wrath in her voice. "You gave me away as though I was a possession. These brave men and women gave their lives to protect me, not for you, but from you, from the results of your actions. I may be your favorite, but I am your favorite thing. You have cost me the only true love of my life and I shall die before I forgive you."

The princess stormed off and Jocund thought about the situation. Though the king, clearly an inbred half-wit, wasn't directly responsible for what had happened, he had given his daughter away to his enemy, was surprised she wasn't happy about it, shocked that she ran away, and grateful to have her back. He wondered how long it would be before the buffoon offered her to another cousin, though he was certain that, despite the man's feeble mind, at least Princess Wanda's idiot father actually loved his offspring.

"Quite a day!" the moronic king said, slapping Jocund on the back with his giant hand made of giant sausage fingers, happily unaware that his daughter loathed him and that he had bits of blood and skull stuck in his beard. "You did a fantastic job keeping my little bird safe."

"Well," Jocund said, deciding he despised the jovial asshole, "perhaps you could demonstrate your appreciation by paying my the money promised as expediently as possible so I can return to Y-Kewnor to contact the families of my soldiers and prepare for their funerals. Oh, and Princess Wanda... she's a woman, not a bird."

Having no patience to converse with idiots, Jocund walked away from the dumbfounded king without waiting for a response and joined Wanda by the milkboy's nude, motionless body. The princess had, with understandable disregard for modesty, turned him onto his back and was wiping the blood and ash from his nude body with her cape, further filthying the once pristine silk.

"He's alive," she said, without looking up, "so my cleaning him isn't a pointless emotional flight of fancy."

"I never suggested it was," said Jocund, kneeling beside her, removing his own cloak to help wipe down Aiwren, his heart smiling at the fool boy's tenacity.

"I should be astounded by what he did," she said. "I know this and I am not ungrateful for his courage, but-"

"Only a fool or a zealot would allow a singular miracle to eclipse today's tragedies," Jocund said.

"And I know," she said, her lip quivering, "no matter how I try, I shall likely never forgive him for Leicester's death, especially after seeing what he was capable of."

"I didn't know your mom was dead," Jocund said.

"Suspecting my father's indiscretions, she drowned herself in the lake," the princess said. "It was an arranged marriage that she took too seriously. Kings have mistresses. She was naive and young, but not young enough for his taste, apparently. I promised myself I wouldn't have that kind of marriage, so there's my naïveté."

"My mother died, too," Jocund said. "I was young, but she's the only person who ever loved me. I thought I could make my father love me. So there's my naïveté. I joined the Kewnorian Guard to make him proud. We were raiding an encampment of smugglers. When they ambushed us, I ran. Everyone died except for me. I was court marshaled. I would have been executed were I not a lordson, but I tarnished my family name and my father has never forgiven me."

Jocund sat with Princess Wanda in silence for a few moments, wrapping Aiwren in his cloak for warmth. He had no idea why he had revealed his shame to her. Perhaps he felt that they were both as exposed as Aiwren was.

"I'm going to fetch our friends' bodies," Jocund said.

"I'm coming with you," she said.

When Jocund and Wanda, scraped and bloody, dragged the final body, Roderick's, from the house, they saw Aiwren, barely covered with the cloak wrapped around his waist, on his knees, sobbing by the corpses of their friends in front of the Old Watusia House. Jocund, dizzied by fury and sorrow and hopelessness, knelt next to the boy.

Jocund hesitated to speak, searching his mind for the right words, then finally said, "This is a shitty world and they gave their lives defending a shitty status quo."

"Is that supposed to make me feel better?" Aiwren asked, choking back tears.

"No," Jocund said with a shaking voice. "What's supposed to make you feel better is knowing that's not why they did it. They did it for you and me and the princess."

"Is that supposed to make me feel better?" he sobbed.

"Yeah, that one was," Jocund said, putting an arm around Aiwren, "I'm fucking terrible at this."

"I hate the way the world is," Aiwren said.

"Me, too," said Jocund, tears welling in his eyes as he noticed Wanda's hands on their shoulders and felt the convulsion of her silent sobs, "Me, too."

THE DREAMS AND THE DARKNESS

It was a full ten suns before The Divine Empress's Knights held the memorial for Sir Vincent Ackaback. Rheo hated that it was being held in tandem with the memorial for Arowyr Malegon or whatever the filthy dragon's actual name was, but he knew how important it was, despite it feeling so wrong, that Malegon be displayed as a hero, since the alternative, announcing there were dragons in the High Council, would tear The Divine Empress's Knights apart. So two coffins were ceremonially burnt in front of the Citadel that morning, one contained Ackaback's body and the other was completely empty. Rheo watched distantly, a decorated hero in the gold armor of a High Knight of the Council, as the pyre's flame reflected in his eyes.

"It had to be done this way," Beatrice said to Rheo, rolling up next to him, wearing dark clothes with a blanket over her lap to keep out the morning chill.

"I know," Rheo replied without looking at her.

"How is she?" Bea asked.

"Better," Rheo said. "She was lucky."

"Hmmm," she frowned dubiously. "Luck."

"When are you going to admit you know more than you're telling me?" Rheo asked.

"Haven't I admitted that?" Bea dismissed casually.

"Lies," Rheo growled. "My knight-father is being honored beside a monster and nobody knows."

"You think you're the only one burdened with unspeakable truths?!" Beatrice said, turning to Rheo with tears in her eyes. "Here's one of my secrets. Your knight-father, Ulysses Cutter, and I we were part of the most powerful force of goodness in all of Allyoshmar and we destroyed it. The incorruptible had been corrupted and we were left with no choice. Since then, everyone involved with that decision has perished. I'm the last person alive responsible for destroying the one thing that could save us and soon, I, too, will have to pay the price."

"What was it?" Rheo asked. "What could save us?"

"Not today, Rheo," she said distantly. "Not today."

Rheo turned to the burning coffins, staring blankly into the fire. He had to look somber, but strong. That was the image Beatrice told him to portray. Rheo stood on the top of the steps to the Citadel, along with the other High Knights of the Council, the Lords of Parliament, and the Generals of the Kewnorian Guard. The lower steps were populated with all of the rest of The Divine Empress's Knights in Y-Kewnor. On the street side of the pyre, a crowd had gathered, hundreds of Kewnorians, perhaps thousands, and Rheo knew many of those people were watching him, so he stuck to the script and made a show of grieving the way he was instructed to grieve.

It was amazing to Rheo how much things had changed in Y-Kewnor after what was being called the second attack on the Citadel. The official story was that one of the dragons who attacked the Citadel had returned and than Arowyr Malegon gave up his life defending the

Citadel. Ultimately, the credit for slaying the dragon went to the beautiful young woman, Matera, who had journeyed from Sima Watusia to take the tests to become a knight. Rheo was credited with tracking and killing Wurm Ahkk-Rhall, the dragon who organized the attacks. The story was agreed upon in closed chambers by Leopold Leonard, Allesander Montgomery, Beatrice Boomswift, and Rheo. Rheo insisted Matera get full credit for killing the dragon in the Citadel and the others reluctantly agreed, but he and Beatrice were the only people who knew her true identity. The story spread across Y-Kewnor and public opinion of the knights soared. Rheo and Matera were heroes. Kewnorians swooned over Rheo and couldn't wait to set their eyes upon the beautiful young dragonslayer, Matera.

Rheo, who once loved adoration, avoided speaking to people about the subject, but his shame was perceived as humility and this only made the people love him more. Hurrying away from the memorial ceremony, he found himself inextricably cornered by Sir Archibald Plune by the entrance to the Citadel.

"I suppose congratulations are in order, Sir Rheodo," Lord Plune said. "You've won the hearts of Y-Kewnor, a task not easily achieved."

"Congratulations to you, as well," Rheo said, "I heard of your son's actions and I'm certain he'll be greeted as a hero when he returns, which ought to help your polling numbers for the upcoming election."

"Well, he wasn't the one who slew the dragon so he shouldn't receive any credit he isn't due," Plune said so pointedly that Rheo was certain he suspected something.

"Yes," Rheo said, "I look forward meeting with him and the young guardsman who slew the beast in Old Watusia to learn the details of that battle."

"As I look forward to learning the details of your battle, Sir Rheodo," Plune replied.

Rheo did his best to deflect Plune's inspection long enough to fabricate a pretext to excuse himself. As soon as he could, he hurried into the Citadel, eager to return to his quarters and see her.

A High Knight of the Council was expected to take a wife, so the knight-fathers' quarters each had several bedrooms to accommodate a family. One of Rheo's extra bedrooms was currently occupied by the princess.

Rheo paused in the open doorway and looked at her standing by the window. Physically, she was, quite miraculously, fine; her recovery was just another lie, one they told until they knew more about her.

"The memorial was beautiful," she said. "Where I'm from, we send the burning coffins of our heroes out into the water."

"Oh," Rheo replied, praying she'd admit who she was so there'd be one person with whom he could be honest. "I hadn't heard of them doing that in Watusia."

"Yes," she said, steadily, "right on the lake."

Rheo stepped into the room. She looked different than she did when he found her killing the dragon or when he first met her in Bridgekeep. Standing in the window, the light dancing across her golden hair, illuminating the profile of her face, and beaming through her white cotton dress to silhouette her body beneath it, she was, perhaps, the most beautiful woman he had ever seen.

"Ahkk-Rhall is secure," he said. "You needn't worry about your safety. My offer to train you still stands, but you don't have to decide anything until you're ready."

"Thank you for making the effort to appear as though you care," she said, still looking out the window.

"I do care," Rheo said and he thought he did.

***

Aiwren was beyond the capacity to make any decisions, so, when Jocund suggested the two of them remain in Sima Watusia for a little while, he numbly acquiesced. They had to at least wait for King Sima Watus to pay them the reward for Wanda so they could take it to Y-Kewnor. The sword, the sword that could only be one of the Crystal Blades from Cutter's story, remained sheathed and, enjoying the luxury of the bed and board provided to him, Aiwren did his best not to think about it or about anything important at all, drinking all night with Jocund and sleeping until well into each day.

There was a fireplace in Aiwren's chamber so large he could have stepped into if he wanted to. King Watus said that a hero such as him should have the best quarters in the castle, other than his own. Jocund didn't seem to mind Aiwren getting the better room, but, having the bigger room, Aiwren was usually the host of his and Jocund's parties. The parties usually started with just Aiwren and Jocund, but, as the night progressed, they were usually joined by scores of people whom neither of them knew or remembered inviting. By the end of the night, the two of them, both drunk, would sit in silence. Jocund would say that he had to go piss, which, Aiwren knew, meant he was going to find a prostitute. Aiwren would then sit by the fire alone, drink, and try not to think.

One night, after their party had burned down to its final embers, Jocund asked, "So, how do you feel now that you've tasted adventure, now that you've slain a dragon?"

"Empty," Aiwren said. "Our whole mission was pointless. Good people died for no good reason."

"You see this?" Jocund said, heaving a large sack onto the table. "This is the reason."

Jocund dumped the bag on the table. It was filled with platinum coins. Aiwren stared at the coins, more coins than he had ever seen before, as Jocund silently separated them into eight little piles. Pointing to each pile, he said the names of the eight people in their platoon and then slid one of the piles to Aiwren.

"So that's what our lives were worth?" Aiwren asked. "Each pile is more than my family makes in an annual, but it still doesn't seem like it's enough."

"It never is," Jocund said. "That's the problem."

"What of Wanda's life?" Aiwren asked.

"All the coins," Jocund said.

"And Leicester?" Aiwren asked.

Jocund paused, then said, "None of them."

"That's not fair," Aiwren said, sliding the pile of coins in front of him back to the center of the table.

"My father said the best thing I could do with my life is die in battle," Jocund said, "even a stupid battle like this one. I'd be honorably out of his hair for good."

"That's terrible," Aiwren said. "My parents would be furious if they found out I did this."

"Do you know what the Y-Kewnor motto is?" Jocund asked, sliding his own pile back to the center.

"No birthright," Aiwren said.

"That's right," Jocund confirmed. "Any man can be a lord and any woman can be a lady, given the right circumstances. Rise to the top. Money. Wealth. Etcetera. Of course, you could just be born into the right family."

Aiwren wasn't sure exactly what Jocund's point was, thinking it might just be random drunken rantings, but he said, "I think you want the same thing I do. To feel as though you matter."

"Blah," Jocund laughed, "I gave up on that long ago. I have everything. There's no honor in being who I am. I ought to have been born a thief."

"You were," Aiwren laughed. "You've been steeling the hearts of prostitutes for annuals."

Both men laughed and, for a moment, if only a moment, things weren't so bad.

"We're living in a time when thieves and milkboys are heroes," Jocund roared hysterically. "Divine Empress help us all!"

Aiwren and Jocund laughed again, even harder, but then Aiwren said, "Today you received a message from that knight in Y-Kewnor, Rheozarccio Rheodo, asking us to meet with him. Do you trust him?"

"He used to be a shithead prick," Jocund said. "Now he's a man of honor who would do what's right no matter the cost."

"So no?" Aiwren joked.

"No," Jocund laughed, "not at all."

"So what do we do, then, when we get back, after we deliver this money to your father?" Aiwren asked.

"Perhaps, we oughtn't go back," Jocund slurred. "Perhaps we oughtn't deliver this money, either. Perhaps we use it to start something that will destroy their pretty little system."

"Are you serious?!" Aiwren asked.

Jocund never answered, but, instead raised his glass and said, "To thieves and milkboys," before excusing himself to go take a piss, leaving Aiwren alone for the rest of the night.

After Jocund left, Aiwren did what he could to stay awake. He kept drinking. With the dreams he had been having, those terrible long dark hallways, always leading to the room with the pool and the Skinless Woman skinning his friends alive, anything was better than sleep. His mind wandered to thoughts of the Order of the Crystal Blade, how the crystal sword had protected him, and how the Order was his only chance of eliminating his nightmares. With Cutter gone, his only connection to the Order was the sword, a sword that had been given to him by his father. He also thought of the girl he had seen in his vision and then by the side of the road. He wished to know more about her just as much as he wished to know more about the Order of the Crystal Blade. Both wishes felt as impossible as his wish that his friends were not really dead and he wondered if this loneliness and regret was what it meant to be a hero.

***

Teryessa silently slipped from Rheo's bed when the sun hadn't yet risen. She didn't want to wake him and have to endure an awkward conversation. She knew what she was doing with Rheo was inappropriate, but she didn't care. They had each gone through a great ordeal and, although she had no interest in sharing her pain with him or learning of his, they both had needs. She wasn't passionate about Rheo, but he fulfilled the need for arms to hold her, the need for her to control her own body, and the need to not be alone at night, even though she almost never allowed herself to fall asleep in his arms. It was an arrangement, nothing more. She told herself, the instant she felt trapped, she'd be gone. Teryessa couldn't stand to lay there that morning, pretending to sleep, waiting for unwanted kisses. She counted to two, got out of bed, dressed as quickly as possible, and silently slipped away.

In her own room, Teryessa stood by her window, allowing the frigid morning air to freeze her skin as she watched Y-Kewnor breath in the purple life of morning. She drank deeply from the wineskin of numbendria she had been keeping by her side, but it didn't ease her pain.

She wondered about herself and the darkness whispering to her. She knew she had done things that, before, in her innocence, she could not have imagined herself doing, but what could she have done differently? Would she be judged for surviving? If so, by whom? The Divine Empress?! Where was The Divine Empress when she was being raped, or mutilated, or fighting for her life? She welcomed the judgement.

Despite her contempt, she was afraid of judgement, but there was nobody who's judgement she feared more than the boy's. That boy she didn't even know. The boy she saw at the side of the road. She knew her actions would break his heart. She would destroy him and have to destroy herself for doing so. That was why she hoped, more than anything else, that she never saw him again and that the fantasy she had of him loving her would eventually decay into a wisp of an impossible dream.

She felt evil and good and strong and frail and scared and it didn't seem to matter. Nothing mattered at all as the first splinter of sunlight illuminated the skyline of Y-Kewnor, painting its buildings with orange light against the dark blue of the lingering night, washing away the dreams and the darkness. It was all so beautiful.

www.ingramcontent.com/pod-product-compliance
Lightning Source LLC
Chambersburg PA
CBHW030922020726
47498CB00001B/69